Julia QUINN

The Other Miss Bridgerton

piatkus

PIATKUS

First published in the US in 2018 by Avon Books,
An imprint of HarperCollins, New York
First published in Great Britain in 2018 by Piatkus

1 3 5 7 9 10 8 6 4 2

A CIP catalogue record for this book
is available from the British Library.

ISBN 978-0-349-41056-2

Printed and bound in Great Britain by
Clays Ltd, Elcograf S.p.A.

Papers used by Piatkus are from well-managed forests
and other responsible sources.

MIX
Paper from
responsible sources
FSC® C104740

Piatkus
An imprint of
Little, Brown Book Group
Carmelite House
50 Victoria Embankment
London EC4Y 0DZ

An Hachette UK Company
www.hachette.co.uk

www.littlebrown.co.uk

For Emily.
When I say I couldn't have done it without you,
I mean it literally.

And also for Paul.
Just tell me again—
Which way is the wind?

Chapter 1

Early summer 1786

For a young woman who had grown up on an island, in Somerset to be precise, Poppy Bridgerton had spent remarkably little time at the coast.

She was not unfamiliar with water. There was a lake near her family's home, and Poppy's parents had insisted that all their children learn to swim. Or perhaps more accurately, they had insisted that all their sons learn to swim. Poppy, the sole daughter of the bunch, took umbrage at the notion that she would be the only Bridgerton to die in a shipwreck and said as much to her parents—in precisely those words—just before she marched alongside her four brothers to the water's edge and hurled herself in.

She'd learned faster than three out of four of her brothers (it wasn't fair to compare her to the eldest; of *course* he'd catch on more quickly), and to this day she was, in her opinion, the strongest swimmer in the family. That she might have achieved this goal as much out of spite as natural ability was irrelevant. It was *important* to learn how to swim. She would have done so even if her parents hadn't originally told her to wait patiently on the grass.

Probably.

But there would be no swimming today. This was the ocean, or at least the channel, and the chilly, bitter water was nothing like the placid lake at home. Poppy might be contrary, but she wasn't stupid. And alone as she was, she had nothing to prove.

Besides, she was having far too good a time exploring the beach. The soft give of the sand beneath her feet, the tang of the saltwater air—they were as exotic to her as if she'd been dropped into Africa.

Well, maybe not, Poppy thought as she nibbled on a piece of the very familiar-tasting English cheese she'd brought along on her hike. But still and all, it was new, and it was a change, and that had to count for something.

Especially now, with the rest of her life the same as it ever was.

It was nearly July, and Poppy's second London Season—compliments of her aristocratic aunt, Lady Bridgerton—had recently drawn to a close. Poppy had found herself ending the Season much as she'd begun it—unmarried and unattached.

And a little bored.

She supposed she could have remained in London for the last dregs of the social whirl, hoping that she might actually meet someone she hadn't met before (unlikely). She could have accepted her aunt's invitation to rusticate in Kent, on the off chance that she might actually *like* one of the unmarried gentlemen who just happened to be invited for dinner (even less likely). But of course this would have required that she grit her teeth and attempt to hold her tongue when Aunt Alexandra wanted to know what was wrong with the latest offering (the least likely of all).

Her choices had been dull and duller, but thankfully she'd been saved by her dear childhood friend Elizabeth, who had moved to Charmouth several years earlier with her husband, the affable and bookish George Armitage.

George, however, had been called to Northumberland for some urgent family matter, the details of which Poppy had never quite got straight, and Elizabeth had been left alone at her seaside house, six and a half months with child. Bored and confined, she'd invited Poppy to come for an extended visit, and Poppy had happily accepted. It would be like old times for the two friends.

Poppy popped another bite of cheese into her mouth. Well, except for the massive size of Elizabeth's belly. That was new.

It meant Elizabeth couldn't accompany her on her daily jaunts to the shore, but that was no matter. Poppy knew her reputation had never included the word *shy*, but conversational nature notwithstanding, she rather enjoyed her own company. And after months and months of making small talk in London, it felt rather nice to clear her head with the sharp sea air.

She'd been trying to take a different route each day, and she had been delighted to discover a small network of caves about halfway between Charmouth and Lyme Regis, tucked away where the foamy waves lapped the shore. Most filled with water when the tide was in, but after surveying the landscape, Poppy was convinced that there had to exist a few that remained dry, and she was determined to find one.

Just because of the challenge, of course. Not because she had any need of a perpetually dry cave in Charmouth, Dorset, England.

Great Britain, Europe, the world.

One really had to take one's challenges where one could, given that she *was* in Charmouth, Dorset, England, and that seemed a decidedly small corner of the world, indeed.

Finishing the last bites of her lunch, she squinted up toward the rocks. The sun was to her back, but the day was bright enough to make her wish for a parasol, or, at the very least, a large shady tree. It was gorgeously warm too, and she'd left her redingote back at the house. Even her fichu, which she'd worn to protect her skin, was starting to get itchy and hot across her chest.

But she wasn't going to turn back now. She'd not come this far before, and in fact had only made it to this point after convincing Elizabeth's plumpish maid, who'd been drafted as her chaperone/ companion, to remain behind in town.

"Think of it as an additional afternoon off," Poppy had said with a winning smile.

"I don't know." Mary's expression was doubtful. "Mrs. Armitage was quite clear that—"

"Mrs. Armitage hasn't had a clear thought since

finding herself with child," Poppy cut in, sending Elizabeth a silent apology. "It's like that for all women, I'm told," she added, trying to get the maid's mind off the subject at hand, namely, Poppy's chaperonage, or lack thereof.

"Well, that's certainly true," Mary said, tilting her head slightly to the side. "When my brother's wife had her boys, I never could get a sensible word out of her."

"That's it exactly!" Poppy exclaimed. "Elizabeth knows that I will be perfectly fine on my own. I'm no spring miss, after all. Hopelessly on the shelf, they say."

As Mary attempted to assure her that that was most certainly not the case, Poppy added, "I'm only going for an easy little stroll by the shore. You know that. You came with me yesterday."

"And the day before that," Mary said with a sigh, clearly not relishing the prospect of another afternoon of exertion.

"And the day before that as well," Poppy pointed out. "And what, all week before that?"

Mary nodded glumly.

Poppy didn't smile. She was far too good for that. But success was clearly right around the corner.

Literally.

"Here," she said, steering the maid toward a cozy tea shop, "why don't you sit down and have a rest? Heaven knows you deserve it. I've quite run you ragged, haven't I?"

"You've been nothing but kind, Miss Bridgerton," Mary said quickly.

"Kind and exhausting," Poppy said, patting Mary's hand as she opened the tearoom door. "You work so hard. You deserve a few minutes for yourself."

And so, once Poppy had paid for a pot of tea and a plate of biscuits, she'd made her escape—two of the aforementioned biscuits in her pocket—and now she was wonderfully, blessedly on her own.

If only there were ladies' shoes that were suitable for climbing across rocks. Her little boots were quite the most practical made for women, but they didn't compare in durability with the sort that sat in her brothers' wardrobes. She took great care to watch her steps, lest she turn an ankle. This area of the beach did not receive much foot traffic, so if she hurt herself, heaven only knew how long it would take for someone to come after her.

She whistled as she walked, enjoying the opportunity to engage in such uncouth behavior (wouldn't her mama be horrified at the sound!), and then decided to compound the transgression by switching to a tune whose words were not suitable for female ears.

"*Oh, the barmaid went down to the oh-oh-oh-ocean,*" she sang happily, "*with an eye toward getting her*— What's this?"

She stopped, peering at a strange formation in the rocks off to her right. A cave. It had to be. And far enough from the water's edge that it wouldn't flood in high tide.

"Me secret hideaway, mateys," she said, winking to herself as she switched direction. It did seem the perfect spot for a pirate, well off the beaten track, its opening obscured by three large boulders. Truly, it was a wonder she'd even spotted it.

Poppy squeezed between the boulders, idly noting that one of them wasn't as large as she'd originally supposed, then made her way into the mouth of the cave. *Should've brought a lantern*, she thought, waiting for her eyes to adjust to the darkness, although Elizabeth certainly would have wanted to know the reason for *that*. Hard to explain why one might need a lantern while walking on a beach at half noon.

Poppy took a few baby steps in, nudging her shoes carefully across the ground, searching out rough spots with her feet since she couldn't possibly see them with her eyes. It was difficult to tell for sure, but the cave seemed deep, stretching out far beyond the light at the opening. She moved forward, emboldened by the thrill of discovery, edging slowly toward the back . . . slowly . . . slowly . . . until . . .

"Ow!" she yelped, wincing as her hand connected with something quite hard and wooden.

"Ow," she said again, rubbing the sore spot with her other hand. "Ow ow ow. That was . . ."

Her words trailed off. Whatever she'd smacked her hand into, it wasn't a natural outcropping of the cave. In fact, it felt rather like the splintery corner of a rough wooden crate.

With tentative movements, she reached her hand back out until it connected—more gently this time—with a flat wooden panel. No doubt about it, it was definitely a crate.

Poppy let out a little giggle of glee. What had she found? Pirates' booty? Smugglers' loot? The cave smelled musty, and it felt unused, so whatever this was, it had probably been there for ages.

"Prepare for treasure." She laughed, saluting herself in the darkness. A quick check confirmed that the crate was far too heavy for her to lift, so she ran her fingers along the edge, trying to determine how she might get it open. Drat. It was nailed shut. She'd have to come back, although she had no idea how she'd explain away her need for a lantern *and* a crowbar.

Although . . .

She cocked her head to the side. If there was a crate—two, actually, one stacked atop the other—in this section of the cave, who knew what might be farther back?

She edged into the gloom, her arms stretched gingerly in front of her. Nothing yet. Nothing . . . nothing . . .

"Careful there!"

Poppy froze.

"The captain'll kill you if you drop it."

Poppy stopped breathing, relief washing over her when she realized that the rough male voice was not directed toward her.

Relief that was instantly replaced with terror. Slowly, she brought her arms back to her body until she'd enveloped herself in a tight hug.

She was not alone.

Using excruciatingly careful movements, she edged as far behind the crates as she could manage. It was dark, and she was quiet, and whoever was here ought not to see her unless—

"Will you light the damn lantern?"

Unless they had a lantern.

A flame blazed to life, illuminating the back portion of the cave. Poppy's brow furrowed. Had the men come in from behind her? And if so, how had they entered? Where did the cave go?

"We don't have much time," one of the men said. "Hurry up and help me find what we need."

"What about the rest?"

"It'll be safe until we get back. It's the last time, anyway."

The other man laughed. "So the captain says."

"He means it this time."

"He'll never quit."

"Well, if he doesn't, I will." Poppy heard a pained grunt of exertion, followed by "I'm getting too old for this."

"Did you move the boulder in front of the opening?" the first man asked, exhaling as he set something down on the ground.

So that was why she'd had to squeeze in, Poppy realized. She should have wondered how such a large crate had fit through the small space.

"Yesterday," came the reply. "With Billy."

"That scrawny mite?"

"Mmph. I think he's thirteen now."

"Never say it!"

Good God, Poppy thought, she was trapped in a cave with smugglers—maybe even pirates!—and they were chattering away like two old ladies.

"What else do we need?" came the lower of the two voices.

"Captain says he won't leave without a crate of the brandy."

Poppy felt the blood leave her body. *A crate?*

The other man laughed. "To sell or to drink?"

"Both, I expect."

Another chuckle. "He'd best be sharing, then."

Poppy looked around frantically. Enough of the lantern's light had filtered in her direction that she could see her immediate surroundings. Where the *hell* was she going to hide? There was a little indentation in the cave wall that she could press herself into, but the men would have to be blind to miss her.

Still, it was better than her current spot. Poppy scrambled back, curling herself into the tiniest ball she could manage, thanking her maker that she'd not worn her bright yellow frock that morning, simultaneously sending up her first true prayer in months.

Please please please.
I'll be a better person.
I'll listen to my mother.
I'll even listen in church.
Please please . . .

"Jesus, Mary, and Joseph!"

Poppy slowly tipped her face toward the man looming above her. "Forsaken," she muttered.

"Who are you?" the man demanded, shoving the lantern closer to her face.

"Who are you?" Poppy shot back, before the relative lack of wisdom of such a retort sank in.

"Green!" the man hollered.

Poppy blinked.

"Green!"

"What?" grumbled the other man—apparently named Green.

"There's a girl!"

"*What?*"

"Here. There's a girl."

Green came running over. "Who the hell is this?" he demanded.

"I don't know," the other man said impatiently. "She didn't say."

Green bent down, jamming his weathered face close to Poppy's. "Who're you?"

Poppy said nothing. She didn't often hold her tongue, but now seemed an intelligent time to start.

"Who are you?" he repeated, this time groaning with the words.

"No one," Poppy answered, finding a little courage in the fact that he seemed more tired than angry. "I was just out for a walk. I won't bother you. I'll just go. No one will ever know—"

"I'll know," Green said.

"And so will I, for that matter," the other one said, scratching his head.

"I won't say a word," Poppy assured them. "I don't even know what—"

"Damn!" Green cursed. "Damn damn damn damn damn."

Poppy glanced frantically between the two men,

trying to decide whether it was in her best interests to add to the conversation. It was difficult to guess their ages; both had that weather-beaten look one got after spending too much time in the sun and wind. They were dressed simply, in rough work shirts and trousers, tucked into those tall boots men liked to wear when they knew they'd be getting their feet wet.

"Damn!" Green bit off again. "The day only needed this."

"What should we do with her?" the other man said.

"I don't know. We can't leave her here."

The two men fell silent, staring at her as if she were the world's largest burden, just waiting to launch itself onto their shoulders.

"The captain'll kill us," Green finally sighed.

"It's not our fault."

"I suppose we should ask him what to do with her," Green said.

"I don't know where he is," the other one replied. "Do you?"

Green shook his head. "He's not on the ship?"

"No. He said he'd meet us on deck an hour before we sail. Had some sort of businesslike thing to take care of."

"Damn."

It was more *damn*s than Poppy had ever heard in one sitting, but there seemed little to be gained in pointing that out.

Green sighed, closing his eyes in what could only be described as an expression of abject misery. "We have no choice," he said. "We'll have to take her."

"What?" the other man asked.

"*What?*" Poppy screeched.

"Good God," Green grumbled, rubbing his ears. "Did that squall come from your *mouth?*" He let out a long-suffering sigh. "I'm too old for this."

"We can't take her!" the other man protested.

"Listen to him," Poppy said. "He's obviously very intelligent."

Green's friend stood up a little straighter and beamed. "The name's Brown," he said, nodding politely at her.

"Er, pleased to meet you," Poppy said, wondering if she ought to extend her hand.

"Do you think I *want* to take her?" Green said. "Bad luck having a woman on a ship, and especially *this* one."

Poppy's lips parted at the insult. "Well," she said, only to be cut off by Brown, who asked, "What's wrong with this one? She said I was intelligent."

"Which only goes to show that *she* ain't. And besides, she talks."

"So do you," Poppy shot back.

"See?" Green said.

"She's not so bad," Brown said.

"You just said you didn't want her on the boat!"

"Well, I don't, but—"

"There is nothing worse than a talky female," Green grumbled.

"There are many things that are worse," Poppy said, "and you're quite fortunate if you've never experienced them."

Green looked at her for a long moment. Just looked at her. Then he groaned, "The captain's gonna kill us."

"Not if you don't take me with you," Poppy hastened to say. "He'll never know."

"He'll know," Green said ominously. "He always knows."

Poppy chewed on her lower lip, assessing her options. She doubted she could outrun them, and Green was blocking her path to the entrance, in any event. She supposed she could cry and hope that her tears might appeal to the softer sides of their natures, but that presumed that they *had* softer sides.

She looked at Green and smiled hesitantly, testing the waters.

Green ignored her and turned to his friend. "What time—" He stopped. Brown was gone. "Brown!" he yelled. "Where the hell'd you go?"

Brown's head popped up from behind a stack of trunks. "Just getting some rope."

Rope? Poppy's throat went dry.

"Good," Green grunted.

"You do not want to tie me up," Poppy said, her throat apparently still wet enough for words.

"No, that I don't," he said, "but I have to do it, anyway, so let's make it easy for the both of us, eh?"

"Surely you don't think I will allow you to take me without a struggle?"

"I'd been hoping."

"Well, you can keep hoping, sir, because I—"

"Brown!" Green hollered.

With enough force that Poppy actually shut her mouth.

"Got the rope!" came the answer.

"Good. Get the other stuff as well."

"What other stuff?" Brown asked.

"Yes," Poppy said nervously. "What other stuff?"

"The other stuff," Green said impatiently. "You know what I mean. And a cloth."

"Oh, the other stuff," Brown said. "Righto."

"What other stuff?" Poppy demanded.

"You don't want to know," Green told her.

"I assure you I do," Poppy said, just as she was beginning to think that maybe she didn't.

"You said you were going to struggle," he explained.

"Yes, but what does that have to do—"

"Remember when I said I was too old for this?" She nodded.

"Well, 'this' includes a struggle."

Brown reemerged, clutching a green bottle that looked vaguely medicinal. "Here y'go," he said, handing it to Green.

"Not that I couldn't manage you," Green explained, popping the cork. "But why? Why make it harder than I have to?"

Poppy had no answer. She stared at the bottle. "Are you going to make me drink that?" she whispered. It smelled foul.

Green shook his head. "You got a cloth?" he asked Brown.

"Sorry."

Green let out another tired groan and eyed the linen fichu she'd used to fill in the bodice of her dress. "We'll have to use your handkerchief," he said to Poppy. "Hold still."

"What are you doing?" she cried out, jerking backward as he yanked the fichu free.

"I'm sorry," he said, and strangely enough, it sounded as if he meant it.

"Don't do this," Poppy gasped, scrambling as far away from him as she could.

But it wasn't very far, given that her back was to the cave wall, and as she looked on in horror, he poured a liberal amount of the noxious liquid onto the whisper-thin linen of her fichu. It became quickly saturated, and several drops fell through, disappearing into the damp ground.

"You're going to have to hold her," Green said to Brown.

"No," Poppy said, as Brown's arms came around her. "No."

"Sorry," Brown said, and it sounded as if he meant it too.

Green scrunched the fichu into a ball and placed it over her mouth. Poppy gagged, gasping against the onslaught of foul fumes.

And then the world slipped away.

Chapter 2

—➤═✳═⫷—

Andrew Rokesby strode along the decks of the *Infinity*, giving the ship one last inspection before they set sail at precisely four that afternoon. Everything appeared to be in order, from bow to stern, and except for Brown and Green, every man was accounted for and well-prepared for the voyage that lay ahead of them.

"Pinsley!" Andrew called out, tilting his head up toward the young man tending to the rigging.

"Yes, sir!" Pinsley called down. "What is it, sir?"

"Have you seen Brown and Green? I sent them out to the cave earlier today for some supplies."

"Supplies, sir?" Pinsley said with a cheeky grin. Everyone knew why Andrew had *really* sent out Brown and Green.

"One little tilt of the wheel, and you'll be hanging by your fingertips," Andrew warned.

"They're below, sir," Pinsley said with a grin. "Saw 'em head down a quarter hour ago."

"Below?" Andrew echoed, shaking his head.

Brown and Green had work to do; there was no reason they should be below.

Pinsley shrugged, or at least Andrew thought he did. It was difficult to tell with the sun in his eyes.

"They was carrying a sack," Pinsley said.

"A sack?" Andrew echoed. He'd sent them for a crate of brandy. Every man had his indulgences, and his were women in port and French brandy at sea. He had one glass every night, following his supper. Kept life civilized, or at least as civilized as he wanted it.

"Looked real heavy-like," Pinsley added.

"Brandy in a sack," Andrew muttered. "*Madre de Dios*, it'll be nothing but shards and fumes by now." He glanced up at Pinsley, who was at work lashing the ropes, and then turned to the narrow staircase that led below.

It was his policy to have a brief word with each member of his crew, no matter how high or low, before the *Infinity* took to sea. It ensured that each knew his role in the mission at hand, and the men appreciated the show of respect. His crew was small but fiercely loyal. Each would have laid down his life for him, Andrew knew that. But that was because they knew their captain was prepared to do the same.

Andrew was unquestionably in command, and there wasn't a man aboard who would dare counter one of his orders, but then again, there wasn't a man aboard who would want to.

"Sir!"

Andrew looked behind him. It was Green, who'd obviously come up the other staircase.

"Ah, there you are," Andrew said, motioning for him to follow. Green was the most senior member of his crew, having joined one day earlier than Brown. The pair had been bickering like old women ever since.

"Sir!" Green said again, running along the deck to catch up with him.

"Talk as we walk," Andrew said, turning his back to him as he strode toward the staircase that led to his cabin. "I need to secure some things in my cabin."

"But sir, I need to tell you—"

"And what the hell happened with my brandy?" Andrew asked, taking the steps two at a time. "Pinsley said you came aboard with a sack. A sack," he added, shaking his head.

"Right," Green said, making a strange sound.

Andrew turned around. "Are you quite all right?"

Green gulped. "The thing is—"

"Did you just gulp?"

"No, sir, I—"

Andrew turned away, getting back to business. "You should see Flanders about that throat. He's got some kind of concoction to cure it. Tastes like the devil, but it works, I can attest to that."

"Sir," Green said, following him down the hall.

"Brown's aboard?" Andrew asked, grasping the handle to his door.

"Yes, sir, but sir—"

"Good, then we'll be ready to sail right on schedule."

"Sir!" Green practically cried out, wedging himself between Andrew and the door.

"What *is it*, Green?" Andrew asked with forced patience.

Green opened his mouth, but whatever it was he wanted to say, he clearly lacked the words to do so.

Andrew placed both his hands under Green's arms, lifted him up, and set him aside.

"Before you go in there . . ." Green said in a strangled voice.

Andrew pushed open the door.

And found a woman lying on his bed, bound, gagged, and looking as if she'd shoot flames from her eyes were it anatomically possible.

Andrew stared at her for a full second, idly taking in her thick chestnut hair and bright green eyes. He let his gaze wander down to the rest of her—she *was* a woman, after all—and smiled.

"A present?" he murmured. "For me?"

IF SHE GOT out of this alive, Poppy decided, she was going to *kill* every damn man on the ship.

Starting with Green.

No, Brown.

No, definitely Green. Brown might have let her go if she'd had a chance to talk him into it, but Green deserved nothing less than a permanent pox on his house.

And that of his every last descendant.

Hmmph. That assumed the odious man could find a woman willing to procreate with him, which Poppy sincerely doubted was possible. In fact, she thought rather viciously, it was going to be physically *im*possible by the time she got through with him. Four brothers taught a woman a great deal about how to fight dirty, and if she ever managed to get her ankles unbound, she was going to plant her knee right in his—

Click.

She looked up. Someone was coming in.

"Before you go in there . . ." she heard a familiar voice say.

The door swung open, revealing not Green, and not Brown, but a man at least a dozen years younger, and so blindingly handsome that Poppy was quite certain her mouth would have dropped open if she hadn't been gagged.

His hair was a rich warm brown, sun-streaked with gold and pulled into a devilish queue at the back of his neck. His face was quite simply perfect, with full, finely molded lips that tipped up at the corners, leaving him with an expression of permanent mischief. And his eyes were blue, so vividly so that she could discern their color from across the room.

Those eyes traveled the length of her, from head to toe, and then back again. It was quite the most intimate perusal Poppy had ever been subjected to, and, damn it all, she felt herself blush.

"A present?" he murmured, his lips curving ever so slightly. "For me?"

"Mmmph grrmph shmmph!" Poppy grunted, struggling against her bindings.

"Er, this is what I was trying to tell you about," Green said, sliding into the room beside the mysterious stranger.

"This?" the other man murmured, his voice silky smooth.

"Her," Green amended, the single syllable hanging heavy in the air, as if she were Bloody Mary crossed with Medusa.

Poppy glared at him and growled.

"My, my," the younger man said, quirking a brow. "I scarcely know what to say. Not in my usual fashion, but fetching nonetheless."

Poppy watched him warily as he came farther into the cabin. He'd uttered barely a handful of words, but it was enough to know that he was no lowborn sailor. He spoke like an aristocrat, and he moved like one too. She knew the sort. She'd spent the last two years trying (but not really trying) to get one to marry her.

The man turned to Green. "Any particular reason she's lying on my bed?"

"She found the cave, Captain."

"Was she looking for the cave?"

"Don't know, sir. I didn't ask. I think it was an accident."

The captain regarded her with an unsettlingly even expression before turning back to Green and asking, "What do you propose we do with her?"

"I don't know, Captain. We couldn't just leave her there. It was still full of our haul from the last voyage. If we let her go, she'd've just told someone about it."

"Or taken it for herself," the captain said thoughtfully.

Poppy grunted at the insult. As if she were unprincipled enough to resort to stealing.

The captain looked at her with an arched brow. "She seems to have an opinion about that," he said.

"She has a great many opinions," Green said darkly.

"Is that so?"

"We took her gag off while we were waiting for you," Green explained. "Had to put it back on after a minute. Less, really."

"That bad, eh?"

Green nodded. "Got me in the back of the head with her hands too."

Poppy grunted with satisfaction.

The captain turned back to her, looking almost impressed. "Should've bound her hands in back," he said.

"I wasn't going to untie her long enough to redo it," Green muttered, rubbing his head.

The captain nodded thoughtfully.

"We didn't have time to unload the cave," Green continued. "And besides, no one's ever found it before. It's valuable even without anything in it. Who knows what we might need to hide there."

The captain shrugged. "It's worthless now," he said, crossing his powerful arms. "Unless, of course, we kill her."

Poppy gasped, the sound audible even over the gag.

"Oh, don't worry," he said, rather offhandedly. "We've never killed anyone who didn't need killing, and never a woman. Although," he added, idly rubbing his chin, "there have been one or two . . ." He looked up, blinding her with a smile. "Well, never you mind."

"Actually, sir," Green said, stepping forward.

"Hmm?"

"There was that one in Spain. Málaga?"

The captain looked at him blankly until his memory was jogged. "Oh, *that* one. Well, that doesn't count. I'm not even sure she was female."

Poppy's eyes widened. Who *were* these people?

And then, just when she thought the two of them might sit down for a leisurely drink, the captain snapped open his pocket watch with precise, almost military, movements and said, "We're to sail in less than two hours. Do we even know who she is?"

Green shook his head. "She wouldn't say."

"Where's Brown? Does he know?"

"No, sir," came the answer from Brown himself, standing in the doorway.

"Oh, there you are," the captain said. "Green and I were just discussing this unexpected development."

"I'm sorry, sir."

"It's not your fault," the captain said. "You did the right thing. But we do have to ascertain her identity. She's finely dressed," he added, motioning to Poppy's blue walking dress. "Someone will be missing her."

He stepped toward the bed, reaching for her gag, but both Green and Brown leapt forward, Green grabbing his arm and Brown actually wedging his body between the captain and the bed.

"You do not want to do that," Green said ominously.

"I beg you, sir," Brown pleaded, "do not remove the gag."

The captain stopped for a moment and looked from man to man. "What, pray tell, is she going to do?"

Green and Brown said nothing, but they both backed up, almost to the wall.

"Good God," the captain said impatiently. "Two grown men."

And then he removed the gag.

"You!" Poppy burst out, practically spitting at Green.

Green blanched.

"And you," she growled at Brown. "And you!" she finished, glaring at the captain.

The captain quirked a brow. "And now that you've demonstrated your extensive vocabulary—"

"I am going to kill each and every one of you," she hissed. "How dare you tie me up and leave me here for hours—"

"It was thirty minutes," Brown protested.

"It felt like hours," she railed, "and if you think I'm going to sit here and accept this type of abuse from a pack of idiot pirates—"

She coughed uncontrollably. The bloody captain had shoved the gag back in.

"Right," the captain said. "I understand perfectly now."

Poppy bit his finger.

"That," he said smoothly, "was a mistake."

Poppy glared at him.

"Oh, and by the by," he added, almost as an afterthought, "we prefer the term *privateer*."

She growled, grinding her teeth around the gag.

"I'll remove that," he said, "if you promise to behave."

She hated him. Oh, how she hated him. It had taken less than five minutes, but already she was certain she'd never hate anyone with quite the same intensity, with the same fervor, with—

"Very well," he said, shrugging. "We set sail precisely at four, if you're interested."

And then he just turned and walked to the door. Poppy grunted. She had no choice.

"Can you behave?" he asked, his voice annoyingly silky and warm.

She nodded, but her eyes were mutinous.

He walked back to the bed. "Promise?" he asked mockingly.

Her chin jerked in a furious approximation of a nod.

He leaned down and gingerly removed the gag.

"Water," she gasped, hating that she was begging.

"Happy to oblige," he said, pouring her a glass from the pitcher on his table. He held it to her lips while she drank, since her hands were still tied. "Who are you?" he asked.

"Does it matter?"

"Not just now, but it may," he said, "when we return."

"You can't take me!" she protested.

"It's either that or kill you," he said.

Her mouth fell open. "Well, you can't do that either."

"I don't suppose you have a gun hidden in your

dress," he said, leaning one shoulder against the wall as he crossed his arms.

Her lips parted with surprise, and then she quickly covered her reaction and said, "Maybe."

He laughed, drat the man.

"I'll give you money," she said quickly. Surely he could be bought. He was a pirate, for heaven's sake. Wasn't he?

He lifted a brow. "I don't suppose you've a purse of gold hidden in that dress."

She scowled at his sarcasm. "Of course not. But I can get you some."

"You want us to ransom you?" he asked, smiling.

"No! Of course not. But if you release me—"

"No one's releasing you," he interrupted, "so just stop your—"

"I'm sure if you think about it—" she cut in.

"I've thought all I need to—"

"—you'll see that it—"

"We are not letting you—"

"—really isn't such a good idea to—"

"I said we're not letting you—"

"—hold me hostage. I'm sure to get in the way and—"

"Can you be quiet?"

"—I eat a lot too, and—"

"Does she ever shut up?" the captain asked, turning to his men by the door.

Green and Brown shook their heads.

"—I'll surely be an inconvenience," Poppy finished.

There was a moment of silence, which the captain

seemed to savor. "You make a rather fine argument for killing you," he finally said.

"Not at all," she quickly put in. "It was an argument to let me go, if you must know."

"Clearly, I must," he muttered. Then he sighed, the tired sound his first sign of weakness, and said, "Who *are* you?"

"I want to know what you plan to do with me before I give up my identity," Poppy said.

He motioned lazily to her bindings. "You're not really in a position to make demands now, are you?"

"What are you going to do with me?" she repeated. It was probably foolish to remain so headstrong, but if he was going to kill her, he was going to kill her, and her display of temper wasn't going to tip the scales either way.

He sat on the edge of the bed, his nearness disconcerting. "I will humor you," he said, "since despite your waspy tongue, you're here through little fault of your own."

"*No* fault," she muttered.

"You never learn, do you?" he asked. "And here I was going to be nice to you."

"I'm sorry," she said quickly.

"Not terribly sincere, but I'll allow it," he said. "And much as it pains me to inform you, you will be our guest aboard the *Infinity* for the next two weeks, until we complete our voyage."

"No!" Poppy cried out, the horrified sound escaping her lips before she could press her bound hands to her mouth.

"I'm afraid so," he said grimly. "You know where

our cave is, and I can't leave you behind. Once we return, we'll clear it out and let you go."

"Why don't you clear it out now?"

"I can't," he said simply.

"You mean you won't."

"No, I mean I can't," he repeated. "And you're starting to annoy me."

"You can't take me with you," Poppy said, hearing her voice crack. Good God, she wanted to cry. She could hear it in her voice, feel it in the burning sensation behind her eyes. She wanted to cry like she hadn't cried in years, and if she didn't get ahold of herself, she was going to lose her control right here in front of this man—this awful man who held her very fate in his hands.

"Look," he said, "I do sympathize with your plight."

Poppy shot him a look that said she didn't believe him for a second.

"I do," he said gently. "I know how it feels to be backed into a corner. It isn't fun. Especially for someone like you."

Poppy swallowed, unsure if his words were compliment or insult.

"But the truth is," he continued, "this ship must depart this afternoon. The wind and tides are favorable, and we must make good time. You should just thank your maker we're not the killing sort."

"Where are we going?" she whispered.

He paused, obviously considering her question.

"I'm going to know when we get there," she said impatiently.

"True enough," he said, his small smile almost a salute. "We sail for Portugal."

Poppy felt her eyes bug out. "Portugal?" she echoed, her throat strangling over the word. "Portugal? Will it really be two weeks?"

He shrugged. "If we're lucky."

"Two weeks," she whispered. "Two weeks." Her family would be frantic. She'd be ruined. Two weeks. A whole fortnight.

"You have to let me write a letter," she said urgently.

"I beg your pardon?"

"A letter," she repeated, struggling to sit up. "You must allow me to write one."

"And what, pray tell, do you plan to include in such a missive?"

"I've been visiting a friend," Poppy said quickly, "and if I don't return this evening, she will call out the alarm. My entire family will descend on the district." She bored her eyes into his. "Trust me when I tell you that you do not wish for this to happen."

His gaze did not leave hers. "Your name, my lady."

"My family—"

"Your name," he said again.

Poppy pursed her lips, then said, "You may call me Miss Bridgerton."

And he blanched. He *blanched*. He hid it well, but she saw the blood drain from his face, and for the first time in the interview, she felt a little rush of triumph. Not that she was about to go free, but still, it was her first victory. A tiny one, to be sure, but a victory nonetheless.

"I see you've heard of my family," she said sweetly.

He muttered something under his breath that she was quite certain would not hold up in polite circles.

Slowly, and with what looked to be great control, he stood up. "Green!" he barked.

"Yes, sir!" the older man said, jumping to attention.

"Kindly fetch *Miss Bridgerton* some writing materials," he said, her name sounding like a dread poison on his lips.

"Yes, sir," Green said, hurrying out the door, Brown hot on his heels.

The captain turned to her with resolute eyes. "You will write precisely what I direct you to write," he said.

"Begging your pardon," Poppy said, "but if I did that, then my friend would know immediately that there was a problem. *You* wouldn't sound like *me*," she explained.

"Your friend will know there is a problem when you don't return this evening."

"Of course, but I can write something that will assuage her," Poppy returned, "and at the very least, ensure that she doesn't notify the authorities."

He ground his teeth together, then said, "It will not be sealed without my approval."

"Of course," she said primly.

He glared at her, his eyes somehow hot and cold and so so blue.

"I'll need my hands untied," Poppy said, lifting her wrists in his direction.

He crossed the room. "I'm waiting until Green returns."

Poppy decided not to argue any further. He appeared about as movable on the point as a glacier.

"Which branch?" he said suddenly.

"I beg your pardon?"

"To which branch of the family do you belong?" His voice was sharp, each word enunciated with military precision.

It was on the tip of her tongue to make an insolent retort, but it was clear from the captain's expression that this would be most unwise. "Somerset," she said quietly. "My uncle is the viscount. They are in Kent."

His jaw clenched, and the seconds ticked by in silence until Green finally reappeared with paper, a quill, and a small pot of ink. Poppy sat patiently while the captain untied her hands, her breath sucking over her lips at the pain as the blood returned to her fingers.

"Sorry about that," he grunted, and she looked sharply at him, his apology taking her by surprise.

"Habit," he said. "Not heartfelt."

"It was difficult to imagine that it might be," she returned.

He made no response, merely held out his hand as she swung her legs over the side of the bed.

"Am I to hop to the table?" she asked. Her ankles were still bound.

"I would never be so ungallant," he said, and before she had any idea what he was about, he swept her into his arms and carried her to the dining table.

And dropped her most unceremoniously into a chair. "Write," he ordered.

Poppy took the quill between her fingers and dipped it gingerly in the ink, chewing on her lip as she tried to figure out what to say. What sort of words would possibly convince Elizabeth not to summon the authorities—and her family—while Poppy disappeared for two weeks?

> *Dearest Elizabeth, I know you will be worried . . .*

"What is taking so long?" the captain snapped.

Poppy looked up at him and lifted her brows before replying. "If you must know, this is the first time I've had the occasion to write a letter explaining—without, of course, actually explaining—my having been kidnapped."

"Don't use the word *kidnapped*," he said sharply.

"Indeed," she replied, shooting him a sarcastic glare. "Which accounts for the delay. I'm forced to use three words where a reasonable person would use only one."

"A skill one would think you've long since mastered."

"Nevertheless," she said, trying to speak over him, "it tends to complicate the message."

"Write," he directed. "And say you'll be gone a month."

"A month?" she gasped.

"I hope to God not," he muttered, "but this way,

when we get you back in a fortnight, it will be cause for celebration."

Poppy was not quite certain, but she thought he muttered under his breath, "*My* celebration."

She decided to let it pass. It was the least of his insults thus far, and she had work to do. She took a deep breath and continued with:

> . . . but I assure you that I am well. I shall be gone for a month, and I must beg you to keep my disappearance to yourself. Please do not alert my family or the authorities, as the former will only worry and the latter will spread the tale so far and wide that my reputation will be forever ruined.
>
> I know this is a great deal to ask of you, and I know that you will have a thousand questions for me upon my return, but I implore you, Elizabeth—please trust me and all shall be explained soon.
>
> Your sister in spirit,
> Poppy

"Poppy, eh?" the captain said. "I wouldn't have guessed it."

Poppy ignored him.

"Pandora, perhaps, or Pauline. Or even Prudence, if only for the irony—"

"Poppy is a perfectly acceptable name," she snapped.

His eyes held hers in an uncomfortably intimate gaze. "Lovely, even," he murmured.

She swallowed nervously, noticing that Green had departed, leaving her quite alone with the captain. "I signed it 'sister in spirit' so that she would know I wasn't coerced. It is how we have always signed our letters."

He nodded, taking the missive from her fingers.

"Oh, wait!" she blurted, taking it back. "I need to add a postscript."

"Do you now?"

"Her maid," Poppy explained. "She was my chaperone for the afternoon, and—"

"There was another person at the cave?" he questioned sharply.

"No, of course not," Poppy retorted. "I managed to be rid of her in Charmouth."

"Of course you did."

His tone was such that she was compelled to shoot him a slitty side-eyed glance. "She was not of sufficient physical constitution to accompany me," she said with exaggerated patience. "I left her at a tea shop. Trust me, we were both happier that way."

"And yet you ended up kidnapped and on your way to Portugal."

Score one for him. Damn it.

"At any rate," she continued, "Mary could be trouble, but only if Elizabeth doesn't get to her before she realizes something is wrong. If Elizabeth asks her not to say anything, she won't. She's fiendishly loyal. Mary, that is. Well, Elizabeth too, but that's different."

He rubbed one hand over his brow, hard, as if he was having trouble following her.

"Just let me write the addendum," she said, and she hastily added:

> *Postscript: Please assure Mary that I am well. Tell her I came upon one of my cousins and decided to join him for an outing. She **must** not talk indiscreetly. Bribe her if you must. I shall repay you.*

"Your cousins?" he murmured.

"I have many," she said, angling for an ominous tone.

Other than a slight lift of his brow, he gave no reaction. Poppy held out her now-finished missive, and he took it, giving the words one last glance before folding it neatly in half.

The motion was crisp, and horribly final. Poppy exhaled, because it was either that or cry. She waited for him to go—*surely* he would take his leave now, but he just stood there looking thoughtful, until he said, "Your name is very unusual. How did you come by it?"

"It's not so unusual," she muttered.

He leaned toward her, and she could not seem to look away as his eyes crinkled merrily. "You're no Rose or Daisy."

Poppy didn't intend to respond, but then she heard herself say, "It had nothing to do with flowers."

"Really?"

"It came from my brother. He was four, I suppose. My mother let him touch her belly while she was carrying me, and he said it felt like I was popping about."

He smiled, and it made him even more impossibly handsome. "I imagine he's never let you hear the end of that."

And that broke the spell. "He died," Poppy said, looking away. "Five years ago."

"I'm sorry."

"Habit or heartfelt?" she asked waspishly, quite before she had a chance to think about her words. Or her tone.

"Heartfelt," he said quietly.

She said nothing, just looked down at the table, trying to make sense of this strange reality she'd been thrust into. Pirates who apologized? Outlaws who spoke as finely as any duke? Who *were* these people?

"Where shall I have this delivered?" the captain asked, holding up her letter.

"Briar House," Poppy said. "It's near—"

"My men will know where to find it," he cut in.

Poppy watched as he walked to the door. "Sir!" she suddenly called out. "Er, Captain," she amended, furious with herself for offering him the respect of a *sir.*

He lifted one brow in silent question.

"Your name, Captain." And she was delighted that she managed to say it as a statement, not a question.

"Of course," he said, sweeping into a courtly bow. "Captain Andrew James, at your service. Welcome aboard the *Infinity*."

"No 'We're delighted to have you'?" Poppy asked.

He laughed as he placed his hand on the doorknob. "That remains to be seen."

He poked his head out the door and barked out someone's name, and Poppy watched his back as he gave instructions—and the letter—to one of his men. She thought he might then depart, but instead he shut the door and leaned against it, regarding her with a resigned expression.

"Table or bed?" he asked.

What?

So she said it. "What?"

"Table"—he nodded at her before jerking his head toward the corner—"or bed."

This could not be good. Poppy tried to think quickly, to figure out in under a second both his intentions and her possible responses. But all she said was "Ehrm . . ."

"Bed it is," he said crisply.

Poppy let out a shriek as he scooped her up again and tossed her onto the bed.

"It will be better for us both if you don't struggle," he warned her.

Her eyes grew wide with terror.

"Oh, for the love of—" He bit off his statement before he blasphemed, then went on to utter something far worse. He took a moment to compose himself, then said, "I'm not going to defile you, Miss Bridgerton. You have my word."

She said nothing.

"Your hand," he said.

She had no idea what he was talking about, but she lifted her hand nonetheless.

"The other one," he said sharply, then grabbed her left hand—the one with which she wrote, despite her governess's best attempts to force her to switch—and pulled it against the bed rail. Before she could count to five, he'd tied her to the long slat of wood.

They both looked at her free hand.

"You could try," he said, "but you won't get it undone." And then he smiled, damn the man. "No one ties knots like a sailor."

"In that case, could you untie my ankles?"

"Not until we're well at sea, Miss Bridgerton."

"It's not as if I can swim," she lied.

"Shall we toss you in the water to test the truth of that statement?" he asked. "Rather like setting a witch afire. If she burns, she's innocent."

Poppy ground her teeth together. "If I drown—"

"Then you're trustworthy," he finished, smiling broadly. "Shall we give it a go?"

"Get out," she said tightly.

He let out a bark of laughter. "I'll see you when we're well at sea, my little liar."

And then, before she had the chance to even think about throwing something at him, he was gone.

Chapter 3

—✦⟫❈⟪✦—

"Bridgerton," Andrew ground out as he strode furiously across the *Infinity*'s foredeck. "Bridgerton!" Of all the women in all the world, the one who stumbled into his cave—which, he might add, had gone undetected for a full three years—had to be a *Bridgerton*.

It would have only been worse if she'd been a bloody Rokesby.

Thank God he'd never used his family surname aboard the ship; his entire crew knew him only as Andrew James. Which wasn't technically untrue; his full given name was Andrew James Edwin Rokesby. It had seemed prudent not to advertise his aristocratic identity when he took command of the *Infinity*, and he'd never been so glad of it before now. If the girl in his cabin was a Bridgerton, she'd know who the Rokesbys were, and that would cause a cascade of misery all around.

"Bridgerton," he practically groaned, earning him a curious look from one of his deckhands. It was impossible to overstate just how well Andrew knew the Bridgertons, at least the portion of the family that resided in Aubrey Hall, in Kent, just a short distance from his own ancestral home. Lord and Lady Bridgerton were practically a second set of parents to him, and they had become family in truth seven years earlier when their eldest daughter, Billie, had married Andrew's older brother George.

Frankly, Andrew was surprised that he and Poppy Bridgerton had never met. Lord Bridgerton had several younger brothers, and as far as Andrew knew, they'd all had children. There had to be dozens of Bridgerton cousins scattered about the English countryside. He vaguely recalled Billie telling him about family in Somerset, but if they'd ever visited, it had not been when Andrew was home to meet them.

And now one of them was on his ship.

Andrew swore under his breath. If Poppy Bridgerton discovered his true identity, there would be hell to pay. Only thirteen people knew that Andrew James was actually Andrew Rokesby, third son of the Earl of Manston. Of those thirteen, nine were members of his immediate family.

And of those nine, zero knew the real reason for the deception.

It had all started seven years earlier, when Andrew had been sent home from the navy to recuperate after he'd fractured his arm. He had been eager to return to his post aboard the HMS *Titania*—he'd worked hard for his recent promotion to first lieutenant, damn it—but the king's Privy Council had had other ideas.

In their infinite wisdom, the members of the council had decided that the best place for a naval officer was a tiny landlocked principality in central Europe. Andrew was told—and this was a direct quote—to be "charming." *And* to make sure that Wachtenberg-Molstein's Princess Amalia Augusta Maria Theresa Josephine was delivered to London in one virginal piece as a potential bride for the Prince of Wales.

That she'd fallen overboard during the channel crossing was not Andrew's fault. That she'd been rescued, however, was, and when she had then declared that she'd marry none but the man who'd saved her, Andrew had found himself at the center of a diplomatic disaster. The final leg of the trip had involved nothing less than a runaway coach, the disgruntled resignation of two sub-members of the council, and an overturned chamber pot. (On Andrew, not the princess, although you'd think it had been the latter from the way she'd carried on.)

It had been his sister-in-law's favorite story to tell at dinner parties for years. And Andrew had never even told her about the ferret.

In the end, the princess didn't marry Andrew *or* the Prince of Wales, but the Privy Council had been so impressed with Andrew's unflappable demeanor that they decided he could serve his country better out of uniform than in. But not officially. Never officially. When the secretaries of state summoned him for a joint interview, they clarified that when they said *diplomatic* they had meant *conversational*.

They didn't want Andrew to negotiate treaties, they wanted him to talk to people. He was young, he was handsome, he was charming.

People loved him.

Andrew knew this, of course. He'd always made friends easily, and he had that rare gift of being able to talk almost anyone into almost anything. But it had felt strange to be ordered to do something so intangible. And so secret.

He had to resign his naval commission, of course. His parents were dumbfounded. Three years later, when he took command of a ship and began the life of a privateer, they had been disappointed in the extreme.

Privateering was not a noble profession. If an aristocratic gentleman wished to take to the seas, he wore a uniform and swore allegiance to King and Country. He did not command a ship of potentially disreputable sailors and smuggle goods for his own financial gain.

Andrew told his parents that this was why he sailed under an assumed name. He knew that they disapproved of his choices, and he did not want to bring dishonor to the family. What his parents didn't know—since he wasn't allowed to tell them—was that he wasn't just a merchant ship captain. In fact, he'd never been *just* a merchant ship captain. He'd assumed command of the *Infinity* at His Majesty's explicit request.

This had happened in 1782, when the government was reorganized, and the Northern and Southern Departments were transformed into the Home and

Foreign Offices. With foreign affairs finally con-
solidated into one department, the new foreign
secretary had begun to look for innovative ways to
pursue diplomacy and protect British interests. He
had summoned Andrew to London almost immediately upon assuming his office.

When Charles James Fox—the first foreign secretary and former leader of the House of Commons—
asked a man to serve his country, that man did not
say no. Even if it meant deceiving his own family.

Andrew did not perform the crown's bidding on
every voyage—there simply weren't enough tasks for
that, and it would have looked odd if he sat in port
twiddling his thumbs until someone at the Foreign
Office asked him to courier some papers to Spain
or collect a diplomat in Brussels. Most of the time
he was exactly what his crew thought he was—an
ordinary sea captain, with mostly legal cargo.

But not this time. The current foreign secretary
had entrusted a packet of papers to his care, and
he'd been tasked with delivering them to the British
envoy in Portugal. Andrew wasn't sure what it was
all about; he was rarely told the contents of the documents he carried. He suspected it had something
to do with the ongoing negotiations with Spain over
the settlements on the Mosquito Coast. It didn't
matter, really. All that mattered was that he'd been
told to get the papers to Lisbon as soon as possible,
and that meant he had to leave now, when the winds
and tides were favorable. He certainly did not have
time to clear out the cave that Poppy Bridgerton had
discovered. Nor did he have the manpower to leave

three people behind—the number it would take to distribute the goods and guard the girl until the job was done.

If it had just been about profits, he would have abandoned the cargo and taken the financial loss. But the cave was also used as a drop point, and hidden in one of the crates was a letter to the prime minister that Andrew had just brought back from an envoy in Spain. Someone from London was due to pick it up in two days' time. It was vital that the cave remained undisturbed, at least until then.

So he was stuck with Poppy Bridgerton.

"Sir!"

Andrew turned to see Brown heading his way.

"I delivered the letter, sir," the seaman said.

"Good," Andrew grunted. "Did anyone see you?"

Brown shook his head. "I had Pinsley hand it to a housemaid. No one knows him hereabouts. And I made him wear that black wig you keep aboard."

"Good."

"Didn't want to leave it on the steps," Brown added. "Didn't think you'd want to chance it not getting read."

"No, of course not," Andrew said. "You did the right thing."

Brown nodded his thanks. "Pinsley says the maid says she'll give it to the lady of the house straight-away."

Andrew nodded sharply. He could only hope that all went according to plan. There would still be hell to pay when Miss Bridgerton was returned in two weeks' time, but he might be able to retain at least a semblance of control over the situation if her friend kept quiet. And if her friend did keep her mouth shut, and no one ever learned that Poppy had gone missing, Andrew just might avoid having to marry the chit.

Oh yes. He was well aware that this was a very real possibility. He was a gentleman, and he'd compromised a lady, however inadvertently. But he was also pragmatic. And as there was at least a remote chance that she'd emerge from her ordeal with her reputation intact, it seemed best that she not be apprised of his true identity.

At least this was what he was telling himself.

It was time to depart, so Andrew found his place at the wheel, his body stiffening with a rush of excitement as they lifted anchor and the *Infinity*'s wind-filled sails propelled them forward. One would think the sensation would grow old, that so many voyages at sea would have left him immune to the thrill of the wind and the speed and the spray of the sea as they raced across the waves.

But it was still exhilarating, every time. His blood surged, and his lungs filled with the tangy salt air, and he knew that at this moment in time, he was exactly where he was supposed to be.

Which was ironic, he supposed, as he wasn't in an actual place, but rather moving swiftly across the water. Did that mean he was meant to be in motion? Would he live his days on the water? *Should* he live his days on the water?

Or was it time to go home?

Andrew gave his head a shake. This was no time to grow maudlin. Philosophy was for the idle, and he had work to do.

He scanned the sky as he steered the *Infinity* past the town of Lyme Regis and into the English Channel. It was a perfect day for sailing, crisp and clear and with a hearty wind. If the weather held as such, they could reach Portugal in five days.

"Please, God," Andrew said, with the sheepish expression of one who didn't often make divine entreaties. But if ever there was a time for prayer, this was most definitely it. He was confident that he could manage Poppy Bridgerton, but still, he'd rather have her off his hands as soon as possible. As it was, her presence meant the eventual end of his career. At some point she would learn his true name; given how close he was to her cousins, it seemed impossible that she wouldn't.

"Sir?"

Andrew nodded, acknowledging Billy Suggs, at thirteen the youngest hand on the ship.

"Sir, Pinsley says there's a woman on the ship," Billy said. "Is that the truth?"

"It is."

There was a pause, and then Billy said, "Sir? Isn't that devilish bad luck, sir? To have a woman aboard, sir?"

Andrew fought the urge to close his eyes and sigh. This was exactly what he was worried about. Sailors were a notoriously superstitious lot. "Nothing but foolish talk, Billy," he said. "You won't even know she's here."

Billy looked dubious, but he headed back to the galley.

"Hell," Andrew said, despite the fact that there was no one close enough to hear, "if I'm lucky, *I* won't even know she's here."

Chapter 4

By the time Poppy heard the door to the captain's cabin open, she was in a ferociously bad mood.

One to which she rather thought she was entitled. Being bound hand and foot tended to lower the spirits. Well, one hand and two feet. She supposed Captain James had shown some degree of kindness when he'd left her right hand free. Not that it had served her any use. He had not exaggerated when he'd boasted about the quality of sailors' knots. It had taken but a minute for her to conclude that she had no hope of wriggling the rope loose. She supposed a feistier female might have persisted, but Poppy was not fond of raw skin or broken nails, and it was quite clear that that was all she'd achieve if she kept working at the knot.

"I'm hungry," she said, without bothering to look and see who had entered the cabin.

"Thought you might be," came the captain's voice. A warm, crusty roll landed on the bed next to her shoulder. It smelled heavenly.

"Brought you butter too," the captain said.

Poppy thought about turning to face him, but she'd long since realized that any change in position involved a rather undignified amount of grunting and twisting. So she just said, "Shall I fill your bed with crumbs?"

"There are so many interesting rejoinders to such a statement," he said, and she could hear the lazy smile in his voice, "but I will refrain."

Score one for him, *again*. Damn it.

"If you'd like," he said mildly, "I'll free you from your bindings."

That was enough to make her twist her head. "We're well out to sea, then?"

He stepped forward, holding a knife. "Far enough that one would have to be far less clever than you to attempt an escape."

She wrinkled her nose. "Compliment?"

"Absolutely," he said, his smile positively lethal.

"I assume you plan to use that knife on my bindings."

He nodded, slicing her free. "Not that the alternatives aren't tempting."

Her eyes flew to his face.

"I jest," he said, almost rotely.

Poppy was not amused.

The captain just shrugged, tugging the rope out from under her ankles. "My life would be far simpler if you were not here, Miss Bridgerton."

"You could have left me in Charmouth," she reminded him.

"No," he said, "I couldn't have done."

She picked up the roll and took a bite of unladylike proportions.

"You *are* hungry," he murmured.

She shot him a look that told him what she thought of his overly obvious statement.

He tossed another roll in her direction. She caught it one-handed and managed not to smile.

"Well done, Miss Bridgerton," he said.

"I have four brothers," she said with a shrug.

"Do you now?" he asked mildly.

She glanced up briefly from her food. "We're fiendishly competitive."

He pulled a chair out from his surprisingly elegant dining table, then sat, resting one ankle on the opposite knee with lazy grace. "All good at games?"

She leveled her gaze onto his. She could be every bit as nonchalant as he. And if she couldn't, she'd die trying. "Some better than others," she said, then finished up the first roll.

He laughed. "Meaning you're the best?"

She lifted a brow. "I didn't say that."

"You didn't have to."

"I like to win."

"Most people do."

She fully intended to respond with a cuttingly witty rejoinder, but he beat her to the punch with "You, I imagine, however, like to win more than most."

She pursed her lips. "Compliment?"

He shook his head, his lips still curved into a vexing little smile. "Not this time."

"Because you're afraid I'm going to best you?"

"Because I'm afraid you're going to make my life a living hell."

Poppy's lips parted in surprise. That was not what she'd expected him to say. She regarded the second roll, then took a bite. "Some would say," she said once she'd finished chewing, "that such language isn't appropriate in the presence of a lady."

"We're hardly in a drawing room," he returned, "and besides, I thought you said you had four brothers. Surely they've managed to blister your ears once or twice."

They had, of course, and Poppy wasn't so high in the instep that she would faint at the occasional curse. She'd scolded the captain mainly just to annoy him, and she rather suspected he knew that.

Which annoyed *her*.

She decided to change the subject. "I believe you said you'd brought butter."

He motioned gallantly to a small ramekin, resting atop the dining table. "Surely you don't want me to toss *this*," he said, "your superior catching skills notwithstanding."

Poppy rose and walked to the table. She was a bit wobbly, but she couldn't tell if it was from the motion of the sea or the blood returning to her feet.

"Sit," he said, the word more of a request than an order.

She hesitated, his politeness far more disconcerting than incivility might have been.

"I won't bite," he added, leaning back.

She pulled out the chair.

"Unless, of course, you want me to," he murmured.

"Captain James!"

"Oh, for heaven's sake, Miss Bridgerton, you're made of sterner stuff than *that*."

"I don't get your meaning," she ground out.

His lips quirked. Not that they'd ever really stopped quirking; the odious man always looked as if he was up to something. "If you were truly my match," he said, his voice lightly taunting, "you'd not be the least put off by my wordplay."

She sat down and reached for the butter. "I don't generally jest about matters relating to my life or virtue, Captain James."

"A wise rule," he said, leaning back, "but I certainly need not feel constrained by it."

She picked up the butter knife and regarded it thoughtfully.

"Not nearly sharp enough to do me damage," the captain said with a smile.

"No." Poppy sighed, dipping it into the butter. "Pity that." She slathered her roll and took a bite. "Do you plan to keep me on bread and water?"

"Of course not," he said. "I am not so ungentlemanly as that. Supper is due to arrive in"—he checked his pocket watch—"five minutes."

She watched him for a moment. He didn't look like he was going anywhere. "Do you plan to eat here with me?" she asked.

"I don't plan to starve."

"You can't go eat with . . . with . . ." She waved her hand about somewhat ineffectually, not really knowing what she was motioning to.

"My men?" he finished for her. "No. We're a

more liberal ship than most, but it's hardly a democracy. I am the captain. I eat here."

"Alone?"

His smile was slow and wicked. "Unless I have company."

She sucked in her upper lip, refusing to entertain him by rising to his bait.

"Are you enjoying your roll?" he asked felicitously.

"It's delicious."

"Hunger can make anything taste good," he remarked.

"Nonetheless," she said honestly, "it's rather tasty."

"I shall convey your compliments to the chef."

"You have a chef aboard?" she asked, surprised.

He shrugged. "He fancies himself French. I've always suspected he was born in Leeds."

"There's nothing wrong with Leeds," Poppy said.

"Not unless you're a French chef."

A tiny laugh crossed her lips, taking her completely by surprise.

"There now, Miss Bridgerton," the captain said as she finished the second roll, "that wasn't so hard, was it?"

"Chewing, you mean?" she asked innocently. "I've always been rather good at that. At least since I grew teeth."

"Sharp ones, I'm sure."

She smiled. Slowly. "Positively wolfish."

"Not the most appealing of images, and I'm sure you knew I was referring to our conversation." He tilted his head to the side, which somehow made his small smile more lopsided—and more devastating. "It's not so terribly difficult to laugh in my company."

"The more pertinent question would be— Why do you wish me to?"

"Laugh, you mean?"

She nodded.

He leaned forward. "It's a long voyage to Portugal, Miss Bridgerton, and at heart, men are lazy creatures. I'm forced to have you aboard, in my very cabin even, for at least two weeks. It will require far less energy on my part if you're not spitting mad the entire time."

Poppy managed a half smile that was every bit a match with his. "I assure you, Captain James, I never spit."

He laughed aloud. "Touché, Miss Bridgerton."

Poppy sat quietly for a moment. She'd finished both rolls, but supper had not yet arrived, leaving her without anything with which to occupy herself. It made the silence awkward, and she hated that she was staring at her hands to avoid staring at him.

It was *hard* to look at him. It wasn't that he was so handsome, although that was certainly true. And while Poppy was usually comfortable in most social gatherings, she was the first to admit that there were some people who were simply *too* beautiful. One almost had to look away, else risk turning tongue-tied and stupid.

But that wasn't why Captain James made her feel so inept. She was pretty enough, but she was used to being around people who were more attractive than she was. London was full of ladies and gentlemen who spent hours upon hours on their appearance. Poppy could barely sit still long enough for her maid to dress her hair.

The problem with Captain James wasn't his beauty, it was his intelligence. More specifically, he had too much of it.

Poppy could see it in his eyes. She'd spent most of her life being the cleverest person in the room. It wasn't braggadocio, it was fact. But she wasn't so sure she had this man beat.

She stood abruptly and walked to the windows, gazing out over the endless sea. She hadn't had the chance to explore the cabin, not really. Her time on the bed had been spent tied up and staring at the ceiling. And when she was writing the letter to Elizabeth, she'd been far too focused on the task— and on keeping up with the clever captain—to truly examine her surroundings.

"These are very fine windows," she said. The glass was of obvious quality, perhaps a little weather-beaten, but not warped or wavy.

"Thank you."

She nodded, even though she wasn't looking at him. "Are all captain's cabins this commodious?"

"I can't say I've done a thorough study on the subject, but of the ones I've been in, yes. Military ships, especially."

She turned. "You've been aboard a military ship?"

He glanced to the side—not even for a full second—but it was enough to let Poppy know that he'd not meant to let such a detail slip.

"I'd wager you were in the navy," she said.

"Would you now?"

"Either that or you were there as a prisoner, and strange as it seems to say this, since you *did* kidnap me, that doesn't seem likely."

"Because of my high moral fiber?"

"Because you're too clever to get caught."

He laughed at that. "I shall take that as the highest of compliments, Miss Bridgerton. Mostly because I know how grudgingly it was given."

"It would be foolish of me to underestimate your intelligence."

"Indeed it would, and if you will permit me to pay you a compliment, it would be equally foolish for me to underestimate you."

A little thrill ran through Poppy's chest. Men so rarely acknowledged intelligence in a woman. And the fact that it was *he* . . .

. . . had nothing to do with it, she told herself firmly. She walked over to his desk, set against the far wall. Like the table, it was a finely crafted piece of furniture. In fact everything about the cabin spoke of wealth and privilege. The books squeezed tightly on the shelf were those of an educated man, and she was fairly certain the carpet was imported from the Orient.

Or maybe he'd gone to the Orient and brought it back himself. Still, it was quality.

She had always thought ship cabins would be tiny and cramped, but this one was quite spacious. Nothing compared to her bedchamber at home, of course, but still, she could take ten paces between the two walls, and she'd always had a lengthy stride.

"Do you get seasick, Miss Bridgerton?" Captain James asked.

She turned sharply, surprised that she had not yet considered this. "I don't know."

This seemed to amuse him. "How do you feel right now?"

"Fine," she said, the word drawn out long as she paused to take stock of her insides. Nothing was churning, nothing was queasy. "Almost normal, I suppose."

He gave a slow nod. "That's a good sign. I've seen men reduced to invalids even here in the calm waters of the channel."

"This is calm?" Poppy asked. They might not be pitching and rolling, but the floor was definitely unsteady beneath her feet. Nothing like the times she'd been rowed out on a lake.

"Relatively," he replied. "You'll know rough waters once we reach the Atlantic."

"We're not—" She cut herself off. Of course they were not yet in the Atlantic. She knew her geography. She just had never had reason to put it to firsthand use before.

She schooled her features back into what she hoped was a composed expression. "I have never been to sea," she said stiffly. "I expect we will soon learn how I fare."

He opened his mouth to speak, but at that moment a knock sounded at the door, and whatever he might have said was supplanted by "That will be supper."

Poppy scooted out of the way as a towheaded boy of perhaps ten or twelve carried in a tray with covered dishes and a carafe of what looked to be red wine.

"Thank you, Billy," the captain said.

"Sir," Billy grunted, setting the heavily laden tray on the table.

Poppy smiled at the boy—there was no need to be rude to everyone—but he was clearly trying to avoid looking her way.

"Thank you," she said, perhaps a little too loudly.

Billy flushed and gave a jerky nod.

"This is Miss Poppy," the captain said, laying a hand on Billy's shoulder before he could flee. "Aside from me, you will be the only person allowed in this cabin to tend to her. Do you understand?"

"Yes, sir," Billy said, still not looking at her. He seemed downright miserable. "Will there be anything else, sir?"

"No, that will be all. You may return in three quarters of an hour to clear the tray."

Billy nodded and practically sprinted from the room.

"He's at that age," the captain said with a wry lift of his brows, "when there is nothing so scary as an attractive female."

"It's nice to know I scare someone," Poppy half muttered.

The captain let out a bark of laughter. "Oh, you

need not worry on that score. Brown and Green are thoroughly terrified."

"And you?" Poppy asked as she took her seat. "Do I scare you?"

She held her breath as she waited for his answer. She wasn't sure what foolish devil had compelled her to ask such a question, but now that she had, her skin prickled with anticipation.

He took his time in answering, but Poppy didn't think it was with the intent to draw out her unease. His expression grew thoughtful as he lifted the lid on the main dish. "Rabbit in wine," he murmured, "and no, *you* don't scare me." He looked up, his eyes meeting hers in a startling blaze of azure.

She waited for him to elaborate, but he did not, instead ladling the fragrant stew into their bowls.

"What does scare you?" she finally asked.

He chewed. Swallowed. "Well, I don't much like spiders."

His answer was so unexpected she gave a little snort. "Does anyone?"

"Must be someone, I imagine," he said with a one-shouldered shrug. "Don't people study such things at university? Naturalists and the like?"

"But if you were a naturalist, wouldn't you rather study something sweet and fluffy?"

He glanced down at his bowl. "Like a rabbit?"

She tried not to smile. "Point taken."

"I'll be honest," he said, uncovering a small serving dish filled with parsleyed potatoes. "I don't think either of us had a point."

This time, she couldn't help it. She did smile. But she also rolled her eyes.

"See," he said, "I'm not so dreadful."

"Neither am I," she shot back.

He sighed.

"What does that mean?" she asked, instantly suspicious.

"What?"

Her eyes narrowed. "You sighed."

"Am I not allowed to?"

"*Captain James.*"

"Very well," he said, sighing again, and for the first time his face looked almost weary. "I was not dissembling. You don't scare me. But I'll tell you what does."

He paused, and she wondered if it was for dramatic effect or simply so he might consider his words.

"I am petrified," he said with slow deliberation, "by everything you represent."

For a moment, Poppy could do nothing but stare. "What does that mean?" she asked, and she didn't think she sounded defensive. She didn't think she *was* defensive. But she was curious. After a statement like that, how could she be otherwise?

He leaned forward, resting his elbows on the table as his hands formed a steeple. "You, Miss Bridgerton, are a lady of gentle birth. I suspect you're already aware that I have some experience with this particular species."

She nodded. It was clear that Captain James had been born a gentleman. It was right there in everything he did, everything he said. She saw it in the way he moved and spoke, and she wondered if a person could ever truly throw off the customs with which he was raised.

She wondered if the captain had wanted to.

"Simply put, Miss Bridgerton," he continued, "creatures such as yourself have no place on a ship."

Poppy gave him an arch look. "I believe I have already concurred on this point."

"So you did. But much to our joint dismay, there are forces at work which precluded my being able to redeposit you ashore."

"Forces such as what?"

He gave her a practiced smile. "Nothing you need worry your pretty head about."

This time she was *quite* sure he was trying to rankle her. But his condescending statement didn't bother her nearly so much as the fact that he'd known it would.

She did not like being so easily read.

She especially did not like that he was the one to do so.

So she smiled prettily and thanked him when he spooned potatoes onto her plate. And when she caught him regarding her with a curious expression, as if he wasn't quite sure what to make of her non-reaction, she allowed herself some small satisfaction. But just a tiny bit, because frankly, she didn't think she would be able to keep it off her face if she allowed herself to truly savor her triumph.

She did not want to think about what it meant that *this* was what now passed for a triumph.

"Wine?" the captain inquired.

"Please."

He filled her glass, and it was all very civilized. They ate in silence, and Poppy was reasonably content to remain in her own thoughts until the captain swallowed the last bite of his food and remarked, "It's a comfortable bed. When one is not tied up, of course."

Her head shot up. "I beg your pardon?"

"My bed," he said, with a little motion in its direction. "It's very comfortable. There is a rail—you pull it up and it clicks into place. It keeps one from falling out in bad weather."

Poppy felt her eyes widen with alarm as she turned toward his berth. It was larger than she might expect for a sailing vessel, but *surely* it did not fit two. He couldn't possibly imagine they would . . . No, he would never. But he wouldn't be sleeping there. He'd said that he was giving her his room.

"Relax," he said. "The bed is yours."

"Thank you," she said.

"I'll be on the floor."

She gasped audibly. "In here?"

"Where else do you propose I lay my head?"

It took a few tries before she managed to get out "Somewhere else?"

He shrugged. "No room."

Her head shook from side to side, the motion tiny and quick, as if she might be able to jostle his words right out of the cabin. "That can't be true."

"There's always the deck," he said, "but I've been told I'm a restless sleeper. I could roll right overboard."

"Please," she begged, "be serious."

His eyes met hers, and once again she was reminded that he was something more than a devil-may-care rogue. There was nothing amusing in his gaze, and nothing amused. "I am serious," he said.

"My reputation—"

"Won't change either way. If it's discovered you're gone, your reputation will be in tatters regardless of where I sleep. If it's not discovered you're gone, no one will be the wiser."

"Your men will know."

"My men know *me*," he said in a voice that brooked no dissent. "If I tell them you are an honorable lady, and that I sleep at the door to protect you, that is what they will believe."

Poppy brought her hand to her mouth, a nervous gesture she indulged in for only the greatest moments of apprehension. Or at least this was the lie she told herself; she probably did it all the time.

"I can see you do not believe me," the captain said.

"I will be honest," she said. "I do not know what to believe."

He regarded her for a long moment. "Fair enough," he said, and somehow it felt like a compliment. He stood then, and walked to the door. "I will summon Billy to clear the dishes. The poor boy is beside himself, I'm afraid. I assured him he wouldn't even know you were here, and now he's required to carry all your meals."

"He had to be assured that he would not see me? Am I really such a gorgon?"

Captain James smiled, but not with humor. "Any woman is a gorgon on this ship. Very bad luck."

"Do *you* believe that?" Surely he didn't. He couldn't.

"I believe it was very bad luck that you came across my cave."

"But—"

"No," he interrupted with sharp authority. "I do not believe that women are inherently bad luck, on a ship or anywhere. But my men do, and I must take that into consideration. Now then, I've work to do. I'll be gone at least three hours. That should give you time enough to prepare yourself for bed."

Poppy's mouth went slack as she watched him reach for the door handle, and he was halfway out before she yelled, "Wait!"

Chapter 5

---

 ndrew allowed himself a long exhale before he turned around. Miss Bridgerton was standing near the bed, a nervous expression on her face.

No, not nervous. Ill-at-ease was probably a more accurate descriptor. She clearly had something she wished to say.

But she wasn't saying it, which should have been cause for alarm.

"Yes?" he finally prompted.

She shook her head. "Nothing."

He had enough experience with women to know *that* wasn't true. "Are you certain?"

She nodded.

Very well. If she insisted. He acknowledged her evasion with a dip of his chin and turned back to the door.

"I just—"

Damn. He'd come so close. He turned again, the very model of patience.

"I don't have anything to wear," she said in a small voice.

He fought the urge to close his eyes, even for just one weary moment. He hadn't thought her so frivolous. Surely she did not see the need for fancy frocks on the voyage to Portugal.

Then she added, "In which to sleep, and, well, for the days too."

"What's wrong with what you're wearing?" he asked, flicking a hand toward her blue confection. The bodice was made of some sort of large-patterned lace, and the skirt was thankfully plain, with no hoops or bustles that might make shipboard life even more difficult for her.

He thought the dress looked quite nice on her. In fact, he'd entertained thoughts of peeling it from her body before he'd discovered her identity.

"There is nothing wrong with it," she replied, "but I can't wear it for two weeks straight."

"My men generally wear the same clothes for the duration." *He* didn't, but his men did.

"Nevertheless," she said, looking very much as if she was trying not to cringe, "I don't think my dress is going to be practical on deck."

Finally. A problem with an easy solution. "You won't be on deck," he told her.

"*Ever?*"

"It's not safe," he said simply.

"I'll suffocate in here." She waved her arm about, looking less like she was motioning to the cabin and more like she was slightly deranged.

"Don't be silly," he said, wincing inwardly at his dismissive tone. She wouldn't suffocate, but she *would* be miserable. He could already tell that Poppy

Bridgerton was not a person who did well with boredom.

But he couldn't have her wandering the length and breadth of the ship. She was a distraction his men could well do without, and furthermore, she knew nothing of safety at sea. Not to mention how superstitious sailors were about women being bad luck on a ship. Half his men would likely be crossing themselves every time they saw her.

On the other side of the cabin, Miss Bridgerton was still visibly distressed. And stammering. "But—but—"

He moved back toward the door. "I am sorry, Miss Bridgerton, but that is the way it must be. It is for your own safety."

"But for a fortnight? Not to see the sun for an entire fortnight?"

He quirked a brow. "You were just complimenting me on my fine windows."

"It is not the same, and you know it."

He did, and he sympathized. Truly, he did. He couldn't imagine being forced to remain in a ship's cabin for two weeks, even one as well-appointed as his.

"Captain James," she said, after what sounded like a fortifying breath, "I am asking you as a gentleman."

"That is where you are in error."

"Do not dissemble, Captain. You may wish to hide it, or perhaps you wish to hide *from* it, but you were born a gentleman. You have already as much as confessed to it."

He crossed his arms. "On this ship, I am no gentle-man."

She crossed hers. "I don't believe you."

And then something inside him snapped. Just snapped. Since the moment he'd first seen her, tied up and gagged on his bed, he'd spent every minute of his time dealing either with *her* or with the myriad problems her presence wrought—and was about to wreak—on a very delicate mission.

"For the love of Christ, woman," he half exploded, "have you no sense?"

Her mouth opened, but he didn't allow her an answer.

"Do you have any concept of your perilous situation? No? Well, allow me to explain. You have been kidnapped. You are trapped on a ship on which you are the only female, and half the men out there"—he waved his arm almost violently toward the door—"think your very presence means that a typhoon is on its way."

"A typhoon?" she echoed.

"There *are* no typhoons in this region," he ground out. "Which should give you some indication of how much they *don't* want you aboard. So in my humble opinion, not that you're likely to heed it, *you* should start speaking with a bit more circumspection."

"I did not ask to be here!" she shouted.

"I am well aware," he shot back. "For the record—*again*—I am not pleased to be hosting you."

Her lips pressed together, and for one terrifying moment he thought she might cry. "Please," she said. "Please do not force me to remain in this cabin for the duration of the voyage. I beg of you."

He sighed. Damn her. It was so much easier to dismiss her concerns when they were yelling at each other. "Miss Bridgerton," he said, trying to keep his voice even, "it is my duty as a gentleman to ensure your safety. Even if it means your discomfort."

He half expected her to say, "So you *are* a gentleman." But she surprised him with restraint, and after a heavy beat of silence, she said, "I will see you later this evening, then."

He gave a curt nod.

"You will be three hours, you said?" Her voice was formal, almost businesslike, and it made him oddly uncomfortable, almost because it didn't sound like *her*.

Which was patently ridiculous. He didn't know Poppy Bridgerton. He hadn't even been aware of her existence until this very afternoon, at least not in a specific sense. She'd been one of many vague and hazy Bridgerton cousins, utterly nameless, and to him, irrelevant.

So he should not know when she sounded unlike herself.

And he should not care that she did.

"I will be ready," she said, with a touch of haughty pride that still wasn't quite right.

But it wasn't entirely wrong either.

"I bid you good evening, Miss Bridgerton," he said. He gave a brief bow of farewell and exited the cabin. Bloody hell. He needed a drink. Or maybe a good sleep.

He glanced back at his door, now closed and

locked behind him. He'd be on the floor tonight. A good sleep was highly unlikely.

A drink it was, then. And not a moment too soon.

MISS BRIDGERTON WAS still fully clothed when Andrew returned three and a half hours later, but she'd removed the pins from her hair, and it now lay across her shoulder in a sleeping plait. She was sitting upright on his bed, the blankets pulled over her lap. A pillow was wedged between her back and the wall behind her.

His pillow.

Andrew noticed that the curtains were still open, so he crossed the cabin and drew them shut. His cabin was port, and he did not think she would enjoy the blazing eastern sun in the morning. They were not far past the solstice; sunrise was blindingly early this time of year.

"Are you ready for bed?" he asked. The most mundane of questions, and yet he found it remarkable that he had been able to utter it in such a normal tone of voice.

Miss Bridgerton glanced up from the book she was reading. "As you can see."

"You won't be too uncomfortable in your dress?" he asked.

She turned slowly to look at him. "I see no alternative."

Andrew had some experience removing such frocks from women; he knew she had to have some sort of shift underneath it that would be far more comfortable for sleeping.

But far too revealing for either of their comfort.

Not that he had *any* intention of bedding her. God help him if he even so much as kissed the girl. But she was rather attractive, objectively speaking. Her eyes were a gorgeous shade of green, somewhere between leaf and moss, and she had the Bridgerton hair, thick and lustrous, with the color of warm chestnuts. Her mien would never be placid enough for conventional standards of beauty, but he'd never liked expressionless females. Hell, he'd never liked expressionless males either, and Lord knew he'd met enough of those when he was out in society. Andrew had never understood why it was so fashionable to appear bored.

Disinterested equaled disinteresting.

He considered that. An excellent new catch-phrase. He'd use it on his family the next time he went home. They'd likely roll their eyes, but they sort of had to. It was what family did.

God, he missed them. He had eleven nieces and nephews now, and he hadn't even met the most recent two. Of the five Rokesby siblings, only he and his younger brother, Nicholas, were still unwed. The other three were blissfully happy and reproducing like rabbits.

Not with each other, of course. With their spouses. He winced, even though he alone was privy to his convoluted thoughts. He was so tired. It had been a hell of a day, and it was about to get worse. He had no idea how he expected to get any sleep tonight. Between his spot on the floor and the simple presence of *her* in the room . . .

She was impossible to ignore. Maybe it would have been better if she'd been frightened and meek. There would have been tears, but at least when she was out of his sight, she'd have been out of his mind.

He walked over to a built-in set of drawers. His nightshirt was there, as were his tooth powder and brush. Billy usually left a small basin of water on the table, but clearly the boy had been too terrified of Miss Bridgerton to enter the room again. He picked up the toothbrush and regarded it, sighing at the lack of necessary liquid.

"I didn't brush my teeth either."

He smiled. So she *had* been watching him. She'd been trying a little too hard to appear absorbed in her book, but he'd been almost certain that she would give up the ruse the moment his back was turned. "We shall both be foul of breath in the morning," he said.

"A charming prediction."

He glanced at her over his shoulder. "I don't plan to kiss anyone. Do you?"

She was too smart to take such obvious bait, so he popped his toothbrush into his mouth and gave himself a powderless cleaning. It was better than nothing.

"I don't suppose you have an extra on board," she said. "A toothbrush, I mean."

"I'm afraid not, but you're welcome to use your forefinger and some of my powder."

She sighed but nodded, and he found himself oddly pleased that she was so unfussy. "There will be water in the morning," he told her. "There is usually some at night, but I believe you have frightened Billy away."

"He did come to remove the dishes."

"Well, there is that." He didn't tell her that he'd had to grab the boy by his collar and shove him in the right direction. But better Billy than anyone else on the ship. Brown or Green would have been acceptable—Andrew had known both of them long enough to know that they'd not imperil her safety— but he doubted either one of them wanted anything to do with her.

Andrew reached into his drawer for his nightshirt, then stopped. Bloody hell, he was going to have to sleep in his clothing too. He couldn't undress unless he did so after snuffing out the lanterns, and there was something that felt undignified about wearing his nightshirt while she remained fully clothed.

"Are you ready for sleep?" he asked.

"I'd been hoping to read for a bit longer. I trust you don't mind that I borrowed a few of your books."

"Not at all. You'll go mad without something to occupy your time."

"How positively liberal of you."

He rolled his eyes but didn't bother to rejoin. "The light of one lantern won't matter. Just make sure you don't fall asleep with it burning."

"Of course not."

He felt the need to reiterate the point. "Aboard a ship there is no greater disaster than fire."

"I understand," she said.

He had half expected her to respond with a bristly

"I *said* I would douse the lantern." That she had not . . .

He was bizarrely pleased.

"I thank you for your good sense," he said. He noticed that she had not pulled up the rail for the bed, so he walked over to take care of it.

"Captain James!" she exclaimed, and she frantically pressed herself against the back wall.

"Have no fear for your virtue," he said in a tired voice. "I was merely intending to do *this*." He yanked up the rail and clicked it into place. It was a solid piece of wood, meant to keep the occupant of the bed *in* bed when the weather was rough.

"I'm sorry," she said. "It was . . . instinct, I suppose. I am on edge."

He felt his brow draw down. That wasn't a rote apology. Her tone had been too full, too . . . something. He turned back to look at her. She had not moved from the corner, and she looked so small— not in size but in expression, if that made any sense.

Not that anything had made sense today.

In a quiet voice, she said, "I am aware that you would not attack me."

That she might think she needed to apologize, or even worse, *reassure* him in some way . . . it made him ill. "I would never harm a woman," he said.

"I—" Her lips parted, and her eyes grew unfocused with thought. "I believe you."

Something inside him grew fierce. "I would never harm *you*."

"You already have," she whispered.

Their eyes met.

"I fear my reputation will not be so fortunate," she said.

He cursed himself for having nothing but platitudes, but still he said, "We shall cross that bridge when we come to it."

"And yet I cannot stop thinking about it."

His chest squeezed. Christ, it felt like someone had taken his heart in their fist. He turned away—cowardly, he knew, but he didn't have the words to respond to her quiet statement, and he suspected he never would. His voice was rough as he said, "I'd best get my bed ready."

He pulled some extra blankets from the wardrobe and laid them on the carpet. He'd told her he'd be sleeping at the door, but that hardly seemed necessary, given the sturdy lock and his unquestionable command over his men. The carpet wasn't much of a cushion, but it was better than the planked wood of the floor. He blew out one lantern, and then another, until all that remained was the one by the bed, illuminating the book that lay open on Miss Bridgerton's lap.

"You should take the pillow," she said. "I don't need it."

"No." He sighed. This was his penance, he supposed. He hadn't wanted to kidnap her, but he could not escape the bitter truth: this wretched situation was far worse for her than it was for him. He didn't bother looking at her as he shook his head. "You keep—"

The pillow hit him mid-chest.

He smiled wryly. She was stubborn even in her generosity. "Thank you," he said, and he lay down on his back, the least uncomfortable position on such a hard surface.

He heard her rustling about, and then the room went dark.

"I thought you were going to read," he said.

"I changed my mind."

It was just as well. In the dark, it would be easier to forget her presence.

Except it wasn't. She fell asleep first, and then he was alone in the night, listening to her move as she slept, hearing her voice in each quiet breath. And it occurred to him—he'd never spent a night with a woman, not an entire night. He'd never listened to a woman sleep, never even imagined the strange intimacy of it.

It was oddly compelling, lying there and waiting for each soft noise to rise through the air. He could not bring himself to close his eyes, which made no sense. Even if the cabin were lit, he would not be able to see her, tucked away behind the bed rail as she was. He did not feel he needed to remain alert, but he could not stop himself from remaining aware.

What had she said earlier? She was on edge.

He knew exactly what she'd meant.

Chapter 6

When Poppy opened her eyes the following morning, Captain James was already gone. She chewed on her lower lip as she took in the sight of his bedroll on the other side of the cabin. He couldn't have had a good night's sleep. She'd given him the pillow, but other than that, he'd had only the carpet to cushion him.

But *no*. She was not going to feel guilty over his discomfort. He was going about his regular business. *She* was the one who quite possibly had an army of people searching for her, fearing that her body might wash up on the beach. And her family—dear heavens, she could not begin to imagine their distress if Elizabeth had gone ahead and alerted them to Poppy's disappearance.

Her parents had already lost one child, and it had nearly killed them. If they thought Poppy had met with an ill fate . . .

"*Please*, Elizabeth," she whispered. Her friend would be frantic with worry, but if she kept quiet, at least she'd be the only one.

"He's a monster," Poppy said aloud, even though she knew it wasn't true. She hated Captain James for any number of reasons, and she did not believe him when he told her that he'd had no choice but to take her to Portugal—because honestly, how was that even possible? But the captain was treating her with far more care than she imagined most men of his profession would, and she knew—because it was impossible not to know—that he was a gentleman, and a man of honor.

What the devil he was doing on a pirate ship, she couldn't imagine.

She noticed that a small basin of water had been set on the table, and she had a brief queasy moment at the thought of Billy entering the cabin while she slept.

She took some comfort in the fact that he'd probably felt worse.

She decided not to feel guilty about that either.

It took her a few tries to get the bed rail down, and once she had her feet on the floor she raised and lowered it several times until she understood how it worked. It was very cleverly made, and she wished she could see the inner workings—hinges and springs and whatnot. One of her brothers had fallen out of bed quite frequently as a child; a contraption such as this would have been brilliant.

She set the rail into its down position, then moved to the basin so she could splash some water on her face. She might as well greet the day, such as it was. The cabin was dim, with only a thin stripe of light filtering in at the curtain's edge. A glance at the clock told her it was already half eight, so she took care with her balance—the captain had been correct; the sea *was* rougher now that they were well into the Atlantic—and wobbled over to the windows to draw back the heavy fabric.

"Oh!"

The sound escaped her lips without conscious thought. She wasn't sure what she'd expected to see—well, to be honest, she'd expected exactly what she did see, which was the ocean, stretching out for miles and miles until it kissed the blue edge of the horizon. But even so, she had not been prepared for the sheer beauty of it, the enormity, the immensity of it all.

Or how very small it would make her feel.

But it was gorgeous. No, it was more than that. It was tremendous, and she could almost be glad for the circumstances that had brought her here to see it.

She leaned her forehead against the cool glass. For ten minutes she stood there, watching the play of the waves, the way they formed frosty tips like meringues. Every now and then a bird flew into view, and she wondered how far they were from land, and how far a bird could fly before it needed to set itself down. And surely some birds could fly farther than others—what made them able to do that? The weight? The wingspan?

There were so many things she did not know, and so many things she hadn't known to ponder, and now she was stuck here in this cabin instead of up on deck where she might have a grander view of the world.

"They can't be *that* superstitious," she muttered, pushing herself back from the window. Honestly, it was ridiculous that the sailors clung to such nonsense in this day and age. Her eyes fell on the tooth powder the captain had left out for her. She hadn't used it yet. It would serve those sailors right if she ignored it and then went above deck and breathed on everyone.

She rubbed her tongue against the roof of her mouth. Good heavens, her morning mouth was appalling.

She cleaned her teeth, deciding that she enjoyed the minty flavor of the captain's powder, then plopped down in a chair by the window with the book she'd started the night before. It was a treatise on navigation, and truth be told, she didn't understand half of it, but it was clear that it had not been written for novices.

She'd managed a few more pages when a knock sounded at the door.

"Billy," she said, because it must be he. She stood as he let himself in.

He was as red-faced as ever, carrying a tray with her breakfast.

"Good morning," she said, determined to get him to speak to her. "Oh, is that tea?"

"Yes, miss," he stammered.

"How heavenly. I hadn't thought—well, in truth I *hadn't* thought."

Billy turned to her with a perplexed expression. Well, not exactly. He still looked as if he wanted to be anywhere but in her company, but now he also looked confused about his chances for escape.

"I had not given any thought to whether there would be tea," she explained. "But if I *had* considered it, I'm not sure I would have thought I'd be so lucky."

Billy seemed not to know what to make of her meandering statement, and he put the tray down and got to work setting her a place at the table. "The captain insists on it. Says it keeps us civilized. That an' brandy."

"How fortunate for us all."

Billy made a noise that could have been a chuckle if he would allow himself to relax. "He doesn't share the brandy. But he's free with the tea."

Poppy blinked at the sheer number of words that had just emerged from the boy's mouth. "Well, it's still fortunate," she said. "I am very fond of tea."

Billy nodded. "You're a proper lady."

Poppy smiled wistfully. He really was a sweet boy. "How old are you, Billy?"

He looked up with surprise. "Thirteen, miss."

"Oh. I'd thought you younger." Then she could have kicked herself; boys of his age never liked to be mistaken for little children.

But Billy just shrugged. "I know. Everyone thinks I'm not even twelve. M'dad says he didn't grow until he was almost sixteen."

"Well then, I'm sure you shall have a spurt soon," Poppy said encouragingly. "I'm not likely to see you again after this voyage, but if I did, I would expect you to grow as tall as the captain."

He smiled at this. "You're not so bad, miss."

"Thank you." It was a bit ridiculous how pleased she felt by his compliment.

"Never met a proper lady before." He shuffled from foot to foot. "Didn't think you'd be so nice t'me."

"I try to be nice to everyone." She frowned. "Except perhaps the captain."

Billy's mouth fell open, and he looked as if he didn't know if he should laugh or gasp.

"Don't worry," she assured him. "I jest."

Well, a little.

"The captain is the best of men," Billy said fervently. "I promise you. You'll not meet finer. I know I said he doesn't share his brandy, but he's right good in all other ways, an' I don't like brandy, anyway."

"I'm sure you're correct," she said with what she called her drawing room smile. It was the one she used when she did not mean to be *in*sincere . . . but she was not quite being honest either. "I'm just a bit vexed that I'm here."

"You're not the only one." Billy clapped a hand to his mouth. "I'm sorry, miss!"

But Poppy was already laughing. "No, don't apologize. It was very amusing. And from what I've heard, true."

Billy scrunched up his face in sympathy. "It's not normal to have a lady on board, Miss Poppy. I've heard fearsome tales of disaster."

"Disaster brought about by the presence of a woman?"

Billy nodded, perhaps a little too vigorously. "But I don't believe it. Not anymore. The captain told me it weren't true. An' he doesn't lie."

"Ever?"

"Never." Billy said this so firmly Poppy thought he might salute.

"Well," Poppy said briskly, "thank you for bringing breakfast. I am quite hungry."

"Yes, miss. If y'want, just leave the tray outside the door. Then I won't have to bother you when I collect it."

Poppy couldn't bring herself to tell him that their conversations were likely to be the high point of her day, so instead she said, "It won't be a bother. And besides, I don't think I'm permitted to open the door."

Billy frowned. "Not even open it?"

Poppy shrugged and held her hands out as if to say, *Who knows?* "The captain and I did not discuss the particulars of my confinement."

"Seems a bit unreasonable," Billy said, scratching his head. "The captain's not usually like that."

Poppy shrugged again, this time tipping her head to the side in an *I-don't-know-what-to-tell-you* expression.

"Well," Billy said with a little bow, "I hope you enjoy your breakfast. I think Cook gave you bacon."

"Thank you again, Billy. I—" She cut herself off when he opened the door. "Oh, one thing!"

He paused. "Yes, miss?"

"Can I peek out?"

"Beg pardon?"

It was ludicrous that she even had to ask. "Can I peek outside the door? I haven't even seen the corridor."

"How'd you get here?"

"I was in a sack."

Billy's face went slack. "But you're a proper lady!"

"Not all the time, apparently," she muttered, and she dashed over to the open door to stick out her head.

"Not much to see," Billy said regretfully.

But she still found it interesting. It was obviously the nicest part of the ship, or at least Poppy assumed it was. The hallway was not lit, but a small patch of sunlight shone down the stairwell, and she could see that the wooden walls were oiled and polished. There were three other doors, all on the other side of the corridor, and each had a well-made brass handle. "Who sleeps in the other cabins?" she asked.

"That one's for the navigator," Billy said with a jerk of his head. "His name is Mr. Carroway. He doesn't say much, 'cept when he's navigating."

"And the others?"

"That one's for Mr. Jenkins. He's second in command. And the other one"—Billy pointed to the door farthest away—"Brown an' Green share it."

"Really?" Poppy would have thought they'd be down below with the rest of the sailors.

Billy nodded. "They've been with the captain the longest. He said he likes to reward loyalty."

"My goodness," Poppy said, craning her neck even though there wasn't much of anything to see. "How positively revolutionary of him."

"He's a good man," Billy said. "The best."

Poppy supposed it spoke well of Captain James that he inspired such devotion, but honestly, the gushing was getting to be a bit much.

"I'll come back for the tray in an hour, miss," Billy said, and with a nod he dashed away and up the stairs.

To freedom.

Poppy gazed longingly at the patch of sunlight. If the light reached the stairwell, didn't that mean one could see the sky from the bottom of the stairs? Surely it wouldn't hurt if she took a quick peek. No one would know. According to Billy, only five men had any business in this area of the ship, and they were all presumably at their stations.

Gingerly, she pulled the door almost closed so that it was resting carefully against its frame. She tiptoed her way to the staircase, feeling foolish but well aware that this was probably the most excitement she'd have all day. When she reached the end of the corridor, she pressed her back against the wall, mostly because it felt like some subterfuge was in order. And then she looked up and angled her body toward the stairs, deciding that even a stripe of blue sky would be a victory.

Just a little farther, and then—

The ship pitched to the side, sending her tumbling to the floor. Poppy rubbed her hip as she hauled herself back upright, muttering, "Of all the—"

She froze.

The door . . .

The door she'd so carefully rested in place against the frame . . .

The lurch of the ship had pulled it shut.

Poppy gasped and ran back to the cabin, but when she pressed down on the door handle, it moved barely

a quarter inch before informing her that she was
locked out.

No no *no*. This couldn't be happening. She leaned
against the door and sank down until she was on
her haunches. Billy had said he'd be back in an hour
for the tray. She'd just wait here, and no one would
be the wiser.

Then she thought about the tea. It would be stone
cold and black as death by the time she got to it.

Somehow that seemed the worst tragedy of all.

Chapter 7

It was a strange combination of exhaustion, irritation, and guilt that prompted Andrew to hand the wheel to Mr. Jenkins and head below to check on Miss Bridgerton. The exhaustion was obvious; he couldn't have got more than three hours' sleep the night before. The irritation was with himself. He'd been in a foul mood all morning, barking orders and snapping at his men, none of whom deserved his temper.

The guilt . . . well, *that* was what had put him in a bad mood in the first place. He *knew* it was in Miss Bridgerton's best interest to remain sequestered in the cabin, but he kept seeing her pained face when she pleaded with him to allow her on deck the night before. She had been honestly distressed, and it ate at his gut because he knew that if he were in her position, he would feel the exact same way.

This unexpected sympathy left him incensed. He had no cause to feel remorse over locking her in the cabin; it wasn't *his* fault she'd gone into the damn cave. And maybe it wasn't *her* fault that the foreign secretary had ordered him to take a diplomatic pouch to Lisbon, but that was beside the point. She would be safest in his cabin. His decision was right and sensible, and as captain, his command must be unquestioned.

But every time he tried to get on with the work of the day, Poppy Bridgerton's sad, trembling face filtered through his mind. He started to write an entry in the ship's log, but his quill hovered over the paper for so long that a fat drop of ink slid from the nib and stained the page. Thinking that good, hard manual labor might be what he needed, he decided he might as well go aloft, and so he left the bridge and headed on deck to climb the rigging.

Once there, however, he seemed to forget why he'd come. He just stood there, hand on the ratline, his thoughts alternating between Miss Bridgerton and his cursed inability to *stop* thinking about Miss Bridgerton. Finally, he let out a stream of invective so vulgar that one of his men actually went bug-eyed and backed carefully away.

He'd managed to offend the sensibilities of a hardened sailor. Under any other circumstances, he'd have taken pride in that.

Eventually he gave in to the guilt and decided to see how she was getting on. Bored out of her skull, he imagined. He'd seen the book she was reading the night before. *Advanced Methods of Maritime Navigation*. He himself read it occasionally—whenever he was having difficulty falling asleep. It never failed to knock him out in under ten minutes.

He'd found something much better—a novel he'd

read a few months earlier and lent to Mr. Jenkins. His sister had liked it. She'd been the one to give it to him, actually, so he thought it might be to Miss Bridgerton's taste.

Down the stairs he went, imagining how grateful she'd be.

Instead—

"What the devil?"

Miss Bridgerton was sitting on the floor with her legs outstretched, her back against the door to his cabin. In the corridor, very clearly *not* where she was supposed to be.

"It was an accident," she said immediately.

"Get up," he snapped.

She did, moving quickly out of his way as he jammed his key into the lock.

"I didn't mean to do it," she protested, yelping when he grabbed her wrist and hauled her into the cabin. "I just took a peek into the hall when Billy left and—"

"Oh, so now you've dragged him into this?"

"No! I would never." Her manner suddenly shifted to something more contemplative. "He's really quite sweet."

"*What?*"

"Sorry. My point was, I would never take advantage of his good nature. He's just a boy."

He didn't know why he believed her, but he did. This did not, however, make him one jot less furious.

"I just wanted to see what it looked like outside the door," she said. "I arrived in a *sack*, if you recall. And then the ship moved—well, it was more of a lurch, really, quite violent, and I was thrown against the opposite wall."

"And the door closed," he said dubiously.

"Yes!" she exclaimed, obviously not comprehending his tone. "That's exactly what happened. And I didn't even get to drink my tea!"

He stared at her. Tea? Really?

"I almost cried," she confessed. "I haven't yet, you know, despite everything, and you have no idea how lucky you are that I'm not a crying sort of female. But when I was out there, and I realized my tea was going cold, I almost cried."

She was so earnest that it was difficult to sustain an appropriate level of anger, but Andrew was determined to try. "You disobeyed me," he said in a curt voice. "I specifically told you not to leave the room."

"But the ship moved!"

"*As they do*," he ground out. "Perhaps you've noticed the ocean?"

Her lips pressed together at his sarcasm. "I am unfamiliar with ships," she said through clenched teeth. "I did not expect such a jolt."

He leaned in menacingly and spoke with the same frosty tone. "You shouldn't have been hanging out the door."

"Well, then I'm *sorry* for that," she ground out, in what had to be the least gracious apology he'd ever heard.

But strangely, he thought it was sincere.

"Don't let it happen again," he said sharply. But he spared her the indignity of having to respond by turning away and moving to his desk. He shoved the novel onto his shelf, not wanting her to think that he'd come down because he was trying to make her detention more pleasant. This was a ship, and bad behavior could not be rewarded. She had disobeyed his explicit instructions; if one of his men had done the same, he'd have been put on rat-catching duty for a week. Or been flogged, depending on the severity of the transgression.

He wasn't sure Miss Bridgerton had learned her lesson—probably not, knowing her—but he rather thought he'd said all there was to say on the matter. So instead he pretended to look for something on his desk. He could only keep up such a ruse for so long, though, and she was just standing there staring at him, so he said, perhaps a bit more harshly than was necessary, "Eat your breakfast."

And then—God above, he would swear it was like his mother was in that very cabin, yanking on his ear and telling him to mind his manners—he heard himself clear his throat, and he added, "Please."

POPPY'S JAW DROPPED. Captain James changed topics with enough speed to make her dizzy. "I—all right."

She watched him for a moment, then walked carefully—why, she did not know; it just seemed like she ought to be extra quiet—back to the table. She lifted the lid to the dish after she sat down. Eggs, bacon, and toast. Stone cold, all of it.

But beggars couldn't be choosers, and technically it *was* her fault that she'd been locked out, so she ate quietly and without complaint. The eggs were less than appetizing, but the toast and bacon held up reasonably well at their lower temperatures.

She supposed she should be glad she hadn't been served porridge.

The captain's desk was on the far side of the cabin, so she had a perfect view of his back as he rummaged about. "Where is that navigation book?" he finally asked.

She took a moment to chew and swallow. "The one I was reading last night?"

"Yes."

"It's still on the bed. Do you need it?"

"For Mr. Carroway," he said brusquely. "The navigator."

"Yes, I know," she said as she rose to her feet and walked over to the bed. "Billy told me about him. Your second in command is Mr. Jenkins, is that correct?"

"Indeed."

"I suppose it is beneficial to know the names of the officers even if I am unlikely ever to interact with them."

His jaw stiffened. "You do like to make that point, don't you?"

"It is one of my few pleasures," she murmured.

He rolled his eyes but didn't otherwise reply, so she retrieved the navigation guide from the bed and handed it to him. "One would hope Mr. Carroway already possesses the skills outlined within."

The captain made no sign of amusement. "I can assure you he possesses all the necessary skills."

And then there it was again. That phenomenally foolish little devil on her shoulder, urging her to prove that she was every bit as clever as he. She curved her lips and murmured, "Do *you* possess the necessary skills?"

Her regret was instant.

He, on the other hand, seemed to relish the question. His smile was languid and vaguely patronizing, and the air between them grew hot.

He leaned forward, and for a moment she thought he was going to reach out and touch her. Instead she found herself awkwardly tucking a lock of hair behind her ear, as if her raised arm could even pretend to offer protection from him.

"Oh, Miss Bridgerton," he purred, "do you really want to pursue that line of questioning?"

Stupid, stupid girl. What had she been thinking? This was not a game she was qualified to play, especially not with him. Captain James was not like anyone of her acquaintance. He had the comportment and speech of a gentleman, and in so many ways he *was* a gentleman, but he took such obvious pleasure in poking at the boundaries of polite behavior. Granted, she had found herself in a situation for which there *were* no rules of polite behavior, but somehow she thought that if she met him in a ballroom, he'd behave in almost exactly the same manner.

Some people broke rules.

Others merely wished to.

Poppy wasn't sure to which category she belonged. Maybe neither. For some reason, that depressed her.

"How old are you, Miss Bridgerton?" the captain inquired.

Poppy was immediately on her guard. "Why do you ask?"

He did not answer her question, of course. He just kept watching her with that heavy-lidded stare. "Humor me."

"Very well," she said, when she could not think of a reason she ought not reveal her age. "I am two and twenty."

"Old enough to be married, then."

There was an insult in there somewhere, even if she wasn't quite sure what it was. "I am not married because I do not wish to be," she said with clipped formality.

He was still standing too close, and she was uncomfortably near the bed, so she tried to put a halt to the conversation by stepping around him. She moved to the window, but he followed her pace for pace.

His voice held equal parts arrogance and amusement when he asked, "You do not wish to be married or you do not wish to be married to any of the men who have asked for your hand?"

She kept her gaze firmly on the azure view. "I do not see how that is any of your business."

"I ask," he murmured, moving slightly closer, "if only to ascertain *your* skills."

She drew back, looking at him despite all of her best intentions. "I beg your pardon?"

"In the art of *flirting*, Miss Bridgerton." He placed a hand over his heart. "Goodness, you jump to conclusions."

She fought to keep her teeth from grinding into

powder. "I am not, as you have so deftly demon-strated, up to your standards in that realm."

"I shall take that as a compliment, even though I'm fairly certain it wasn't meant as such." He stepped away then, giving her his back as he wandered over to his desk.

But Poppy had not even managed to exhale before he abruptly turned around and remarked, "But surely you agree that flirting is an art, and not a science."

She had no idea what they were talking about anymore. "I will agree to no such thing."

"You think it a science, then?"

"No!" she almost yelled. He was baiting her, and they both knew it, and she hated that he was win-ning this twisted competition between them. But she knew she had to remain calm, so she took a moment to compose herself. Several moments, actually. And one very deep breath. Finally, with what she felt was admirable gravity, she tipped her chin up by an inch and said, "I don't think it's either, and it's certainly not an appropriate conversation between two un-married individuals."

"Hmmm." He made a show of considering this. "I rather think two unmarried individuals are pre-cisely the sort of people who ought to be having such a conversation."

That was it. She was *done*.

If he wanted to talk, he could do so until his eyes bled, but she was through with this conversation. She returned to her breakfast, buttering her toast with such fervor that the knife poked through and jabbed her hand. "Ow," she muttered, more at the surprise than the pain. It was just a butter knife, too dull to break her skin.

"Are you hurt?"

She took an angry bite of toast. "Don't talk to me."

"Well, that's rather difficult, seeing as how we're sharing a cabin."

Her hands came down on the table with startling force and she jerked herself to her feet. "Are you *trying* to torture me?"

"You know," he said thoughtfully, "I rather think I am."

She felt her mouth grow slack, and for a moment she could do nothing but stare at him. "Why?"

He shrugged. "You annoy me."

"Well, you annoy me too," she shot right back.

And then he laughed. He laughed as if he couldn't help it, as if it were the only possible reaction to her words. "Oh come now, Miss Bridgerton," he said when he caught her watching him as if he'd gone mad, "even you must admit we've hit a new low." He chuckled some more, then added, "I feel as if I've been tossed back into a childhood spat with one of my siblings."

She felt herself thawing, but only a little bit.

He offered her a conspiratorial grin. "I have the most astonishing urge to pull your hair and say, 'You annoy me more.'"

She pressed her lips together, because she didn't want to say what she was dying to say, which was "You annoy me even *more*."

He looked at her.

She looked at him.

Eyes went narrow on both sides.

"You know you want to say it," he goaded.

"I'm not talking to you."

"You just did."

"Are you *three*?"

"I believe we have already concluded that we are both acting like children."

"Fine. You annoy me even more. You annoy me more than all of my brothers put together. You annoy me like a wart annoys the bottom of one's foot, like rain annoys a garden party, like misquoted Shakespeare annoys my very soul!"

He looked at her with renewed respect. "Well," he murmured, "nothing can come of nothing."

She glared at him.

"What? That was perfectly quoted. *King Lear*, I believe." He cocked his head to the side. "Also, do you have warts?"

She threw up her arms. "Oh my God."

"Because if you do, it would be only polite to inform me. They're highly contagious, you know."

"I'm going to kill you," she said, her statement more of an incredulous conclusion than a rant. "By the end of this voyage, I will have strangled you. I am quite certain of it."

He reached down and swiped a piece of her bacon. "It's harder than you think, strangling a man."

She shook her head in disbelief. "Dare I inquire how you know such a thing?"

He tapped his chest and said, "Privateer," as if that were explanation enough. "One often ends up in unsavory locales. Not that *I've* strangled anyone, mind you, but I've seen it attempted."

He spoke so offhandedly, as if he were discussing village gossip or an impending change of the weather. Poppy couldn't decide if she was appalled or fascinated. This had to be somewhere on the list of Things One Ought Not to Bring Up at Breakfast, but still . . .

She couldn't resist. "I know I shouldn't ask but—"

"I intervened," he said, taking the lid off the tea and peeking inside. He glanced up, the blue of his eyes glinting devilishly through his lashes. "That *was* your question, I assume."

It was unsettling how easily he deduced her thoughts, but surely anyone of sound mind would have had the same question. "It was," she confirmed, "but I assure you I don't want to know the details."

"Please, Miss Bridgerton. You know that you do." He rested his hip against the edge of the table and leaned roguishly toward her. "But I shan't tell you the story. You'll have to beg for it later."

Poppy shook her head, refusing to be trapped into another juvenile exchange. At this rate they'd be stuck in an endless loop of *will-not, will-too* until they reached Portugal. Besides, she'd seen enough of his skill with double entendre not to make a fuss over any statement containing the word *beg*.

"Is that a pelican?" he asked, his arm reaching out even as he looked toward the window.

She slapped his hand. "Not the bacon."

So he took her last triangle of toast. "It was worth a try."

"Captain James," she asked, "how many siblings do you have?"

"Four." He bit off one corner of the toast. "Three brothers and one sister. Why do you ask?"

She cast a cynical glance at the purloined toast, bitten down into a slightly off-kilter rhombus. "I knew you had to have several."

He grinned. "Aren't you perceptive."

"I'd wager you're not the oldest."

"Well, that much is obvious. If I were the heir, I'd not be out here on the water, would I?"

Not the heir . . . "Interesting," she murmured.

"What?"

"You referred to your brother as the heir. One has to come from a specific sort of background to do that."

"Not necessarily," he said, but she knew he was trying to cover his tracks. He'd let slip another detail of his background, which meant she now knew two things about him: he had served in the navy, and his family were likely members of the landed gentry.

He had not confirmed either detail, of course, but she had faith in her conclusions.

"Regardless . . ." she said, deciding not to pursue it further for now. Better to tuck the tidbit away for future use. "You don't act like the oldest."

He nodded in a most courtly manner, acknowledging her point.

"But I'd also wager you're"—she touched a finger to her mouth as she pondered this—"not the *youngest*."

He seemed to find this amusing. "But . . . ?"

"The second to youngest. Most definitely."

"Why, Miss Bridgerton, you are correct. May I ask how you came to your conclusion?"

"You're not spoiled," she said with an assessing eye, "so I wouldn't think you the youngest."

"You don't find me spoiled? I'm touched."

She rolled her eyes. "But as you've so ably just demonstrated, you're highly irritating. Enough so to be the second youngest."

"Highly irritating?" He let out a bark of laughter. "From you I take that as the highest of compliments."

She nodded graciously. "Please do, if it gives you comfort."

He leaned toward her, his voice growing husky. "I am always in need of comfort," he murmured.

Poppy's cheeks caught fire. Score another one for him, damn it.

His grin made it quite clear that he was not oblivious to her distress, but he must have taken pity on her, because he popped the last bite of toast into his mouth and said, "And now I must ask where you fall in your own family order."

"Right in the middle," she replied, relieved to have returned to the previous topic. "Two brothers on one side, and two on the other."

"No sisters?"

She shook her head.

"Well, that explains a lot."

She rolled her eyes. Again.

He looked mildly disappointed that she did not ask him to elaborate, but knowing him, he probably assumed she'd beg for that story later too. "I'll be on my way, then," he said. "The ship won't steer itself."

"But surely Mr. Jenkins or Mr. Carroway can do so."

"Indeed they can," he allowed. "But I do like to keep an eye on things. I rarely spend much time in my cabin during the day."

"Why *did* you come down?"

He looked at her blankly for a moment, then said, "Oh yes, the book." He picked it up, made a little emphasizing motion with it in the air, and said, "Must give this to Mr. Carroway."

"I would tell you to give him my regards, but of course I do not know him."

He gave her a wry half smile. "Your greatest pleasure."

"For now, at least."

He acknowledged her quip with an approving nod. "Well done, Miss Bridgerton."

Out the door he went, leaving her alone with her breakfast and her thoughts, which unfortunately consisted of one part pleasure at his compliment and twelve parts annoyance with herself for feeling that way.

She supposed she'd better get used to such inner conflict. She had a hunch it would be with her the rest of the voyage.

Chapter 8

⟶⬥⧓⬥⟵

$\mathcal{T}$he rest of the day passed uneventfully. Poppy found a novel she hadn't noticed on the shelf the night before and gave it a try, moving—as boredom dictated—from the bed to a chair, to a different chair, and then back to the bed. When the sky began to dim, she went to the windows, but they must have been facing east, because the sky went from blue to dark blue to black without even a speck of orange or pink.

There might have been a moment of indigo in there somewhere, but that was probably just wishful thinking.

It stood to reason, though, that if she was facing east on the way to Portugal, she'd be facing west on the way back. She consoled herself with the knowledge that there would be sunsets galore as she voyaged home. She supposed she could rouse herself early to watch the sun rise, but she knew her habits well enough to know *that* was not going to happen.

Billy's timid knock sounded at the door, and even

though Poppy knew he had a key, she got up to greet him. It seemed only polite, as she assumed he was carrying a heavy tray.

"Good evening, miss," he said when he saw her.

Poppy moved aside to let him pass. "Come in. Dinner smells delicious."

"Chicken in sauce, miss. I had some earlier. 'Twas good, it was."

"What kind of sauce?"

Billy set the tray on the table and frowned. "I don't right know. It's kind of a brown, I think."

"Brown sauce," she said with a friendly smile. "It is one of my favorites."

Billy grinned back, and she suspected he'd be calling whatever this dish was *Chicken in Brown Sauce* for the rest of his life.

"Will the captain be dining here tonight?" she asked.

"I don't know, miss. I brought enough food for two, but he's very busy above deck."

"Busy? I hope nothing is wrong."

"Oh no," he said reassuringly. "He's always got a lot to do. We just thought you'd be getting hungry."

"We?"

"Me an' Brown an' Green," Billy said. He took an empty plate from the tray and began to set her a place. "We've been talking about you."

"Do I want to know what you've been saying?"

"Well, *I've* had only nice things."

Poppy winced. "Brown and Green and I did not get off to the best of beginnings."

"Well, *you* can't be blamed for being angry," Billy said loyally.

"That's very ki—"

"And *they* was just doing their jobs."

Poppy decided not to push the issue. "So they were."

"The captain said they're allowed to come see you. If I'm busy, that is." Billy gave her a sympathetic look. "He said no one else, though. But he said it in an awful strange way."

"What do you mean?"

"He said—" Billy made a scrunched-up grimace. "I'm probably going t'get this wrong. He speaks right fancy sometimes."

"What did he *say*, Billy?"

"He said . . ." Billy paused again, his head bobbing up and down as he mouthed the words before actually saying them. "He said 'twould be his greatest pleasure if you did not have occasion t'meet any of the other men."

Poppy clapped a hand over her mouth, but she couldn't quite stifle her bubble of laughter.

"I think it might mean he fancies you," Billy said.

"Oh no," she said with great alacrity. "I assure you it does not."

Billy shrugged. "He's never talked about any other lady before."

"Quite possibly because I'm the only one who has ever had cause to be aboard," Poppy replied, with no great lack of irony.

"Well, that's true," Billy confirmed, "at least as

far as I know." He went back to setting her place, then did the same for the captain. "In case he comes for supper. That is t'say he *will* come and dine. He has to eat, and he always takes his meal in his cabin. It just might not be at the same time you do." He stepped back, then motioned to the covered dish at the center of the table. "It's one of his favorite meals. Chicken in brown sauce. He loves it."

Poppy stifled a smile. "I'm sure it will be delicious."

"I'll come back for the tray at— Well, no I won't," Billy said with a frown. "I don't know when I'll come back for the tray, seeing as how I don't know when the captain will be eating." He thought for a moment. "Don't worry, I'll figure out something."

"I have every faith in your powers of deduction," Poppy said gamely.

"I don't know what that means," Billy said with great enthusiasm, "but I think it's good."

"It's very good," Poppy said with a laugh. "I promise."

He gave her a friendly nod and let himself out. Poppy just smiled and shook her head. She could hardly believe he was the same boy who wouldn't even look at her the day before. She considered it a personal victory that she'd got him to speak to her. A rather fortunate personal victory considering that Billy was now her only friend on the ship.

"Be glad you *have* a friend," she admonished herself. This could be worse. That was what she had been telling herself all afternoon. Back in England, her entire life might already have fallen apart—she wouldn't know for sure until she returned—but for now she was in good health, unmolested, and—she took the lid off the serving dish and took a whiff of her supper—being fed remarkably well.

"Chicken in brown sauce," she murmured. It was as good a description as any. She put a piece on her plate, along with a serving of an unfamiliar rice dish, then set the lids back in place so that the food would remain warm for Captain James.

Not like her eggs. Or her tea.

That wasn't his fault, she reminded herself. There was a preposterous number of other things that *were* his fault, but she could not blame him for her breakfast.

She ate in silence, staring out the window at the fathomless sea. There must have been a moon, because she could see its ethereal reflection on the waves, but it didn't do much to illuminate the night. The sky was inky dark and endless, with stars peeking through like pinpricks. The heavens felt huge out on the water, so different from at home. Or maybe it wasn't different at all, and it was just that right now she felt so very much more alone.

How different this voyage might have been under more auspicious circumstances. She tried to imagine taking to the sea with her family. It would never happen, of course; neither of her parents cared for travel. But Poppy imagined it all the same—standing on deck with her brothers, laughing as the wind and the waves set them off-balance. Would any of them have grown seasick? Richard, most likely. There were any number of foods that did not agree with him. In their childhood, he'd thrown up more than the other four put together.

Poppy chuckled to herself. What a thing to think about. If she were home, she'd say as much to her mother, if only to hear her shriek. Anne Bridgerton did have a sense of humor, but it did not extend to bodily fluids. Poppy, on the other hand, had been far too influenced by her brothers to be so fussy.

Roger had been the worst. And of course, the best. He was her fiercest protector, but he'd had far too much mischief and humor to ever be stern. He was clever too, as clever as she was, but he was the oldest, and his extra years of experience and education made it impossible for the others to keep up. For example, he would never just leave a toad in his brother's bed. That would have been far too pedestrian.

No, when Roger turned to amphibians, he made sure they fell from the sky. Or at least from the ceiling, and onto Richard's head. Poppy still wasn't sure how he'd managed that with such accuracy.

Then there was what he called his crown jewel. He spent six months secretly tutoring Poppy in false vocabulary, and she dutifully complied, writing such things in her primer as:

TINTON, NOUN. THE DELICIOUS CRUST MADE BY BURNT SUGAR ON A PUDDING.

and

FIMPLE, ADVERB. ALMOST, NEARLY.

He declared his life complete the day she approached their mother and asked, "Is the apple cream fimple out of the blackbox? You know how much I chime when it gets a tinton."

Her mother had fainted on the spot. Her father, upon learning the extent of Roger's preparation, mused that he was not sure he could bring himself to mete punishment for such a well-thought-out plan. He'd even opined that perhaps such diligence ought to be rewarded. Indeed, Roger might have received that new épée he'd been coveting had not Mrs. Bridgerton overheard. With strength no one knew she possessed, she smacked her husband on the back of his head and demanded, "Have you *heard* your daughter? She's talking to the maids about plumwort and farfar!"

"She's especially fond of plumwort," Roger said with a smirk.

Mr. Bridgerton turned to him with a sigh-crossed groan. "You realize now that I *have* to punish you?"

Poppy was never quite certain just what punishment her father had chosen, but she did recall that Roger smelled remarkably like the chicken coop for several weeks, and, proving that punishment occasionally did fit its crime, her mother had required him to write, "I will not farfar my sister," one thousand times in *his* primer.

But he'd only had to do so nine hundred times. Poppy had sneaked in to help him, taking the quill and doing a hundred lines for him.

He was her favorite brother. She would have done anything for him.

She wished she still could. Even now, after five years, it was so hard to believe he was gone.

With a sigh, and then another and another, she wandered aimlessly around the cabin. Captain James had not told her what time he normally took his dinner, but after the clock struck seven, then eight, then nine, she decided there was no point in saving the pudding. Poppy took the larger of the two slices of pie, then pulled a chair up close to the window so she could gaze out as she ate.

"My compliments to the chef," she murmured, casting an eye back to where the other piece of pie sat on the table. "If he's not back by . . ."

Ten, she decided. If the captain didn't return by ten, she'd eat his pie. It was only fair.

In the meantime, she'd take very small bites. She might be able to make it last until—

She looked down at her empty plate. Never mind. She'd never been able to make her sweets last. Richard had been just the opposite, savoring each bite until the very end, at which point he moaned with pleasure, not because the pudding was especially delicious (although it was; their cook had had a particular talent for baking), but rather to torture his less patient siblings. Poppy had swiped one of his biscuits once, as much out of irritation as hunger, and when he'd noticed he'd walloped her.

Then her father had walloped him.

It had been worth it. Even when her mother had taken her aside for a lecture on ladylike behavior, it had been worth it. The only thing that would have made it better was if Poppy had got to do some walloping herself.

"Wallop," she said aloud. She liked that word.

It sounded rather like its meaning. Onomatopoeia. Another word she liked.

Strangely, *it* didn't sound like its meaning. An onomatopoeia ought to be one of those crawly things with fuzzy legs, not a literary device.

She looked down at the dish in her hand. "Plate," she said. No, it didn't sound anything like what it was. "Bowl?"

Dear God, she was talking to crockery.

Had she *ever* been so bored?

She was on a *ship*, for heaven's sake. Heading to exotic climes. She ought not to feel as if her brain was desiccating. She ought to feel—

Well, what she ought to feel was terror, but she'd already done that, so didn't she now deserve a little excitement? Surely she'd earned it.

"Yes, I have," she said firmly.

"Have you?" came the amused voice of Captain James.

Poppy shrieked with surprise and jumped nearly a foot in the air. It was a wonder she didn't drop her dessert plate. "How did you enter so quietly?" she demanded.

Although honestly, it did sound more like an accusation.

The captain just shrugged. "Have you eaten?" he asked.

"Yes," Poppy said, still waiting for her pulse to return to normal. She waved her hand to the table. "I saved some for you. I don't know if it will still be warm."

"Likely not," he said, heading straight for the

table. He didn't sound concerned. "Ah . . ." He sighed appreciatively. "Chicken in brown sauce. My favorite."

Poppy's head whipped around.

He gave her a queer look. "Is something amiss?"

"Chicken in brown sauce? That's what you actually call it?"

"What else would you call it?"

Poppy's mouth opened, and it hung that way for about two seconds too long. Finally she made a steadying motion with her hands and said, "Never mind."

The captain shrugged, indifferent to the meanderings of her conversation, and he dug into his food with the speed of a man who had put in a hard day of work.

"Chicken in brown sauce," Poppy said to herself. "Who could have known?"

The captain paused with his fork halfway between plate and mouth. "Do you have a problem with the food?"

"No," she said. "No. It's—" She shook her head. "It's nothing. I have been talking to myself all day."

He took a bite and nodded. "As opposed to all those people you'll never have occasion to meet?"

She pressed her lips together, trying—and probably failing—to look stern. "Now you're just taking all my fun away."

He grinned unrepentantly.

"I can see you are troubled by the thought."

"Miss Bridgerton, you *always* trouble me."

She allowed herself a lofty tip of her chin. "Then I can count this a good day's work."

The captain took a long sip of his wine, then covered up a belch with his hand. "You do that."

Poppy tapped her hand against her thigh, trying not to look as if she had nothing to do but watch him eat (when of course they both knew she had nothing to do but watch him eat). She felt ridiculously awkward, so she turned back to the window and pretended to look out. She supposed she actually *was* looking out, but the vista hadn't changed for the last two hours, so really, it was more of a staring at the glass sort of thing. "You're quite late," she finally said.

His voice came from behind her, warm, rich, and terribly provoking. "Did you miss me?"

"Of course not." She turned around, trying to maintain a disinterested air. "But I was curious."

He smiled, and it was a devastating thing. Poppy could easily imagine dozens of ladies swooning in its wake. "You're always curious, aren't you?" he murmured.

She was instantly suspicious. "You're not saying that as if it were an insult."

"It's not an insult," he said plainly. "If more people were curious, we'd be far more advanced as a species."

She took a step toward him without realizing it. "What do you mean?"

His head tipped thoughtfully to the side. "Hard to say. But I like to think we'd be traveling the world in flying machines by now."

Well, that was the most ridiculous thing she'd ever heard. So she plunked herself right down across from him and said, "That's the most ridiculous thing I've ever heard."

He chuckled. "Clearly you're not curious *enough*."

"I'll have you know—" Poppy frowned as a contraption with wings, wheels, and maybe some fire shot through her imagination. It was enough to distract her from her initial response, which had been to defend herself.

She'd grown up with four brothers. Defending herself was always her initial response.

"Do you think it's possible?" she asked. She leaned forward, arms crossed on the table in front of her. "Flying machines?"

"I don't see why not. Birds do it."

"Birds have wings."

He shrugged. "We can build wings."

"Then why haven't we done so?"

"Men have tried."

She blinked. "They have?"

He nodded.

People had built wings and tried to fly and she didn't *know*? The injustice was astounding. "No one tells me anything," she grumbled.

He barked out a laugh. "I have difficulty believing that to be true."

Her eyes narrowed for what had to have been the tenth time in their conversation. "Why?"

"Your aforementioned curiosity."

"Just because I *ask* doesn't mean people tell me things."

He cocked his head to the side. "Did you *ask* anyone about men building wings?"

"Of course not."

"Then you can't complain."

"Because I didn't *know* to ask," she protested, jumping right in over his words. "One needs a certain base of knowledge before one can ask sensible questions."

"True," Captain James murmured.

"And it goes without saying," Poppy continued, only somewhat mollified by his easy agreement, "that I have not been given the opportunity to study physics."

"Do you want to?"

"Study physics?"

He made a courtly gesture with his hand.

"That's not the point," she said.

"Well, it is, actually, as pertains to aerodynamics."

"My point exactly!" She jabbed her finger toward him with enough suddenness that he blinked. "I didn't even know that was a word."

"It's self-explanatory," he said. "One doesn't need—"

"That's not the point."

"Again with the points," he said, sounding almost impressed.

She scowled. "I can deduce the meaning once you *say* it. That's not the—" She bit her tongue.

"Point?" he offered helpfully.

She gave him a look. "Women ought to be allowed an equal education," she said primly. "For those who want it."

"You'll get no objection from me," the captain said, reaching for his pie. "Awfully small piece," he muttered.

"It's very good, though," she told him.

"It always is." He took a bite. "Your slice was larger?"

"Of course."

He gave her a vaguely approving nod, as if he'd expected no less, and Poppy sat quietly as he finished his pie.

"Do you always dine so late?" she asked, once he had sat back in his chair.

He glanced up, almost as if he'd forgotten her presence. "Not always."

"What were you doing?"

He seemed slightly amused by the question. "Other than captaining the ship?"

"I was hoping you might tell me what captaining a ship *entails*."

"I will," he surprised her by saying. "Just not tonight." He yawned and stretched, and there was something astonishingly intimate about the motion. No gentleman of her acquaintance would *ever* have done such a thing in her presence—aside from her family, of course.

"Forgive me," he murmured, blinking as if he'd only just remembered that he no longer had sole free rein of his quarters.

She swallowed. "I think I'll get ready for bed."

He nodded. He suddenly looked exhausted, and Poppy was struck by the most inconvenient burst of compassion. "Was it a particularly tiring day?" she heard herself ask.

"A bit."

"Was it because of me?"

He cracked a wry smile. "I'm afraid I can't blame everything on you, Miss Bridgerton."

"Much as you would like to?"

"If you can conspire a way to take responsibility for a torn topgallant sail, a vexing wind, and three cases of putrid stomach, I would be much obliged."

Almost apologetically, she said, "I'm afraid the wind requires a supernatural talent I do not possess."

"As opposed to the torn sail and the putrid stomachs?"

"I could manage those, given a bit of time to plan." She made a vaguely sarcastic motion with her hand. "And access to the deck."

"Alas, I am too cruel."

She leaned her elbow on the table, her chin resting thoughtfully in her hand. "And yet I don't think it is your nature."

"To be cruel?"

She nodded.

He smiled, but just a little, as if he were too tired to make a proper go of it. "It has been but a day, and yet you already know me too well, Miss Bridgerton."

"Somehow I think I have barely scratched the surface."

He regarded her curiously. "You almost sound as if you wish to."

Their voices had softened, the hard edges of the conversation worn down by fatigue. And maybe respect.

Poppy stood, unsettled by the thought. She did not respect Captain James. She could not. And she certainly shouldn't *like* him, no matter how likeable he could be.

She was tired. Her defenses were low. "It's late," she said.

"Indeed," he replied, and she heard him rise from his chair as she made her way over to the basin of water Billy had brought sometime between her entrée and dessert. She needed to clean her face and teeth, and brush her hair. She did so every night, and she was determined to maintain her routine at sea, no matter how odd it felt to be performing her ablutions in front of a man.

And yet it was strangely *less* odd than it should have been.

Needs must, she told herself as she retrieved the tooth powder. That was all. If she was getting used to his presence, it was because she *had* to. She was a practical woman, not given to hysterics. She prided herself on that. If she had to brush her teeth in front of a man she'd only just met, she certainly wasn't going to cry over it.

She glanced over her shoulder, sure that the captain somehow knew she was thinking about him, but he seemed to be immersed in his own tasks, riffling through some papers on his desk.

With a resigned exhale, Poppy looked down at her finger and sprinkled some of the minty powder on it. She wondered if she should switch hands with each brushing. All this tooth powder might irritate her skin.

She took care of her teeth, splashed some water on her face, and, after making sure the captain was not watching, pulled the pins from her hair and ran her fingers through it, doing her best approximation of the boar bristle hairbrush she used at home. Once she'd fashioned a sleeping plait, there was nothing left to do except get into bed.

She turned, taking a step toward the bunk, but then there he was, somehow much closer than she'd expected.

"Oh!" she yelped. "I'm sorry, I—"

"No, it's my fault entirely. I didn't think you were going to turn and—"

She stepped left.

He stepped right.

They both made awkward noises.

"Sorry," he grunted.

He stepped left.

She stepped right.

"Shall we dance?" he joked, and she would have made a similar riposte, but the ship swept up and then down on a wave, sending her stumbling to the side, saved only by two warm hands at her waist.

"Now we really are—" She looked up, and it was such a mistake. "Dancing," she whispered.

They did not move, did not even speak. Poppy was not sure if they even breathed. His eyes held hers, and they were so bright, so astonishingly blue, that Poppy felt herself being drawn forward, pulled in. She didn't move, not an inch, but still, she felt it, the pull.

"Do you like to dance?" he asked.

She nodded. "When there is music."

"You don't hear it?"

"I *can't* hear it." She wondered if he knew that she really meant she *must* not. Because it was there, and she felt it on her skin—the soft music of the wind and the waves. If she were anyone else—no, if *he* were anyone else—this would be a moment made of romance and breathless anticipation.

In another lifetime, another world, he might lean down.

She might look up.

They might kiss.

It would be daring. Scandalous. How funny to think that if she were back in London, she could be ruined by a single kiss. It seemed so trivial now, compared with, oh, being kidnapped by pirates.

And yet as she stared into the captain's eyes, it didn't seem trivial at all.

She lurched back, aghast at the direction of her thoughts, but his hands were still there, large and warm on her hips, holding her, if not in place, then at least steady.

Safe.

"The water," he said in a rough voice. "It's choppy tonight."

It wasn't, but she appreciated the lie.

"I'm steady now," she said, setting her hand on the table to reassure him. Or maybe herself.

He released her and took a polite step back. "I beg your pardon," he said. "I am not usually so clumsy."

Another lie. Another kindness. He hadn't been clumsy. To the contrary; she had been the one to stumble. She should have repaid his generosity with her own by saying so, but all she could manage was "I'm done with the tooth powder."

It took him a moment longer than she would have expected to respond, and when he did, it was with a distracted "Of course." He took a step, and this time she made sure to wait a half second so that she could see his direction and step out of his way.

"Thank you," he added.

It was all very awkward. Which, Poppy thought, was how it ought to be. "I'll just get into bed now," she said.

He was busy with his teeth, but he turned his back to give her privacy. Why, she wasn't sure, as they both knew she would be sleeping in her clothes. Still, it was a considerate gesture, and yet another indication of his status as a gentleman.

"I'm in," she called out.

He finished with his teeth and turned back around. "I'll have the lanterns off shortly."

"Thank you." She pulled the covers up to her chin so that she could loosen the sash of her dress without him seeing. She was going to burn this frock when she got back home. She might have an identical one made up, because she did rather like the fabric, but this one . . .

To the fire pit.

She rolled onto her side and faced the wall, affording him the same privacy he'd given her. She could hear his every move, though, setting up his sleeping area, pulling off his boots.

"Oh, the pillow!" she suddenly remembered. She grabbed it from beneath her head and lobbed it over her shoulder. "Here you are!"

She heard a soft thunk, and then a soft grunt.

"Impeccable aim," he murmured.

"Did I hit you?"

"Square on."

Poppy smiled. "Face?"

"You should be so lucky."

"I couldn't see," she demurred.

"Shoulder," he told her, snuffing the last of the lanterns. "Now be quiet and go to sleep."

Amazingly, she did.

Chapter 9

The problem, Andrew realized as he turned the ship the following morning just enough to keep the sails flush with wind, was that Poppy Bridgerton wasn't awful.

If she'd been awful, he could have shut the cabin door and forgotten about her.

If she'd been awful, he might have even taken some vaguely undignified pleasure in her predicament.

But she wasn't awful. She was a bloody miserable nuisance—or rather, her presence was—but she wasn't awful.

And that made all of this so much more complicated.

The girl's safety was surely worth the price of her boredom, but somehow that didn't make him feel any better about having sequestered her in the cabin, with nothing but a few books and an ocean view to keep her company.

Andrew had been up and about for several hours already; he rarely slept past sunrise. Billy would have brought her breakfast by now, so that was something. The boy wasn't the most sparkling of conversationalists, but now that he'd got over his terror of their female guest, surely he could provide a few moments of diversion.

At least she wouldn't have to eat a cold breakfast. Miss Bridgerton wouldn't make that mistake again.

She wasn't the kind to ever make the same mistake twice.

Still, he should check on her. It was only polite. She was his guest.

In a way.

Regardless, he was certainly responsible for her. And that included her mental well-being along with the physical. Besides, he'd thought of something that might alleviate the monotony. He didn't know why it had not occurred to him earlier—probably because he'd still been so aghast at their unexpected predicament.

He had a wooden puzzle, modeled after the dissected maps that had become all the rage in London. But his was considerably more intricate. It had taken him several hours to put together when he'd given it a go. It wasn't much, but it would help her fill her time.

She'd love it. He knew this with a certainty he couldn't explain, except that *he'd* loved it, and he and Miss Bridgerton seemed to have the same sort of analytical, problem-solving mind. He rather suspected they'd have been jolly good friends if she hadn't put national secrets at risk when she trespassed in his cave.

Or if he hadn't kidnapped her. That too.

"Jenkins, take the wheel," he called out, ignoring the speculative look on his second's face. Andrew had given over far more of his wheel time than usual. But there was no law saying that a captain had to spend a prescribed amount of time in—

"Oh for the love of God," he muttered. He didn't need to explain himself to anyone, much less himself.

Jenkins, thankfully, assumed command without comment, and Andrew took the steps two at a time down to the main deck, and then triple-pace down to his cabin.

He gave a sharp rap before inserting his key into the lock, letting himself in before Miss Bridgerton had a chance to call out a greeting.

She was seated at the table, her chestnut hair pinned somewhat haphazardly on her head. The scant remains of her breakfast—three berries and a bit of toast—sat on the tray in front of her.

"You don't like strawberries?" he asked, plucking the largest of the three off her plate.

She glanced up from the book she was reading. "They make me ill."

"Interesting." He took a bite. "My sister-in-law is the same. I've not seen it, but Edward—that's my brother—says it's a sight to behold."

She marked her place in the book—a slim guide to Lisbon, he noted; rather practical of her even if he had no plans to let her so much as touch a toe to Portuguese soil—then set it down. "I imagine it's a sight one wishes *not* to behold."

"Indeed." He shuddered. "I believe the word

gruesome was used, and my brother is not given to hyperbole."

"Unlike you?"

He laid a hand over his heart. "I exaggerate only when absolutely necessary."

"Your brother sounds delightful."

"He's married," Andrew immediately retorted.

"This makes him less delightful?" She seemed to find this terribly amusing, which should have irritated him, but instead he felt . . . awkward?

Green?

It had been a long time since his glib tongue had failed him so.

Thankfully, however, Miss Bridgerton did not seem to require a response. Instead she pushed her plate in his direction. "Have the rest if you wish."

Andrew accepted her offering and ate one whole, leaving only the green leafy cap in his fingers. Setting it down on her plate, he rested his hip against the side of the table and asked, "Are *you* gruesome?"

She let out a surprised laugh. "Right this minute?"

He tipped his head, a small salute to her riposte.

"No," she said, a touch of humor making her voice delightfully warm. "I get rather itchy, though, and somewhat short of breath. Two things I'd rather avoid, frankly, while confined in a cabin."

"I'll tell the cook," Andrew said, finishing off the last berry. "He can give you something else."

"Thank you. I'd appreciate that."

He regarded her for a moment, then said, "Alarmingly civil, aren't we?"

"Alarming that we find it so alarming," she returned.

"There is much to dissect in that comment," he said, pushing off from the edge of the table, "but alas, I haven't the time."

"And yet you spared some for me," she remarked. "To what do I owe this pleasure of your company?"

"A pleasure, is it?" he murmured, heading over to his wardrobe. He did not let her reply before adding, "No? It will be."

"What are you talking about?"

He enjoyed her befuddled tone, but he didn't bother with further conversation as he dug through his belongings. It had been some time since he'd brought out the puzzle, and it was wedged at the back of the wardrobe behind a broken kaleidoscope and a pair of socks. The wooden pieces were stored in a velvet pouch, purple with a gold drawstring. All in all, quite regal.

He set it down on the table. "I thought you might enjoy this."

She looked at the velvet pouch and then at him, her brows arched in question.

"It's a dissected map," he told her.

"A what?"

"Have you never seen one?"

She shook her head, so he opened the pouch and let the pieces spill out onto the wooden tabletop. "They were very popular about ten years ago," he explained. "A cartographer by the name of Spilsbury fixed a map onto a wooden board and then cut the countries and seas at their borders. He thought it would help to teach geography. I believe the first few went to the royal family."

"Oh, I know what you're talking about," she exclaimed. "But the ones I've seen had nowhere near so many pieces."

"Yes, this one is unique. I had it commissioned myself." He took a seat diagonal to her and spread out a few of the pieces, flipping them over so that the map side was up. "Most of the dissected maps are cut along borders—national boundaries, rivers, coasts—that sort of thing. I already know my geography, but I rather like to put things together, so I asked if mine could instead be cut into many random small shapes."

Her lips parted with wonder, and she picked up one of the pieces. "And then you have to fit them together," she said almost reverently. "That's brilliant! How many pieces are there?"

"Five hundred."

"Never say it!"

"Give or take," Andrew admitted modestly. "I haven't counted them."

"I'll count them," Miss Bridgerton said. "It's not as if I don't have the time."

She didn't seem to have said it as a complaint, so he turned a few more pieces over and said, "The best way to get started is to look for—"

"No, don't tell me!" she cut in. "I want to figure it out for myself." She picked up a piece and squinted at it.

"The writing is small," he said.

"My eyes are young." She looked up, afore-mentioned eyes glinting with delight. "It says *IC*. Not terribly helpful. But it's blue, so it could be the Baltic. Or the Atlantic."

"Or the Pacific."

She looked surprised. "How big is the map?"

"The known world," he told her, a little surprised by the boastfulness in his voice. He was proud of the puzzle; as far as he knew, no other map had been dissected into quite as many pieces. But that wasn't why he'd been bragging, and it wasn't because she was so obviously happy for the first time since he'd met her. It was—

Dear God, he'd wanted to impress her.

He jolted to his feet. "I have to get back."

"Yes, fine," she said distractedly, far more interested in the puzzle than anything he had to say. "I'll be here, as you know."

He watched her as he walked to the door. She didn't glance at him even once. He *should* be glad that she had not noticed his abrupt change in disposition. "Billy will bring you something to eat this afternoon," he said.

"That will be nice." She picked up another piece and examined it, taking a sip of tea before setting it down to study another.

He tapped the handle of the door. "Do you have any preferences?"

"Hmmm?"

"For food. Do you have any preferences? Other than the strawberries, of course."

She looked up and blinked, as if she was surprised he was still there. "I'm not terribly fond of asparagus, if that's what you're asking."

"You're unlikely to encounter that on board," he said. "We do try to keep fruits and vegetables, but never anything that expensive."

She shrugged and turned back to the puzzle. "I'm sure anything will be fine."

"Good." He cleared his throat. "I'm pleased you're getting on so well. I realize it is not an ideal situation."

"Mmm-hmm."

He cocked his head to the side, watching her as she started flipping pieces over so the map side faced her. "It's really too bad I don't have another one of those puzzles," he said.

"Hmmm."

"I'll be going, then."

"Hmm-mmm." This one came out with an up-and-down lilt, as if she were saying good-bye.

"Well," he said gruffly. "Good-bye."

She lifted a hand in farewell, even as her attention remained fixed on the wooden pieces. "Bye!"

Andrew stepped out of the cabin and into the corridor, making sure the door closed and locked behind him. She could get out, of course. It would have been irresponsible of him to have left her there without a means to evacuate. The *Infinity* had never had a problem, but one had to be careful at sea.

He unlocked the door and barged back in. "You do know you have a key?"

This got her attention. "I beg your pardon?"

"A key. Right over there in the top drawer. It's

highly unlikely, but if there were an emergency, you would be able to leave the cabin."

"You wouldn't come get me?"

"Well, I would try . . ." He suddenly felt most awkward. It was not a pleasant—or a familiar—sensation. "Or I could send someone. But it's important that you have the ability to evacuate if necessary."

"So what you're saying," she said, "is that you are trusting me not to leave the cabin."

He had not quite thought of it that way, but— "Yes," he replied. "I suppose I am."

"That is good to know."

He stared at her. What the devil did that mean?

"Thank you for the puzzle," she said, changing the topic with unsettling speed. "I'm not sure if I actually said as much. It really was most thoughtful of you."

"It was nothing," he said, and his head and shoulder did a little twitch. His cheeks felt warm too.

She smiled—a lovely, warm thing that thoroughly reached her eyes, and he started to think that their color was more moss than leaf, although it might just be the light coming through the windows . . .

"Didn't you say you were needed?" she reminded him.

He blinked. "Yes, of course." He gave his head a little shake. "I was just thinking for a moment."

She smiled again, this time with a vague air of amusement. Or maybe impatience. She clearly wished to be rid of him.

"I'll take my leave, then." He made a quick bow with his head and moved toward the door.

"Oh, wait!" she called.

He turned around. But not eagerly. Not eagerly at all. "Yes?"

She motioned with her hands toward her breakfast. "Would you mind removing the tray? I'll need more room for the puzzle, wouldn't you think?"

"The tray," he echoed dully. She wanted him to carry her tray. He was the captain of his own bloody ship.

"I would very much appreciate it."

He took the tray. "Until this evening, Miss Bridgerton."

Until this evening. Absolutely. He would not be going back to check on her before then. Certainly not.

POPPY WAS JUST about a quarter of the way through the puzzle when she heard a single sharp rap on the door, followed by the sound of the key turning in the lock.

"Captain James!" she said with some surprise. As usual, he looked ridiculously handsome. What was it with men and windblown hair? And unlike this morning, his shirt was open at the neck. She didn't mind, really, but out of politeness, she averted her eyes and turned her attention back to the puzzle piece in her hand. She thought it might belong in Canada. Or maybe Japan.

"Did you think I was Billy?" he asked.

"No, he would never knock with such authority. But you said you'd not be back until evening."

He cleared his throat and motioned toward the far wall. "I need to retrieve something from my wardrobe."

"A cravat, perhaps," she murmured. She'd only ever seen her brothers in such a state of undress. But her brothers had not looked like *this*. Or if they had, she'd hardly cared.

The captain, on the other hand—well, she had already admitted to herself that he was good-looking. As long as she did not admit it to *him*, she had nothing to worry about.

He touched his throat, and she suspected he'd forgotten that he'd removed his neckpiece. "We often dispense with formalities on board."

"Is it very warm today?"

"When one is in the sun."

That was probably how his hair had come to be so liberally streaked with gold. She'd wager that it had not been so lustrous when he was living year-round in England.

Lustrous? She gave herself a mental shake. Adjectives such as that had no business in her head while she was stuck on this ship. It was fanciful and silly and . . .

True, dash it all. Weren't pirates meant to be filthy and coarse? Captain James looked like he might take tea with the queen.

Provided he wore a cravat.

She watched as he rummaged about in his wardrobe. (His back was to her and thus she had no reason not to stare.) After a few moments, he pulled something out, but he tucked it into his pocket before she could see what it was.

She turned back to the puzzle just as he turned around.

"How is it coming along?" he asked.

"Very well, thank you," she said, relieved that he had not caught her watching him. "I started with all of the edge pieces." She gazed down at her work. She was rather proud of the rectangular frame she'd created.

His voice came from right behind her. "Always a sound plan."

She startled. She hadn't realized he was so close. "Ehrm . . . I've been trying to sort the rest of the pieces by color. It's difficult, though. Most are very pale, and . . ."

Why was he so warm? He wasn't even touching her, and yet she could feel the heat radiating from his body. She dared not turn around, but how close *was* he?

She cleared her throat. "I'm finding it difficult to tell the difference between pink and this shade." She held up a piece that obviously contained both water and land. One corner was light blue, and the rest was something slightly peachy.

"This one is definitely pink," he said near her ear, and then he leaned forward, his arm stretching past her as he reached for a triangular piece at the back of the array. The linen of his shirt whispered against the back of her head, and for a moment she could not remember how to breathe.

She could not remember if she *knew* how to breathe.

He set the piece into her pink pile and drew his arm back, lightly grazing her shoulder.

Her skin tingled.

It was the heat. It had to be. The sun had finally traveled high enough so that it was no longer streaming through the windows, but the cabin had had the entire morning to warm up. She'd been so engrossed in the puzzle that she hadn't really noticed it. But now she had that prickly feeling one got when one needed a cool drink. And much the way she could never ignore hiccups when her mother said, "Just forget about them, and they'll go away," she could not stop being so aware of the sensation.

And of him, scandalously close.

The captain reached for another piece, this one lavender, but it was farther than the other one had been, and when she turned, she saw that his head was right next to hers. If he turned . . . If she turned . . .

It would be a kiss.

"Stop!" she cried out.

He straightened. "Is something wrong?"

"No," she said, utterly mortified by her outburst. "No. *No.*" She tried to make the last *no* sound droll, but she had a feeling she had not succeeded. She cleared her throat, giving herself an extra few seconds to compose herself before she spoke again, and when she did, her hands were spread out like starfish on the table to steady her. "It is simply that I wish to complete this on my own. I don't want any help."

He'd moved out from behind her, and when she looked at his face she was relieved to see that there was nothing roguish or teasing or even *knowing* in his expression. Instead, he almost looked sheepish.

"Sorry," he said. "I love things like this."

"It's—it's all right," she said, hating the stammer in her voice. "Just . . . no more."

He stepped away, and she thought he was headed for the door, but suddenly he stopped and turned around, resting his hands on the back of the chair across from her. "Why are you being so agreeable?"

She blinked. "I beg your pardon?"

"You're remarkably amiable today." His eyes narrowed, but he didn't *quite* look suspicious.

"As opposed to . . ."

His head tilted to the side, as if he hadn't considered this. "When you arrived, I suppose."

"You mean in a *sack*?"

He waved that off. "Is it the puzzle?"

"Well . . ." Poppy paused, unsure of how to answer his question. Why *was* she being agreeable? The maddening man was holding her against her will—not that she could do anything about it, here on the open ocean. Perhaps she would behave differently if she was at an inn or a house—someplace from which she could reasonably envision escape. But here on the ship there was nothing to be gained from being contrary. Not when she had to spend a fortnight in his company.

She looked over at the captain, hoping that she'd stalled long enough for him to have moved on, but no, he was still staring at her with bright blue expectation, awaiting her answer.

"I suppose," she said carefully, "it's simply because I have no good reason not to be agreeable. I can't go anywhere. I certainly can't escape, and I'd have to be an idiot to think I'd fare better on my own in Portugal than with your protection. So like it or not, I'm stuck with you."

He nodded slowly. "As I am with you."

"*Oh*," she added with particular emphasis, "and I *don't* like it."

His chin drew back, adding to the air of puzzlement that marked his face.

"I said 'like it or not,'" she explained. "I want to make it clear that I don't. Like it, I mean."

"So noted," he remarked.

"But," she added, coming to her feet, "you have treated me with a small measure of respect, so I am endeavoring to do the same."

One of his brows arched. "Just a small measure?"

She met this expression with her own. "You still sleep in this room, do you not?"

"For your protection," he reminded her.

"The door locks."

"I'm *not* sleeping below."

"As I have yet to see an inch of the ship other than this cabin and the corridor outside, I could not say if the berths below would be appropriate."

He smiled condescendingly. "Trust me when I tell you that even if you did have free rein of the *Infinity*, you would not be permitted anywhere near the sailors' quarters."

She tipped her head toward the door. "I counted three other cabins on this deck."

"So you did. They are very small."

"But large enough for two men, I would think. Don't Brown and Green share?"

"Neither Brown nor Green is the captain of this ship."

"So what you're actually saying is that it is your pride that is too large to share a cabin."

"I'm sharing one with *you*."

"A decision I still cannot comprehend." She snorted. "You do realize that if we were anywhere else, you'd have to marry me."

This made him grin, and it was a lethal, devilish thing. He leaned toward her. "Why, Miss Bridgerton, are you asking for my hand?"

"No!" she practically howled. "You're twisting my words."

"I know," he said, almost sympathetically. "You make it so easy."

She scowled. "I take back everything I said about your being a gentleman."

Still, he kept smiling. The wretched man found this *amusing*. Or more to the point, he found *her* amusing, which was considerably worse.

"As it happens," he said, "I have decided to sleep in my navigator's cabin tonight. There are indeed two berths there."

"You just said—"

He held up a hand. "A wise man never argues when he's getting his way. The same goes for women, I should think."

He was right, damn it. Still . . . "What brought on this change of heart?" she asked suspiciously.

"Oh, let's see . . . My sore neck, my aching back, and the fact that I nearly fell asleep at the wheel this morning."

"*Really?*"

"No, not really," he retorted. Then he might have groaned. "But I wanted to."

Poppy tried to appear contrite. She really did. But there was something delicious about the thought of him falling asleep while on duty, and she hadn't been able to keep *all* the glee from her voice.

Schadenfreude, meet Poppy Bridgerton.

"I have taken measure of the crew's mood," Captain James said, "and I am confident that you will remain unbothered."

She nodded demurely. She had won. She had won! But she knew men, and she knew she had to let him think the victory was his. So she gave him a pretty smile and said, "Thank you."

He crossed his arms. "You will, of course, keep the door locked."

"As you wish."

"And you must understand that this is still my cabin, and I will be in and out during the day."

"All of your things are here," she murmured agreeably, although she might have ruined it when she added, "See how agreeable I am?"

Chapter 10

❦

Agreeable, indeed. The chit was up to something. Although what, Andrew could not envisage. He'd believed her when she said she wasn't plotting an escape. She was far too intelligent for that. He supposed she might try something when they were back on British soil, but certainly not before.

But when they *were* back on British soil . . . well, he wanted to be rid of her then, didn't he?

"Is something wrong?" he heard her ask. "You look very skeptical all of a sudden."

He looked over at her. Brown hair, green eyes, blue dress . . . everything was the same. And yet *he* felt different.

But it wasn't because of *her*, he told himself. True, her presence had turned this voyage into one like no other, but she was not the reason for his unease. He'd been feeling not quite right for several months now.

Something inside of him had jolted out of place. He felt off-center.

Restless.

It was a sensation that he usually took to mean it was time to set sail. His wasn't a soul that was meant to remain too long in one place. This was a basic fact of his existence, as much a part of him as his cheeky humor, his blue eyes, or his fascination with all things mechanical. It was why he'd begged his parents to allow him to withdraw from Eton in his final year and join the navy. It was why they'd let him, even though he knew they would rather he'd finished his studies.

They didn't even try to suggest that he go on to Cambridge, despite the fact that Andrew had always had a passion for engineering and architecture and could have probably used some tutelage.

He could never have made it through three years at university. Not then, at least. He could barely sit still. Lectures and seminars would have been absolute torture.

But it was a different sort of restlessness that had recently taken root in his chest. A need for change, yes, but not *constant* change. He saw that cottage again, the one that had been lurking for so long at the back of his mind. It altered a little each time he thought of it . . . a trellis here, new stonework there . . . And of course he was never quite sure how large it ought to be. Did he want to live by himself? Have a family?

It couldn't be too small, he decided. Even if he never had a family of his own, he'd want plenty of room for his nieces and nephews. Children needed room to run wild, to explore. His own childhood had been magnificent. The Rokesby and Bridgerton children had formed their own little tribe, and they'd had the entirety of two estates to roam. They'd fished and climbed, and created all sorts of sketches of the imagination with princes and knights, pirates and kings. And of course Joan of Arc and Queen Elizabeth, because Billie Bridgerton had refused to be cast as a damsel in distress.

When it rained, they played games and built houses out of cards, and Andrew supposed there had to have been lessons in there at some point, but even those had been made enjoyable by his parents' expert picks for tutors. They had understood that learning could be fun, that there was nothing to be gained by a slavish devotion to discipline, at least not with children whose ages remained in the single digits.

His parents were remarkably wise people. How ironic and, he supposed, logical that none of their children would truly realize this until they too were adults.

He really needed to get back to see his family. It had been much too long.

"Captain James?"

Miss Bridgerton was standing next to him now; he had not even realized she'd got up from the table.

"Captain James?" she said again. "Are you all right?"

"Sorry." He gave himself a mental shake. "I was just thinking . . ." Well, honestly, there was no reason not to tell her the truth. "I was thinking about my family."

"Ah yes, your brother," she said, her eyes crinkling with something approaching mischief. "The one who does not exaggerate. Married to a gruesome hater of strawberries."

And just like that, she made him laugh. "I assure you, she's hardly gruesome. You'd like her, actually. She—"

He stopped. He'd been about to tell her how Cecilia had crossed an ocean to look for her wounded brother, how she had feigned marriage to a man who had lost his memory so that she might continue to nurse him through his injuries. Cecilia had not thought herself particularly daring or headstrong— she still didn't—and she often said that she'd be happy never to travel more than fifty miles from her home again. But when she needed it—when *others* had needed it—she had found her strength.

But he could not reveal more information about his family. He shouldn't even have mentioned Edward's name, but honestly, what family *didn't* have an Edward in a recent branch of their tree? If he started talking about George and Nicholas and Mary, however . . . That combination of names was considerably more distinctive. And with the aforementioned George married to Poppy's cousin Billie . . .

"Do you miss them?" Miss Bridgerton asked.

"My family? Of course. All the time."

"And yet you've chosen a life at sea."

He shrugged. "I also like the sea."

She considered this for a moment, then said, "I don't really miss mine."

He looked at her with frank astonishment.

"I mean, of course I *miss* them. But I wasn't meant to be with my family right now, anyway."

"Ah yes," he recalled. "You were visiting your friend in Charmouth. Mrs. Armitage."

She blinked in surprise. "You remember her name?"

"I have to return you to her, don't I?"

Her mouth opened, but then he saw her expression and realized—

"For the love of Christ, woman, you didn't think I was just going to drop you at the docks, did you?"

Her lip caught between her teeth. "Well . . ."

"What sort of man do you think I am?" He stalked away, furious at her assessment of him. "Bloody hell, woman, you're the one who keeps insisting I'm a gentleman. How could you think I would not see you safely to your friend's doorstep?"

"You did kidnap me," she pointed out, almost politely.

"That again," he ground out.

Her eyes widened, and she made a sound that clearly translated to: *You did not just say that.*

He planted his hands on his hips. "We have already established that I had no choice."

To that she responded with a one-shouldered shrug. "So you say."

He supposed she had a point there, but it wasn't as if he could explain himself to her. His own parents didn't even know that he had spent the last seven years in secret service to the crown.

Still, he wasn't going to rise to her bait and get into another argument about how and why she'd come to be on the *Infinity*. "Regardless," he said, his tone pointedly firm, "you will not be left at the docks like some unwanted cargo. I'm not yet certain *how* we will see you home, but we will, you have my assurance."

He stared her down, waiting for her response.

Which she gave.

"Technically," she said, with the careful expression of one who is picking through needles, "I *am* unwanted cargo."

It took him a moment to digest this. "*That* is the point you wish to argue?"

"Well, I'm certainly not going to argue that you *shouldn't* return me safely to Briar House. Although you might wish to be careful." Her brows rose, calling to mind the many times Andrew's sister—and his sister-in-law and his *other* sister-in-law—doled out unnecessary advice.

"Elizabeth is not so willing as I to bend rules," Miss Bridgerton said. "She may very well have summoned the authorities."

Not to mention the entire Bridgerton family, he thought grimly.

She walked back over to the table. "It would probably be unwise of you to approach the house."

He almost smiled. "Are you worried I might be arrested?"

She snorted. "I have every faith you'll escape the law."

He wasn't sure it was a compliment. But he also wasn't sure that it wasn't. And he definitely wasn't sure which he would rather it be.

He cleared his throat. "I should be getting back. There is much that requires my attention."

She nodded absently, inspecting several puzzle pieces. "I would imagine so. I'm surprised you have remained in the cabin as long as you have."

Not as surprised as he was.

"You should know that I still intend to take my evening meal here," he said with a nod to the table, "although it does appear that you've quite taken over with the puzzle."

She smiled without regret. "I'm afraid I cannot apologize for that."

"Nor would I expect you to." He looked down, saw a piece that was clearly the Orkney Islands, and set it into place.

She swatted his hand. "Stop it! You've done this before!"

"I know, but I can't help that I'm better at it than you are."

Her scowl was so marvelous he had to do it again. "Did you open the windows?" he asked innocently.

She twisted in her seat. "They open?"

He grabbed another piece and set it into place. "No." He grinned when she turned back around to glare at him. "Sorry. Can't help myself."

"Obviously not," she grumbled.

"It was Norway," he said helpfully.

"I can see that." And then, in what had to be an admission so grudging it deserved applause, she added, "*Now.*"

"I've never been," he said in his most conversational tone. Which was to say, his usual timbre.

"To Norway?" She tried to fit a piece into the southernmost tip of Africa. "Nor I."

He smiled at that, since they both knew she had never set foot outside England. At least not on dry land. "It won't fit," he said, all helpfulness. "You've got South America there."

Miss Bridgerton frowned at the puzzle piece in her hand. It was shaped like a rhombus, with a green triangle of land jutting out from one of the short sides. The rest was pale blue water. "Are you sure?" she asked. She squinted at the tiny writing. "There's an *H* and an *O*. I thought it must be the Cape of Good Hope."

"Or Cape Horn," he said.

"Well, that's confusing," she said with some irritation. She set it back down on the table with a snap. "You'd think they could have come up with names that didn't sound *exactly* the same."

He grinned at that. He had to.

She pressed the tip of her forefinger on one of the pieces, sliding it aimlessly in a figure eight. And then she shocked him utterly by saying, "I lied earlier."

He turned. Softly, he said, "Tell me."

It took her a moment to speak, and when she did, her voice was solemn in a way he'd not heard before. "I do miss my family. Not the way I think you do. I'm—I'm not away from them as frequently as you are, or for the same duration. But I miss my brother. The one who died. I miss him all the time."

She allowed him to see her face for only a second before turning away, but even if he had not seen the grief in her eyes, he would have known it by the bleak stance of her shoulders, the way some of the life seemed to have leeched from her limbs.

"I'm very sorry for your loss," he said.

She nodded, her throat working as she looked down at the puzzle pieces, focusing on nothing. "He was my favorite."

"What was his name?"

She looked at him, and in her eyes he saw a tiny flash of gratitude that he'd asked.

"Roger," she said. "His name was Roger."

Andrew thought about his own siblings. He didn't have a favorite, or at least he didn't think he did. But even though his were all living, Andrew could more keenly imagine her pain than one might think. His brother Edward used to be an army officer, and he had gone missing in America, during the war. Andrew had believed that he'd perished. He had not said as much to anyone; his mother in particular would have blistered his ears if he'd so much as hinted at the fact that he had lost hope.

In his heart, though, Andrew had begun to mourn.

He'd believed his brother dead for almost a year, and he would have liked to offer words of empathy to Poppy, but he could not. The story of Captain Edward Rokesby's return from the dead was too well-known. And so Andrew just sat beside her and said again, "I'm sorry."

She acknowledged this with a jerky nod. But then, after only a few moments, her mouth tightened resolutely. She tapped her fingers several times on the table, then reached out to grab the puzzle piece she'd recently had in her hand.

"I have to say," she told him, in a voice that made it clear she was changing the subject, "it doesn't much look like a horn."

Andrew took the piece from her fingers with a smile. "I believe it is named for Hoorn."

"For who?"

He chuckled. "Hoorn. It is a city in the Netherlands."

This did not seem to impress her. "Hmmph. Well, I've not been *there* either."

He leaned toward her, just enough for his shoulder to make a conspiratorial bump against hers. "Nor I."

"That *is* surprising," she said, glancing ever so slightly in his direction. "I'd assumed you'd been everywhere. Except Norway, apparently."

"Alas, no. My business keeps me on familiar routes." It was true. Most of Andrew's time was spent ferrying documents to the same three or four countries. Spain and Portugal, most of all.

"How do you spell it?" she suddenly asked.

"Hoorn? *H-O-O-R-N.* Why?"

"Just wondering if there is a city of Good *H-O-O-P-E* out there somewhere."

He laughed at that. "If so, I should like to visit."

She was not, however, done with her queries. "Do you know which was named first?"

"Of the capes? I think it was Good Hope. If I recall correctly, the name was bestowed upon it by a Portuguese king."

"Portuguese, you say? It's settled then. We'll stop in Good Hoope on the way back from Lisbon." Her eyes lit with merriment. "Do you think Mr. Carroway knows the way?"

"If he's read that bloody awful navigation guide he will."

She laughed gaily at that, and it was a marvelous sound, rich with humor and joy. It was the sort of sound Andrew wasn't used to hearing while he was at sea. The sailors had their jokes, but they were coarse, masculine things, nothing so clever as Poppy Bridgerton's bon mots.

Poppy. The name really did suit her. What a shame it would have been if she'd turned out drab and pinched.

"Good Huuuupe," she chortled, adopting an accent he was quite sure existed nowhere but inside this cabin. "Guuuuuuuud Huuuuuupe."

"Stop," he said. "I can't bear it."

"Guud Huuuuuuuuuuuuupe," she practically sang. "The most hopeful spot in Portugal."

"Honestly, your accent might be the most frightful thing I have ever heard."

She turned with mock outrage. "You don't think I sound like a Dutchwoman?"

"Not even a little bit."

She let out a mock huff. "Well, that is disappointing. I was trying so hard."

"That much was clear."

She jabbed him with her elbow, then motioned with her head toward the puzzle pieces. "I don't suppose you see the Cape of Good Hope among this mess."

He glanced sideways at her. "I thought you didn't want help."

"I don't want *unsolicited* help," she clarified.

"I'm afraid I only like to offer help when it is not wanted."

"So you *don't* see it."

He grinned unrepentantly. "Not at all."

She laughed again, her head falling back with her mirth. Andrew was transfixed. He'd thought she was pretty, but in that moment she became something much more. *Pretty* was a dull, static thing, and Poppy Bridgerton could never be that.

"Oh my goodness," she said, wiping her eyes. "If you'd told me when I arrived that I'd be laughing . . ."

"*I* certainly wouldn't have believed you."

"Yes, well . . ." Her words trailed off, and he could see the moment her thoughts forced her back to propriety. Her expression grew shuttered, and just like that, the magic was gone. "I would still rather be at home."

"I know," he said, and he had the most intense urge to cover her hand with his.

But he didn't.

She spoke haltingly, her words coming out in small batches, and though she lifted her eyes to his, she did not hold them there for long before shifting her gaze toward a spot somewhere past his shoulder. "I don't want you to think . . . that just because I might occasionally laugh . . . or even appreciate your company . . ."

"I know," he said. She didn't need to finish the sentence.

He didn't want her to finish the sentence.

But she did anyway. "You shouldn't think that I forgive you."

He knew that too, but as blows went, it was still spectacularly well aimed.

And surprisingly deep.

He stood. "I should go."

She didn't say anything until he reached the door. Her good manners must have got the best of her, though, because before he could leave she said, "Thank you again. For the puzzle."

"You're most welcome. I hope you enjoy it."

"I will. I . . ." She swallowed. "I am."

He bowed, a crisp, regimented dip of his chin that offered every respect he had to give.

And then he got the hell out of the cabin.

ANDREW WAS ALREADY on deck before he took a moment to pause and take a breath. He hadn't meant to leave so suddenly, but Miss Bridgerton had got under his skin, and—

Oh bloody hell, who did he think he was kidding? He hadn't even been planning to go down to his cabin until evening, but for some idiotic reason he'd wanted to see how she was getting on with the puzzle, and then he'd had to make up an excuse for his being there.

He didn't even know *what* he'd grabbed from his wardrobe. He reached into his pocket and pulled out . . .

A pair of his smalls.

Good God.

He briefly considered tossing them over the side. The last thing he needed was one of his men coming across him holding his undergarments like some sort of demented laundress.

But he could not bring himself to dispose of a perfectly good piece of clothing just because *she* . . .

No, because *he* . . .

It was certainly not because *they* . . .

He balled up the linen and shoved it in his pocket.

This, he thought. *This* was the curse his men kept yammering about. A woman on board wasn't going to cause lightning to strike the mast or bring on a plague of rats and locusts. Instead, he would go mad. By the time they reached Portugal he'd have lost half his mind, and by the time they made it back to England he'd be a stark, raving lunatic.

Stark. Raving—

"Something wrong, Captain?"

Andrew looked up, not even wanting to imagine what expression he'd made so that one of his men felt emboldened to inquire such a thing. A newish young sailor named John Wilson was just a few feet away, watching him with either curiosity or concern, Andrew couldn't tell which.

"Nothing," Andrew said sharply.

Wilson's already ruddy cheeks took on more color and he gave a jerky nod. "'Course. M'pologies for asking."

Bloody hell, now Andrew felt the worst sort of heel. "Er, what duty have you today?" he asked, hoping the show of interest would take the sting out of his previous tone. Besides, the inquiry was not out of character. It was entirely normal that he might ask this upon coming across one of his men.

When he didn't have a pair of his own smalls stuffed in his pocket.

Because he couldn't admit he'd wanted to see a girl.

God in heaven, this voyage could not be over soon enough.

"Been aloft," Wilson said, with a nod toward the rigging. "Checking the ropes."

Andrew cleared his throat. "All in order?"

"Yes, sir. Only one in need of repair, and it wasn't nothing serious."

"Excellent." Andrew cleared his throat. "Well. I won't be keeping you."

"It's no trouble, sir. My shift just ended. I was just heading below. It's my turn for a hammock."

Andrew gave a nod. Like many similar ships, the hammocks were shared. The men did not all sleep at the same time; they could not. The bridge could never be left unattended, and a skeletal portion of the crew was required to work through the night. The wind did not stop when the sun went down.

The sleeping quarters were already crowded. It would have been a waste of space to have provided enough hammocks for every sailor to have his own. Andrew wasn't sure what sort of rotation the men had worked out to share them. He'd seen it done in different ways on different ships. But regardless, he had not been joking when he told Poppy he refused to sleep below. He'd done his time in the hammocks, back when he'd first entered the navy.

He was captain of the *Infinity*. He'd earned the right not to sleep in some other man's sweaty ropes.

But Mr. Carroway's spare berth would have to do for the rest of the voyage. Andrew was no stranger to discomfort, but why sleep on the floor when there was a perfectly good bed across the hall? Maybe not as nice as *his* bed, but as *his* bed was currently occupied by Poppy Bridgerton . . .

His bed.

Poppy Bridgerton.

Something clenched within him. Something suspiciously close to lust.

"No," he said aloud. "No."

"Captain?"

Bloody hell, Wilson had still been in earshot.

"Nothing!" Andrew snapped, this time not caring if he scared the piss out of the man with his tone.

Wilson scurried away, and Andrew was left alone.

With a terrible sense of foreboding.

And a pair of underwear in his pocket.

Chapter 11

◆━━►∗◄━━◆

$\mathcal{T}$he next few days passed without incident. Poppy finished the puzzle, took it apart, and then put it together again. It wasn't nearly as satisfying the second time, but it was a better pastime than her other options, which, since she had already finished reading the bookshelf's sole work of fiction, consisted of such gems as *Engineering Methods of the Ancient Ottomans* and *Agrarian Masterpieces of Kent.*

Why a ship captain needed a guide to agrarian masterpieces, she couldn't imagine, but she did get a few moments of pleasure from the section on Aubrey Hall, the country estate where her father had grown up, and where her cousins still lived.

Poppy had visited Aubrey Hall several times, although not recently. When her family gathered with their aristocratic cousins, they were more likely to do so in London. It made sense, Poppy supposed. Lord and Lady Bridgerton of Kent maintained a magnificent residence in the capital, which meant that Mr. and Mrs. Bridgerton of Somerset did not have to. The current viscount, her father's older brother, was a generous man, and he would not hear of his siblings and their families staying anywhere else. Fortunately, he had plenty of room. Bridgerton House was a grand, stately manse with a sizable ballroom and over a dozen bedchambers, right in the heart of Mayfair.

It was where Poppy had lived during both of her London Seasons. Her parents had remained in the country; neither was particularly fond of city life. It was probably why they had happily accepted Lady Bridgerton's offer to supervise Poppy's presentation and debut. That and the fact that Aunt Alexandra was a viscountess, and thus a powerful sponsor for a young lady looking for marriage.

Although apparently not powerful enough, as Poppy had gone through two Seasons without finding a spouse. That wasn't Aunt Alexandra's fault, though. Poppy *had* received a proposal, and while the gentleman had means and looks, he'd possessed a moralizing side that Poppy feared would strengthen and grow mean with age. Even Aunt Alexandra, who was eager to see her charge well-settled, had agreed with her on this.

Several other gentlemen had also expressed interest, but Poppy had not encouraged them. (Aunt Alexandra had not been nearly so agreeable about *this*.) But Poppy had held firm. She was going to have to spend the rest of her life in the company of her future husband, whoever he turned out to be. Was it too much to hope for someone who was interesting to talk to? Someone who could make her laugh?

The people she'd met in London seemed to talk only about one another, and while Poppy was not wholly averse to gossip (honestly, it was a liar who said he was) surely there was more to life than discussions of horse races, gambling debt, and whether a certain young lady's nose was too large.

Poppy had learned not to ask the questions that so frequently popped into her head. It turned out that the young ladies her aunt had selected as suitable companions were not interested in why some animals had whiskers and some didn't. And when Poppy had wondered aloud if everyone saw the same blue sky, three separate gentlemen had looked at her as if she were having some sort of madness attack, right in front of their eyes.

One had even backed nervously away.

But honestly, Poppy could not imagine why *everyone* did not think about this. She had never been inside anyone else's mind. Maybe what she thought was blue was what they thought was orange.

There was no way to prove it wasn't.

But Poppy didn't want to live out her life as a spinster. And so she'd resigned herself to another Season in London the following year, provided Aunt Alexandra was willing to sponsor her again.

But all that had changed. Or perhaps it would be more accurate to say that it *might* change. Who knew what the state of her reputation would be when the *Infinity* returned to England? There was still the chance that she might slip back into Briar House with no one (except Elizabeth Armitage) the wiser, and Poppy held on to that possibility, but it was a slim hope, indeed.

Perhaps she should count herself lucky that she seemed to have landed among the world's only band of scrupulous pirates. Or privateers, or traders, or whatever they wished to call themselves. She supposed she *was* lucky; her situation could have been far worse. She could have been beaten. She could have been violated.

She could be dead.

But she wasn't going to be grateful. She refused to feel *gratitude* for the men who had most probably ruined her life forever.

The hardest part—for now, at least—was the uncertainty. This was not a case of *Will I enjoy the opera tonight, or will I find it tedious?* It was *Will my life continue on as normal, or will I forevermore be an outcast to society?*

The strangest thing was, she had a sense she would feel differently if she *knew* that Elizabeth had managed to keep her disappearance quiet. If she *knew* that no one would ever point to her and say, "There's the wicked, fallen girl who ran off with pirates." (Because they would say that; it was far more delicious than the truth, and in matters of reputation the woman was always to blame.) If Poppy could be certain that she'd regain precisely the same life she had left behind . . .

She might think she was enjoying herself.

Oh, she was still bitter that she was stuck in this cabin and had not had so much as a breath of fresh air in nearly a week. She *really* would have liked to have explored the rest of the ship. Poppy doubted she would have the occasion to take such a voyage again, and she'd always been curious about the way things worked. A sailing ship was full of such puzzles: How did the men hoist the sails, for example? Did it take more than one? More than three? How was the food stored, and had anyone done a review to determine if it could be done in a more hygienic manner? How was the work distributed, and who made the schedule?

She'd asked the captain dozens of questions, and to his credit, he'd answered most. She'd learned about hardtack, and why she should be grateful that she didn't have to eat it. She now knew that the sun rose and fell more quickly near the equator and that a massive ocean wave was called a tsunami, and no, Captain James had never experienced one, but he'd met someone who had, and the description still gave him nightmares.

Poppy loved to ask him about the sailors on the *Infinity*, and he told her that they hailed from twelve different countries, including two from the Ethiopian Empire. (Which she could now locate easily on a map.) Captain James had tried to describe them to her, explaining that their features were quite different from the men he'd met from the western side of the continent, but Poppy was much more interested in their customs than how they looked.

She wanted to talk with these men who had grown up on a different continent, to ask them about their lives and their families, and how to pronounce their names (because she was fairly certain Captain James wasn't doing it right). She was never going to have an opportunity like this again. London was a cosmopolitan city, and during her two Seasons in the capital, Poppy had seen many people of different races and cultures. But she had never been allowed to speak to any of them.

Then again, until this week, it had never occurred to her that she might wish to. Which made her feel . . . odd. Odd and uncomfortable.

It wasn't the nicest of feelings, and it made her wonder what else she'd never noticed. She had always thought herself open-minded and curious, but she was coming to realize how impossibly small her world had been.

But instead of Ethiopia, she got to learn more about Kent. (*Engineering Methods of the Ancient Ottomans* turned out to be far more about engineering than it was about the Ottomans and was thus not only *not* exotic, but also completely indecipherable.)

And so Poppy was examining the illustrations of the Aubrey Hall orangery after dinner—for perhaps the dozenth time—when Captain James came in, alerting her as usual with one sharp rap before entering.

"Good evening," she said, glancing up from the chair she'd dragged over to the windows. The view didn't change, but it was beautiful, and she'd become devoted to it.

The captain didn't look as tired as he had the last few nights. He'd said that all of the sailors had got over their putrid stomachs and were back on duty, so maybe that was it. She imagined everyone would have to work harder when three men were out sick.

"Good evening," he said in polite return. He headed straight for the table, lifted the lid off one of the dishes, and inhaled deeply. "Beef stew. Thank you, Lord."

Poppy couldn't help but chuckle. "Your favorite?"

"It's one of Monsieur LaBaker's specialties," the captain confirmed.

"Your cook's name is LaBaker? Truly?"

Captain James sat down and dug into his meal, taking two very happy bites before saying, "I told you he was from Leeds. I think he just put a *La* in front of his name and called it French."

"How very enterprising."

The captain glanced at her over his shoulder. "He can call himself a potato if he wishes as long as he keeps cooking for me."

Poppy being Poppy, she immediately began to wonder what Mr. LaBaker *couldn't* call himself and still have a job cooking for him.

Captain, probably. It was difficult to imagine Captain James tolerating *that*.

"What are you grinning about?" he asked.

Poppy shook her head. It was just the sort of meandering thought there was no point in trying to explain.

He turned his chair so that he could see her without twisting in his seat. Then he sat back with that effortless masculine grace of his, long legs stretched out as a devilish smile played across his lips. "Are you plotting against me?"

"Always," she confirmed.

This made him grin—truly, and Poppy had to remind herself she did not care if she made him smile.

"I've yet to meet with success, though," she said with a sigh.

"Somehow I doubt that."

She shrugged, watching as he went back to his supper. After three bites of stew, half a roll, and a sip of wine, she asked, "Do your men eat the same meals you do?"

"Of course." He looked somewhat offended she'd asked. "It's served more plainly, but I'll not give them substandard fare."

"A hungry man cannot work hard?" she murmured. She had heard it said, and she was sure it was true—she herself was worthless when she was hungry—but it did feel a somewhat self-serving statement, as if a man's food was only worth the labor he might provide to his betters.

The captain's eyes narrowed, and for a moment it felt as if he were judging her. And perhaps not favorably.

"A hungry man quickly loses his spirit," he said in a quiet voice.

"I agree," Poppy swiftly responded. She felt no need to impress this man—if anything, it ought to be the other way around—but it did not sit well to think that he thought badly of her.

Which was nonsense. She shouldn't care.

But apparently she did, because she added, "I did not mean to say that *I* think a man's potential for hard work is the only reason to feed him well."

"No?" he murmured.

"No," she said firmly, because his tone had been *too* mild, and she feared it meant he did not believe her. "I agree with you that a hungry man loses his spirit. But many men don't care about the spirits of those they consider beneath them."

His voice was sharp and perfectly enunciated when he said, "I am not one of those men."

"No," she said. "I didn't think you were."

"There are many reasons to feed one's men well," he said, "not the least of which is the fact that they are human."

Poppy nodded, mesmerized by the quiet ferocity of his voice.

"But there is more," he continued. "A ship is not the same as a mill or a shop or a farm. If we do not work together, if we do not trust one another, we die. It is as simple as that."

"Is that not the reason why discipline and order are so essential in the navy?"

He gave a sharp nod. "There must be a chain of command, and ultimately there must be one man in charge. Otherwise it will be anarchy."

"Mutiny."

"Indeed." He used the side of his fork to cut a potato, but then he seemed to forget that he'd done so. His eyes narrowed, and the fingers of his free hand drummed along the table.

He did that when he was thinking. Poppy wondered if he realized this. Probably not. People rarely recognized their own mannerisms.

"However," he said so suddenly that she actually jerked to attention, "this is not the navy, and I cannot invoke King and Crown to foster loyalty. If I want men who will work hard, they must know that they are respected, and that they will be rewarded."

"With good food?" she asked dubiously.

This seemed to amuse him. "I was thinking more about a small share in the profits, but yes, good food helps too. I don't want to lead a ship of miserable souls. There's no pleasure in that."

"For you *or* the souls," she quipped.

He tipped his fork at her in salute. "Exactly. Treat men well, and they will treat you well, in return."

"Is that why you have treated me well?"

"Is that what you think?" He leaned forward, a warm, lazy smile on his face. "That I've treated you well?"

Poppy forced herself not to react to his expression. He had a way of looking at her as if she were the only human being in the world. It was intense, and thrilling, and she'd had to learn how to steel herself against it, especially since she knew she could not possibly be its sole recipient.

"Have you treated me well?" she echoed. "Aside from the actual fact of the kidnapping, yes, I suppose you have done. I cannot say that I have been mistreated. Bored out of my skull, perhaps, but not mistreated."

"There's an irony there," he remarked. "Here you are on what will probably be the biggest adventure of your life, and you are bored."

"How kind of you to point that out," she said dryly, "but as it happens, that exact thought has already entered my mind. Twice."

"Twice?"

"An hour," she ground out. "Twice a bloody hour. At least."

"Miss Bridgerton, I did not know you cursed."

"It's a relatively new habit."

He smiled, all white teeth and mischief. "Formed in the past week?"

"You are so astute, Captain James."

"If I might be permitted to pay you a compliment . . ."

She inclined her head graciously; it seemed expected.

"Of all my conversational sparring partners, you rank easily in the top five."

She quirked a brow. "There are four other people in this world who find you as vexing as I do?"

"I know," he said with a woeful shake of his head. "It's hard to believe. But"—at this he raised his fork, complete with carrot speared to the end—"the counterpart to that is there are four people in the world who vex me as much as you do."

She considered that for a moment. "I find that reassuring."

"Do you?"

"Once I'm back home, never to see you again . . ." She clasped her hands over her heart and sighed dramatically, as if preparing herself for her final soliloquy. "It will warm my heart to know that somewhere in this big, cruel world, *some*one is irritating you."

He stared at her for a moment, stunned into silence, and then he burst into laughter. "Oh, Miss Bridgerton," he said, getting the words out when he was able, "you have risen to the number one spot."

She looked over at him with a tipped-up chin and a clever smile. "I do try to excel in all of my endeavors."

Captain James lifted his glass. "I do not doubt that for a moment." He drank, seemingly in her honor, then added, "And I have no doubt that you succeed."

She thanked him with a regal nod.

He took another long drink, then held the glass in front of him, watching the dark red liquid as he swirled it about. "I will confess," he said, "that for all of my egalitarian views, I don't share my wine."

"You did with me."

"Yes, well, *you* are a special case."

"Aren't I just," Poppy grumbled.

"I might even have shared my brandy," he continued, "if I had any." At her questioning look he added, "*That* was what Brown and Green were supposed to get at the cave."

"And instead you got me."

Poppy wasn't positive, but she thought he muttered, "God help us both."

She snorted. She couldn't help it.

"Watch your manners," he said without any bite whatsoever. "I could give you grog."

"What *is* grog?" She'd heard Billy talking about it. He seemed to like it.

The captain tore off a piece of his roll and popped it into his mouth. "Mostly just watered-down rum."

"Mostly?"

"I try not to think about what else might be in there. I had enough of it when I—"

He stopped.

"When you what?" Poppy asked. He did that sometimes—started to tell her something, then cut himself off.

He set down his fork. "Nothing."

And that was what he always said when she probed his silences.

But Poppy kept asking. It wasn't as if she had anything better to do.

Captain James stood and walked to the window, hands on his hips as he gazed at the indistinguishable horizon. "There's no moon tonight."

"I had wondered." She'd been sitting by the window for hours, and she'd not seen one drop of moonlight flickering along the waves. It made for a slightly different seascape than the previous evenings.

"It means the stars will be staggeringly brilliant."

"How nice of you to let me know," she muttered.

She was fairly certain he'd heard her, but he did not react. Instead he asked, without turning around, "What time is it?"

Poppy shook her head. Was he so lazy that he could not twist his neck to look at the clock? "It is half ten." *Your Highness.*

"Hmm." It was a rather short *hmm*, one that said he accepted her words as true and was now pondering a related issue.

How she knew how to interpret his grunts, she did not know, but she would have bet real money that she was correct.

"Most of the men will be below by now," he said. He turned back to face her, leaning against the spot where the wall met the windows. "They work in shifts. They each get eight hours for sleep, but more than half take it at night, from nine to five."

It was interesting—she liked these sorts of details—but she could not imagine why he was telling her this now.

"I think," he said with a slow, deliberate tilt of his lips, "that if I were to take you up to see the stars, it would not cause such a large commotion."

Poppy went very still. "What did you just say?"

He looked at her, something in his expression hinting at a smile.

And something hinting at something more.

"You heard me," he said.

"You need to say it," she whispered. "You have to say the words."

He took a small step back, just enough so that he could offer her a courtly bow.

"My dear Miss Bridgerton," he murmured, "would you like to join me on deck?"

Chapter 12

◆─❧✳☙─◆

Poppy set down her book, never once taking her eyes from the captain's face. She had the strangest notion that if she did, if she broke that contact for even a moment, his suggestion would pop in the air like a soap bubble.

She made the tiniest of nods.

"Take my hand," he said, reaching out.

And even though everything within her that was sensible and true screamed that she ought not touch this man, she ought not let her skin even so much as brush against his . . .

She did.

He was still for a moment, looking down between them as if he couldn't quite believe she'd done it. His fingers curled slowly around hers, and when their hands were truly clasped, he brushed his thumb against the tender skin of her wrist.

She felt it everywhere.

"Come," he said. "Let's go above."

She nodded dumbly, trying to make sense of the strange sensation that was unfurling within her. She felt light, as if at any moment her heels would rise from the floor, leaving her tiptoed and ungrounded. Her blood seemed to fizz beneath her skin, and she tingled . . . not where he touched her—her hand felt warm and secure in his—but everywhere else.

Every spot of her.

She wanted . . .

Something.

Maybe she wanted everything.

Or maybe she knew what she wanted and was afraid to even think it.

"Miss Bridgerton?" he murmured.

She looked up. How long had she been staring at their hands?

"Are you ready?"

"Do I need a shawl?" she asked. (Then realized the irrelevance of her question and blinked.) "I don't have a shawl. But do I need one?"

"No," he said, his voice warm with amusement. "It's quite mild. The breeze is light."

"I do need shoes, though," she said, pulling her hand from his. She paused, for a moment forgetting where her short black boots even were. She had not bothered to put them on since she'd arrived. When would she have needed to?

"In the wardrobe," the captain said. "At the bottom."

"Oh yes, of course." How silly of her. She knew that. He'd put them there on her second day, after he'd tripped on them three times.

She grabbed her boots and sat down to lace them up. She'd sworn to herself—just this evening!—that she would not feel gratitude to any of the men on the ship, no matter how kind they were, but she could not seem to quell the traitorous urge inside her to throw her arms around him and gush *thank you thank you* until . . .

Well, maybe just twice. Any more would be ridiculous.

But the point was—

She paused. She had no point. Or if she did, she no longer knew what it was.

He did that to her sometimes. Jumbled her thoughts, tangled her words. She, who prided herself on her gift of conversation, her ready supply of wit and irony, was rendered without speech. Or at least without intelligent speech, which she rather thought was worse.

He turned her into someone she didn't know— but only sometimes, which was the most baffling part. Sometimes she was precisely the Poppy Bridgerton she knew herself to be, quick with a rejoinder, mind sharp. But then other times—when he'd turn to her with a heavy-lidded blue stare, or maybe when he walked too close and she felt the air around her grow warm from his skin—she lost her breath. She lost her sense.

She lost herself.

And right now? He had disarmed her with a kindness, that was all. He knew that she was desperate to leave the cabin. Maybe he was even just doing this to butter her up for some future injustice he would commit. Hadn't he once said that his life would be easier if she wasn't spitting mad?

She'd told him she never spit. *That* was Poppy Bridgerton. Not this scatterbrained peahen who couldn't find her own shoes.

"Is something wrong with your laces?" he asked.

Poppy realized she'd stopped tying her laces halfway through her left boot. "No," she blurted, "just lost the thread of my thought." She finished up quickly and stood. "There. I'm ready."

And she was. Somehow, with her sturdy shoes on her feet, she had regained her balance. She gave a little jump.

"Your boots look very practical," the captain said, looking at her with a combination of amusement and curiosity.

"Not as practical as yours," she said, with an eye toward what were surely custom-made tall boots. Such well-crafted footwear did not come cheap. In fact, all of the captain's attire was exquisitely made. Privateering must be more lucrative than she'd imagined. Either that or Captain James came from a *lot* of money.

But that didn't seem realistic. He was certainly wellborn, but Poppy doubted his family was rich. If they were, why on earth would he have gone into trade? And *such* a trade. There was nothing respectable about his profession. She could not even imagine her parents' reaction if one of her brothers had done the same.

Her mother would have died of shame. Not literally, of course, but she would have declared her death by shame often enough that Poppy would have feared her *own* demise by repetitive aural torture.

And yet, Poppy could not see anything within the captain that warranted such disappointment. True, she did not know the nature or extent of his business dealings, but she saw the way he treated his men— or at least Billy and Brown and Green. She saw the way he treated her, and she could not help but think of all the so-called gentlemen of London—the ones she was supposed to adore and admire and want to marry. She thought of all the cutting remarks, the cruelty and unkindness they displayed toward the men and women who worked for them.

Not all of them, but enough to make her question the strictures and standards that declared one man a gentleman and the other a rogue.

"Miss Bridgerton?"

The captain's voice wiggled its way into her thoughts, and she blinked, trying to remember what she'd been talking about.

"Are you ready?"

She nodded eagerly, took a step, and then grinned so suddenly it took her by surprise. "I haven't worn shoes for days."

"You will certainly need them on deck," he said. "Shall we be off?"

"Please."

He tipped his head toward the door. "After you."

After they exited the cabin, she followed him up the short flight of stairs to the deck. They emerged into a covered area, and he took her hand again to guide her forward.

But Poppy was not so easily led. "What is this?" she asked, just steps into the open air. She tugged her hand free and touched what looked like a lattice of ropes—something she might have tried to climb when she was a child.

Actually, she'd try to climb it now, except that it didn't look like it was meant for such a thing.

She turned back to Captain James, and he said, "Rope."

She smacked his shoulder, and not lightly. He wore a cheeky grin on his face, making it clear he'd said that to needle her.

"It's called a shroud," he said, smiling at her impatience.

She touched the ropes, marveling at the strength and thickness of the fibers. "*A* shroud?" she asked. "Not *the* shroud?"

"Very astute," he said. "It is one of many. They are part of the standing rigging, used to support the mast from side to side."

Yet another nautical term she did not know. "Standing rigging?"

"As opposed to the running rigging," he told her. "The standing rigging refers to the ropes that do not generally move. The ropes that *do* move—or rather, the ones we move in order to control the sails—are called the running rigging."

"I see," she murmured, although in truth she did not. She had seen only one small portion of the ship, and already there were so many unfamiliar mechanisms and gadgets. Even the items she thought she knew well—ropes, for example—were being used differently than she was used to. She could not imagine how long it took to truly master the art of sailing.

Or was it the science of sailing? She didn't know.

Poppy walked on, a few steps ahead of the captain, craning her neck to look up the length of one of the masts. It was amazingly tall, stabbing the night so majestically she almost thought it could pierce the sky.

"This has to be why the Greeks and Romans devised such fanciful tales of the gods," she murmured. "I can almost imagine the mast breaking through to the heavens."

She looked over at the captain. He was watching her intently, his every attention on her words, her face. But this time she did not feel self-conscious. She didn't feel awkward or embarrassed. Or reminded that in games of flirtation, she could not compete with this man.

Instead she felt almost buoyed. Maybe it was the ocean, or the salt breeze on her skin. She should have felt tiny under the vast starry sky, but instead she was invincible.

Jubilant.

More herself than she had ever been.

"Imagine the mast rips a hole in the sky," she said, waving her hand toward the dark night above. "And then out fall the stars." She looked back at Captain James. "If I lived in ancient times, with no notion of astronomy or distance, I might have devised such a myth. Surely a god could create a boat so tall that it touches the sky."

"A clever theory for the birth of the stars," he mused, "although it does make me wonder how they came to be spread out so evenly."

Poppy stood beside him, and together they gazed upward. The stars did not make an even pattern, of course, but they were scattered to every corner of the sky.

"I don't know," Poppy said thoughtfully. She kept her eyes on the stars, taking in the vastness of it all. Then she bumped him with her elbow. "You'll have to come up with that part of the story. I can't do all the work."

"Or," he said dryly, "I can sail the ship."

She could do nothing but grin in return. "Or you can sail the ship."

He motioned toward the bow, urging her forward, but instead she pressed her palm against the mast and swung around, like a ribbon on a maypole. When she was nearly back to her starting point, she peeked over at him and asked, "Is it made from a single piece of wood?"

"This one is. Actually, all of ours are. But we are not such a large vessel. Many of the navy's ships have masts constructed from several pieces of wood. Come," he said, urging her forward. "This is not even our tallest mast."

"No?" She looked ahead, eyes wide. "No, of course it isn't. That would have to be one of the center ones." She skipped forward, but he was faster, and by the time she'd reached the tallest mast, he had to turn around to offer his hand.

"Here," he said, "come with me. I promised you the stars."

She laughed, although not because it was funny. Just because she felt joy. "So you did," she said, and once again, she placed her hand in his. But they'd gone only two steps before she saw yet another interesting object. "Oh, what's that?"

The captain didn't even bother to look. "I'll tell you later."

Poppy grinned at his impatience and let him pull her forward, past yet another mast (the mizzenmast, he'd told her without breaking his stride). They went up a short set of stairs, and then forward *still*.

"The view is best up this way," he told her.

Her face was already tipped to the heavens, even as she stumbled along behind him. "It's not the same everywhere?"

"It *feels* best on the beakhead."

"On the *what*?"

"Just come with me," he said, tugging her hand.

She laughed again, and it felt *marvelous*. "Why is part of your ship named after a chicken?"

"Why are you named after a flower?" he countered.

She considered that for a moment. "Touché."

"The beakhead is the foremost part of the deck," he explained as he pulled her along. "Slightly lower in elevation. It's where the men stand when they work the sails of the bowsprit."

Beakhead? Bowsprit? "Now you're just making things up," she teased.

"Life at sea has a language all its own."

"Let's see, I'll call *that*"—she didn't actually point to anything—"a winchknob. And that over there shall be a mucklebump."

He paused for just long enough to give her an admiring glance. "It's not a bad name for it."

As Poppy hadn't been referring to anything in particular, she had no idea what *it* he was talking about, but she nevertheless asked, "Which one? The winchknob or the mucklebump?"

"The winchknob, of course," he said with a perfectly straight face.

She chuckled and let him tug her forward. "You would certainly know better than I."

"I shall treasure that statement. I'm not likely to hear it again."

"Certainly not!" But she said it with a grin, her cheeks nearly hurting from the joy of it. "I'm very good at making up words, you know. It runs in my family."

His brow crinkled with good humor and curiosity. "I can't even begin to imagine what you mean by that."

She told him about her brother, about tintons and farfars, and sneaking into Roger's room to write lines and help him complete his punishment, even though she was the one he'd wronged.

And the captain laughed. He laughed like he couldn't imagine anything better, with such joy that it almost felt to Poppy as if he'd been there, as if he'd seen the whole thing and was now remembering it with merriment rather than hearing it for the first time.

Had she told anyone about Roger's antics before? She must have done, if only in good-natured complaint. But not recently, probably not since he'd passed.

"I think your brother and I would have been

good friends," the captain said once he'd caught his breath.

"Yes," Poppy said, electrically aware that Roger had been her favorite brother, and Captain James might have been his finest friend. "I think you would have liked him a great deal. I think he would have liked you."

"Even though I kidnapped his sister?"

It should have stopped the conversation, ground it to parched, insidious dust. But somehow it didn't, and before Poppy gave it a second thought, she said, "Well, he'd make you marry me."

She looked at him.

He looked at her.

And then, with astonishing nonchalance, she added, "But then he'd have been satisfied. He wasn't the sort to hold a grudge."

The captain's fingers tightened around hers. "Are you?"

"I don't know," Poppy said. "I've never been wronged quite so dearly."

She hadn't said it to wound him, and she took no satisfaction when he winced. But it was the truth, and this was a moment that deserved no less.

"I wish it had not happened," he said.

"I know."

His eyes pressed into hers. "I wish you would believe me when I tell you I had no choice."

"I . . ." Poppy swallowed. *Did* she believe him? She had come to know him over the past few days, perhaps not like someone she'd known for years, but certainly more than she'd known any of the gentlemen who'd courted her in London. More, even, than the man who'd asked her to marry him.

She did not think Andrew James was a liar, and she did not think he was the sort of man who would allow someone to be hurt in the pursuit of his own expediency and profit.

"I believe that you believe you had no choice," she finally said.

He was silent for a moment, then said, "That is something, I suppose."

She gave him a helpless shrug. "I cannot understand what you will not tell me."

His nod was one of resignation, but he said no more on the subject. Instead he motioned with his arm, urging her a few more steps forward. "Careful," he murmured.

Poppy looked to her toes. The deck came to an abrupt halt in front of her, its elevation dropping by several feet.

The captain hopped down. "The beakhead, my lady," he said with a gallant wave to the triangular deck that formed the pointy front of the *Infinity*. He reached up and placed his hands on her hips to help her down.

But when she was steady, he didn't let go.

"This is as far forward as one can stand on deck," he told her.

She pointed to a spot a few feet ahead. "What about—"

"As one can stand *safely* on deck," he amended. He adjusted their position so that he was standing behind her. "Now close your eyes."

"But then I can't see the stars."

"You can open them later."

She tilted her head to the left, right, and back again, as if to say, *Oh, very well*, but she closed her eyes.

"Now tilt your head up. Not all the way, just a bit."

She did, and maybe it was that motion, or maybe it was just because she'd closed her eyes, but she felt instantly off-balance, as if something far greater than the ocean had stolen her equilibrium.

The captain's hands tightened on her hips. "What do you feel?" he asked, his lips coming close to her ear.

"The wind."

"What else?"

She swallowed. Licked her lips. "The salt in the air."

"What else?"

"The motion, the speed."

He moved his mouth closer. "What else?"

And then she said the one thing that had been true from the beginning.

"*You.*"

Chapter 13

Andrew wasn't sure what devil had convinced him to bring Poppy up to the deck.

Perhaps it was simply that he couldn't think of a compelling reason not to.

The sea was calm. The stars were out.

Most of the crew were below.

When he'd come down for supper and had seen her sitting by the window, he'd somehow known that she had been in that position for hours, staring at the sea and the sky, and never understanding how it felt to be truly a part of either.

It seemed a crime.

When he had reached out to her, and she placed her hand in his . . .

It was a benediction.

Now, as they stood at the very front of the ship, the wind riffling its salt and spray through their hair, he felt renewed.

He felt *new*.

The world turned endlessly on its axis—this he understood. So why did it feel as if it had just turned *more*? As if it had taken a greater rotation, or the direction had reversed. The salt air was crisper, the stars uncannily sharp in their inky canvas. And the feel of her—the gentle curve of her hip, the soft radiant heat of her body . . .

It was as if he had never touched a woman before.

It was strange how content he was simply to gaze upon her face. Poppy watched the sky, and he watched her, and it was perfect.

No. Not perfect. Perfect was complete. Perfect was *done*.

This wasn't perfect. He didn't want it to be.

And yet he felt perfectly wonderful.

You, she'd said, when he'd asked what she felt.

His fingers slid forward, perhaps an inch, just enough so that his steadying grip became something closer to an embrace. Just enough to pull her against him, if he dared.

You, she'd said.

He wanted more.

You.

He was not a romantic man, or at least he hadn't thought so. But the moment had become a poem, the wind whispering its lines as the water rose and fell in mysterious meter.

And if the world beneath his feet had become a sonnet, then *she* was the sublime.

Had she become his muse? Surely not. Poppy Bridgerton was vexing, exasperating, and far too clever for his peace of mind. She was an inconvenience wrapped in an impending disaster, and yet when he thought of her—which was all the time, damn it—he smiled.

Sometimes he grinned.

He told himself that she was a thorn in his side, that she was worse than that—the equivalent of a damn stab wound—but it was hard to maintain his own lies when all he wanted at the end of the day was to sit down with his supper and a glass of wine and see what he could do to make her flirt with him.

Maybe *that* was why he'd finally brought her above deck.

He'd just wanted to see her smile.

And in that pursuit, in that mission . . .

His success had been absolute.

She had not stopped smiling, not from the first moment he'd pulled her through the doorway and out of the cabin. She had smiled so hard and so well that it might as well have been a laugh.

He had made her happy, and that had made him happy.

And *that* should have been terrifying.

"How many stars do you think there are?" she asked.

He looked down at her. She'd opened her eyes and was now gazing up at the heavens with such intensity that for a brief moment he thought she might be intending to count.

"A million?" he said. "A billion? Surely more than our eyes can see."

She let out a little noise, something like a hum, if

a hum could be crossed with a sigh and then colored with a smile. "It's so big."

"The sky?"

She nodded. "How can something be so unfathomable? I can't even fathom how unfathomable it is."

"Isn't that the definition of the word?"

She kicked him lightly with her heel. "Don't be a spoilsport."

"You would have said the same thing, and you know it."

"Not here," she said in a voice that was almost dreamy. "And not now. All of my sarcasm has been suspended."

This he did not believe for a second. "Really."

She sighed. "I know it can't always be this lovely and wonderful on deck, but will you lie to me, just this once, and tell me so?"

He couldn't resist. "What makes you think I haven't lied to you before?"

She poked him with her elbow.

"It is always this lovely and wonderful on deck," he parroted. "The sea is never turbulent, and the skies are always clear."

"And your men always comport themselves with propriety and discretion?"

"Of course." He adjusted his pressure on her hips, turning her just a little to the left. "Do you see that?" he asked, nodding toward a hole in the decking ahead of them.

"See what?" She turned her head to peer up at him, and he motioned again, this time making sure she could follow his gaze.

"That round opening, right there," he said. "It's a privy."

"*What?*"

"Well, we call it the head," he clarified. "I told you we had our own language on board."

She jerked a little, although not enough to dislodge her from his grasp. "Right here? A privy? Out in the open?"

"There's one on the other side too."

She gasped, and Andrew was brought back to all the times he'd tortured his sister with things creepy, crawly, and repulsive.

It was just as good now as it had been then.

He brought his lips a little closer to Poppy's ear. "You didn't think we all have lovely and wonderful chamber pots in our cabins, did you?"

He was very glad that he'd tilted to the side so he could see her face, because her lips bent and stretched in a marvelous expression of hygienic horror before she finally said, "You're telling me you just squat down and situate yourself over—"

"*I* don't," he interrupted, "but the men do. It's an ingenious design, really. The hull of the ship curves inward, of course, so the waste just drops straight down into the ocean. Well, unless there's a particularly strong wind, but even then—"

"Stop!" she squealed. "It's disgusting."

"But you're always so full of questions," he said with all innocence. "I thought you wanted to know how the ship worked."

"I do, but—"

"I assure you, such matters are most critical to the

successful running of a ship. No one ever wants to talk about the unglamorous. It's a common downfall of would-be architects and engineers, I tell you. It's all very well and good to design the elegant bits, but it's the things you can't see in a structure that make it truly great."

"I can see *that*," she muttered with a nod toward the head.

He fought a chuckle. "A compromise, if you will. In this case, the men trade a bit of their dignity for a far cleaner ship. Believe me, it gets rank enough on board during a long voyage."

She made a little frown—the kind that was accompanied by a tilt of the head when people decided they approved of something. Still, she said, "I can't believe I am having this conversation."

"Likewise."

"*You* brought it up."

"So I did." He frowned, trying to remember why. "Oh, right. It was because you had commented on the delicate manners of my men."

"*This* was your way of refuting my claim?"

"It worked, didn't it?"

She frowned. "But you said *you*—"

"I used to," he admitted. "Not on the *Infinity*, but on other ships, when I wasn't in command."

She gave a little shudder.

"The King of France sits on the chamber pot in front of his entire court," Andrew said cheerfully.

"He does not!"

"He does, I swear. Or at least the last one did."

She shook her head. "The *French*."

Andrew burst out laughing.

"What's so funny?"

"You are, as you know."

She tried to scowl, but it didn't work. She was clearly too proud of herself. Andrew thought she looked delightful.

"I suppose you've been to France," she said.

"I have," he confirmed.

"All over, or just to Paris?"

"And the ports."

"Of course." Her eyes flicked sheepishly to the side. "You can't sail a ship of this size all the way to Paris."

"Not generally, no. We can go as far as Rouen. Sometimes we do, sometimes we dock at the coast. In Le Havre, usually."

Poppy was quiet for a moment, long enough for the wind to pull a wispy lock of her hair from behind her ear. It tickled Andrew's skin, almost made him sneeze.

"What will you do when you've done everything?" she finally asked. Her voice was more serious now, thoughtful and curious.

He thought that a most interesting question, one he could not imagine anyone else asking of him. "Is that possible?" he wondered. "To do everything?"

Her brow drew down as she thought about that, and even though Andrew knew the lines that formed were due to thought and not worry, he had the hardest time keeping his fingers from smoothing them out.

"I think it might be possible to do *enough*," she finally said.

"Enough?" he murmured.

"So that nothing feels new anymore."

Her words echoed his own recent thoughts so closely it nearly pulled his breath from his body. It wasn't that his work was no longer exciting, or that he never got to do anything new. It was more that he was starting to feel ready to go home. To be with the people he loved.

With the people who loved him.

"I don't know," he said, because her question deserved honesty, even if he didn't have a proper answer. "I don't think I've reached that point yet," he said. "Although . . ."

"Although?"

He might be getting close.

But he didn't say that. He let himself lean forward, just far enough so that he could imagine setting his chin on the top of her head. He fought the urge to move his hands forward, to wrap them around her and pull her against him. He wanted to hold her in place, just the two of them against the wind.

"I should like to go to Ethiopia," she said suddenly.

"Really?"

Poppy Bridgerton was more adventurous than most, but this surprised him.

"No," she admitted. "But I like to *think* that I'd like to go there."

"You'd like to . . ." He blinked. "What?"

"I've had a great deal of time to myself lately," she said. "There is little else to do besides imagine things."

Andrew generally thought himself an intelligent

man, but he was having the *damnedest* time following her. "So you imagine going to Ethiopia?"

"Not really. I don't know enough to imagine it properly. I can't imagine what little I've heard is accurate. In England people speak of Africa as if it's one big happy place—"

"Happy?" It wasn't the word he'd have used.

"You know what I mean. People speak of it as if it's one place, like France or Spain, when in actuality it's *huge*."

He thought of the dissected map, of how much fun she'd had while putting it together. "So says the map," he murmured.

She nodded her agreement, then befuddled him completely when she said, "I imagine being the sort of person who would *want* to go to Ethiopia."

"There's a difference?"

"I think so. Perhaps what I mean is that I'd like to be the *type* of person who wants to do such things. I think someone like that would be brilliant at parties, don't you?"

Andrew was dubious. "So you're saying your goal is to be brilliant at parties."

"No, of course not. My current goal is to avoid such gatherings at all costs. That's why I was in Charmouth, if you must know."

"I suppose I must," he murmured, mostly because there didn't seem any other appropriate response.

She gave him a look that was half peeved and half indulgent before carrying on. "What I'm trying to say is that if I went to a ball and met someone who had been to Ethiopia on purpose—"

"*On purpose?*"

"I don't think it counts if one goes under *duress*."

Andrew turned her around. He needed to see her face. It was far too difficult to follow the conversation otherwise.

He studied her, looking for what, he did not know. Signs of mischief? Of madness? "I have absolutely no idea what you are talking about," he finally admitted.

She laughed, and it was a glorious thing. "I'm sorry, I'm not being terribly clear. But that's your own fault for leaving me to my own devices for so long. I've had far too much time to do nothing but think."

"And this has led you to sweeping conclusions about social discourse and the Ethiopian Empire?"

"It has." She said it quite grandly, stepping back as if that might broaden her stage. Not that there was anyone else to listen; they'd passed only two crewmembers on the way to the beakhead, and both men had wisely made themselves scarce.

It wasn't often they saw their captain hand-in-hand with a lady, even if it was just so he could pull her along behind him.

But Poppy's step back meant that he had to release his hold on her hips, which was a damn shame.

When she was confident of his attention, she made her pronouncement. "There are two types of people in this world."

"Are you sure about that?"

"For the purposes of this conversation, yes. There are people who want to visit Ethiopia, and people who don't."

Andrew fought very hard to maintain an even expression. He failed.

"You laugh," she said, "but it's true."

"I'm sure it must be."

"Just listen to me. Some of us have an adventurous, wandering soul, and some of us don't."

"And you think a person has to want to travel to the east of Africa to prove he has a thirst for adventure?"

"No, of course not, but as an indicator—"

"You, Miss Bridgerton, have an adventurous soul."

She drew back with a pleased smile. "Do you think so?"

He swept his arm through the air, motioning to the sea and the sky, to their spot at the bow of a cleverly crafted pile of wood that could somehow carry them from one land to another, across liquid depths no man could withstand on his own.

"It doesn't count if it's under duress," she reminded him.

Enough. He planted his hands on her shoulders. "There are two types of people in this world," he told her. "The ones who would curl up in a ball and sob their way through this sort of unexpected voyage, and—"

"Those who wouldn't?" she interrupted.

He shook his head, and he felt the tiniest of smiles tugging at his lips as he touched her cheek. "I was going to say *you.*"

"So it's me against the world?"

"No," he said, and something began to tumble inside him. He was weightless, and it was like the time he'd fallen from a tree, except there was nothing below, just an empty expanse of space and *her*.

"No," he said again. "I think I'm on your side."

Her eyes grew wide, and although it was clearly too dark to make out the color of her irises, it still somehow *felt* as if he could see it, the dark moss giving way to flecks of something paler. Younger, like new shoots in the grass.

Something light and luminous began to rise within him. That heady, fizzy feeling of infatuation, of flirtation and desire.

No, not desire. Or not *just* desire.

Anticipation.

The moment *before*. When you could feel the beat of your heart in every corner of your body, when every breath felt as if it reached all the way down to your toes. When nothing could quite compare to the perfect curve of a woman's lips.

"If I kissed you," he whispered, "would you let me?"

Her eyes grew soft, with something like amusement.

Amusement?

"If you kissed me," she replied, "I would not have the opportunity to let you or not let you. It would be done."

Trust this one to split hairs. He would not allow her to get out of the question so cleanly.

"If I leaned toward you, like this . . ." He followed his words with actions, and the space between their faces grew smaller. "And if my eyes dropped to your mouth, in what we all know is a universal signal that one is pondering a kiss, what would you do?"

She licked her lips. He doubted she even realized that she'd done so. "I'm not sure," she whispered.

"But it's happening right now. I've leaned in." He reached out, brushed her skin. "I'm touching your cheek."

She turned almost imperceptibly into his hand.

Andrew felt his voice grow husky, even before he formed words. "It's no longer what would you do but what *will* you do."

He moved even closer, so close that his eyes could no longer focus on her face. So close that he could feel the light touch of her breath on his lips.

But still not a kiss.

"What will you do, Poppy?"

And then she leaned. She swayed. Just a little, but that was all it took for her lips to brush softly against his.

It was the lightest of kisses.

It shot through his heart.

His fingers landed on her shoulders, and some very small corner of his mind realized it wasn't to pull her close, but rather to keep himself from doing so. Because if he did . . .

And heaven knew he wanted to.

Dear God, he wanted so much. So much of *her*.

He wanted the length of her body against his. He wanted the curve of her back beneath his hand, the heat of her as he nudged his leg between hers.

He wanted to press himself against her, so that she would feel his desire, so that she would *know* it, and she would know what she had done to him.

He wanted all that, and then he wanted more,

which was why he drew an unsteady breath and stepped back.

To continue would be heaven.

To continue would be madness.

He turned away, needing a moment to catch his breath. That kiss . . . it had lasted less than a second, but he was undone.

"I'm sorry," he said, his voice rough and scratchy in his throat.

She blinked several times. "You are?"

He looked back at her. Her fingers were lightly touching her lips, and she looked dazed, as if she wasn't quite sure what had just happened.

Welcome to the club.

"I shouldn't have done that," he said, because it seemed slightly kinder than saying it shouldn't have happened. Although he wasn't sure why.

"It's . . ." Her brow wrinkled, and she looked as if she was thinking very hard about something. Either that or she couldn't figure out what she ought to be thinking about.

"Poppy?"

Her eyes flicked back to his, as if something inside her had woken up. "It's all right," she said.

"All right?" he echoed. That sounded . . . tepid.

"It's not your fault," she said. "I kissed *you*."

"Please," he said patiently, "we both know—"

"I kissed you." She said it firmly, between her teeth. "You dared me to."

"I—" But he said no more. Was it the truth? *Had* he dared her? Or had he just been making sure she had wanted it too? Because even just one kiss . . . it could ruin her.

It may well have ruined him.

"That's what happened," she said. "That's what happened, and I don't regret it."

"You don't?"

"No. Weren't we just discussing the irony of my being bored while on the adventure of my life? You are many things, Captain James, but you are not boring."

His mouth might have gone slack. "Thank you?"

"But we will never speak of it again."

"If that is your wish." It wasn't *his* wish, but it should be.

She regarded him with an oddly penetrating expression. "It has to be, don't you think?"

He had no idea *what* he thought any longer, but he wasn't going to tell her that. "I bow to your judgment, Miss Bridgerton."

She gave a little snort, as if she didn't believe that for a second. He supposed he deserved it; he was usually employing some degree of irony when he said such things.

"Very well," he said. "We shall pretend it never happened."

She opened her mouth as if she might argue—and in fact he was quite certain she wanted to argue; he'd seen that expression on her face enough times to know what it meant. But in the end she didn't say anything. She snapped her mouth shut and nodded her agreement.

That seemed to be the end of the conversation, so Andrew just stared off at the horizon, barely discernible in the moonless night. They'd made good time; barring an unexpected change in the weather, they'd be in Lisbon by morning. Which meant that he needed to get some sleep. He had to be off the ship and into town first thing.

"I'm afraid I need to take you back down below," he said to Poppy.

She could not hide her disappointment, but at the same time, it was clear she'd been expecting this. "Very well," she said with a sigh.

He held out his hand.

She shook her head. "I can manage."

"At least allow me to help you up from the beakhead."

She did, but the moment she was on the main deck, she pulled her hand from his grasp. He let her lead the way back, and soon enough, they were at his cabin door.

"I just need to gather a few things before I go to Mr. Carroway's cabin," he said.

"Of course." She stepped to the side as they entered, and it was all very polite, and strangely not awkward.

Rather like nothing had happened.

Which was how they wanted it.

Wasn't it?

Chapter 14

Poppy awakened the following morning with the strangest feeling. It was almost vertigo, and she grasped the bed rail for several seconds before she realized—

They were not moving.

They were not moving!

She leapt out of the bunk and rushed to the window, inexplicably stumbling on the stillness. With an excited breath, she pulled back the curtains to reveal . . .

Docks.

Of course.

She wasn't sure why it hadn't occurred to her that she would not be able to see the proper center of Lisbon from her ship's window. The docks in London weren't anywhere near the sights of the capital.

Still, it was something to look at that wasn't the endless water of the Atlantic, and Poppy took it all in eagerly. She could see only a small sliver of what was surely a large canvas, but even so, the scene before her was buzzing with life and activity. The men—and they were all men; she did not see a woman among them—moved about with strength and efficiency, carrying crates, pulling on ropes, performing all manner of tasks, the purpose of most Poppy could not deduce.

And how strange and different the men were . . . and at the same time, not different at all. They were performing all the same tasks she assumed English dockworkers did, jostling and laughing and arguing in the manner of men, and yet even if she had not been aware that she was in Portugal, she would have known that these men were not English.

It was not their looks, although it was true that many had darker hair and skin than most of Poppy's countrymen. It was more in their movements, their gestures. When they spoke, she could tell just by looking at them that their words were of a different language. The men's mouths moved differently. They used different muscles. They made different expressions.

It was fascinating, and she wondered if she would have noticed it if the sounds of their voices had not been brought to such a low volume by the wall and windows between them. If she could hear them—really *hear* the sound of the Portuguese language—would her eyes have found the changes in their faces?

There was so much to think about. So much to see.

And she was stuck in this cabin.

Captain James had made it clear that she would not be permitted to disembark in Lisbon. He'd said it was too dangerous, he wasn't there to serve as a guide, he had business to conduct, this wasn't a pleasure voyage . . .

He was just full of reasons.

Then again, he had also told her that under no circumstances would she be allowed on deck.

And last night he had changed his mind.

Poppy leaned her forehead on the window, the glass cool and soothing against her skin. As she'd lain in bed the night before, reliving every moment up under the stars, she'd allowed herself to hope that *maybe* he would relent and take her into town.

Something had changed the night before, and she wasn't thinking of the kiss.

Well, no, she was *certainly* thinking about the kiss. She might have declared that they should never speak of it again, but she'd been aghast when the captain had suggested that they pretend it never happened. She'd almost told him so, was going to say in no uncertain terms that it was exactly the sort of thing a person should take care to remember, if only to make sure it wasn't repeated.

That had seemed petty, though, and maybe even mean, so then she almost said that it was her first kiss, and a girl only got one of those, and he was mad if he thought she was going to pretend it never happened.

But that was exactly the sort of thing he'd misunderstand. She didn't want him to think she was lying in bed thinking about him, even if she was.

For now.

It wasn't as if she had plans to lie in bed and think about him for the rest of her life. She would be back in England in less than a week, and then she'd never see him again. If Elizabeth kept her mouth shut, Poppy's life would continue as normal, which meant that eventually she would marry some nice gentleman her family approved of, and she'd lie in bed and think about *him* for the rest of her life.

And if Elizabeth *didn't* keep her mouth shut, and Poppy's social standing drew down to zero, she'd have far bigger problems keeping her awake than the devastatingly handsome Captain Andrew James.

Poppy glanced over at the clock to check the time, and as if on cue, Billy knocked on her door. She did not need to hear his voice to know it was he. Billy and the captain were the only two people who ever came to see her, and their knocks were as different as chalk and cheese.

"Come in!" she called, because unlike the captain, Billy always waited for her permission to enter. Her hair was still in its sleeping braid, but she'd given up caring about that. And since she slept in her clothes, it wasn't as if anyone would ever see her improperly dressed.

"I brought breakfast, miss," he said, carrying his usual tray. "It's nothing fancy. Just some toast, tea, an' apples. Most of the men will be going ashore to eat."

"Will they?" Poppy murmured, her envious eyes wandering back to the window.

Billy nodded as he set down the tray. "They have to finish up on board, of course, an' they can't all leave the ship at once, but the captain makes sure everyone has a chance to stretch his legs."

"Everyone, eh?"

Billy missed her undertone and sailed on. "Oh yes, though it's a right confusing place if you don't know what's what. It's not just the language, though it's good to know a few words. *Sim* for *yes*, *no* for *no*."

"Well, that's handy," Poppy remarked.

"*No* seems to be *no* in just about every place we go," Billy said with a cheeky grin. "It's spelled different, I think, but it sounds close enough."

Poppy took her usual seat at the table, then adjusted it to give the best view of the port. "In German it's *nein*."

"Is it?" Billy scratched his head. "I've not been there. They don't have a coast, I think."

Poppy poured herself a cup of tea. "Hamburg," she said absently.

"Eh?"

She looked up. "They speak German in Hamburg. It's a busy port city near the Baltic Sea. I would show it to you on the map, but I've already disassembled it."

Billy nodded; he'd seen her working on the dissected map earlier in the week. "Maybe I should give it a try," he said. "Be useful to know something more of geography. I can read, y'know," he said proudly. "An' I can do sums better than half the men on the ship."

"That's wonderful," Poppy said. Maybe they could work on the puzzle on the voyage back. It would be her third time, but it would be great fun to have company. She would have to petition Captain James to release Billy from some of his duties, but if she explained that it was for the boy's education . . .

He would say yes to that. She was sure of it.

"Tell me more about Lisbon," she said with an encouraging smile. "I want to hear everything."

"Oh, it's a lively city, miss. Y'can't really tell from here." He plopped down in the chair across from her and motioned toward the window. "This is just the waterfront. We're moored in real close this time, so you've got a right good view, but it's not the city. The city is grand."

"Grand?" Poppy murmured. She took a careful sip of her tea. It was still a little too hot.

"Oh yes, and a real different sort of place. Nothing like home, not that there's anything *wrong* with home. It's just—it's nice to see things that are different."

"I'm sure," Poppy murmured, bringing her teacup to her lips to mask whatever sarcastic tone she'd not been able to keep from her words.

"Everything looks different," Billy continued. "Well, most everything, and the food isn't the same. Takes some getting used to, but it's good, the food. I've been here six times now, so I know my way around."

Poppy managed a small smile.

Billy paused, finally noticing her expression. "I could, ah . . . Well, I could ask if we could bring you something. They make a nice rice pudding, though that's not so easy to carry. An' there's these little

bready things that sometimes come rolled in sugar."
His eyes actually rolled back in his head as he re-
lived his culinary ecstasy. "I could bring you one of
those, if you want."

"From the looks of you," Poppy said, "I think I
might want more than one."

Billy laughed. "They won't be as good as when
they're fresh hot, but you'll still like 'em. An' the
cook will be getting provisions, so he might make
something that's a little Portuguesey."

"This is all very kind of you, Billy."

He gave her a sympathetic smile. "The captain's
not a bad man for making you stay on board. It
wouldn't be safe for you to go out on your own.
Wouldn't be safe even if we were docked back in
London. The ladies here near the water . . ." He
blushed, powerfully, and his voice lowered as he
said, "Not all of them are ladies, if you get what I
mean."

Poppy decided not to inquire further about
that. "What do you think would happen if I went
ashore with Captain James?" she asked. "Surely
Lisbon is not such a dangerous city that he could
not protect me."

"Well . . ." Billy pondered this for a moment, his
mouth pursing on one side as he thought. "I suppose
he could just take you through the docks area and
over to the nicer bits."

Poppy's mood brightened considerably. "Brilliant! I—"

"But he's not here."

Well, damn. "Not here?"

Billy shook his head. "Was the first one off the ship. Had some sort of business. He usually does."

"Do you know when he will be back?"

"Hard to tell," Billy said with a shrug. "It usually depends on what he's carrying."

"Carrying?" Poppy echoed.

"Sometimes it's a package, sometimes just papers. And of course, sometimes nothing at all."

Sometimes nothing at all? Poppy found this interesting, although she couldn't say why. Probably just because she had nothing better to wonder about. She'd already been through just about every permutation of her return to England (ninety percent involved her ruin; the other ten percent required a spectacular and unlikely combination of good luck).

So, yes. She *was* going to wonder why the captain sometimes carried packages and sometimes carried papers. She was going to do her damnedest to think only about things of this sort until she got home and had to deal with far more serious issues.

"Does he often carry papers?" she asked.

Billy stood and pushed his chair back into place. "Sometimes. Don't know, really. He doesn't tell any of us what his business is that's not the ship's business."

"He has business that's not the ship's business?"

He shrugged. "He has friends here. Has to. He's been so many times."

Poppy knew that Billy had been on the *Infinity* for only nine months; he'd told her that the second time he brought her breakfast. If he had been to

Lisbon six times already, Poppy could only imagine how often Captain James had visited over the years. According to Billy (because just about everything she knew was according to Billy), he'd been captaining the ship since 1782.

It seemed like an awful lot of trips to Portugal, but then again, what did she know about privateering? Maybe it made sense to stick with a dependable, loyal network of traders.

And just like that, she was thinking like a criminal. Good heavens.

Poppy sipped her tea, which had finally cooled to an acceptable temperature. "Have a good time in town," she said. "I assume you're going."

"Oh yes. Soon, actually. One of the men said he'd take me with him." Billy looked at her with a sheepish expression. "The captain doesn't let me go by myself either."

The captain, Poppy was coming to realize, had a softer heart than he wanted others to realize. It was difficult to imagine another ship captain worrying over the welfare of a thirteen-year-old boy.

Not that she had experience with any other ship captains, but still.

"I'd best be going," Billy said. "I've got to finish my duties before I can go ashore, an' I don't think Mr. Brown will wait if he's ready before I am."

Poppy nodded and bid him farewell. She made quick work of breakfast—there were only so many ways to bite a pattern into a toast triangle—then took her tea to the window to watch the show.

It was rather like going to the theater. Not any

theater she'd had occasion to attend, but she was determined to enjoy it all the same. At first she tried to take in the entire panorama, but there was too much happening at once, so she decided to follow the path of just one man, watching as he went about his tasks.

"I shall call you José," she announced. It was the name of a recent king, so surely it was appropriate to the region. "José Goodhope. You shall have three children, four dogs, and a rabbit."

She frowned. He'd probably eat that rabbit. Best not get too attached to it.

"Are you married, Mr. Goodhope? Or widowed?" She watched her mystery man as he lifted a crate from a wagon and carried it toward a ship. "Widowed," she said decisively. "Much more dramatic."

Shakespeare would be proud. It was a play, after all.

"And your poor motherless children. You must work so hard to feed them. My goodness, they're hungry."

She thought about that.

"But not hungry enough to eat the rabbit," she said firmly. This was her story, and she wanted to save the rabbit. It was white and fluffy and thoroughly nonexistent, but that was the beauty of writing one's own tale. She could do whatever she wanted.

She'd always wanted to be an evil overlord.

Or a nice one. She had no real preference. Just so long as she was in charge.

José set down his crate and returned to the wagon, wiping his brow with his sleeve. He picked up another crate, this one heavier than the first if his posture was any indication. After he set that one down, he stood straight and rolled his neck a few times.

Poppy did the same. There was something about watching someone stretch that made her need to do it too.

When she was once again facing forward, she saw that José had twisted to call out to someone over his shoulder. Then he reached down to the hem of his shirt . . .

And took it off.

Poppy leaned forward. Now *this* was interesting.

Did dockworkers routinely perform their duties shirtless? Was this a Portuguese custom? It was certainly warmer here than it was in London, but then again, she'd never been to the London docks. Maybe the men ran around all the time with their chests bare as day.

And if that was the case, why had no one told her?

"Oh, José," she murmured, setting down her teacup. "It's a very hot day, isn't it?"

This seemed reason enough to stand and move closer to the window. Maybe she needed to re-engineer her plot. Did she really want José to be a widower? Wouldn't it make more sense to make him a never-married bachelor?

With no children. Maybe a dog. And the rabbit could stay.

It was so lovely and fluffy. Who wouldn't want to keep it in the story?

"Are you courting anyone, José?" She caught

her lower lip between her teeth as she watched his muscles flex with exertion. First it was his arms, as he reached down to grip the crate, but then once he reached the ship she had a good view of his back.

She had no idea a man's back could be so interesting. She'd seen her brothers shirtless, but not recently, and none of them had looked as sculpted as José.

"Sculpted," she said aloud. Another word she thought sounded a bit like its meaning. But only if one was working in a soft medium. She squeezed her hands in the air as if molding clay. *Sculpting*. It sounded like the motion of scooping and mashing.

She shook her head. She was getting entirely off topic, and José was *right there* on the dock. What were those muscles called? The ones on a man's chest that made it so . . .

Her hands wiggled in the air, still sculpting.

So . . . defined.

Poppy had taken drawing classes, of course; all young ladies did. Her instructor had talked about the muscles of the body, but he'd never mentioned the ones on a man's chest. What were they called?

She glanced at Captain James's bookshelf. Somehow she doubted she'd find the answer in *Agrarian Masterpieces of Kent*.

Poppy moved closer to the window. She didn't think anyone would be able to see her from the dock. It was much brighter outside than in.

"How old are you?" she wondered. José was taking a break now, sitting atop one of the crates he'd just moved. He didn't look very much older than she was. Certainly not more than thirty. And he had all his hair. It was dark—darker than the captain's, of course—but just as thick. It would probably also have that soft, springy quality.

She'd touched the captain's hair a few days earlier when the ocean had taken a dip and set her off-balance. She'd lurched forward and grabbed the first thing she could, which turned out to be the captain's head.

It was entirely accidental, of course.

José's hair had a similar wave. Poppy decided she liked it. If the breeze hit it just so, it would fall rakishly over his forehead. There had been a gentleman like that in London, and all the ladies had swooned. There was something about a mussed man, one of Poppy's acquaintances had said. It meant he was so very *vigorous*. Poppy had thought she was talking her usual nonsense, but now, looking at José, vigor was taking on an entirely new meaning.

She had a feeling José was *most* vigorous.

He was handsome, her José. Nothing on the captain, of course, but not every man could be as beautiful as Andrew James.

"But José," she said aloud, "I think you come close."

"Close to what?"

Poppy jumped nearly a foot, almost knocking her teacup off the table. Captain James was standing by the door, watching her with arched eyebrows and an amused expression.

"You didn't knock!" she accused.

"I did," he said plainly. "And who's José?"

Poppy just stared at him like an idiot, which was probably not a bad thing, since she doubted she could have managed anything that was either intelligent or nonincriminating. She couldn't believe she hadn't heard him knock.

Or the door opening.

Or closing.

She cleared her throat and bid him good morning. It seemed the best course of action.

But Captain James was undeterred. "What are you watching that has you so entranced?"

"Nothing!" she said, far too loudly. "I mean, just the docks, of course. I'm sure it's not interesting to *you*, but it's the first thing I've had a chance to look at that's not just water."

He took off his tricorn hat. "Did you miss me?"

"Of course not."

He acknowledged this with a slightly sardonic nod, then ambled over to join her at the window. Poppy found herself trying not to squirm as he tilted his head to the side and perused the scene.

"It looks like an ordinary day loading cargo," he said.

Poppy resisted the urge to babble some sort of agreement and instead just made a few meaningless noises and nodded.

Outside, José had gone back to work, but thankfully Captain James was looking elsewhere. He motioned with his hand toward a nearby ship and said, "The *Marabella*'s off to South America tomorrow."

"Really? That sounds exciting."

"It's a longer voyage than I've ever made."

"I imagine so," Poppy responded, trying to keep her attention from wandering back to José, who was still laboring without a shirt.

"I don't think I'd want to do it," the captain said, his tone thoughtful.

"You could see Cape Horn," Poppy pointed out.

He shrugged. "Hardly anyone goes that far south. The *Marabella* is heading for Salvador."

"Salvador?" Poppy echoed. José was walking right toward her.

"In Brazil," the captain confirmed.

Poppy tried to remember if Salvador had been marked on the dissected map, but out of the corner of her eye she saw José stretching again, and—

"Why, Miss Bridgerton," the captain drawled, "are you ogling a naked man?"

"He's not naked," Poppy retorted.

In retrospect, it would have been far wiser to have denied the *other* part of the question.

Captain James smiled. Broadly. "So you *are* ogling him."

"I'm not ogling anyone."

"He does look like a fine specimen of man," the captain said, stroking his chin.

"Stop."

"Very muscular."

Poppy's face began to burn. "*Stop.*"

"*Now* I understand," the captain said with unmistakable delight. "That's José!"

"I don't know what you're talking about," Poppy mumbled.

"You chose well, Miss Bridgerton. He seems a hard worker."

Poppy wanted to die.

He patted her shoulder. "Very industrious, your José."

"How could I possibly know his name?"

The captain positively snorted with laughter. "I'd wager you've already given him a name, a family history, and a tragic backstory."

Poppy was surprised her mouth didn't fall open. How did this man know her so well after less than a week at sea?

Captain James leaned back against the wall, crossing his arms in a most satisfied manner. There was something supremely masculine about him as he regarded her, and just like that, poor José was back to having three children and a rabbit.

"Why are you watching me like that?" Poppy said suspiciously.

"Oh, this is the most entertaining thing I've seen all day."

"It's only half nine," she muttered.

"My dear Miss Bridgerton," he continued, "if you wanted to see a man without a shirt, I would have been happy to oblige you."

Her eyes grew very narrow. "You are a monster."

"But a lovable one."

"How does your family put up with you?"

And there was that lethal smile again. "Haven't you realized I'm endlessly charming?"

"Hmmph."

"Ask anyone."

She gave him a look. "I would, except the only person I've spoken to all week is Billy."

"And me," he pointed out cheerfully.

"You're hardly an unbiased source." Neither was Billy, for that matter.

The captain chuckled again as he finally left her side, crossing the cabin to his desk. "Oh, Miss Bridgerton," he said. "I fervently wish we had not crossed paths in this manner, but if I had to have an inadvertent captive on board, I'm very glad it's you."

Poppy could only stare. "Thank you?"

"It's a compliment," he assured her as he went about his business at his desk. He used a key to open the top drawer, removed something from his coat pocket, and slid it inside, then shut the drawer again. He locked it, of course. He always locked it.

As Poppy watched him, she finally realized that he was dressed somewhat more formally than normal. He'd donned a waistcoat, for one, and his boots appeared to have been polished. His cravat too was tied with uncharacteristic precision.

"Billy said you left quite early this morning," she said.

"Indeed I did. Just after sunrise. It enabled me to conduct my business rather quickly."

Poppy's mind went to the locked top drawer. "And what business was that?"

"Come now, Miss Bridgerton, you know better than to ask questions I will not answer."

"Perhaps I hope to catch you in a weak moment."

"I believe I already caught *you* in a weak moment this morning."

She blinked.

"Have you forgotten José so quickly? Ah, the inconstancy of women."

Poppy rolled her eyes to show him what she thought of *that*.

He put his hand over his heart. "*O, swear not by the moon, th' inconstant moon, That monthly changes in her circled orb, Lest that thy love prove likewise variable.*"

Shakespeare? Really?

"*Romeo and Juliet*," he said, as if she wouldn't have recognized it. "And not in the least bit misquoted."

Oh, he had no idea who he was up against. She lifted her chin a notch. "*Sigh no more, ladies, sigh no more, Men were deceivers ever; One foot in sea, and one on shore, To one thing constant never.*"

He acknowledged her parry with a nod, then said, "I never claimed men were any *more* constant. *And* I think you're making much ado about nothing."

Poppy was impressed despite herself.

"I know," he said, correctly interpreting her expression. "I'm ridiculously good at this."

She quirked a brow. "As am I."

"I have no doubt."

Their eyes remained locked in silent battle until the captain said, "I can't think of another Shakespeare line about inconstancy, can you?"

"Not a one," she admitted.

They both stood there, trying not to laugh. Finally, the captain gave in. "Oh, Miss Bridgerton"—he drew out the moment by stalking across the room and stopping in front of her with a cat-in-cream smile—"I think you will be very pleased today."

Her suspicions went on every possible alert. "What do you mean?"

"The weather is especially fine."

"Yes, I'd gathered as much." She gave him a patently false smile. "Through the window."

"But you can't tell everything through the window. You can see the sun, I suppose, but you can't feel breeze, you can't be sure of the temperature."

Poppy decided to humor him. "Is there a breeze today?"

"Indeed there is."

"And the temperature?"

"As you can tell from José's lack of attire, it's quite pleasantly warm."

Poppy made a growling sound. Really, he needed to let this go.

"Might I offer advice?" he murmured, leaning in just enough to make the air tingle between them.

"As long as you won't be offended if I don't take it."

"Sheathe your sarcasm, if only for this afternoon. We are friends of a sort, aren't we?"

It required a magnificent display of fortitude, but she managed to say, "Of a sort."

"Well then, Miss Bridgerton, as your friend—of a sort—I was wondering if you might like to join me in Lisbon today."

She froze. "What?"

He smiled. "Shall I repeat myself?"

"But you told me—"

"I changed my mind."

"Why?"

"Does it matter?"

Actually, she rather thought it did, but not enough to quibble when she was finally getting off the ship.

"I want to see everything," she said as she sat down to pull on her boots.

"That is patently impossible."

She glanced up, but only for a second. She wanted to get her boots laced as quickly as she could. "Everything that's possible, then."

"Everything that's possible." His mouth curved into a hint of a smile. "I promise."

Chapter 15

—— ⋗✳⋖ ——

"Don't turn around," Andrew whispered in Poppy's ear, "but José is watching you."

For this he was rewarded with an elbow in his ribs. Which prompted him to add, "He hasn't put his shirt back on."

"Pffft!" Poppy did a thing with her eyes that was more a flick than a roll. All in all, it was an impressive display of *I hardly care*, but he knew better.

"It does beg the question," Andrew mused. "Why?"

He waited. It took her a moment but she took the bait.

"What do you mean, why?"

"Why hasn't he put his shirt back on? It's not *that* hot."

He wasn't sure, but he thought he heard her growl. And not with appreciation.

"Do you know what I think?" he asked.

"I'm sure you're going to tell me."

"I'm glad you asked," he said brightly. Then he leaned toward her, his lips just a few inches from her ear. "*I* think he knows you're watching him."

She made an exasperated motion with her free hand, as if to point out that she was clearly focused on the road ahead. "I'm not watching him."

"Well, you're not *now*."

"I wasn't before."

"Come now, Miss Bridgerton, you could hardly *not* look at a half-dressed man. Frankly, I'd think less of you if you didn't."

This time she did roll her eyes.

"You can't really blame him," he went on, steering her through the waterfront area toward a spot where hackney drivers liked to wait to take on customers. "It's not often such a finely dressed lady disembarks a trading vessel."

Poppy looked down at her dress with a grimace. "It's hardly fine any longer."

"You look lovely," he said. It wasn't a lie. *She* looked lovely, even if her dress no longer did. It had held up fairly well, all things considered, but it had not been made to be worn all day and all night for a week. The blue fabric was now spectacularly wrinkled, and, since Poppy never wore shoes in the cabin, a dull layer of dust ringed the hem. There was also an oily spot on the side of the skirt he thought might have once been butter, but if she hadn't noticed it yet, he certainly wasn't going to point it out.

"Is José really looking at me?" She was taking his don't-look-now warning seriously; all of this was said out of the corner of her mouth. She didn't even turn her head enough to look at Andrew.

So naturally he said, "*Everyone* is looking at you."

She stumbled. "Are you serious?"

"As scurvy," he said cheerfully.

This seemed to give her pause. "Did you really just say 'serious as scurvy'?"

"There's not a whole lot more serious on a ship than scurvy. Exhaustion, pain . . . and that's just on the inside. Eventually the gums start receding, and then the teeth fall out." He tilted his head toward her as if to confide. "That's assuming they haven't already done so. Unfortunately, seamen aren't generally known for their dental hygiene."

Poppy's mouth whorled in thought. "Hmmm."

A surprisingly mild response. He countered with "Hmmm?"

Because he was witty and articulate that way.

But really, he'd spent a ridiculous amount of time dangling all measure of disgusting things (both literal and not) in front of the women of his family. Tales of bloody gums and rotten teeth usually merited more of a reaction.

"Have *you* had scurvy?" she asked.

He grinned, showing his teeth. He had them all, which was no mean feat. He was a sailor; he had frequented his fair share of dockside taverns. Couldn't do that without getting punched in the face a few times.

Poppy, however, was unimpressed with his toothsome display. "That doesn't mean you haven't had it. I'm sure not everyone loses his teeth."

"True," he replied, "but mine is a rather fetching smile, don't you think?" He grinned again, better to make the point.

"*Captain James.*"

"How beleaguered you sound," he teased, "but to answer your question, no, I have not had scurvy. But it would be surprising if I had. I've never undertaken an exceptionally long voyage."

"Scurvy is more common on longer trips?"

"Very much so. The *Infinity* generally keeps to European waters, and we almost never see it."

She thought about that for a moment. "What sort of journey would qualify as exceptionally long?"

"India could take a good four months. Parts of South America the same."

Poppy shuddered. "That sounds awful."

"I agree." Andrew frequently thanked his maker (or more often his king) that he'd never been asked to carry out a mission outside Europe. He loved the sea, but he *adored* the moment of stepping onto dry land. And while he regularly marveled over just how much of the world was covered with water, he was very much aware that he had never experienced the true infinity of the ocean.

Ironic, really, that that was the name of his vessel.

"Ships often make stops along the way," he told Poppy, "but not always. I heard of one recent voyage to India that took twenty-three weeks."

She gasped. "Without a single stop?"

"That's what I'm told. At any rate, I insist upon fruit on every voyage, even short ones such as this."

"Fruit?"

"It seems to keep the disease at bay."

"Why?"

"I have no idea," he admitted. "I'm not sure anyone does, to be honest. But I'll not argue with results."

"Fruit," she murmured. "How fascinating. I wonder how they figured it out."

"Simple observation, I should think."

She nodded absently, the way she did when she was lost in thought.

He enjoyed watching her; sometimes he would swear that he could almost *see* her thinking.

Andrew had never given much thought to the fact that women were not permitted a higher education, but it was a crime that Poppy Bridgerton had not been able to go to university. Her curiosity was endless. She asked questions about everything, and he had no doubt that she kept all the answers stored neatly away for later use.

Or for further examination. He often caught her just *thinking*. Poppy was as sharp a conversationalist as anyone, but she spent a great deal of time pondering great and deep questions.

Or at least he assumed they were great and deep questions. It was just as likely she'd been plotting his demise.

"Why are you smiling?" she asked suspiciously.

"Because I don't have scurvy?" he quipped.

She elbowed him. She did *that* a lot too.

"If you must know, I was reflecting upon the fact that you seemed lost in thought, which led me to wonder just what it was you were thinking about. Which in turn led me to wonder if you were plotting my demise."

"Oh, I haven't done that for days," she said blithely.

"I do improve upon association."

She snorted.

"I'll take that as an agreement," he said. "But if I might ask, what *were* you thinking so deeply about?"

"Scurvy," she said.

"Still?"

She shrugged. "There's a lot to think about. Do any of your books mention it? I could read about it on the way back. It would be far more interesting than Ottoman engineering."

Personally, Andrew found Ottoman engineering fascinating, but he was well aware that few shared this particular passion. "I don't think so," he said, "but now that you mention it, I probably should acquire a medical text." There was no doctor on board the *Infinity*; it was far too small a vessel for that. A guide to diseases would be helpful the next time someone fell ill.

"Can one buy English-language books in Lisbon?" she asked.

"If so, I doubt you'd find something so specific."

She made a gesture that seemed to say, *It was worth a try*, and then she was quiet, her thoughtful frown once again making twin furrows between her brows.

Thinking again. Or still. Andrew smiled. If he leaned toward her, would he hear the wheels and gears of her mind spinning away?

"I wonder . . ." she said slowly.

He waited. She did not finish the thought. "You wonder . . ." he finally urged.

She blinked, as if she'd forgotten that he might be listening to her. "I think the problem must be one of two kinds: either the body is lacking in some kind of nutrient—presumably something one doesn't get on a long voyage but exists in fruit—or the disease is spread from one man to another, and there is something in fruit that acts as a cure."

"Actually," he told her, "the fruit seems to act as both a prevention and a cure."

"Really?" She looked almost disappointed. "That's too bad. I mean, of course it's *good* that it does both, but from an investigative standpoint, it would be much easier to figure out why if it was just one or the other."

"Not necessarily. If it's a case of the body not getting a certain nutrient that is within the fruit, that would account for it being both the prevention and the cure."

"Of course!" Her whole face lit up. "You're brilliant!"

"Alas, I have finally convinced you."

She didn't even notice his quip. "I wonder what it is *in* the fruit, though. And is it all fruit? What about vegetables? Would a juice made of fruit do the trick?"

"I would think so. Some ships put lemons in the grog."

That seemed to interest her. "Does it make it taste any better?"

"Not really." He chuckled as he turned them onto the road. Up ahead he could see several hackneys, and he mentioned that he planned to hire one.

"We cannot walk?" Poppy inquired. "It is such a fine day, and I am so happy to be out of doors."

"It's not too far to walk," he admitted, "but some of the areas on the way are somewhat unsavory."

Her eyes narrowed as she considered this. "*Somewhat* unsavory or"—she paused here—"unsavory?"

"Is there a difference?"

"Quite a bit, I would imagine."

Trust her to split such hairs. "Very well," he conceded, "it is only somewhat unsavory." He'd thought to save time by hiring a carriage, but Poppy was right. It was far too fine a day to be confined in a dusty carriage, even if only for ten minutes.

They headed toward the Baixa, which he explained to her was what the Portuguese called the central neighborhood. There wasn't a whole lot of interest along the way, but Poppy was fascinated by everything.

"Billy told me to try the food," she said. "Especially the sweets. There was some sort of fried doughy treat he was especially fond of."

"*Malasadas*," Andrew confirmed. "They're divine."

"Divine?" she teased. "I had not pegged you for a man to speak of food in such spiritual terms."

"As it happens, *malasadas* are customary before Easter, although I'm not really sure why. Probably something to do with Catholic Lent. We should be able to find you one, though."

Sure enough, on the next corner they saw a man standing before a vat of hot oil, a large bowl of dough on the table behind him.

"Your *malasada* awaits," Andrew said, waving his arm in a courtly horizontal arc.

Poppy looked positively giddy as she approached the vendor, who immediately launched into a sales pitch in rapid Portuguese.

"No, no, I'm sorry," Poppy said helplessly. "I don't speak—" She turned to Andrew with those widened eyes that said, *Help me.*

He stepped forward. "*Dois malasadas, por favor.*"

"*Só dois?*" The vendor looked scandalized. He placed a theatrical hand over his heart and resumed his testimonial, this time indicating with his fingers the size of the *malasadas*.

"What's he saying?" Poppy asked.

"He's speaking too quickly for me," Andrew admitted, "but I'm fairly certain he's trying to convince us that the *malasadas* are too small for us to eat only one each."

"*Pequeno,*" the man said earnestly. "*Muito pequeno.*"

"*Quatro,*" Andrew said, holding up four fingers.

The man sighed dramatically and returned the gesture with six fingers. "*Seis.*"

"I can eat three," Poppy chirped. "I could probably eat six."

Andrew gave her a look. "You don't even know how big they are."

"I could still eat six."

He held his hands up in a gesture of defeat. "*Seis*," he said to the street vendor. He turned to Poppy. "Do you want yours rolled in sugar?"

She drew back, clearly aghast at the question. "Of *course*."

"Sorry," he said, not bothering to hide his amusement. "That was a stupid question."

"Really."

It was hard not to laugh, but Andrew managed to contain his mirth to a smile, watching Poppy as she watched the Portuguese man scoop chunks of dough from the bowl, then expertly roll them into identically sized spheres. One by one—but still quite quickly—he dropped them into the oil, motioning for Andrew and Poppy to step back, away from the splatter.

"The dough is very yellow," Poppy said, rising to her tiptoes as she peered in the bowl. "He must use a great many eggs."

Andrew shrugged. He had no idea what went into *malasadas*. He just knew he liked to eat them.

"Do you know how to say *egg* in Portuguese?"

"I'm afraid not."

"I thought you needed to understand the language for your business here."

For once he didn't think she was fishing for information about his work. "I don't actually need to know much," he said. "And eggs rarely enter the conversation."

"It smells so good," Poppy said with an almost sensual sigh. "How long does he need to cook them?"

"I would think not much longer," Andrew said, trying to ignore the little bolt of electricity her groan had lit within him.

"Ooooooh . . . I can't wait." She was nearly jumping with excitement, rocking on her feet, rising to her toes and then back down again.

"One would think we didn't feed you on the *Infinity*."

"You don't feed me *these*." Poppy arched her neck to peer into the vat. "I think they're almost done."

Sure enough, the street vendor picked up a long pair of tongs and extracted the first *malasada*. It glistened golden brown as he held it up and asked Andrew, "*Açúcar?*"

Poppy would likely stage a full-force revolt if he refused the sugar, so Andrew said, "*Sim, por favor.*"

The vendor dropped the *malasada* in a bowl of spiced sugar and then repeated his actions until all six had been removed from the oil. Using the tongs, he rolled them around in the sugar bowl until they were coated with the sweet powder.

As Andrew reached into his pocket for a few coins, he glanced over at Poppy, who was still practically vibrating with anticipation. Her hands were up near her chest, her fingers rubbing against her thumbs as if she was trying to keep herself from reaching out and grabbing a treat.

"Go ahead," he said, unable to suppress the amusement in his voice. "Take one."

"They won't be too hot?"

"There's only one way to find out."

With a giddy grin she reached out and plucked

one of the *malasadas* from the bowl. She brought it to her lips and took a tiny, careful bite. "Not too hot," she announced, then took a real bite.

"Oh," she gasped.

"Like it?"

"*Oh.*"

"I'll take that as a yes."

"*Ohhhhh.*"

Andrew suddenly felt the need to adjust his cravat. And maybe his breeches. Dear God, he'd been with women who'd climaxed with less passion.

"All right!" he said, a little too brightly. "We need to be off." He handed the street vendor what was surely too many coins, then grabbed the rest of the *malasadas* out of the sugar and gave Poppy a little shove toward town.

"We don't want to be late," he said.

"For what?"

He handed her two *malasadas*. "I said I was going to show you everything possible, didn't I? If I'm to keep my promise, we need to get going."

She shrugged and smiled agreeably, then ate another one. "I could never live here," she said, eyeing her final ball of dough with something approaching wistfulness. "I would eat fourteen of these every day and be fat as a house."

"Fourteen?"

"Or more." She licked the sugar from her fingers. "Probably more."

Andrew's lips parted as he watched her tongue dart out for the sugar. He was mesmerized, nearly paralyzed by the urge to kiss the sugar from her lips himself. He couldn't let himself move, not even an inch, or he'd . . .

He didn't know *what* he'd do. Something he shouldn't. Not here. Not with her.

But she looked so goddamn beautiful out here in the sunshine.

No, not beautiful. Radiant. Whatever it was that had him so transfixed, it came from the inside. She was so happy, so full of joy and delight, she almost seemed to glow with it, pulling in everyone within her orbit.

It was impossible to be near her and not feel the same joy.

"What are you looking at?" she asked, still grinning.

"You have crumbs on your face," he lied.

But he quickly realized what a foolish idea that had been, because she immediately brought her hand to her face and said, "Where? Here?"

"Er, no, over . . . ah . . ." He made a vague motion that would tell her absolutely nothing.

"Here?" she asked dubiously, touching a spot near her ear.

"Yes," he said, with perhaps a little more enthusiasm than was warranted. But he wasn't lying this time; the act of trying to locate the nonexistent crumbs had actually deposited a few of them on her skin.

Poppy brushed them away. "All better?"

No.

"Yes," he said. He wasn't sure he was going to feel all better unless he hauled her around the corner and kissed her.

Which was *not* going to happen.

Or so he kept telling himself.

Chapter 16

Poppy was in heaven.

Or it might have been Lisbon.

To hell with it, she decided. Tomorrow heaven could go back to being whatever it really was, with angels on high and whatnot. For today, it was Lisbon, Portugal, and no one could convince her otherwise.

She still could not quite believe that Captain James had changed his mind and taken her ashore with him. It was almost enough to make her rethink her pledge against gratitude.

Almost.

Or . . .

She looked around, at the blue sky and the magnificent ruined castle up on the hill, and the little grains of sugar and cinnamon that were stuck under her fingernails.

Maybe she could rethink her vow for just one day.

For today—for as long as heaven had been transformed into a city in Portugal—Poppy Bridgerton would feel grateful to Captain James for having taken her there.

Tomorrow she could go back to trying not to think about what might await her at home.

That reminded her . . . She had no idea how long he planned to remain in Lisbon. "Do we sail tomorrow?" she asked him. "Have you completed your business?"

"I have. Normally we would remain in Lisbon for a few days, but given our current situation"— the captain accompanied this with a wry nod in her direction—"I think it is best that we return as quickly as possible, don't you?"

"Of course," Poppy said, and she meant it. Every day she was gone added to the probability that Elizabeth would report her disappearance. That Poppy would spend the rest of her life under a cloud of scandal.

But she could not help but think how much she would enjoy another day in Lisbon. She was having a marvelous time, and she did not think it was only because she had finally escaped the (admittedly comfortable) confines of the cabin.

There was so much more to it. As she walked through the lively streets of the Portuguese capital, it occurred to her that this wasn't just the first time she had been to a foreign land, it was the first time she had traveled to a place that was so wholly unfamiliar.

Which wasn't the same thing at all.

Poppy had been to a number of locations within England, but even if the towns were new, they had never felt as if they were unknown. Her ears heard the same language she herself had always spoken; her eyes saw the sorts of shops and churches she could find in her own home village. Anything that was new to her was still easily understood.

But today it was as if someone had taken her world and twisted it like a rotating tray on a table, depositing her into a place where nothing was quite as she knew it.

She could not read the signs—well, she could *read* them, of course; the Portuguese used mostly the same alphabet as the English—but she rarely could figure out what they meant.

It was strange—and thrilling—to listen to the chatter of another language, to realize that hundreds of people were having ordinary conversations, and she hadn't a clue as to the meaning. She thought of all the times she'd overheard the chatter of passersby as she and her aunt had walked through London (the only place she'd ever been that was more crowded than Lisbon). She never meant to eavesdrop, but it was impossible not to hear bits and pieces: two women discussing the price of wool, a child begging for a sweet.

Now she could only guess, based on the facial expressions and the tones of voice. A man and a woman were arguing across the street—nothing too vehement, but to Poppy's mind, they were husband and wife, and the woman was cross with her husband for coming home so late the night before.

From the man's sheepish expression, Poppy did not think he had a good excuse.

Up ahead, at the door to a fashionable milliner's establishment, two young ladies were speaking with great animation. They were clearly well-to-do; off to their right stood an older lady with an expression of utmost boredom—surely she was one of their chaperones.

At first Poppy thought the ladies might be discussing the hats they had just purchased, but she quickly revised her theory. Their eyes were flashing with too much excitement; the blonde in particular looked almost as if she might burst with joy.

She was in love. Poppy was sure of it. They were talking about a gentleman, she decided, and whether he was about to propose marriage.

From the excited giggles, Poppy predicted that he was.

The people and the language weren't all that was foreign. The city was vivid in a way that London never could be. Maybe it was the crystal clarity of the sky, or the bright red roofs of the buildings.

Or maybe it was the four *malasadas* she'd eaten just an hour earlier.

Poppy was entranced.

Captain James was proving to be a most charming and informative guide. He did not complain when she stopped to peer in every shop window, or when she insisted upon going inside a church to gaze upon each and every stained glass window. In fact, he seemed to take joy in her delight.

"Oh, look at these," she said, for what she knew had to have been the tenth time in the last five minutes. At every shop or stall she'd found something worth pointing out.

This time it was a bolt of fine, pale linen, exquisitely embroidered at the hem. It could be used for a dress, Poppy thought, with the intricate cutwork at the hem, or maybe for a tablecloth, although she'd be terrified someone would spill wine on it. She'd never seen needlework of this particular style before, and she had spent more than her fair share of time in the most elegant shops in London.

"You should buy it," the captain said.

She gave him a doubtful look. "I don't have any money, and furthermore, how on earth would I explain its existence when I return home?"

He shrugged. "You could say you got it in Cornwall."

"Cornwall?" Where had *that* idea come from? And furthermore—"Do they even make such things in Cornwall?"

"I have no idea. But that's the beauty of it. I doubt anyone else does either."

Poppy shook her head. "I can't very well go around saying I went to Cornwall for two weeks. That's almost as improbable as Portugal."

"Almost?" he echoed, not *quite* mocking her.

"It would be equally difficult to explain," she said.

He did not look convinced.

"You have no idea what awaits me back in England," she told him. Honestly, she was a little put off by his flippancy.

"You don't know what awaits you either," he said. And although he was correct, and his words were not unkind or argumentative, she thought the statement belied a lack of understanding of her predicament.

No, that wasn't it. He understood her predicament perfectly. What he did not appreciate was how difficult it was for her to blindly await her fate.

Maybe he was the kind of person who could wait until he had all of his information before making plans, but she was not. If it meant she had to come up with a dozen ideas for every one she actually carried out, so be it.

To wit:

She had considered the (wonderful) possibility that Elizabeth hadn't told anyone Poppy had gone missing.

She had considered the possibility that Elizabeth had told Poppy's family but no one else.

But what if Elizabeth's husband had returned home early?

What if Elizabeth's maid promised Elizabeth she would keep quiet but then said something to her sister?

What if the maid didn't have a sister? What if she was alone in the world except for her dearest childhood friend and frequent correspondent who happened to live in London and worked for the Duchess of Wyndham?

Poppy had only met the duchess once, and she did not think the great lady had liked her very much. Certainly not enough to keep *that* sort of news quiet.

But what if the Duchess of Wyndham had gambling debts that she didn't want her husband to know about? Poppy had never heard rumors to this effect, but it was certainly *possible*. And if the duchess did have gambling debts, her thoughts might turn to blackmail over profit.

These were the questions that—well, no, they did not keep Poppy up at night. In truth, she was sleeping quite well; the ocean seemed to rock her like a cradle. But she stewed about these questions all day long. She stared at the ocean and stewed and stewed and stewed.

But she did not want to argue, not today at least, so she did her best not to sound combative when she said, "It is true that I do not know what awaits me. It could be that every single thing that could have gone right *has* gone right. And wouldn't that be splendid? But that hasn't stopped me from imagining every possible outcome, then trying to devise a plan to deal with each."

He looked at her with a frank, penetrating stare. "Tell me," he said.

She blinked. "I beg your pardon?"

"Tell me one of your plans."

"Now?"

He shrugged, as if to say, *Why not?*

Her lips parted with surprise as she glanced around the shop. It seemed an unlikely spot for so delicate a conversation.

"No one can understand us," he said. "And even if someone could, you don't know anyone here."

"Later," she said. She was glad that he had asked,

but she certainly wasn't prepared to discuss her future in the middle of a Portuguese fabric shop. She was almost amused that he had suggested it. It was such a *man* thing to do.

"At supper," he said. "I shall remind you."

She nodded her agreement. "Will we be taking our supper back on the ship?"

"I would not do that to you," he said gamely. "This is your one day in Lisbon. We will go to a tavern I like to frequent. I think you will like it. Now then"—he motioned to the bolt of fabric—"shall I buy this for you?"

Under normal circumstances Poppy would not consider accepting such a gift from a gentleman. But although these were not normal circumstances, she still had to refuse. "I can't," she said regretfully. "But I shall try to remember the details. I might be able to learn this type of stitching."

"You embroider?" He sounded surprised. She didn't know why; most women did some sort of needlework.

"Not *this* well," she told him, lightly brushing her fingers over the elegant parade of stitches. "But I enjoy it. I find it soothing. It clears my mind."

Now he *looked* surprised. "Forgive me if I have difficulty believing that your mind is ever clear."

Well, if that wasn't just the oddest statement. If it had been said in any other tone of voice, Poppy might have taken it as an insult. "What do you mean by that?"

"You're *always* thinking."

"Isn't that what it means to be human?"

"You're different," he said, and strangely, she rather liked that he felt that way.

"Do you have anything like that?" she asked. "Something you can do with your hands so that your mind can become quiet?"

He looked at her with a curiously intense stare, and she wasn't sure if he understood what she'd meant.

"The sort of thing you can do and still carry on a conversation if necessary, but it . . . settles you." She gave a helpless little shrug. "I don't know how else to explain it."

"No, I understand," he said. He hesitated for a moment, or maybe he was simply choosing his words with care. But then he reached out and touched the drawn-thread embroidery she had just been admiring.

"I like to build houses out of playing cards," he said.

She was momentarily struck speechless. "I beg your pardon?"

"Have you never made a house of cards? You use regular playing cards, and then you set the first two into a *T*-shape." He demonstrated with his hands, as if he were holding actual cards. "Then you bring in a third, and make an *H*. There's really no other way to start. Well, I suppose you could try building in triangles, but that's very advanced. I would not recommend it."

Poppy just stared at him. She wouldn't have thought he would take such a thing so seriously.

She wouldn't have thought that *anyone* would

take such a thing so seriously. But she found it rather charming that he did.

"Once you have that stable," he continued, "you can build to your heart's content." He paused. "Or until one of your brothers comes and knocks the whole thing down."

Poppy chuckled; she could well imagine a similar scene in her own household. "I don't think I've ever done that," she said. "It never even occurred to me that one could build with playing cards."

"You need more than one deck," he said with authority. "If you wish to make things interesting."

"Alas, my life has been nothing but interesting lately."

He gave a laugh at that. "Maybe I can find a deck or two here in Lisbon and show you tomorrow."

"On the *ship*?"

"Oh, right." Sheepishly, he pressed his lips together. "That's not going to work."

They wandered out of the shop and back out into the bustling streets of the Baixa. It was truly a lovely area, but then something occurred to Poppy, and she turned to the captain and asked, "Why does this part of the city look so new?"

"Ah." He stopped walking and turned to her with an almost professorial air. "There was an earthquake here about thirty years ago. It was devastating. Much of the old city was destroyed."

Poppy immediately glanced this way and that, as if she could possibly see signs of the earthquake thirty years after the fact.

"This area was completely rebuilt," the captain said.

"How grand these avenues are," Poppy murmured, gazing down toward the waterfront. "So straight." She wasn't sure there was a street so straight and long in all of England.

"The new city was laid out on a grid." He swept his arm in a wide horizontal arc. "See how much light it allows. The air quality is improved too, because it does not get trapped in stagnant pockets."

Poppy had not noticed it before, but there was indeed a lovely, fresh breeze tickling at her skin. She tried to remember ever experiencing such a thing in London. She could not.

"It's remarkable," she said, craning her neck to peer up and down the street. There was something about the collection of buildings that was very harmonious. Each was *almost* exactly the same, four or five stories tall, with an arched arcade on the ground floor. The windows were uniform—of the same size on each level of every building, and they all measured the exact same distance apart.

It should have created a dull monotony, but it did not. Not at all. Each building had its own character, with tiny differences that gave the street such joy. Some buildings were painted, some not. One was even covered with tile. Most had balconies on the first story above the shops, but a few had flat façades, and then a few more sported balconies on every window up to the top. And they were not all of the same width. The grander buildings measured six or eight windows across, but many others had just three.

And yet still, for all the differences, they *fit*. As if they could not possibly have been built anywhere else.

"It's beautiful. So very modern." She looked over at Captain James. He was watching her with a curious intensity, as if he truly cared what she thought about the architecture. Which was preposterous. Because why would he? This wasn't his home; he'd had nothing to do with the designs.

And yet, with his eyes on hers, so brilliantly blue and inquisitive, it seemed almost imperative that she share her thoughts. "What I find most interesting," she said, looking back down the street for a moment, "is that there is no single element that is unfamiliar. The windows, the arches . . . They are of the neoclassical style, are they not?"

He nodded, and she continued. "But when it is all put together in this way, it makes something entirely new. I don't think I've ever seen anything like it."

"I agree," he said. "It's truly original. I try to visit this area every time I'm in Lisbon. It's not always possible. Sometimes I never make it past the port. And the old city also has its charms. But this . . ." He waved his arm out again, as if putting modernity on display. "This is the future."

Suddenly Poppy could not imagine why he'd chosen to be a sailor. He'd never been so animated when talking about the sea. He had not seemed *un*-happy, and in fact she suspected there were many aspects of life as a sea captain that he loved. But this—these buildings, this architecture—this was his true passion. She wondered if he realized this himself.

"But this is not even the most remarkable thing," he said suddenly. "Here, come." He grabbed her hand and pulled her along the pavement, and when he glanced back to look at her, she saw that his eyes were even more lit with excitement. She couldn't imagine what new detail had him so aglow, but then he led her inside one of the elegant new buildings.

"Look," he said. "Is it not amazing?"

"I'm not sure what you're talking about," she said carefully. They were in some sort of governmental building, stylish and new, but not otherwise exceptional.

"No, you can't see it," he said, even as he motioned to . . . a wall? A doorway?

"You just told me to look," she said to him.

He grinned. "Sorry. It's what is within the walls that is revolutionary. Each is built over a Pombaline cage."

She blinked. "A Pomba-what?"

"A Pombaline cage. It's—well, it doesn't matter what it's called. It's an entirely new type of construction meant to make buildings safer in earthquakes. You start with a wooden cage—"

"A *cage*?"

"Not like in a prison," he said, chuckling at her reaction. "Think of it more as a framework. A three-dimensional lattice, if you will. It's built into the walls, and then covered with other material. So if the earth shakes, it helps to distribute the force."

"Force?"

"Of the earthquake. If you can spread it out"—he made a motion with his hands rather like Moses parting the Red Sea—"it's less likely to cause major damage."

"I suppose that makes sense." She frowned, trying to envision the concept in her head.

But the captain clearly wanted to make sure she understood. "Think of it this way. If I pull your hair—"

She jumped back. "What?"

"No, bear with me, I promise there's a physics lesson in this, and didn't you recently bemoan your lack of study in the field?"

She rolled her eyes. Trust him to remember that. "Very well. Get on with it, then."

"Right. It's all about the distribution of force. If I pull just a small lock of your hair, it will hurt quite a bit."

He reached up and pinched a lock between his fingers. It wasn't hard to do, what with her inexpert work pinning it up.

"Wait, are you *actually* going to pull my hair?"

"Not any harder than your brothers likely did."

She thought back to her childhood. "That does not reassure me."

The captain's face came a little closer to hers. "I will not hurt you, Poppy. I promise."

She swallowed, and she wasn't sure whether it was the earnest look in his eyes or the fact that it was the first time he had used her given name, but she believed him. "Carry on."

He gave a little tug, not so that she felt pain, but just enough that she knew she would have done, if he had yanked harder.

"Now," he said, "imagine that I grabbed a whole hunk of your hair." His hand curved and made a claw shape in the air, as if approximating the amount of hair she was meant to imagine.

"*Oh no.*" There was no way her coiffure could survive that.

"I won't do it, don't worry," he said, displaying his first ounce of sensibility all afternoon. "But imagine that I did. It wouldn't hurt."

He was right. It wouldn't.

"That's because the force would be spread across a larger area of your scalp. Therefore, each affected spot receives less of the tug. And consequently, less pain."

"So what you're also saying is that if you wished to cause equal pain you would need to pull much harder if you had a larger amount of hair in your hand."

"Exactly! Well done."

It was ridiculous how pleased she was by his compliment, especially since she was the one who now had an errant lock of hair jutting out from the side of her head.

"Now," he continued, oblivious to her attempts to subtly pin her hair back into place, "you can't just erect any wooden framework and expect it to work. I beg your pardon, I suppose anything would be better than nothing, but if you apply the laws of physics, you can create a structure that is incredibly strong."

Poppy could only stare as he went on about St. Andrew's crosses and braces and trusses and someone named Fibonacci who she thought was probably dead, but the captain was so involved in his explanation, Poppy couldn't bring herself to interrupt and ask.

As she watched him—and the truth was, she was doing far more watching than listening; he'd lost her when he started talking about geometry's golden ratio—she realized that he had become a different person, right in front of her eyes. His entire bearing changed. She'd seen him as the captain, standing with complete confidence and authority, and she'd seen him as the rogue, all lanky limbs and smooth motions.

But now his arms moved through the air as if drawing pictures and plans, and he practically hopped in place as he illustrated his invisible canvas and drew equations in the air. Poppy hadn't the slightest idea what he was talking about. Honestly, she couldn't follow a word.

But he was magnificent to watch.

He wasn't the captain, and he wasn't the rogue. He was just Andrew. That was his given name, wasn't it? He'd told it to her that first day. "Captain Andrew James, at your service," he'd said, or something similar. And she'd not thought of it since, not thought of him as anything but Captain James or "the captain."

"Do you see?" he asked, and she realized it was actually important to him that she did.

"I—no," she admitted, "but I lack the imagination to picture such things in my head. If I saw it on paper, I think I might understand it."

"Of course," he said, looking almost glum.

"I think it's very interesting," she said hastily. "Revolutionary, even. You said no one has done such a thing before. Think of how many lives might be saved."

"It will work, too," he told her. "There has not been another earthquake of the same force, but if God forbid there was, these buildings would stand. The engineers tested it."

"How could they possibly do that?" It wasn't as if they could snap their fingers and summon an earthquake.

"Soldiers." Andrew's eyes widened with excitement. "They brought in hundreds and had them stamp about."

Poppy thought her mouth might have fallen open. "You're joking."

"Not even a little bit."

"They had the soldiers stamp about, and that shook the ground well enough to approximate an earthquake?"

"Enough for them to call the design a success."

"Now *that* is something I love," Poppy said. "To take a problem with *no* solution, none at all, and then to solve it in such a sideways fashion. To me, that is true genius."

"And that's not all," he said, taking her back outside and onto the wide pedestrian street. "Look at the façades. You might think them plain—"

"I don't," Poppy cut in eagerly. "I find them quite elegant."

"I do too," he said, and he seemed quite pleased with her statement. "But what I was going to say is that most of these buildings, or rather, most *parts* of each of these buildings were put together else-where."

Poppy looked at one of the buildings and then back at Andrew. "I don't understand what you mean."

He gestured to a nearby façade. "Most of the pieces of the buildings were put together at another site, one with a great deal more room, where stone-masons and carpenters could all work on one type of thing at a time. There is great economy—both of time and of money—in doing, for example, all of the window frames at once."

Poppy peered up and down the street, trying to imagine some vast field filled with unconnected walls and window frames. "And then they brought all of the pieces here? On carts?"

"I imagine so. More likely by barge."

"I've never heard of such a thing."

"It's not often done. They call it pre-fabrication."

"It's fascinating." Poppy shook her head in slow wonder, taking it all in—the architecture, the fact that she was actually in Lisbon and people were speaking Portuguese, and—

"What?" she asked. Andrew was looking at her in the strangest fashion.

"It is nothing," he said softly. "Not really. It's just that most people don't find this interesting."

"I do," she said with a shrug. "But then again, I'm curious about most things."

"It's what got you into this mess," he said wryly.

"Isn't it just." She sighed. "I really should have walked the other way down the beach."

He nodded in slow agreement, but then surprised her utterly by saying, "And yet right now—just this afternoon, mind you—I'm rather glad you didn't."

It was all Poppy could think about for the rest of the afternoon.

Chapter 17

~❊~

Andrew took Poppy to a small tavern near the port. He'd eaten there countless times, as had most of his crew, and while he would never take a lady to a comparable establishment in England, the rules did not seem to apply in the same way here in Portugal.

Plus, the tavernkeeper's wife was a superb cook, and he could think of no better place to take Poppy for true Portuguese cuisine.

"This will not be quite what you're used to," he warned as he reached out to open the door.

Her eyes lit up. "Good."

"The patrons can be a bit uncouth."

"My sensibilities are not so tender."

Andrew opened the door with flair. "Then by all means, let us go forth."

They were greeted immediately.

"Captain!" Senhor Farias, the middle-aged owner of the establishment, came bustling over. He had learned some English over the years, and he spoke it far better than Andrew did Portuguese. "Is so good to see you. I am told that your ship is here and I wonder where you are."

Andrew grinned. It was always a joy to be greeted like an old friend. "Senhor Farias, it is my pleasure entirely. Tell me, how fares your family?"

"Very good, very good. My Maria is now married, you know. I will soon be—how do you call it—not father, but . . ." He rapidly snapped his fingers in the air, his preferred motion whenever he was trying to think of something. Andrew had seen him do it many times.

"*Avô, avô,*" he said. "Not father, but—"

"Grandfather?"

"Yes! That's it."

"Congratulations, my friend! Senhora Farias must be very pleased."

"*Sim!* Yes, she is very happy. She loves the little babies. But who is this?" Senhor Farias finally noticed Poppy standing just a little behind and to the side of Andrew. He took her hand and kissed it. "Is this your wife? Have you been married? *Parabéns*, Captain! Congratulations!"

Andrew stole a glance at Poppy. She was blushing furiously, but she did not seem to be truly embarrassed.

"She is my cousin," Andrew said, since that seemed the safest lie. If his men had not already come to Taberna da Torre for a meal, they would soon, and would surely impart the news that the *Infinity* had been sailing with a woman on board. "She is a guest on our voyage."

"Then she is a guest in my *taberna*," Senhor Farias said, leading her to a table. "I will bring only our best food."

"Are you telling me that some of your food is not the best?" Andrew teased.

"No," Senhor Farias said with conviction. "My wife cooks nothing bad. It is all best. So I will bring your cousin everything."

Poppy opened her mouth and for a moment looked as if she might refuse, but instead she said, "That would be *wonderful*."

Senhor Farias planted his hands on his hips. "Does the captain not feed you?"

"The food on the *Infinity* is very good," Poppy said, allowing Senhor Farias to link his arm in hers. "But I have never tried Portuguese food—well, except for *malasadas*—and I am very curious."

"She is a very curious lady," Andrew called, trailing after them.

Poppy shot him a look. "That can be interpreted in several ways."

"They're all accurate."

She did a funny thing with her mouth that was clearly the equivalent of rolling her eyes, and then happily went with Senhor Farias to his best table.

"Sit, sit," he urged. He looked from her to Andrew and back. "I will bring wine."

"He's lovely!" Poppy gushed as soon as they sat down.

"I thought you would like him."

"Are all the Portuguese so friendly?"

"Many, but none so much as he."

"And he's going to be a grandfather!" Poppy clasped her hands together, her smile enough to light the room. "It makes me so happy and I don't even know him."

"My mother often says that it is the mark of a truly good person if she is happy for those she has never met."

She frowned. "That's odd. My aunt says the same thing."

Andrew bit the inside of his cheek. Damn it, of course Lady Bridgerton said the same thing. She and his mother were the closest of friends. "It's a common phrase," he said. This was probably a lie, but maybe not. For all he knew, all the ladies in his mother's set said the same thing.

"Really? I've never heard anyone else say it, but then again, my circle of acquaintances is not so broad." And then, alleviating any worry he might have had that she'd found his comment suspicious, she leaned forward with an eager expression and said, "I can't wait to see what Senhor Farias brings. I'm so hungry."

"As am I. Two *malasadas* do not a meal make."

She wagged a finger in his direction. "It was your choice to let me have one of yours."

"Three would not have done either. And apparently," he said, wagging his finger right back at her, "nor does four."

She only laughed, smiling at Senhor Farias when he came to pour wine. When the tavernkeeper left, she leaned forward with gleaming eyes and said, "I want to try everything."

Andrew lifted his glass. "To everything," he said.

She smiled as if it were the most charming toast she'd ever heard. "To everything."

Andrew sat back, watching her with a strange sense of pride. It had been a long time since he'd shown someone the sights of a city—any city. Most of his business—whether for the government or not—was conducted on his own. And when he did venture into town with men from his ship, it was not the same. They were friends, but they were not equals, and that would always stand between them.

But with Poppy every moment had been a delight. And he was beginning to think that perhaps her presence on the *Infinity* would not be as much of a disaster as he'd feared.

He'd known at the start that he might have to marry this girl, but he was starting to wonder if this really was such a burden. Where was he going to find someone else who found Pombaline cages interesting? Who could take every one of his dry statements and twist it, turn it upside down, and toss it back with even greater wit?

She was a clever one, his Poppy.

And she'd kissed him. She'd kissed him with the tiniest, most fleeting touch of the lips he'd ever felt. Yet somehow it was *more*.

Poppy Bridgerton had kissed him, and it was monumental.

He felt it in his blood, he felt it across his skin. And when he finally found sleep later that night, it had burned through his dreams. He woke up aching and hard, nothing like his usual morning erection. He couldn't even do anything about it, since he was bunked in his navigator's cabin.

Carroway was a solid chap, but every friendship had its limit.

Come to think of it, every friendship had *this* limit. Or if it didn't, it damn well should.

"What are you thinking about?" Poppy asked.

There was no way he was going to tell her the truth, so he said, "I was wondering if we ought to bring a meal to José. He was working with such vigor this morning."

She gave him an exasperated look. "You're terrible."

"You keep saying so, but you've yet to convince me."

"I can hardly believe I'm the first to try," she said with a snort.

"Oh, certainly not. My family has long since given up the attempt to instill a sense of propriety in my soul."

She looked at him shrewdly. "That's an awful lot of words to say that you behave very badly."

"Indeed it is. And probably why I get away with it so well." He leaned toward her with a wicked smile. "Silver tongue and all that."

"All that indeed."

He chuckled at her waspy tone. "Did I tell you that I hold the record for the most times getting sent down from Eton?"

"You went to Eton?"

"I did," he confirmed, and it occurred to him that he didn't much care that he'd revealed such a distinguishing fact about his background.

She stared at him for a moment, her eyes shining almost emerald with her curiosity. "Who *are* you?"

It wasn't the first time she'd uttered the question. It wasn't even the first time she'd done so in that same incredulous voice. But it *was* the first time his response was something more than a flashed grin or condescending chuckle.

It was the first time the answer had to be teased out of his heart.

"It's an odd thing," he said, and he could hear in his voice that the words were coming from some untapped corner of his spirit, "but I think you know me as well as anyone now."

She went still, and when she looked at him, it was with an astonishingly direct gaze. "I don't know you at all."

"Is that what you think?" he murmured. She didn't know his true name, and she didn't know his history, or that he'd grown up alongside her cousins in Kent. She didn't know that he was the son of an earl, or that he worked clandestinely for the crown.

She didn't know any of these details, but she knew *him*. He had the most terrifying feeling that she might be the first person who ever had.

But then he realized that it wasn't terrifying at all, that he thought it *should* be terrifying, but in reality it was . . .

Rather nice.

His family had always viewed him as something of a jokester, and he supposed he had done little to convince them otherwise. He *had* been sent down from Eton on multiple occasions—never for academic failings, though. He had been far too restless a boy to earn top marks, that was true, but he'd acquitted himself tolerably well in his studies.

His transgressions had always been of the behavioral variety. A prank intended for a friend that somehow ended on the doorstep of a tutor. A prank intended for a tutor that somehow ended on the doorstep of the head of school. Inappropriate laughter in the dining hall. Inappropriate laughter in church. Inappropriate laughter, frankly, just about everywhere.

So if his family saw him as silly, or at the very least unserious, he supposed they had cause.

But that wasn't *all* he was. He did important things. Important things that no one knew about, but that couldn't be helped.

It didn't bother him.

Well, it didn't bother him much.

He looked across the table at Poppy, marveling that all of this had flashed through his mind in under a second.

"Do you think you know *me*?" she asked.

"I do." He didn't even need to think about it.

She let out a snort. "That's preposterous."

"I know you like puzzles," he said.

"Everyone likes—"

"No they don't," he cut in. "Not like you and me."

His vehemence seemed to surprise her.

"I also know," he said, "that if you set yourself a task, you cannot rest until you have completed it."

At her nonplussed expression he added, "Again, not everyone is that way. Even among those of us who like puzzles."

"You're the same," she said, a touch defensively.

"I'm aware." He shrugged. "It doesn't bother me."

Her chin rose a notch. "Nor me."

He couldn't help but be amused by her attitude. "I'm not accusing you of something nefarious. To my mind, it's a compliment."

"Oh." She blushed a little, and it was really rather entertaining the way she seemed to fidget within herself, as if she couldn't quite absorb the praise. "What else do you think you know about me?" she asked.

He felt himself smile. "Fishing for compliments?"

"Hardly," she scoffed. "I have no reason to expect that your answers will be uniformly flattering."

"Very well." He thought for a moment. "I know that you don't like to hide your intelligence."

"When have you ever known me to do so?"

"Precisely," he said. "But you haven't had to. I know enough of society to know that you're under far different strictures in London than on the *Infinity*."

"I should say I'm under no strictures," she said pertly, "except for the one that confines me to one cabin."

"Says the lady dining in a Lisbon café."

"Touché," she admitted, and he thought she might be biting back a smile.

He leaned toward her, just a bit. "I know that you can't speak French, that you don't get seasick, and that you miss your brother Roger with all your heart."

She looked up, her eyes somber.

"I know that you adored him even though he tortured you as all good older brothers do, and I know that he loved you back far more fiercely than you ever knew."

"You can't know that," she whispered.

"Of course I can." He tipped his head, quirked a brow. "I'm a brother too."

Her lips parted, but she seemed not to know what to say.

"I know you're loyal," he said.

"How could you know that?"

He shrugged. "I just do."

"But you—"

"—have spent much of the last week in your company. I do not need to witness a display of loyalty to know that it is a characteristic you possess."

She blinked several times, her lashes sweeping up and down over unfocused eyes. She seemed to be staring at a spot on the far wall, but it was clear that everything she saw was inside her own head. Finally, just when he was about to give her a verbal nudge, she straightened and brought her gaze to his.

"I know about you," she said.

He did not point out that she had just said that she didn't know him at all. He was far too curious to hear what she had to say.

But before he could ask, Senhor Farias arrived at the table with a plate of cod fritters.

"*Bolinhos de bacalhau!*" he announced. "But you must wait. They are much too hot."

Poppy peered at them. "Goodness, they are still sizzling."

Senhor Farias was halfway back to the kitchen, and he didn't even turn around as he snapped his fingers over his head and called out, "Too hot!"

Poppy grinned, and Andrew knew that he ought to allow their conversation to turn to the glorious meal ahead of them, but she had been about to say something important, and he could not let it go.

"You said you know me," he reminded her.

"Hmm?" She reached out and gingerly touched a fritter.

"Too hot!" Senhor Farias yelled.

Poppy snapped to attention, her head whipping back and forth as she looked for the tavernkeeper. "How did he see that?" she marveled. "He's not even here."

"Poppy."

"Do you think they're ready?"

He said it again: "Poppy."

She finally looked up, smiling pleasantly as she met his gaze.

"Before Senhor Farias arrived with the fritters," he said. "You said you know me."

"Oh yes, that's right. I did."

He made a rolling motion with his hand, his usual visualization of *Well?*

"Very well." She straightened, almost as if she were a schoolteacher, preparing to deliver a lesson. "I know that you are not as hard-edged as you would like others to believe."

"You think so?"

She gave him an arch look. "Billy told me that you will not permit him to go out and about in Lisbon by himself."

"He's a *child*."

"Who has left home and is living on a *ship*," she retorted. "Do most boys in his position face similar restrictions?"

"No," Andrew admitted, "but he doesn't speak the language. And he's very small for his age."

Her smile was lopsided but triumphant. "And you care about him."

Andrew tugged at his cravat. It was ridiculous to feel embarrassed by such a thing. He was only protecting a small boy. Everyone should aspire to such behavior.

"You also treat your men very well," she said.

"That's just good business. We talked about that."

She laughed. Right in his face. "Please. You said quite specifically that the main reason to feed one's men well is not because it is good business, but rather because they are human."

"You remember that, eh?" he muttered.

"I remember everything."

This, he did not doubt for a second. But he was oddly uncomfortable with her praise—for this sort of thing, at least. Which was utter bollocks. He was only doing right by his crew. But men were taught to take pride in their strength and power, not in their good works, and he wasn't quite sure how to simply say thank you.

"I think they're ready," he said, nodding toward the fritters.

Poppy, who had been so eager to try them she'd nearly burned her finger, just shrugged.

"You don't want to eat?" He knew that she did. She was just trying to make some convoluted, completely unimportant point.

He motioned again to the food on the table. "We're wasting time."

"Is that what you think?" she murmured, and her tone was so precisely the same as his had been when he'd uttered the same words a few minutes earlier, it could not have been coincidence. Not from her.

He reached out and stabbed a fritter with his fork.

"Are we not meant to use our fingers?"

"Just being careful in case they're—"

"Not too hot!" Senhor Farias called out.

Andrew looked up and grinned. "Fingers it is."

Poppy took one and bit into it, drawing back in surprise as she tasted it. "I thought it would be sweet!"

He laughed, only then realizing that neither he nor Senhor Farias had told her—in English—what they were. "Salted cod," he told her. "It is a huge favorite here, and it is said that the Portuguese have as many recipes using it as days of the year. This is one of the most common preparations."

"It's a bit like—" Poppy smacked her lips a few times, half a fritter still pinched daintily between her fingers. "Never mind, I'm not exactly sure what it's like. But— Oh, look!" She waved her free hand toward the door. "There is Billy!"

She smiled and beckoned him over.

"Miss Poppy! The captain let you out!" Billy's

eyes went wide with horror when he realized he'd blurted this out in front of his employer. "Begging your pardon, sir. I didn't— That is to say . . ."

Billy swallowed, his small Adam's apple bobbing in his throat. "I've been telling her you're not so bad, sir. In fact, I told her you're the best of men. I promise."

Andrew looked over at Poppy, raising one eyebrow and then the other in an exaggerated attempt to pretend that he was judging Billy's statement. "What do you say, Miss Bridgerton? Is Master Suggs telling the truth?"

"Is that your surname?" Poppy asked the boy. "I don't think I ever knew it."

Billy nodded nervously, and Andrew decided to take pity on him. "There is no need to apologize, Billy. I did indeed 'let her out.'"

Poppy leaned forward with a conspiratorial air. "And you can rest assured he's going to 'put me back in' for the voyage home."

Billy's chin drew back, and his eyes went comically wide.

"It's a joke, Billy," Poppy said. "Well, it's not a joke, I suppose, since it's true, but I was joking *about* it."

"Ehrm . . ." Billy looked to Andrew for help, but he only shrugged. Best that the boy learn early that women could be deuced hard to follow in conversation.

"Did you come here alone?" Poppy asked. "I was just praising Captain James for his requirement that you be accompanied by an adult."

Billy shook his head with vehemence. "Brown brought me on his way into town. Said he'd come to collect me in a bit."

Poppy looked perplexed. "You wished to spend time by yourself *here*?"

"Senhor Farias lets me feed his cat," Billy explained with a grin. "His name is Whiskers. Well, that's what I call him. He's got a name in Portuguese, but I can't pronounce it. He's awful friendly, though. Lets me rub his belly and everything."

As Billy dashed out the side door, Andrew turned to Poppy and said, "He comes here every time we're in Lisbon. Spends hours with that creature."

"He really is a little boy at heart," she murmured. "I forget sometimes— I suspect he's had to grow up faster than I did."

Andrew nodded in agreement. When he was Billy's age, he was still running wild with his siblings and neighbors. His biggest concern was how cold the lake would be if his brother pushed him in.

"Don't you have a cat on the ship?" Poppy asked.

He looked up, about to explain that the ship's cat was a wretched, unpleasant beast, when a sudden movement to his left caught his attention. He glanced discreetly over his shoulder, but all he saw was Senhor Farias. Except . . .

That was odd.

The jovial tavernkeeper was standing still. Too still.

Senhor Farias never stood still. He greeted customers, he poured wine, but he never stood still. Certainly not as he now was: shoulders pressed stiffly against the wall, eyes twitching back and forth.

Something was not right.

"Poppy," he said in a quiet voice, "we need to go."

"What? No. I haven't fin—"

He kicked her under the table. "*Now.*"

Her eyes went wide, and she gave a tiny nod.

Andrew made eye contact with Senhor Farias. Andrew then looked to the door, signaling his intention to leave. Senhor Farias flicked his eyes to a rough-looking trio of men by the far window, signaling the source of the problem.

Andrew stood, but not so quickly as to appear in a rush. "*Obrigado*," he said in a hearty voice, reaching out and grabbing Poppy firmly by the hand. "I will see you next time I am in Lisbon, yes?"

He hauled Poppy to her feet as Senhor Farias nodded and said, "*Sim, sim,*" with perhaps a little too much enthusiasm.

"Thank you, senhor," Poppy said as she hurried to match Andrew's pace.

Senhor Farias smiled tightly, and they almost made it. They really did. But when they were just a few feet from the door, Poppy suddenly jerked her hand free of Andrew's and exclaimed, "Oh, but Billy!"

Andrew lunged forward to grab her hand again, but she was already hurrying toward the side door. "Poppy," he called out, taking care not to sound panicked. "We can get him later."

She shook her head, clearly unwilling to leave the young boy in a place of danger. She said something—

probably about Billy being right outside; Andrew couldn't hear clearly—and poked her head out the back.

Damn it all. Billy was far safer where he was. Whatever—or whomever—these men wanted, it wasn't a thirteen-year-old boy from Portsmouth. But that didn't mean he was safe. If Billy got in their way, they would cut him down without a moment's thought.

Andrew stalked after Poppy. They could leave out the back. It would take longer to reach the relative safety of the busy street, but it would have to do.

"Oh!" he heard Poppy exclaim. "Pardon me."

But her voice was off, and when Andrew reached the door, his blood ran cold. Two more men stood in the alley. One had his hand on Billy's shoulder.

The other had his hand on Poppy.

For the rest of his days, Andrew would remember that moment as if it had unfolded in quarter time. Yet even though every moment felt impossibly slowed down, he could not recall actually *thinking*. Words, language . . . they were gone, replaced by a world washed red with rage.

He lunged forward, and Poppy was knocked to the side as he wrapped his hands around the brigand's throat. But within seconds, he was surrounded, and he only managed to get in two kicks before he found himself pinned against the tavern wall, each arm immobilized by members of the rough-looking gang he'd spotted inside the tavern.

He looked urgently about, trying to assess the situation. It was clear that the three men he'd seen earlier were but a few of a larger group. Andrew could not be sure how many there were in total. He counted four in the alley, but from the noises coming through the open doorway, there were at least that many inside as well.

The four men exchanged words in Portuguese too rapid for Andrew to follow, and then the one who'd had his hand wrapped tightly around Poppy's arm adjusted his position and hauled her back against him, his beefy arm making a pointed elbow around her throat.

"Get your hands off her," Andrew roared, but the foul cretin only laughed, and Poppy let out a strangled cry as she was pulled even more tightly against his chest.

"You son of a—" But Andrew's growl was choked off when he was slammed back against the stone wall of the tavern.

The man holding Poppy laughed anew, and he wrapped a lock of her hair around his finger before tickling the underside of her chin.

He would be the first to die.

Andrew had no idea how he would do it, but as God was his witness, he was going to disembowel him.

"Let her go!"

Billy. Dear God, he'd forgotten about the boy. And apparently everyone else had as well, because no one was restraining him when he ran forward and kicked Poppy's captor in the shin.

"Billy, no!" Andrew yelled, because anyone could see that he did not stand a chance.

But the thirteen-year-old urchin from the wrong

side of Portsmouth had the heart of a gentleman, and he would not allow his lady's honor to be be-smirched.

"Let her go!" Billy screamed again. And then— *Holy Mother of God, they were going to kill him for this*—he sank his teeth into the large man's arm.

The howl of pain that ensued was enough to curdle blood, and whether it was revenge or reaction, Andrew would never know, but the man's fist came down on Billy's head like a cudgel.

The boy dropped like a stone.

"Billy!" Poppy cried.

And then, as Andrew watched in horrified awe, Poppy went *mad*.

"You brute!" she snarled, and she delivered a double blow—first slamming her foot onto her captor's instep, then jabbing her pointy elbow into his belly.

The foot did nothing, but the elbow stunned him enough to let her go, and Poppy dropped to the ground, cradling Billy's head as she tried to rouse him.

"He's a child!" she hissed.

"*Ele me mordeu!*" The man who'd been holding her shoved his injured arm in her face.

Poppy looked up from Billy just long enough to snap, "Well, that's your own bloody fault."

The other brigands were laughing, which did nothing to soothe his temper, and he let out a stream of curses.

Funny how Andrew could understand *that*.

"Billy," Poppy said, smoothing the boy's hair from his face. "Please wake up. Can you answer me?"

Billy did not move.

"I hope that bite becomes infected," Poppy said in a malevolent growl. "I hope your arm turns black and falls off. I hope your bollocks turn gree—"

"Poppy!" Andrew barked. He didn't think any of these men spoke English, but if they did, *bollocks* was likely the first word they'd learned.

"Do any of you speak English?" he asked. "*Inglês?*"

They grunted their *no*s, and one of the men poked his head back into the tavern and yelled something. A few moments later, one of the men Andrew had first seen in the tavern led Senhor Farias into the alley.

With a knife to his throat.

Chapter 18

ᘒᗊᕮᗕ

"Billy?" Poppy murmured, lightly stroking his cheek. "Billy, please wake up."

But the boy didn't stir. He didn't look ill, or pale, or any of those things Poppy thought would come from such a fierce blow to the head. He looked almost peaceful, as if his sleep was natural, and all he needed was a little nudge and reminder that it was time to open his eyes.

Water, she thought. Maybe some water splashed on his face would help. She knew the word for *water*. She'd learned it earlier that day.

"*Agua*," she begged, looking from man to man among the bandits. "*Agua por* the boy."

But her mangled sentence went unheard. A commotion broke out inside the tavern—shouting, followed by the crash of broken wood and overturned tables. The man who had hit Billy rushed to the open doorway and disappeared inside.

There was more talk between the bandits, their voices quick and sharp and utterly incomprehensible to Poppy's English ears.

She felt so bloody helpless. Earlier in the day it had all been so charming—the music of the Portuguese language swirling about her ears. It had been a game to wonder what they were saying, a marvel to consider just how huge the world really was.

Now she just felt illiterate. And lost. She might as well be an infant for all that she could tell what was happening around her.

She turned toward Andrew, not that he was likely to understand the fast chatter much better than she could. She'd spent the entire day with him; she had some idea of how much Portuguese he knew.

More than most, but far from fluent.

"Andrew." She whispered his name, but she didn't think he heard her. The two largest bandits had him pinned tightly against the wall, and just the sight of it caused Poppy's throat to constrict. One of them had an elbow pressed hard into Andrew's belly; the other held his jaw in a viselike grip. Both used the full weight of their bodies to keep him in place.

Andrew. This time she only thought his name. She couldn't have got his attention, anyway. He was staring at the doorway, his face locked in an expression that was almost devoid of emotion.

Devoid. Another word she thought sounded like its meaning.

Devoid. She despised it.

It was a word that should never be used to describe Captain Andrew James. He was full. He was replete. He was *alive*.

She thought he might be more alive than anyone she'd ever met.

And . . .

And . . .

She blinked, bringing her vision into focus. Andrew was still looking away from her, but it didn't seem to matter any longer. She did not need to see his eyes; she knew they held more blue than the ocean. She did not need to hear his voice; she knew it would wash across her with the warmth of the sun.

What he'd said earlier in the day—he was right. She *knew* him.

Andrew James did not merely exist. He *lived*.

And he made her want to be the same way.

The realization took her breath away. She'd thought she was quick and adventurous and full of wit, and maybe she was, but when she was with Andrew, she was *more*. More of all that, and more of everything else, and more of things she'd not even known she might want.

It was not that he'd changed her; all of the seeds were already there.

But with him, she grew.

"Poppy." Andrew's voice. Low, and tight with warning. The noises emanating from the tavern had changed. Footsteps. Someone was coming toward them.

"Senhor Farias," Poppy whispered. The tavern-keeper emerged first, propelled stiffly forward by a man who held his upper body immobile with one beefy arm wrapped tightly around his chest.

And a knife at his throat.

A third man hopped down the steps behind

them—the leader of the bunch, Poppy thought. He said a few words in a chilling tone of voice, and then Senhor Farias said, "Do not fight them, Captain! They are many, and they have many weapons."

"What do they want?" Andrew asked.

"Money. They say they want money. They see you are English, that you are rich."

Poppy's eyes darted from man to man, even as her hand kept stroking Billy's cheek. Why would these men think they were rich? Well-to-do, certainly; it was obvious they were not laborers. But there was no way they could know that she was related to a wealthy viscount, that she had a family who would pay a king's ransom for her safe return.

Not that her parents could afford such a ransom. But her uncle . . . he would pay.

If he knew she'd been kidnapped.

But he did not know she was in Lisbon. No one did. Not a soul who had ever mattered to her knew where she was. Funny how she'd never quite thought of it that way before.

Funny.

Maybe tragic.

Probably not both.

She looked back down at Billy. He mattered to her now, she realized, and so did Andrew. But if she disappeared into the dark side of Lisbon, so would they, and her family would never know her fate.

"I have some coin in my coat," Andrew said, his voice slow and deliberately even. He nodded toward his chest. "If they reach into my breast pocket, they will find it."

Senhor Farias translated, but Poppy did not need to understand Portuguese to know what the gang's leader thought of Andrew's suggestion. His reply was sharp, his expression malevolent.

And Senhor Farias blanched with fear.

"He says it is not enough," the tavernkeeper said. "I ask how he knows it is not enough, and he says he knows who you are. He knows you captain *Infinity*. You have goods and cargo that don't fit in a pocket."

A muscle worked in Andrew's face, and Poppy could see how hard he was working to remain in control of his temper when he said, "Tell them that if they let us go, they will be amply compensated."

Senhor Farias's mouth trembled as the man holding him pressed the knife more firmly to his throat. "I do not know that word, *amplycomp*—"

"I will pay them," Andrew said sharply, grunting as he took an elbow to the gut. "If they let us go, I will pay them."

Senhor Farias translated, and Poppy's blood ran cold when the leader threw back his head and laughed. Once he'd wiped his eyes, he said a few words, and Senhor Farias turned back to Andrew.

"He says he will take you. He will get more that way."

"Only if he releases—"

The leader cut him off with a few barked words. Senhor Farias swallowed convulsively.

"What did he say?" Andrew demanded.

The tavernkeeper's voice shook down to a whisper. "He says . . . he also takes the lady."

A look came over Andrew that was positively feral. "Over my dead—"

"No!" Poppy cried.

Andrew's eyes did not stray from the leader of the gang as he said, "Stay out of this, Poppy."

"I'm already in it," she shot back. "And a fat lot of good you'll do me if anything has to be done over your dead body."

Andrew looked down at her with a glare.

She returned the expression.

"Captain?" Senhor Farias's voice choked with terror, and when Poppy looked at him she saw a tiny trail of blood slipping down his neck.

Andrew's response was absolute. "She. Goes. Free."

"Captain, I do not think they will agree to—"

"*Basta!*" The leader of the gang whipped a gun from his pocket and pointed it at Billy's head.

"No!" Poppy threw herself over the boy. She didn't want to die—*please God, please*—she didn't want to die. But she could not let them shoot Billy. He had wanted only to protect her. And he was so small.

He just wanted to play with the cat.

The leader snorted with disgust, spat a few words toward Senhor Farias, and stalked away.

"What did he say?" Poppy whispered.

Senhor Farias's lips trembled, and he shook his head.

"Do you know them?" Poppy asked.

He nodded. "I must pay them every month. For protection."

"From whom?"

A bitter sound choked its way out of the tavern-keeper's throat. "From them. We all must do it. Everyone in my—*how do you say it*—the streets near my house."

"Neighborhood?"

"Yes. Neighborhood. We all pay. But they never do this before. They have hurt people, but not people like you."

Somehow Poppy did not find that reassuring. Then again, she didn't think Senhor Farias had meant it to be.

"Senhor."

They all turned to Andrew, still held immobile by the wall, his chin tipped into an awkward position by the man pinching his jaw.

But his voice was sure when he said, "What did he say?"

Senhor Farias looked to Poppy and then back to Andrew. "He says they take all three." The tavern-keeper's lips trembled. "You, the lady, and the boy."

Poppy gasped. "What? No! Billy—"

"They take all three," Senhor Farias said, cutting her off before she could finish her objection. "Or they shoot two. Two of you . . . and me."

The world went silent. Maybe people were still talking, maybe the sounds of the nearby street continued as usual. But Poppy heard nothing. The space between her ears felt thick, as if she'd dunked herself underwater and people were speaking above.

Slowly, she rose to her feet. She looked to Andrew.

She didn't say anything. She simply didn't think she needed to.

He gave a single grim nod. He understood.

Fear was a strange beast. When Poppy was a child, she and her brothers had often played *What if?* and *How would you?*

What if you were being chased by a boar?

How would you react if someone pointed a gun at your head?

Didn't all children play these games? Didn't all adults?

She remembered one time with all four of her brothers—somehow the game had metamorphosed into *What if* Poppy *were being chased by a boar?* and *How would* Poppy *react if someone pointed a gun at her head?*

She'd countered with a pert: *Which one of you would come to my aid?*, but she'd been swiftly informed that this was not within the parameters of the game. After settling on the gun conundrum, Richard and Reginald had both decided she'd scream. This wasn't entirely unexpected; Poppy didn't often scream, but it had to be said—when she did, she was *damn* good at it.

Ronald had said that he thought she'd faint. When she pointed out that she'd never fainted in her life, he pointed out that she'd never had a gun to her head.

Which Poppy had to concede was relevant, even if she did not agree with his conclusion.

The game had dissolved shortly thereafter; Richard

sniffed the air, declared that he smelled Cook's apple tarts, and that was that. Later, though, Poppy had asked Roger why he hadn't offered an opinion.

"I don't know, Pops," he'd said with an uncharacteristically serious expression. "I hardly know how I would react in such a situation. I don't think we really *can* know until it happens."

It was happening now.

And fear was indeed a strange beast, because whatever Poppy had thought she might do, however she'd thought she might react when her life was in danger, it wasn't *this*.

It was almost as if she wasn't there.

She was numb.

Detached.

Her movements were slow and careful, but nothing felt deliberate. She was not thinking *I will move slowly, I don't want to startle anyone*.

She just did it. And she waited patiently for the bandits to do what they would.

Andrew was subdued first, his hands pulled roughly behind his body and bound with rope. "Do not hurt her," he warned, just as a coarse burlap sack was lowered over his head.

As Poppy watched, dread slid through her body like a wraith. There was something about being blinded—about *him* being blinded—that was terrifying. If he couldn't see her, he couldn't help her, and, dear heaven, she did not want to face this on her own.

She opened her mouth, but she didn't know what to say, and at any rate, she did not seem able to make a sound, at least not until one of the men grabbed her roughly by the wrist. His fingers pressed into her skin with enough bite that she let out a little yelp.

"Poppy?" Andrew struggled against his bindings. "What did they—"

His captor spat out a few words and slammed him into the wall.

"I'm fine!" Poppy yelled. "I'm fine. I promise. I was only surprised."

She looked at the man holding Andrew. "Please don't hurt him."

He stared back as if she were an idiot. Which she probably was. She knew he couldn't understand her.

But still, she had to try.

"The boy," she said, directing her entreaty to the one with the kindest face. "Please be gentle."

"*Suavemente*," Senhor Farias said.

"*Suavemente*," Poppy repeated, even though the man who was now covering Billy's head had surely heard Senhor Farias himself. "Please."

Poppy swallowed as she watched him tie the unconscious boy's hands together. "Must they do this?" she entreated Senhor Farias. "They have the captain, and they have me. He's just a boy."

Senhor Farias looked at her with a pained expression.

"He probably won't remember any of this," Poppy said.

Senhor Farias let out a shaky exhale and said something to the man on the ground with Billy. Poppy's eyes darted back and forth as the two men spoke in urgent tones. Finally, Senhor Farias turned to her and said, "He says the boy is too much trouble. They will leave him with me."

Poppy almost smiled. She almost laughed, she was so relieved.

"But you must not fight them," the tavernkeeper warned. "You must not give them trouble. You too, Captain," he said. "You must not make trouble when they take you away or they will send someone back and—"

He made a cutting motion across his throat.

Poppy recoiled. She looked up at Andrew, who could not see, and realized she had to translate the gesture. She swallowed, forced herself to say the words. "They will kill him. They will slit Billy's throat if we make trouble."

"And they will set him free if we don't?" Andrew said from beneath the burlap sack.

"*Sim*."

Yes. One of a handful of Portuguese words Poppy now understood. "I will cooperate," she said.

The tavernkeeper's sad nod was the last thing Poppy saw before a sack was roughly pulled down over her head too.

She froze. She hadn't expected it to be so instantly dark.

Or hot.

She tried to breathe.

The air around her face turned thick. She exhaled, and the heated air bounced back onto her mouth and nose. She tried to draw breath, but she couldn't—no, she could, and she thought she *did*, but nothing was reaching her lungs.

No one was holding her throat. Why wasn't she getting air?

She could hear herself breathing, could feel the rapid rise and fall of her chest, but it wasn't *working*. She was dizzy, disoriented. Unable to see her own feet, she suddenly wasn't sure how to stand.

She needed to hold on to something.

"Poppy?" she heard Andrew call out. "Poppy, are you with me?"

He sounded very far away.

"*Poppy!*"

"I need to hold his hand," she gasped. And then when no one did anything, she screamed it. "Let me hold his hand!"

There was a rush of movement around her, a crisp cadence of voices, one of them belonging to Senhor Farias. And then, miraculously, she felt her hand being placed between Andrew's hands.

It was awkward. His hands were bound behind his back. She could barely link her fingers with his.

But it was a lifeline.

"You're all right, Poppy," he said. "I promise."

"I can't breathe."

"You can."

"I'm not."

"Clearly, you are." There was gentle humor in his voice, almost enough to pierce her panic. He squeezed her fingers. "I need you to be strong."

"I'm not strong."

"You're the strongest person I know."

"I'm not. I'm really not." She didn't know why she sounded like she was begging.

He squeezed again, and she heard him chuckle. "This isn't even your first time being abducted."

"It's not the same," she snapped. She twisted her head around to where she thought she might be facing him. "Honestly, Captain. That's the falsest equivalence imaginable."

"And you say you're not strong," he murmured.

"You—" She stopped. Felt his fingers curl around hers.

"Poppy?"

It took her a moment to realize what he'd done.

"Are you breathing now?"

She nodded, then remembered he couldn't see her and said, "I am." And then: "Thank you."

"We will make it through this," he said.

"Do you really think so?"

He paused for a moment too long before saying yes.

But at least Poppy was breathing.

Chapter 19

———— ✳ ————

Andrew had no idea where they were.

Back at the tavern, he and Poppy had been loaded unceremoniously into a wagon. They'd traveled well over an hour, but with a hood over his head—and a heavy blanket thrown over both of them—he could hardly have made sense of the journey.

The only thing of which he was certain was that they had gained elevation. But that was hardly a distinguishing fact. They'd started at sea level; they could hardly have gone any direction *but* up.

They were moved inside a building, then up a steep flight of stairs, and then to a room at the rear. A door shut and a lock turned, and then someone grabbed Andrew's hood from the back and pulled it over and off his head, the angle ensuring that the burlap scraped roughly across his skin. He'd prepared himself to be blinded by sunlight, but the air was murky and dim. The room contained but one window, and it was covered by exterior wooden shutters—closed tightly and presumably nailed shut.

He turned just in time to see one of the men take hold of Poppy's hood and pull it off. She took a massive gulp of air the moment it was lifted, but although she looked a bit shaky, she appeared unharmed. It had been hot and sticky under that blanket, and after her reaction to the burlap hood, he'd been terrified that she would have another breathing attack. He'd tried to talk to her in the wagon—that seemed to have helped before—but he was rewarded with a slap to the head from the man who was riding along with them in the back. It hadn't hurt—the blanket had absorbed a great deal of the impact—but if it was meant as a warning, it had worked. Andrew kept his mouth shut and didn't try anything.

He'd had no other choice.

Which was galling.

It had brought to mind the time when—it must have been the first or second day after Poppy had come aboard the *Infinity*—he had asked her why she was being so agreeable. She had replied that she had no good reason not to be agreeable. She couldn't very well escape while they were at sea.

At the time he'd thought her eminently sensible. He still did, he supposed.

But now he realized how colossally he'd missed the point. How impotent she must have felt, to be forced into meekly accepting her fate. There was nothing satisfying about choosing one's best option when all of the options were terrible.

He could not have left her in England—not with such strict orders to ferry the diplomatic pouch to Portugal *and* keep the cave's location a secret until the prime minister's emissary got there for the documents he'd brought from Spain. Truly, he'd had no choice but to take Poppy with them on the journey.

But he could have been more understanding. More . . . compassionate?

More something. He could have been more something.

Maybe more honest. She did not even know his true name.

He looked over at her, trying to speak with his eyes since he dared not yet make a sound. She seemed to understand; her own eyes opened wide and her lips pinched up at the corners. The two men who had brought them into the house still stood by the door, speaking to each other in rapid Portuguese.

As the men talked, Andrew took stock of their surroundings. They were in a bedchamber—nothing large or luxurious, but as best as he could tell, tidy and clean. The decor was a step or two above what one might find in a posting inn; whoever lived here had a small measure of wealth.

Andrew caught a few words from the conversation—*money, man, woman.* He thought one of them might have said *seven,* although he wasn't sure what that might be in relation to. And maybe it wasn't that at all. It was entirely possible that the only reason he'd recognized *man, woman,* and *money* was because he'd been expecting to hear them.

Tomorrow.

Stupid.

Home.

He thought he heard these words too.

Abruptly, the men turned toward them, and one of them flicked his hand in their direction as he barked out an order.

He wanted them to move. Andrew nudged Poppy with his shoulder, and they edged backward until the backs of their legs hit the bed.

Poppy looked at him with wide, apprehensive eyes, and he gave his head a tiny shake. No questions. Not yet.

The men grew animated as they spoke, and then Andrew saw the glint of a knife.

He didn't think.

He didn't have *time* to think. He just leapt, trying to cover her body with his own. Except that with his hands bound, he was clumsy and off-balance. Poppy let out a grunt as she stumbled back onto the bed, and Andrew fell to the floor, feeling the veriest fool.

The man with the knife strode over and actually rolled his eyes as he grabbed Poppy's wrists and sliced through her bindings.

He looked down at Andrew. "*Idiota.*"

And then he left, taking his friend with him.

Andrew closed his eyes. He needed a moment. Surely he deserved a moment to pretend he wasn't lying on a floor with his hands bound behind his back somewhere in the vicinity of Lisbon.

He tasted blood. He must have bitten his tongue.

"Captain?"

He sighed.

"Captain?"

She sounded a little panicked the second time, so he forced himself to open his eyes. Poppy was standing over him, her brow knit with worry.

"I'm fine," he said flatly.

She reached down to help him to his feet. "I can try to untie you."

He shook his head. Whoever had bound his wrists had done so with knots worthy of the most seasoned of sailors.

There was irony there.

Sod it.

"They should have retied them in front of your body," Poppy said, once he was back upright.

"*Or,*" he said in a brittle voice, "they should have not kidnapped us."

"Well . . . yes." She laughed nervously.

"How are you?" he asked. It should have been the first thing he'd asked. It should have been the first thing he'd *thought*, not some rot about feeling sorry for himself and wanting to keep his eyes closed.

"I . . ." It seemed to take her some time to choose her answer. "I am all right," she finally decided. "I'm not sure what happened to me when they put that sack over my head. I have never experienced anything like it. When we were in the cart, I spent half the time trying to remember to breathe and the other half trying to remember *how* to breathe."

"I'm sorry," he said, and he wasn't even sure what he was apologizing for. His list of transgressions was grotesquely long.

But Poppy did not seem to have heard the thickness in his voice. "It was so strange," she went on.

"It happened so fast. I could not breathe. And yet, I think I *was* breathing. But I didn't *know* that I was. I know— I'm not making any sense."

"Such things rarely do." He cleared his throat. "I have seen it before. What happened to you. One of my men cannot take more than a step into the cave."

"The cave?" she echoed, blinking with surprise. "I had no trouble with the cave."

He shrugged, since his tied-up hands precluded him from making any of his usual gesticulations. "I would imagine it's different for everyone. For all I know, he can sit happily for days with a bag over his head."

Poppy's lips parted as she considered that. "I suppose you're right. It's silly to expect logic in something so entirely illogical."

He nodded slowly and sat down on the bed. He was exhausted. Now that the immediate danger was gone—all the knives and guns (and the people holding the knives and guns) were on the other side of a door—it was as if the energy had just drained from his body.

Or poured. Draining sounded slow. This had been instant. One moment he was poised and ready to fight, and the next he had nothing.

For a moment Poppy looked as if she might sit beside him, but then she turned and awkwardly hugged her arms to her body. "It was very helpful," she said haltingly. "When you spoke to me. It calmed me down. Thank you."

"Do not thank me," he said roughly. He did not want her gratitude. He could not bear it.

If they got out of this room alive, if he was the one to make that happen, *then* she could say thank you. But until then, he was just the man who might get her killed.

"Do you know where we are?" she finally asked.

"No."

"I—" She swallowed, then looked toward the blocked window. "How long do you think we were in the cart? An hour? We are probably rather far out of town by now."

"Or they retraced their path six times and we're right around the corner from the tavern."

Her eyes widened. "Do you really think so?"

"No," he admitted, "not right around the corner. But we might be much closer than the length of our journey would indicate."

Poppy went to the window and pressed her ear to the glass.

"Can you hear anything?"

She gave a nod—a tiny one, meant to shush him as much as it did to signal agreement. "I can't make much out," she said, "but it's not silent. Wherever we are, it's not isolated."

Andrew made his way to her side and leaned his ear against the window. Facing each other, they listened. She was right. It wasn't quiet outside. There was . . . life. Things were happening.

It was just about the least specific descriptor he could have imagined—*things were happening*—and yet it said so much.

"I think we're still in the city," he said slowly. "Or at least not very far out."

Poppy made a murmuring sound of agreement and pressed herself more firmly against the glass. "Some of those voices are female," she said.

Andrew raised a brow. "Somehow I don't think our captors have a secret female division of their gang."

"Which means they must have brought us to a very ordinary part of town. Or near the town."

"That is very good news. The less remote we are, the better."

"The greater the chance someone will be able to find us?"

"The greater the chance we might escape." At her questioning look, he added, "It's much easier to hide in a city."

She nodded, then pushed herself off the window and took a few steps toward the center of the room. "I think I will sit down."

"That's a good idea."

She moved toward the bed, then stopped and turned around. "Is there anything I can do to help you?"

"I don't suppose you have a knife hidden in your dress," he muttered.

"Nor a gun," she said, her eyes telling him that she remembered him saying almost the same thing on the day she'd arrived on the *Infinity*. "Nor a purse of gold. Alas."

"Alas," he agreed.

Damn it.

Two hours later

THERE WAS NOTHING to do but stare at the door.

Someone had come for Andrew a few minutes earlier. He'd been half pushed, half pulled out the door, and she'd not seen him since. Poppy had not heard anything either, which she thought was a good sign. Gunshots were by definition loud, and if they tried to injure him in some other way—surely that would make noise.

Wouldn't it?

She'd searched the room for something she might use as a weapon, but the only movable objects of heft were the chairs.

"Needs must," she muttered, and she pulled one close to the door. If she had to, she could heave it into the air and bring it down upon someone's head. It might even knock someone unconscious.

Hopefully not Andrew.

She wasn't sure how long she stood there, waiting and listening. Ten minutes? Twenty? Certainly not thirty. She'd never been good at estimating the passage of time.

And then finally—

Footsteps. She gripped the top rail of the chair. She had no idea how she'd know whether to attack or not. If she heard Andrew's voice? If she didn't hear his voice?

She was just going to have to wait until the door opened. See who walked in.

The noises drew closer.

She picked up the chair. Held it over her head.

A key turned in the lock.

She held her breath.

The door swung open.

And Andrew stumbled in.

Poppy caught herself mid-swing, halting the downward motion of the chair just before it crashed onto his head.

"Aaaaaa!"

He yelled.

She yelled.

They both yelled, and then so did someone in the hallway, presumably to tell them to shut the hell up.

"Get that away from my head," Andrew shouted, bringing his hands up in defense.

"They untied you!" Poppy exclaimed. He'd been pushed into the room with enough force to land him on the floor, and she'd not immediately noticed that he'd been freed.

"The chair," he ground out.

"Oh, sorry." The bottom of one of the legs was but an inch from his eye. She hastily set it down behind her. "Are you all right?" she asked. "What happened? Are you all right?"

He nodded. "Let me just get up."

"Oh yes, I'm sorry." She helped him to his feet. "Wh—" She bit her tongue. She'd been about to ask him what happened again.

"They brought in someone who speaks English," he said once he'd dusted himself off.

"And?"

"And he pretended to be my friend. Said he was appalled at our treatment, insisted my hands be untied."

Poppy wondered why his tone was so close to a sneer. "That's . . . good? Isn't it?"

"Probably not. It's a well-known tactic when taking prisoners. One person acts kindly. Tries to gain your trust."

"Oh." Poppy considered this. "Still, it's better that than everyone treating you badly, isn't it?"

His head cocked to the side in a considering manner. "I suppose. Most other methods of interrogation involve a great deal of blood, so yes, this is preferable."

She pressed her lips together but did not chide him for such a flip comment. "Did they tell you what they want? I mean, I know they want money, but did they tell you how much?"

"More than I can easily amass."

Poppy's lips parted. She didn't know why, but it had not occurred to her that they might not be able to meet a ransom demand. "I have money," she said haltingly.

"In Portugal?" His answer was sarcastic, almost derisive.

"Of course not. But if we told them—"

"Don't be naïve."

She felt her teeth press together. "I'm just trying to help."

"I know." He raked his hand through his hair. "I know."

Poppy watched him carefully. His second "I know" had been louder than the first, more emphatic.

Angry, even.

She waited a moment, then asked, "Are you going to tell me what happened?"

"I was trying to."

She shook her head. "I wasn't asking what happened. I was asking if you're going to tell me. Because if you're not, if you're going to leave parts out because you think it's for my own good, I'd like to know."

He stared at her as if she'd started speaking German. Or Chinese. "What the devil are you talking about?"

"You keep secrets," she said simply.

"I've known you a week. Of course I keep secrets."

"I'm not scolding you for it. I just want to know."

"For God's sake, Poppy."

"For God's sake, Captain," she returned, letting her voice turn singsong.

He gave her a look of supreme annoyance. "Really? That's what we're doing?"

"What else can I do? You won't tell me anything."

"I was *trying* to," he ground out. "You won't stop harping about my keeping secrets."

"I have never harped in my life. And I never said you shouldn't keep secrets! I just want to know if you *are*."

She waited for his retort, because surely he had one—that's what they *did*. But instead he just made a sound—something strange and unfamiliar and ripped from the very heart of him. It was a growl but it wasn't, and while Poppy watched with fascinated trepidation, he turned roughly away.

He planted his hands against the wall above his head, almost groaning as he pressed forward. There was something wild in him, something Poppy should have found frightening.

She should.

But she didn't.

Her hand tingled. As if she should touch him. As if she might die if she didn't.

Her whole body felt strange. Needy. And though she might be an innocent, she knew this was desire. Inappropriate and ill-timed, but still there, unraveling within her like a needy beast.

She took a step back. It was self-preservation.

It didn't help.

What did it mean that she felt this way now, when he was at his most uncivilized?

Back on the ship she'd felt hints of awareness. She'd wondered for hours what would have happened if she'd swayed closer when they'd kissed on deck. She'd dreamed about his skin, the wicked little patch of it that was revealed when he left off his cravat.

It wasn't just his neckpiece. He rolled up his sleeves too, and she was mesmerized by his arms—the play of muscles beneath his skin. Most of the men she knew didn't work. They rode, they fenced, they walked the perimeter of their property, but they didn't *work*. It made her wonder at the strength of him, what those arms could do that hers could not.

And she was always aware of his heat. There was a cushion of air around his body that was always a few degrees warmer than the rest. It made her want to move closer, and then closer still, to see if it grew hot when she was just a whisper away.

She knew such thoughts were scandalous. Wicked, even. But all of that— No, *none* of that had brought her to such a quivering point as this.

She watched as he took a long breath, his body taut, as if he were protesting some invisible restraint. His hands had become claws, only the fingertips pressing into the wall above his head.

"Captain James?" she whispered. She wasn't sure if he heard her. He was close enough—the room was far too small for even the softest murmur to go unnoticed. But whatever was going on in his head—it was loud. It was loud, and it was primal, and it had left him on the edge of something very fierce.

"Capt—"

He took a step back. Closed his eyes as he took a breath. And then, with composure that was far too even and restrained, he turned to her.

"I beg your pardon," he said.

Poppy didn't know what to say.

"Where were we?"

She had no idea.

"Right," he continued, as if she weren't goggling at him like a speechless loon. "I might have convinced them to let you bring the ransom note to the *Infinity*."

Her mouth fell open. Why hadn't he said that *first*?

He raked his hand through his hair and strode to the other side of the room. It was only a few steps, but he seemed rather like a caged cat. "It was the best I could do," he said.

"But—" Poppy fought for words. All she came up with was: "Me?"

"It would be a show of good faith."

"I was not aware that they had good faith."

"And proof of life," he added in a more brittle tone.

"Proof of— Oh," she said, suddenly understanding the term. "That's a terrible phrase."

He rolled his eyes at her naïveté. "The man I talked with has to consult someone else. We won't have their answer until tomorrow morning."

Poppy looked toward the window. Earlier, there had been a narrow sliver of light between the wooden shutters.

"Night has fallen," Andrew confirmed.

"One would think such men would prefer to work under the cover of darkness."

Again, he rolled his eyes. And again, there was no levity in it, nothing to say that they were in this together. "I have little insight into the workings of their minds," he said.

Poppy held her tongue for a few seconds, but that was all she could manage. "Why are you being so mean?"

A look of impatient incomprehension swept over his face. "I beg your pardon?"

"I'm just saying that you could be a little kinder."

"Wh—" He shook his head, apparently unable to complete the word.

"You have done nothing but growl and snap since you got back."

He gaped as if he could not believe the cheek of

her. "We are being held captive by God-knows-who and you're complaining that I'm not being *kind*?"

"No, of course not. Well, yes, I am. Every time I try to make a suggestion—"

"You have no experience in such things," he cut in. "Why should I listen to you?"

"Because I'm not stupid, and the worst that could come of listening to me is that you'll disagree with what I have to say."

Andrew pinched the bridge of his nose. "Poppy," he said, the word as much of a growl as it was a sigh. "I cannot—"

"Wait," she interrupted. She thought back to what he'd just said. "Do you mean to say that you *do* have some experience in such things?"

"Some," he admitted.

"What does *that* mean?"

"It means this is not the first time I have had to deal with unsavory characters," he retorted.

"Is it the first time you've been kidnapped?"

"Yes."

"The first time you've been tied up?"

He hesitated.

She gasped. "*Captain Ja—*"

"In this manner," he said quickly. And with great volume and emphasis, as if he needed to cut off her query about as much as he needed, for example, air.

Her eyes narrowed. "What does that mean?"

"Don't ask that question."

It was possibly the first time she had seen him *truly* blush, which should have been enough to make her want to force him to answer. But given the circumstances, she decided to let it pass. For the most part.

She gave him a shrewd look. "Can I ask you that question later?"

"Please don't."

"Are you sure?"

There was a noise people sometimes made—it was halfway between a laugh and a cry but it just ended up sounding like irony.

Andrew made that noise, right before saying, "Not even a little bit."

Poppy took a step back. It seemed wise. After a few moments of wary silence, she asked, "What do we do tonight?"

He looked almost relieved she asked, even if his tone was blunt. "I'm going to inspect the room more carefully now that my hands are untied, but I don't anticipate finding a means to escape."

"So we just wait?"

He gave a grim nod. "I counted at least six men downstairs, plus two across the hall. I don't like doing nothing, but I'm even less fond of suicide."

That sound he had made earlier—the one with the laughing and the crying and the horrible irony . . .

She made it too.

Chapter 20

❖

Several hours later—after Andrew and Poppy had eaten the bread and cheese the kidnappers had tossed at them, after a comprehensive inspection of the room yielded absolutely nothing, after a long stretch of silence eased them into a tacit truce—Andrew sat down. He put his back to the wall, stretched his legs out long in front of him, and sighed.

"You don't want the chair?" Poppy asked. She was on the bed. She'd opened her mouth to protest when he had told her to take it a few minutes earlier, but he'd held up his hand and given her such a stare of *Do not argue* that she did not say a word.

He shook his head. "Somehow it looks less comfortable than this."

She looked at the chair, then back at him. "I can see that."

He smiled wryly.

"The bed isn't— Well, it's not uncomfortable, but it's not, well, an excellent bed."

At this, he actually laughed. "You're a terrible liar."

"It's not a lie, exactly. It's all in how you phrase it."

He snorted. "Said every politician in London."

This made her smile, which brought him such an absurd amount of joy that he could only ascribe it to the fact that making someone smile under such circumstances could be treated as nothing short of a triumph.

"Here," she said, grabbing her pillow, "you should have it."

He did not try to catch it; there was something much more pleasing about letting it sail through the air and clip him on the shoulder. "Just like old times," he murmured.

"How I wish."

He looked up at her. She was sitting cross-legged, her knees bumping out the sides of her blue skirt until the frock formed something of a triangle. He tried to remember the last time he'd sat in such a position. He didn't think he'd ever seen her do it either.

It made perfect sense. No one sat that way in public. It was for home. For unguarded moments.

"I'm sorry," he said. The words came slowly, not because he was reluctant to say them, but rather because he felt them more keenly than he expected. "For being so short of temper earlier."

She went still, her lips parting as she absorbed the sudden change of topic. "It's all right," she said.

"It's not."

"It *is*. This is . . ." She looked up toward the ceiling, shaking her head. She looked like she couldn't quite believe her predicament. "Anyone would be short of temper. It's probably a small miracle *I* haven't strangled *you*."

He smiled. "It's not easy, you know, to strangle a man."

Her head fell to her chest as she laughed. When she looked up she said, "I've learned that recently."

"Really. Where would a gently bred woman such as yourself learn such a thing?"

"Well." She leaned forward, elbows on knees, chin in her hands. "I've fallen in with a band of pirates."

His gasp was worthy of the stage. "Never say it."

She responded in kind, with wide eyes, breathless drama, and a hand to her heart. "I think I might be ruined."

And because something inside him felt like it was falling back into place, he gave her a crooked smile and said, "Not yet."

A week earlier such a quip would have offended her sensibilities, but this time she didn't even try to pretend. She just rolled her eyes and shook her head and said, "It's a pity I don't have another pillow to throw at you."

"Indeed." He made a show of glancing at the floor around him. "I would be living in luxury."

"Did you ever have pillow fights with your siblings?"

He'd been adjusting the pillow she'd thrown at him behind his back, but at this, he paused. "You have to ask?"

She giggled. "I know. Stupid question."

"Did you?" he asked.

"Oh, of course."

He looked at her.

"What?" she asked.

"I was waiting for you to tell me that you always won."

"To my desperate shame, *that* would be a false-hood."

"Do my ears deceive me? Was there a contest in the Bridgerton household that Poppy Bridgerton did not win?"

"Poppy *Louise* Bridgerton," she said officiously. "If you're going to scold, you should do it correctly."

"My apologies. Poppy *Louise*. But tell me, who emerged victorious?"

"My two older brothers, of course. Mostly Richard. Roger said I wasn't worth the effort."

"Too easy for him to beat you?"

"He was a full head taller," she protested. "It could never have been a fair fight."

"Good of him to bow out, then."

She pressed her lips together peevishly. "He was hardly so gallant. He said he had more interesting ways to torture me."

"Oh yes." Andrew grinned. "He was the one who taught you a new language, didn't he?"

"A new language, indeed. You'd better watch out or I'll farfar you."

He snorted right into a laugh. "I wish I'd known your brother. I would have worshipped at his feet."

"I wish that too," she said with a sad smile, and he knew that what she really meant was that she wished Roger were still alive, still able to make new friends and, yes, devise new ways to torture his little sister.

"How did he die?" he asked. She'd never told him that, and until now it felt too intrusive to ask.

"Infection." She said it so plainly, as if everything tragic had long since been wrung out of the word and the only thing left was resignation.

"I'm sorry." He'd seen more than one man succumb to infection. It always seemed to start so simply. A scrape, a wound . . . His brother knew a man who'd worn an ill-fitting pair of boots and then died of a purulent blister.

"He was bitten by a dog," Poppy said. "It wasn't even a very bad bite. I mean, I've been bitten by a dog before, haven't you?"

He nodded, even though he hadn't.

"It didn't heal properly. It looked like it was going to. It was completely fine for a few days, maybe just a little red. Swollen. And then . . ." She swallowed and looked to the side.

"You don't have to finish," he said softly.

But she wanted to. He could see it in her face.

"He had a fever," she continued. "It came on overnight. He went to bed, and he seemed fine. I was the one who brought him a mug of hot cider, so I know."

She hugged her arms to her body, closing her eyes while she drew a long breath. "He was so hot. It was unnatural. His skin was like paper. And the worst part was, it wasn't even fast. It took five days. Do you know how long five days can be?"

It was one day less than her time aboard the *Infinity*. Which suddenly didn't seem like very much time at all.

"Sometimes he was insensible," she said, "but sometimes he wasn't, and he knew—he *knew* he was going to die."

"Did he tell you that?"

She shook her head. "He would never. He kept saying, 'I'll be fine, Pops. Stop looking so worried.'"

"He called you Pops?" Andrew tried not to smile, but there was something irresistibly charming about it.

"He did. But only sometimes." She said that in a way that made him think this had not occurred to her before. She cocked her head to the side, her eyes tipping up and to the left as if she might find her memories there. "It was when he was serious, but he was perhaps trying to sound as if he wasn't."

She looked over at Andrew, and he was relieved to see that some of the bleakness had left her face. "He was rarely serious," she said. "Or at least that's what he wanted people to think. He was very observant, and I think people were less guarded around him because they thought he was a scapegrace."

"I have some experience with that particular dichotomy," he said in a dry voice.

"I would imagine you do."

"What happened next?" he asked.

"He died," she said with a tiny helpless shrug. "To the very end, he tried to pretend it wasn't going to happen, but he never could lie about important things."

Whereas Andrew had *only* lied about important things. But he was trying so hard not to think about that right then.

Poppy let out a sad little puff of a laugh. "The morning before he passed, he even boasted that he was going to massacre me in the egg roll at the next May fair, but I could see it in his eyes. He knew he would not live."

"Massacre?" Andrew echoed. He liked this particular choice of words.

She gave a watery smile. "It would never have been enough just to beat me."

"No, I expect not."

She nodded slowly. "I knew he was lying. He knew I knew it too. And I wondered . . . Why? Why would he cling to his story when he knew he wasn't fooling me?"

"Perhaps he thought he was doing you a kindness."

She shrugged. "Maybe."

She did not seem to have more to say on the subject, so Andrew went back to fussing with his pillow. It was both flat *and* lumpy, and it was impossible to get into the right position. He tried mushing it, pushing it, folding it . . . Nothing worked.

"You look very uncomfortable," Poppy said.

He didn't bother glancing up from his efforts. "I'm fine."

"Are you going to lie to me like Roger did?"

That got his attention. "Why would you say such a thing?"

"Just come over and sit on the bed," she said in an exasperated voice. "It's not as if either of us will sleep tonight, and if I have to watch another moment of your fidgeting I'm going to go mad."

"I wasn't—"

"You were."

They held each other's stare for a moment or two, narrow-eyed and quirky-browed.

She won.

"Fine." He got up. "I'll sit on the other side." He moved round to the far side of the bed and sat near the edge. She was right. It wasn't a particularly excellent bed. Still, it was a far cry better than the floor.

"Do you think it's strange," she asked once he was settled, "that we're having such an ordinary conversation?"

He glanced at her sideways. "Bickering about where to sit?"

"Well, yes, and talking about childhood pranks, and my brother's passing. I suppose that's rather sad, but it's certainly ordinary. It's not as if we were having great philosophical discussions about the meaning of—"

"Life?" he supplied.

She shrugged.

He turned so that he could see her without twisting his neck. "Do you *want* to spend the evening having great philosophical discussions?"

"Not really, but don't you think it seems as if we should? Given our precarious situation?"

He leaned back against the headboard and allowed just enough time to pass to give his next words the air of an announcement. "When I was in school they made us read this book."

She turned with her whole body, so curious was she at his abrupt change of subject.

"It was awful," he told her.

"What was it?"

He thought for a moment. "I don't even remember. That's how bad it was."

"Why did they make you read it?"

He shrugged one shoulder. "Someone once said it was important."

"Who gets to decide such things?" she wondered.

"Which books are important? I have no idea, but in this case, they made a grave mistake. I tell you, every word was torture."

"So you read it, then? The whole book?"

"I did. I hated every moment of it, but I read the blasted thing because I knew we would be quizzed upon it, and I did not wish to disappoint my father." He turned and looked at her with a dry expression. "That's a bloody bad reason to read a book, don't you think?"

"I suppose."

"A person should read a book because it speaks to something in his heart." Andrew said this with a passion that belied the fact that he'd never actually thought about this before. At least not in this way. "Because it fills a thirst for knowledge that is *his*, not that of some man in a tower two hundred years ago."

She regarded him for a moment, then said, "Why are we talking about this, exactly?"

"Because we shouldn't have to talk about whether the universe can fit into a man's soul if we don't want to."

"I do not," she said with wide eyes. "I truly do not."

"Good." He settled back into his position and they sat in silence for a bit. It was all rather peaceful and banal until she said—

"We might die."

"What?" Everything snapped—his voice, his head as he whipped around to face her. "Don't talk that way."

"I'm not saying we *will* die. But we could. Don't lie to me and deny it."

"We're worth too much," Andrew told her. "They won't kill us."

But did the men realize the prize they'd captured? Thus far, everything pointed to a normal (if there was such a thing) kidnapping. It was not inconceivable the Portuguese gang had seen two obviously well-to-do foreigners and figured that someone would be willing to pay a ransom for them.

But on the other hand, it was possible that someone had uncovered his role in the government. If that was the case, and the men holding them were politically motivated, then Andrew became a different sort of prize.

(And God only knew *which* politics might motivate them; there were fringe groups the world over who detested the British.)

Captain Andrew James was not entirely unknown in Lisbon. He had met with Robert Walpole—the British envoy—just that morning. He had employed no special subterfuge; he'd long since learned that on his sorts of missions, it was most effective to hide in plain sight. He put on his finer clothes, walked and talked like an aristocrat, and strolled right up to Mr. Walpole's home.

"They won't kill us," he said again. But he wasn't sure he meant it.

"I don't know if that's true," Poppy said.

Andrew blinked. "What?"

"What you said. About our being too valuable. We're only valuable if they know we're valuable."

"They know I have a ship in the harbor."

But then again, if they knew he carried secrets for the crown, they might see more value in his elimination than any riches he might bring.

"We really won't know anything until morning, will we?" she asked.

He sighed. "It's not likely. But as I told you, I think I may have convinced them to let you go."

She nodded.

"Do *not* insist upon staying with me," he added.

"I would never," Poppy said.

Andrew paused. "You wouldn't?"

"Of course not. How can I help you from within this prison? If I leave, I might be able to do something to get you out."

"Precisely." Andrew was pleased by her swift grasp of the situation, and yet at the same time slightly pricked that she was quite so eager to depart.

Still, if he did manage to get her out, she would *not* be returning to rescue him. He had connections in Lisbon who could get her back to England; he needed only to deliver her to them.

Or as the case would likely be, she needed to deliver herself.

He thought of all the causes he'd thought were worth dying for. Not a one of them meant a thing compared to the life of this woman.

Was this love? Could it be? All he knew was that he could no longer conceive of a future without her.

She was laughter.

She was joy.

And she might die because he'd been too bloody selfish to leave her on the ship.

He'd known it was safer to keep her on board. He'd *known* it, and still he'd brought her ashore.

He'd wanted to see her smile. No, it was far more selfish than that. He'd wanted to be her hero. He'd wanted her to look at him with worship in her eyes, to think the sun rose and set on his face.

He closed his eyes. He had to make this up to her. He had to *protect* her.

She wasn't his to protect, and now she might never be, but he would see her safe.

Even if it was the last thing he did.

ANDREW WAS NOT sure how long they sat in silence, resting side by side at the head of the bed. Every now and then he thought Poppy might say something— she would make one of those small but sharp and sudden moves, as if she were about to speak. Finally, just when he thought they'd settled into the stillness of the night, she spoke.

"Last night . . . I don't think I told you, but it was my first kiss."

He went still. He'd assumed as much, but it had seemed rude to ask, especially since she'd declared they would never speak of it again.

"Captain—"

"Andrew," he cut in. If indeed this was their last night, he was damn well going to spend it with someone who called him by his name.

"Andrew," she repeated, and it felt like she was trying it out on her tongue. "It suits you."

It seemed an odd thing to say. "You knew that was my name," he pointed out.

"I know. But it's different to say it."

He wasn't sure he understood what she meant by that. He wasn't sure she knew either. But it was important. Somehow they both knew that.

"You were talking about the kiss," he said quietly.

She nodded, and he could see tension in her throat as she swallowed. She was nervous; of course she was. He himself was terrified. This was not the first time he'd found himself in a dangerous situation. It was not even the first time he'd thought he might die.

But it was the first time he thought he might take an innocent soul with him.

"It was my first kiss," she said, "and it was lovely. But I know there's more."

"More?" he echoed. He cast a wary look at her.

"Not *more* more. I know a bit of that."

"You know a bit of . . . what?"

"Not *know* know."

"Dear God," he said under his breath.

"I know what happens between a husband and wife," she said, almost as if she wished to reassure him.

He could only stare. "I can't believe I'm about to say this, but are you trying to tell me that you *know* know?"

"Of course not!" She flushed; even in the dim light of their candle he could see that.

"Surely you can see my confusion."

"Honestly," she muttered, and he could not tell if she was embarrassed or chagrined.

He let out a breath. Surely this was the end of the conversation. He'd not led a saintly life, but he'd done nothing to deserve *this*.

But no. Poppy pressed her lips together, and in an uncharacteristically officious voice said, "My cousin told me."

He cleared his throat. "Your cousin told you."

She gave him an exasperated look. "Why do you keep repeating everything I say?"

Because he had a feeling he was going stark, raving—

"It's probably a sign of how much I do not wish to have this conversation," he said instead.

She ignored this. "My cousin Billie is married, and—"

He fought the urge to howl with bitter, inappropriate laughter. He knew Billie Bridgerton—Billie Rokesby now. She was his sister-in-law and one of his oldest friends.

"Billie is a woman," Poppy said, obviously misinterpreting the horror on Andrew's face. "It's a very unusual nickname, I know. But it suits her. Her given name is Sybilla."

"Of course it is," he muttered.

She looked at him with a queer expression. Or rather, she looked at him as if *he* had a queer expression. Which he undoubtedly did. He felt a little sick, to be honest. She was talking about Billie, and if there had ever been a time for him to tell her who he really was, this was it.

And yet he couldn't do it.

Or maybe he could.

Would it make her safer? Could the knowledge of his true identity somehow give her a tool that would help her get home? Or was the opposite true? Perhaps she was better left in the dark.

"Andrew. Andrew!"

He blinked.

"You're not listening to me. This is important."

Everything was important now. Every moment.

"My apologies," he said. "My thoughts are racing."

"As are mine!"

He took a moment to compose himself. It didn't work. He took a breath, then another, then adopted a bland expression and looked her in the eye. "How can I help you?" he said.

His resolute affability seemed to take her off guard. But only for a moment.

And then Andrew saw his downfall unfold on her face.

Was it possible that he'd once thought that he loved to watch her think? He was an idiot, clearly.

Her lips parted and then pursed. Her gaze flitted up and to the right as was so often her habit. She turned her head—not a tilt but a turn—to the side.

He'd seen her do all these things. He'd thought them enchanting. But now, as she turned back to look at him, her dark eyelashes sweeping up until her green gaze met his, he knew that his life was about to be forever altered.

"Kiss me," she said.

He froze.

"Please," she added, as if *that* were the reason he had made no response. "I know there is more to a kiss."

Her words hung in the air. It was like one of those awkward moments when all conversation stops, and one person is talking too loudly, and then everyone hears a shout.

Except Poppy had not been shouting.

"Isn't there?" she asked.

He didn't move. He couldn't even bring himself to nod.

"If I'm going to die, I'd like to have a proper kiss."

"Poppy," he finally managed to say. "I—"

She looked at him expectantly, and God help him, his gaze dropped to her lips.

The universal signal.

He wanted to kiss her *so* bad.

But he said, "This isn't a good idea."

"Of course it isn't. But I want to do it anyway."

So did he. But he wasn't going to.

One of them was insane. He was sure of it. He just didn't know which.

"Do you not *want* to kiss me?" she asked.

He nearly burst out in laughter at that. Not want to kiss her? At that moment he wanted it more than he wanted to *breathe*.

"I want— Bloody hell, Poppy, I want—" He swore, again, and the vehemence of it seemed to turn his head. He looked past his shoulder, down to the hardwood floor. His words, when he found them, felt ripped from his soul. "I've already wronged you in so many ways."

"Oh, *now* you're trying to be a gentleman."

"Yes," he practically barked. "Yes, I am. And my *God*, you're making it difficult."

She smiled.

"Don't," he warned.

"It's just a kiss," she said.

"That's your tactic now?" He mimicked her tone. "*It's just a kiss.*"

She deflated. "I'm sorry. I don't know what to say. I've never tried to convince a man to kiss me before."

Andrew closed his eyes and groaned. This need he felt for her—it had been simmering for days, a low, steady flame he knew how to control.

Until now.

He might be able to withstand her if they were back on the ship. Or if the flicker of the candlelight didn't send such tantalizing shadows dancing across her chest.

He could stay firm if they weren't sitting on a *bed*, for God's sake, if she had not turned to him with those perfect lips and endless green eyes and asked him to *kiss* her.

That slow burn . . . the one so quiet and constant he'd almost gotten used to it . . .

It wasn't quiet anymore.

"If I kiss you," he said, each word its own brand of torture, "I'm afraid I won't be able to stop."

"Of course you will," she said, almost brightly.

He could only stare. Was she trying to *reassure* him?

"You're a gentleman," she said, as if that were enough explanation for her. "You will stop the moment I ask you to."

He let out a rough, humorless laugh. "Is that what you think?"

"It's what I know."

It took a moment for him to realize that his head was shaking in disbelief. "You don't know what you're saying," he said hoarsely. Hell, he wasn't sure he knew what he was saying either. He barely knew what he was *thinking* right now.

But she was undeterred. "I know exactly what I'm saying, and I know *you*."

"Poppy . . ."

"Earlier today you said that I know you as well as anyone. I'm telling you, I know that you will stop the moment I ask you to."

And then, before he could formulate a reply, she said, "You will probably stop *before* I ask you to."

"*Christ*," he burst out, practically jumping off the bed. "You have no idea. No bloody idea. Do you know anything of what it means to be a man?"

"I might die," she whispered.

"That's no reason to barter away your innocence."

She climbed down from the bed and stood in front of him. "All I want is a kiss."

He grabbed her. Pulled her close. "It won't be just a kiss, Poppy. It could never be just a kiss between us."

And then—God help him—she whispered, "I know."

Chapter 21

$\mathcal{P}$oppy did not close her eyes.

She could not miss this moment. She would not. And indeed, she saw exactly when Andrew gave in, the very second he realized he could no longer deny her.

Or himself.

But if she saw that moment, she did not see the next. He moved so quickly, he literally stole her breath. One instant she was watching passion spark and flare in his eyes, and the next his mouth was on hers, fierce and hungry.

Relentless.

It was a kiss that made the other one—under the stars, on the deck of the *Infinity*—seem a different species.

If her first kiss had been magic, this one was a beast. Poppy felt enveloped, overwhelmed, almost overtaken.

He kissed her like a man possessed, maybe even like a man with nothing to lose.

His mouth was demanding, almost unforgiving, and whatever part of her that still retained sanity wondered if he was punishing her for having pushed him too far.

It should have scared her. His passion, finally unleashed, was a primal, dangerous thing.

But she felt dangerous too.

Reckless.

She felt *amazing*.

So she kissed him back. She had no idea what she was doing, but it seemed like instinct. All she knew was that she wanted more. More of his touch, more of his heat. More of *him*.

And so when his tongue swooped into her mouth and explored, she did the same with her own. When he nipped at her bottom lip, she nipped at his top. And when his hands slid down her back and cupped her bottom, hers did the same.

He drew back, almost smiling. "Are you copying me?"

"Shouldn't I?"

He squeezed, lightly.

So did she.

He brought one of his hands to her hair, winding a thick lock around his fist.

She sank both of her hands in his unruly mane, pulling him down for another kiss.

"You always were a quick study," he murmured against her lips.

She chuckled, loving the way it felt to laugh right into his skin. "You say that as if you've known me longer than a week."

"Is that all it's been?" He twisted them around

until Poppy's back was to the bed. "I think I've known you forever."

His words rang inside her, unlocking something she'd been afraid to examine. It did feel as if she'd known him forever, as if there were things she could say to him that she could not share with anyone else.

If she asked a silly question he might laugh, but only because he found joy in her curiosity, not because he thought her a curiosity herself.

He had secrets, of that she was certain, but she *knew* him. She knew the man within.

"How did you do that?" he murmured.

Poppy wasn't sure what he was asking, but she didn't care. She brought her arms back up to his neck, the motion causing her hips to tilt forward, pressing against his powerful thighs.

"Poppy," he moaned. "My God, Poppy."

"Andrew," she whispered. She'd used his name so infrequently. It felt like a caress on her lips.

"I love your hair," he said, using it to tug her face toward his. "Every night it was torture, watching you taking it down and braiding it."

"But I tried to do that when you weren't watching."

"*Tried*," he emphasized. "I'm a sneaky bastard. I couldn't decide how I liked it best. Down, so I could watch the play of light on every strand"—he dropped the lock in his hand, letting it bounce against her back—"or up, so I could imagine taking the pins out myself."

"What about the braid?"

"Oh, I loved that too. You have no idea how much I wanted to pull it."

"So you could dip it in a pot of ink?" she teased, remembering how her brothers had liked to do that to her.

"Now that would be a crime," he murmured. "Didn't I just tell you I love to watch all the colors?" He ran his fingers through her hair. Poppy couldn't imagine what he found so interesting, but he clearly loved it, and God help her, it made her feel beautiful.

"At first," he said, bringing the ends to his lips for a kiss, "I wanted to yank it because you were so . . . bloody . . . annoying."

"And now?"

He pulled her more tightly against him. "Now you vex me in a different way."

Poppy felt her body arch, instinctively seeking his heat. He was hard, and strong—every bit of him— and she felt the evidence of his desire pressing insistently against her belly.

She knew something of the mechanics of intercourse. As Andrew liked to tease, she was curious about everything. When her cousin Billie told her a little bit of what to expect when she married, Poppy had been confused enough that she asked for more details. Honestly, it had not made much sense the first time Billie had explained it.

But then, with a lot less embarrassment than Poppy would have predicted, Billie had explained that the male member changed when it became aroused. It lengthened, it grew harder. And then when it was done, it went back to normal.

Poppy had thought this most peculiar. Imagine if some part of *her* mutated when she felt passion or desire. She'd laughed at the thought of her ears suddenly developing points or her hair springing up into curls. Billie had laughed too, but it had been a different kind of laughter—not unkind, just different. She told Poppy that some things could not be explained, only experienced.

Poppy had been dubious, but now it almost made sense. She felt so different on the inside that it was impossible to believe she might be physically unchanged. Her breasts felt heavy, and yes, bigger. Her nipples had ruched into tight peaks, much like when the temperature dropped, and when his hand had skimmed across the material of her bodice, not even touching her skin, it had sent jolts of electricity to her very core.

That had not happened the last time she'd been cold.

She felt hungry . . . hungry at her core. She wanted to wrap her legs around him and pull him close. She wanted to feel that hardness pressed against her. She needed contact. She needed pressure.

She needed him.

As if he'd read her mind, his hands dipped past her bottom to the tops of her thighs, and he hoisted her up, only to then tumble her down upon the bed. He was above her in under a second, moving like a cat, predatory and sleek.

His eyes devoured her.

"Poppy," he groaned, and her heart soared at the sound of her name on his lips. It didn't seem to matter that he'd said it before; it felt different now, as if the two simple syllables had become part of the very structure of his kisses.

The weight of him pressed her into the mattress, and even though he was the one who had her pinned, she felt powerful. It was thrilling to think that she had brought him to this point. That she was the reason this unflappable man was nearly out of control.

And that power . . . it did something to her. It made her bold. It made her hungry.

It made her crave his touch, his strength.

She wanted to be as audacious as he was, to reach out and take what she wanted. But she didn't know—couldn't have known—where to start.

She wanted to learn.

She brought her eyes to his. "I want to touch you."

"Do it," he commanded.

He'd long since disposed of his cravat, and so she reached out and touched the warm skin of his neck, trailing her fingers along the tightly corded muscles that ran down to his shoulder.

He shuddered.

"Do you like that?" she whispered.

He moaned. "So much."

She caught her lip between her teeth, fascinated by his reaction. When her fingers dipped under the edge of his shirt, his body jerked. She started to pull away, but his hand immediately came to cover hers.

Their eyes met. *Don't go*, his seemed say.

Slowly, he lifted his hand, and she resumed her lazy exploration, drawing circles and scribbles on his skin. She could have done this all night, might even have tried to, but he let out a hoarse groan and pulled himself back.

He sat upright, straddling her as he yanked his shirt up and over his head.

Poppy stopped breathing.

He was beautiful.

He had the body of a man who used it, a man who worked, and worked hard. His muscles were exquisitely sculpted under his skin, and she could not help but wonder what movement had built each one.

"What are you thinking?" he whispered.

She looked up, only then realizing that she'd been staring at him.

"I was wondering how you got *this*." She laid her hand over his breast, marveling over the way the hard curve of his muscle filled her palm.

He sucked in his breath. "Jesus, Poppy."

"What sort of movement builds each muscle?" She moved her hand to his upper arm. It flexed beneath her fingers, the bulge of it sliding and changing shape under his skin.

Their eyes met again. *Keep going*, his seemed to say.

She drew lightly downward, over his elbow to the softer skin of his inner arm. "How does one get this sort of muscle?" she wondered, sliding around to the muscle just below his elbow. "Lifting a crate?"

"Gripping the wheel."

She looked up. He'd sounded breathless.

She'd made him sound that way. Again, she felt power.

She *was* power.

"Which do you use when lifting a crate?"

"My back," he murmured. "And my legs." He brought his hand to her upper arm, his long fingers nearly encircling it. "And this."

She looked down, mesmerized by the contrast between his skin and hers. He'd spent hours in the sun, and his skin had been burnished to a golden tan. The texture too told of time spent out of doors—in the wind, in the water. It was rough, and calloused. And beautiful.

"I like your hands," she said abruptly, taking one between both of hers.

"My hands?" He smiled, and his eyes crinkled at the corners.

"They're perfect," she said. "Large and square."

"Square?" He sounded amused, but in the best possible way.

"And *capable*." She brought his hand to her chest, placed it over her heart. "They make me feel safe."

He drew a shaky breath, and his touch seemed to grow heavier on her skin. His palm rotated, inching down her torso until his hand lay over her breast. He squeezed gently, and she moaned with surprised pleasure.

His eyes caught hers. "Are you asking me to stop?"

No.

"Not yet," she whispered.

She'd loosened her dress earlier, trying to make

herself more comfortable, and now, when he curled his finger under the edge of the bodice, the fabric slid easily over her shoulders.

"You're so beautiful," he whispered.

"So are—"

"Shhhh." He put a finger to her lips. "Do not contradict me. If I want to call you beautiful, I will do so without interruption."

"But—"

"Shush."

"I—"

His mouth found hers again, hungry and mischievous, nibbling at the edge of her lips as he murmured, "There are many ways to silence you, but none so pleasant as this."

Poppy had only wanted to say that he was beautiful too, but as he kissed his way down to the edge of her gown, it no longer seemed so imperative. And when she felt the fabric slide ever further down her body, almost baring her breasts, she could do nothing but arch her back to ease the way.

He looked up, his eyes hot but clear. "Do you want me to stop?"

No.

"Not yet," she whispered.

And then his lips found her, closing over the peak of her breast in a kiss more intimate than she could ever have dreamed. She gasped his name and arched off the bed, barely able to comprehend the electricity he seemed to spark within her.

He kissed and touched and stroked, and Poppy was helpless against his onslaught. He knew exactly where to kiss, exactly how to touch—firmly, gently, with his teeth. Everything he did brought pleasure—but it was an agonizing pleasure, because she needed more.

Something was building inside her.

"What are you doing to me?" she gasped.

He went still. Looked up. "Do you want me to stop?"

No.

"Not yet," she whispered.

And then his hand moved between her legs, touching her more intimately than she had ever done herself.

She was wet, unnaturally so—or so she thought. She nearly scooted out from under him, so embarrassed was she by the flood of moisture between her legs. But then he groaned and said, "You're so wet for me. So ready."

And she realized that maybe it wasn't so unnatural. Maybe it was what her body was supposed to do.

His fingers slid inside, and she gasped again. She knew this was where he would eventually join with her, but still, it was a surprise. She felt stretched, and tickled, and it was downright bizarre that someone might be able to touch her from the inside. Bizarre, and yet still . . . right.

"Do you like that?" he whispered.

She nodded. "I think so."

His fingers went still, but he did not pull them away. "You're not sure?"

"It's just very strange," she admitted.

He rested his forehead against hers, and though she could not see his expression at such close distance, she felt him smile. "That could be interpreted in many ways," he said.

"No, I . . . I like it. I just . . ." She could not remember the last time she'd been so inarticulate. But if she'd ever had cause, this was it. "It just feels like it is all moving forward and I don't know where. Or how."

He smiled again. She felt it.

"I know where," he said.

His words seemed to reach inside her body, arousing her from the inside out.

"And I know how." His lips found her ear. "Do you trust me?"

He should have known by now that she did, but she still was grateful that he asked. So she nodded, and then when she wasn't sure he saw, she said, "Yes."

He kissed her once, lightly on the mouth, and then his fingers began to move again. It was everything, and it wasn't enough, and when she gasped, he only seemed to redouble his efforts, bringing her closer . . .

And closer . . .

"Andrew?" She sounded panicked. She hadn't meant to sound panicked. But she didn't know what was happening. Her body was no longer her own.

"Just let go," he murmured.

"But—"

"Let go, Poppy."

She did.

Something inside her clenched and then burst open, and she had no idea what had just happened to her, but she rose off the bed with enough power to lift him with her.

She could not speak.

She did not breathe.

She was suspended . . . transformed.

Then she collapsed.

She still could not speak, but at least now she was breathing. It took a moment for her eyes to focus, but when they did, she saw Andrew gazing down at her, smiling like a cat in cream.

He looked very proud of himself.

"I saw stars," she said.

This made him chuckle.

"Actual stars. On the insides of my eyelids, but still." She closed her eyes again. "They're gone now."

His chuckle grew, and he flopped down onto the bed beside her, shaking the mattress with his mirth.

Poppy lay boneless. She had no words to describe what had just happened, although if she thought about it, *I saw stars* came pretty close.

"Not bad for a first kiss," Andrew said.

"Second kiss," she murmured.

It made him laugh. She loved to make him laugh.

She turned to look at him. His beautiful chest was illuminated by the candlelight, and he was watching her with a tenderness that made her long for something more.

She wanted time.

She wanted more time right now, but mostly she wanted a guarantee of tomorrow.

She reached out to touch his shoulder, and he sucked in his breath at the contact.

"Did I hurt you?" she asked, confused.

"No, I'm just . . . a little . . ." He adjusted his position. "Uncomfortable."

Poppy frowned at the cryptic words, until—

She swallowed awkwardly. How selfish she was. "You didn't . . ."

She couldn't finish the sentence. He would know what she meant.

"It's all right," he said.

She wasn't sure that it was, though. If this was their final night on earth, shouldn't he get to experience the same pleasure that she had?

"You . . ." She had no idea how to say this, wasn't even sure if she meant it. "Maybe I—"

"*Poppy.*"

There was something in his voice. She went silent.

"There is a chance that you will reach safety and I won't," he said.

"Don't say that," she whispered, tugging her dress back over her shoulders. She sat up. This was the sort of conversation for which one ought to be upright. "We are *both* going to escape."

Or neither, she thought. But she would not give voice to that. Not now.

"I'm sure that's true," he said in a tone that she knew was meant to reassure. "But I'll not leave you with an illegitimate child."

Poppy swallowed and nodded, wondering why she felt so hollow when he had done exactly what she'd asked of him. He'd shown far more sense and restraint than she had. Just as she'd predicted, he had stopped *before* she'd asked him to. He had known, even when she did not, that if he had pressed forward, she would not have refused him.

She would have welcomed it and hang the consequences.

She could no longer deny the truth exploding in her heart. She loved him. And even now, knowing that she might indeed reach safety without him, some very impractical corner of her heart wanted to take a piece of him with her.

Her hand went to her abdomen, to the spot where there was most assuredly *not* a child.

"It turns out you were right about me," Andrew said. His lips curved into a tiny smile, but he sounded sad. Sad and ironic.

Regretful.

"I am a gentleman," he said. "And I will not compromise you if I cannot give you the protection of my name."

Poppy James. She could be Poppy James.

It was strange to her ears, and yet somehow lovely.

Maybe not impossible.

But not likely.

"Poppy, listen to me," Andrew said, his voice taking on a new, sudden urgency. "I'm going to give you an address. You must memorize it."

Poppy nodded. She could do that.

"It is the home of the British envoy."

"The Brit—"

"Please," he said, holding up a hand. "Let me finish. His name is Mr. Walpole. You must go alone and tell him I sent you."

She stared at him in disbelief. "You know the British envoy?"

He nodded once, curtly.

Her lips parted, and the silence between them stretched taut. "You're not just a ship's captain, are you?"

His eyes met hers. "Not just, no."

She had a hundred questions. And a thousand theories. She was not sure if she was angry—or if she was, whether she even had a right to be. After all, why would he have told her about his secret life? She'd come aboard as a prisoner. He'd had no reason to trust her until recently.

But still, it pricked.

She waited, holding her tongue for a moment or two, hoping he would elaborate. But he did not.

When she finally spoke, her words felt stiff. "What else should I tell him?"

"Everything that has happened since we docked," he said. "Tell him precisely what happened at the Taberna da Torre. To me, to you, to Senhor Farias and Billy. Everyone."

She nodded.

He got out of bed and pulled on his shirt. "You must also tell him who you are."

"What? No! I don't want anyone to know who—"

"Your name carries weight," he said sharply. "If ever there was a time you must use it, it is now."

She got down from the bed; it felt awkward to be so indolent while he was pacing about the room. "Won't it be enough that I'm a gentlewoman?"

"Probably. But the Bridgerton name will lend greater urgency to the matter."

She acquiesced. "Very well." It could end in disaster for her, but if it meant Andrew had a greater chance of rescue, she would tell the British envoy who she was.

"Good," Andrew said briskly. "Now listen, there is one more thing you must say."

She looked at him expectantly.

"You must say that you long for blue skies."

"Blue skies?" Poppy gave a dubious frown. "Why?"

Andrew's eyes bore down on hers. "What will you say to him?"

"Is it some sort of code? It must be a code."

He closed the distance between them and his hands landed heavily on her shoulders, forcing her to look up at him. "What will you say to him?" he repeated.

"Stop! Fine. I'll say that I long for blue skies."

He nodded, slowly, and with something that almost looked like relief.

"But what does it mean?" she asked.

He didn't say anything.

"Andrew, you can't expect me to deliver a message when I don't know what it means."

He started tucking his shirt into his breeches. "I do it all the time."

"*What?*"

He shot her a glance over his shoulder. "Do you think I know what was in the packet of papers I gave to the British envoy yesterday?"

Her mouth fell open. "*That's* what you—"

"Do you think I ever know?" He started pulling on his boots, and Poppy could only stare. How could he act as if all of this was *normal*?

"How often do you do this?" she asked.

"Often enough."

"And you're not curious?"

He'd been tying his cravat, his fingers expertly looping and tucking the fabric. But at this he went still. "My job—no, my duty—is to transport documents and carry messages. Why do you think I could not delay our departure for Portugal? It wasn't about *me*. It was never about me."

He had to deliver a message. He was working for the government. Poppy's brain was spinning. Everything was starting to make sense.

"This is how I serve my country," he said. "It is what you must do, as well."

"You're telling me that I am somehow doing a service to the crown by telling a man I've never met that I long for blue skies?"

He looked her straight in the eye. "Yes."

"I . . ." She looked down. She was wringing her hands. She hadn't realized it.

"Poppy?"

She let out a long breath. "I will do as you ask. But I must warn you. I don't think I will be able to lead him back. I'm sure I will be blindfolded again when they take me back to the ship."

"You won't need to. When you are released you'll be given some sort of message from the men holding us. Give it to Mr. Walpole. He will know what to do from there."

"And then what will I do?"

"Keep yourself safe."

Poppy felt her jaw clamp into a rigid vise. It was not in her nature to sit idly by when she could be helpful, but in such a situation, she had to wonder— *could* she be helpful? Or would she just get in the way?

"Do not do something stupid, Poppy," he warned. "As God is my witness—"

"I can barely fire a rifle," she said testily. "I'm not going to come swishing back with delusions of saving you myself."

He smiled a bit at that.

"What?"

"I'm just imagining you swishing. I'm not sure what it is."

She glared at him.

"Listen to me." He took her hand. "I appreciate your concern more than I could ever say. And without you—without your going to see the envoy—my situation would be very bleak. But you must not do more than that."

"I know," she mumbled. "I would be in the way."

He did not contradict her. She had kind of hoped he would.

"Poppy," he said, his voice urgent, "I—"

They both froze at the sound of heavy footsteps on the stairs. Their captors were coming back, earlier than they'd expected.

Andrew dropped her hand and took a step back. His demeanor changed, as if his every muscle had been put on alert. His eyes darted to the door, and then to Poppy, then did a quick sweep of the room before landing on her little half boots, on their sides by the table where she'd kicked them off hours before. He scooped them up and handed them to her. "Put them on."

She did. Quickly.

The footsteps drew close, followed by the sound of a key being inserted into the lock.

Poppy turned to Andrew. She was terrified. More than she'd been throughout the entire ordeal.

"I will get out of here," he vowed, even as the doorknob made an ominous turn. "And I will find you."

And then all Poppy could do was pray.

IN THE END, it was simple. Terrifying, but simple. Minutes after the bandits came back, Poppy was blindfolded and returned to the *Infinity*. The journey took no more than a quarter of an hour; it seemed Andrew had been right about their circuitous route the day before.

It was still dark when she reached the ship, but the deck was already teeming with sailors, more than Poppy would have expected so early in the morning. But this was no ordinary morning. Their captain had been taken prisoner, and they had to be ready for anything.

The first person she saw was Green, which was fortunate, since he was one of only three people on board she actually knew. He and Brown insisted upon escorting her to the address Andrew had provided, and after a quick check on Billy, who was still groggy but otherwise recuperating, Poppy headed back out into the city.

"D'you think they're watching us?" Brown asked, his bushy brows drawing down as he flicked his eyes from one side of the street to the other. The sun had only just come up, the pinkish light casting a mysterious air over the city.

"Probably," Poppy said. "Captain James told them that I would need to meet with someone to secure the funds. So they're not expecting me to remain on board."

"I don't like it," Brown muttered.

Neither did Poppy, but she didn't see how she had a choice.

"This is what the captain told her to do," Green said. "If he told her to do this, then he must've had a reason."

"He indicated that the gentleman I'm going to see would be able to help," Poppy said.

Green looked at Brown with one eyebrow raised and an expression on his face that clearly said, *See?*

"I don't like it," Brown said again.

"I didn't say I *did*," Green returned.

"Well, you sounded like—"

"None of us like it," Poppy snapped.

They both looked at her.

She planted her hands on her hips. "Am I wrong?"

"Er, no," one of them mumbled, while the other said, "No, no, not wrong at all."

"Should we take a funny route?" Green asked. "Take 'em round in circles and whatnot?"

"Maybe," Poppy said. "I don't know. It's probably just as important that we deliver the message quickly." She thought of Andrew, of the men still holding him, all of them with guns, knives, and unpleasant dispositions. "Straight there," she decided. "As quickly as we can."

A quarter of an hour later, Poppy was standing in front of a gray stone building in a quietly elegant section of the city. "This is it," she said. She had already made it clear to Brown and Green that they could not accompany her inside.

"Good-bye, then," she said after thanking them once again for their assistance. She took a breath. She could do this.

"Er, Miss Poppy!" Brown called out.

She paused halfway up the steps, and turned.

"Good luck," he said. "If anyone can save him, it's you."

She blinked, startled by the unexpected compliment.

"You're tough," he said. "Er, in a good way."

"Mr. Farias told us what you did for Billy," Green said. "It's . . . ehrm . . . You . . ."

Brown let out an exasperated snort. "He means thank you."

Green nodded. "God will surely look kindly on you. It was a proper good thing you did."

"And we're sorry about the sack," Brown added. "And the, er . . ." He motioned toward his mouth. "The stuff. You know, that we used to . . ."

She gave him a wry smile. "Render me unconscious?"

His already ruddy cheeks turned a bright red as he mumbled, "Yes, that."

"It is already forgotten," she said. Which wasn't *exactly* the truth, but considering everything that had happened after, it hardly seemed of consequence. "Now, go." She shooed them away. "You can't be seen loitering on the streets when I knock."

They stepped reluctantly away, and then Poppy was truly on her own. The door was opened mere seconds after she brought the knocker down on its brass plate, and she was immediately taken to wait in a small but comfortable drawing room. After a few minutes, a gentleman entered.

She stood at once. "Mr. Walpole?"

He regarded her with some aloofness. "I am he."

"My name is Poppy Bridgerton. I was told to come see you by Captain Andrew James."

He did not react at her mention of either name—hers or Andrew's—and in fact seemed almost bored as he walked over to the sideboard to pour a glass of brandy.

Poppy did not remark upon the earliness of the hour. If he thought he needed brandy before breakfast, who was she to argue?

He held out an empty glass, tipping it in her direction.

"No, thank you," she said impatiently. "It's really most important that—"

"So you spoke with Captain James," he said, his voice pleasantly bland.

"Yes," she said. "He needs your help."

She told him everything. There was nothing in his demeanor that encouraged such frankness, but Andrew had told her to trust him.

And she trusted Andrew.

At the end of the tale, she handed Mr. Walpole the note she'd been given by the bandits. "It's written in Portuguese," she said.

His brows rose. "You opened it?"

"No one told me not to." At Mr. Walpole's censorious look, she muttered, "It's not as if it was sealed."

Mr. Walpole's mouth tightened, but he said no more on the subject. Poppy watched as he read the missive, his eyes moving from left to right six times before reaching the end.

"Will you be able to help him?" she asked.

He refolded the note, creasing it much more sharply than before.

"Mr. Walpole?" She wasn't sure how much more of this she could tolerate. The man was all but ignoring her. Then she remembered Andrew's most urgent directive.

She cleared her throat. "I was told to tell you that I long for blue skies."

The envoy's head snapped up. "That's what he said?"

Poppy nodded.

"That's what he said *exactly*?"

"Yes. He made me repeat it."

Mr. Walpole swore under his breath. Poppy blinked with surprise. He had not seemed the type. Then he looked up as if a thought had just occurred to him. "And you said your name is Bridgerton?"

"Have you even been listening to me?"

"You are related to the viscount?"

"He is my uncle."

Mr. Walpole swore again, this time not even trying to muffle it. Poppy watched him warily as he muttered to himself, seemingly trying to work out a problem in his head.

Finally, just when she was about to say something, he strode to the door, wrenched it open, and yelled, "Martin!"

The butler appeared immediately.

"Escort Miss Bridgerton to the yellow bedroom. Lock the door. Under no circumstances is she to leave."

"What?" Poppy wasn't sure what she'd expected the British envoy to do, but it wasn't this.

Mr. Walpole gave her a quick glance before heading out the door. "It's for your own good, Miss Bridgerton."

"No! You can't— Stop that!" she snarled when the butler took hold of her arm.

He sighed. "I really don't want to hurt you, miss."

She shot him a belligerent look. "But you will?"

"If I have to."

Poppy closed her eyes in defeat. She was exhausted. She hadn't the energy to fight him, and even if she had, he outweighed her by at least six stone.

"It's a nice room, miss," the butler said. "You'll be comfortable there."

"All my prisons are comfortable," Poppy muttered.

But they were prisons, nonetheless.

Chapter 22

A few weeks later

It was strange, Poppy thought, how so much could change in a month.

And yet nothing changed at all.

She was changed. She was not the same person who had attended soirees in London and explored caves on the Dorset coast. She would never be that girl again.

But to the rest of the world, she was the same as she ever was. She was Miss Poppy Bridgerton, niece to the influential viscount and viscountess. She was a well-bred young lady, not the biggest matrimonial catch (it was her uncle with the title, after all, not her father, plus she'd never had a massive dowry), but still, a good prospect for any young man looking to make his mark.

No one knew that she'd gone off to Portugal.

No one knew she'd been kidnapped by pirates.

Or by a gang of Portuguese bandits.

Or, for that matter, by the British envoy to Portugal.

No one knew that she'd met a dashing sea captain who should have been an architect, or that he'd probably saved her life, and she might have sacrificed his.

Bloody British government. Mr. Walpole had made it clear that she was to keep her mouth shut when she returned to England. Indiscreet questions could hamper his efforts to rescue Captain James, he'd told her. Poppy had asked how that was possible, given that Captain James was in Portugal and she would be in England.

Mr. Walpole found nothing to celebrate in her curiosity. In fact he had said to her, "I find nothing to celebrate in your curiosity."

To which Poppy had replied, "What does that even *mean*?"

"Just keep your mouth shut," he had ordered her. "Hundreds of lives depend upon it."

Poppy rather suspected this was an exaggeration, possibly even an outright lie. But she could not take that chance.

Because *Andrew's* life might depend upon it.

When Poppy had knocked on Mr. Walpole's door, she had never dreamed that she would be shuttled out of Portugal before learning of Andrew's fate. But the envoy had wasted no time returning her to England. He'd got her onto a ship the very next day, and five days after that she was deposited at the Royal Dockyards in Chatham with a purse holding enough money to hire a carriage to take her to Lord and Lady Bridgerton's home in Kent. She supposed she could have gone all the way home, but it was only a two-hour journey to Aubrey Hall, and Poppy was certainly not equipped to make an unchaperoned overnight stop at an inn on the road to Somerset.

It should have been amusing that she was worried about *that* when she had spent six days as the only female on a ship to Lisbon.

And then a night alone with Captain James.

Andrew. Surely he was now Andrew to her.

If he was even still alive.

It had taken a few days and more than a few lies for Poppy to sort out all of the details—or rather, the lack of details—regarding her two-week absence, but her cousins now thought she'd been with Elizabeth, Elizabeth thought she'd been with her cousins, and to her parents she'd sent a breezily ambiguous letter informing them that she'd accepted Aunt Alexandra's invitation after all and would be in Kent for an unspecified amount of time.

And if anyone doubted any of that, they weren't asking. At least not yet.

Her cousins were blessedly tactful, but eventually their curiosity would win out. After all, Poppy had arrived—

Unexpectedly.

With no luggage.

And wearing a wrinkled, ill-fitting frock.

All things considered, Poppy supposed she should be grateful it had fit as well as it had. Her blue dress had been beyond repair by the time she reached

Mr. Walpole; a housemaid had to be sent out to purchase something ready-made to replace it. It was nothing Poppy would have picked out for herself, but it was clean, which was a whole lot more than Poppy could have said for herself at that moment.

"Oh, there you are!"

Poppy looked up to see her cousin Georgiana on the far side of the garden. Georgie was only one year younger than Poppy, but she had somehow managed to avoid a Season in London. Aunt Alexandra had said it was due to Georgie's delicate health, but aside from a pale complexion, Poppy had never seen anything particularly sickly about her.

Case in point: Georgie was presently striding across the lawn at a fierce clip, beaming as she approached. Poppy sighed. The last thing she wanted just then was to sit and have a conversation with someone so obviously cheerful.

Or any conversation, really.

"How long have you been out here?" Georgie asked once she'd sat down at Poppy's side.

Poppy shrugged. "Not long. Twenty minutes, perhaps. Maybe a little more."

"We have been invited to Crake for dinner this evening."

Poppy nodded absently. Crake House was the home of the Earl of Manston. It was just a mile or so away. Her cousin—Georgie's older sister Billie— lived there. She had married the earl's heir.

"Lady Manston has returned from her trip to London," Georgie explained. "And she's brought Nicholas."

Poppy nodded some more, just to show she was listening. Nicholas was the youngest Rokesby son. Poppy didn't think she'd ever met him. She hadn't met any of the Rokesby sons, actually, except for Billie's husband, George. She thought there were four of them. Or maybe five.

She didn't really wish to go out to dinner, even if it would be nice to see Billie. Supper on a tray in her room sounded so much easier. And besides—

"I haven't anything to wear," she told Georgie.

Georgie's blue eyes narrowed. Poppy had woven a compelling tale (if she did say so herself) to explain her lack of luggage upon her arrival, but she had a feeling Georgie found the whole story *most* suspicious.

Georgiana Bridgerton was a lot shrewder than her family seemed to give her credit for. Poppy could easily imagine her sitting in her room, throwing mental darts at Poppy's story, just to find the holes.

It wasn't that Georgie was malicious. She was just curious.

A malady with which Poppy was well-acquainted.

"Don't you think your trunk should have arrived by now?" Georgie asked.

"I do," Poppy said with wide-eyed earnestness. "I'm shocked, in fact, that it hasn't."

"Maybe you should have taken the other lady's trunk."

"That doesn't seem fair. I don't think she took mine on purpose. And anyway"—Poppy leaned in with a bit of a smirk—"her taste in clothing was abysmal."

Georgie eyed her skeptically.

"It's better this way," Poppy said blithely. "The coaching company said they would find her and make the switch."

She had no idea if the coaching company would behave with such largesse; likely they would tell her it was her own fault for not noticing that someone had taken her trunk. But Poppy didn't have to convince the coaching company, just her cousins.

"Lucky for me we're of a size," she said to Georgie. In actuality Poppy was an inch taller, but as long as they did not socialize, she could get away without adding lace to the hems of Georgie's gowns.

"You don't mind, do you?" Poppy asked.

"Of course not. I just think it's strange."

"Oh, it is. It absolutely is."

Georgie's face took on a thoughtful expression. "You don't feel somewhat . . . rootless?"

"Rootless?" It was probably an innocent question, but Poppy was so tired, so just plain exhausted of trying to keep her stories straight. And it wasn't like Georgie to wax philosophical, at least not with Poppy.

"I don't know," Georgie mused. "Not that *things* should be the measure of a person, but I can't help but think it must be disorienting to be separated from one's belongings."

"Yes," Poppy said slowly. "It is." And yet, what she wouldn't give to be back aboard the *Infinity*, where she'd had nothing but the clothes on her back.

And Andrew. For a brief moment, she'd had him too.

"Poppy?" Georgie asked with some alarm. "Are you crying?"

"Of course not," Poppy sniffled.

"It's all right if you are."

"I know." Poppy turned to brush away something on her cheek that was *not* moisture. "But it doesn't matter because I'm not."

"Ehrm . . ." Georgie seemed not to know what to do when confronted with a crying female. And why would she, Poppy thought. Her only sister was the indomitable Billie Rokesby, who once rode a horse *backward*, for heaven's sake. Poppy was fairly certain Billie had never cried a day in her life.

As for Poppy, she wasn't sure when she'd shed a tear. She had been so proud of herself for not crying when she'd been hauled aboard the *Infinity*. At first, she supposed it was just because she was so bloody angry—the rage had blotted out everything else. After that, it was more because she refused to make such a show of weakness in front of Andrew.

She'd wagged her finger and told him he should thank his lucky stars that she wasn't a crying sort of female. Now she almost laughed at that. Because all she wanted to do was cry.

And yet somehow the tears never came.

She felt as if everything inside her had been scooped out and left somewhere far, far behind. Maybe Portugal, maybe the Atlantic, thrown overboard on the miserable journey home. All she knew was that here, in England, she was numb.

"Hollow," she whispered.

Beside her, Georgie turned. "Did you say something?"

"No," Poppy said, because how could she explain it? If she told Georgie what she was feeling, she'd have to tell her *why*.

Georgie didn't believe her; *that* was easy enough to see. But Georgie didn't press, and instead she said, "Well, if you ever decide that you *are* crying, I am happy to . . . do . . . whatever it is you need."

Poppy smiled at her cousin's awkward attempt at solace. She reached out and squeezed Georgie's hand. "Thank you."

Georgie nodded, recognizing that Poppy didn't wish to talk about it, at least not yet. She glanced up at the sky, shading her eyes even though the sun was mostly obscured by clouds. "You should probably come in soon. I think it's going to rain."

"I like the fresh air," Poppy said. She'd been stuck in her cabin on the way back to England too. Mr. Walpole had been in too much of a rush to find her an English-speaking chaperone, so she had traveled with the same Portuguese housemaid who had picked out her dress. And her sister, since the housemaid couldn't very well travel back to Lisbon on her own.

Regardless, both girls refused to step foot outside their cabin. Which meant Poppy was shut in too. Mr. Walpole had assured her that the captain could be trusted with her safety and virtue, but after all that had happened, she hadn't wanted to risk it.

The food hadn't been as good as on the *Infinity* either.

And she didn't know what had happened to Andrew. Mr. Walpole had told her she *wouldn't* know either. "You will be well on your way back to England, Miss Bridgerton. He will not follow for some time, I imagine."

If ever. He did not include that in the sentence, but it had hung heavily in the air.

"But even then," she'd pressed, "for my peace of mind. Will you send word? James is a very common surname. It would be impossible for me to find out on my own . . ."

She'd trailed off at his look of disdain.

"Miss Bridgerton. Do you really think that his surname is truly James?" At her blank look, he'd continued, "This is in service to your king. You have already been told never to breathe a word of this. For you to go searching for a man who does not exist would draw what I am sure is unwanted attention to these weeks that will undoubtedly be questionable in your calendar."

As set-downs went, it was blistering, but when he'd delivered his next sentence, all energy for retort washed out of her.

"It is unlikely you will ever see Captain James again."

"But—"

Mr. Walpole silenced her with a mere gesture. "Whether we extricate him or not, it will be in the interest of national security that he not go looking for you. And whether you are inept at following orders is irrelevant, Miss Bridgerton, because I assure you he is not."

She had not believed it. No, she had not *wanted* to believe it. Andrew had said he would escape. He said he would find her.

But she wasn't that hard to find. So either he was dead—which she could hardly bear to contemplate—or everything Mr. Walpole had said was true, and she would never see him again.

He followed orders. She knew that he did—it was why he'd taken her to Portugal instead of clearing out the cave and leaving her in Charmouth. It was why he did not read the messages he carried.

It was why he would not come for her even if he wanted to.

And why she had no idea whom she was so angry with—him, for sending her away even though she knew it was the right thing to do; Mr. Walpole, for making it so painfully clear that she would never see Andrew again; or herself.

Because she felt so damn helpless.

"Were you outside last night?" Georgie asked.

Poppy turned lethargically toward her cousin. "Just looking at the stars."

"I thought I saw someone from my window. I had not realized you were a student of astronomy."

"I'm not. I just like looking at the stars." They hadn't been as brilliant as out at sea, though. Or maybe it was just that the sky seemed to hold more power and sway when one stood on the deck of a ship, face tipped to the heavens.

Andrew's hands had been on her hips. She had felt the heat of his body, the strength of it.

But she hadn't understood.

So much. There was so much she hadn't understood.

And now . . . It was laughable, really. Here she was, lamenting her younger, innocent self as if she were such a lady of experience. She still knew nothing. Almost nothing.

"Well, I'm going to go in," Georgie said as she rose to her feet. "I want to have enough time to dress for dinner. Are you coming?"

Poppy started to say no; dinner wasn't for several more hours, and she felt no great need to fuss over her appearance. But Georgie was right—it did look as if it might rain. And as hopeless and numb as she felt right then, she had no wish to catch her death in a downpour.

"I'll come with you," she said.

"Wonderful!" Georgie linked her arm through Poppy's, and they began their stroll back to the house.

Dinner with the neighbors was a good idea, Poppy decided. She didn't *want* to go, but what she wanted lately hadn't seemed to make her feel any better. She'd have to put on a good front, pretend she was happy and cheerful and the same Poppy she'd always been. Maybe if she tried hard enough, she'd start to believe it.

She turned to Georgie as they walked past the gazebo. "Who did you say was coming to dinner?"

ANDREW WAS EXHAUSTED.

It had taken almost two weeks for Robert Walpole to extricate him from the house on the hill. During that time he'd been mostly ignored, but he had not slept well. Nor had he been given much to eat.

He did not know how long it would take for him to regain his full strength, but recuperation would have to wait.

He needed to find Poppy.

His original plan had been to bypass his home in Kent and head straight to Dorset, where he assumed she had returned to the home of Elizabeth Armitage. If Poppy had already gone home, it was an easy journey from there to Somerset.

But the *Infinity* had been ordered back to England without him, and no one in Lisbon was sailing to Dorset. The quickest journey would be to Margate, which was close enough to Crake House that it would be foolish not to stop there first. He could reach Poppy much faster on a mount from the Rokesby stables than he could in a carriage hired at the port.

And as eager as he was to find her, the notion of a bath and a fresh change of clothing had obvious appeal.

It had started to rain by the time he was dropped off at the end of the drive to Crake, so he was somewhat damp and squishy when he let himself in through the front door. He had not a clue who might be home. His mother never stayed in London this far into summer, but she'd been known to gad about the countryside visiting friends. His older brothers were probably home—George lived at Crake with Billie and their three children, and Edward was just a few miles away with his brood.

No one was in the entry when he walked in, so he set his wet hat on a table and took a moment to take in his surroundings. It seemed almost surreal to be here, in his home, after such a tumultuous few weeks. There had been several moments that he'd feared were his last, and even after his rescue, he'd not been able to enjoy any of life's luxuries. The bandits had not, in fact, turned out to be politically motivated, but they were part of a larger syndicate, powerful enough that Robert Walpole had advised Andrew to keep his head down until he departed Lisbon.

And never return. Walpole was clear about that. Captain Andrew James might be an important courier for the crown, but he could no longer count on aid and protection on the Iberian Peninsula.

It was time to go home, but more than that, it was time to *stay* home.

"Andrew!"

He grinned. He'd know that voice anywhere. "Billie," he said warmly, enveloping his sister-in-law in a hug. She wouldn't care if he got her wet. "How are you?"

"How am *I*? How are *you*? We've seen neither hide nor hair of you in months." She gave him a cautioning glance. "Your mother is displeased."

Andrew winced.

"You *should* be afraid," she said.

"You don't think the joy of my unexpected arrival will soften her temper?"

"For an hour, perhaps. Then she'll remember your lack of correspondence."

"There were extenuating circumstances."

"I'm not the one you need to convince," Billie said with a shake of her head. "I hope you're not planning to leave anytime soon."

"I *was* going to go tonight—"

"*What?*"

"I'd already decided otherwise," he told her. "I'll wait until morning. I don't relish riding in the rain."

"Would you like my advice?"

"Is there any way I can prevent you from giving it?"

"Of course not."

"Then I would be delighted."

She rolled her eyes at his sarcasm. "Don't tell your mother you were thinking of leaving this evening. In fact, I'd avoid mentioning your morning departure if at all possible."

"You know it will be the third thing she asks."

"After 'How are you?' and 'Why haven't you written?'"

He nodded.

She shrugged. "I wish you luck, then."

"You are a cruel woman, Billie Rokesby."

"You would never have escaped before dinner in any case. Nicholas is down from London. Everyone is coming to dine."

Everyone surely included the Bridgertons. Andrew supposed his delay wasn't a complete loss. He might be able to get some information about Poppy. Her whereabouts, for example.

Or if she'd been ensnared in a scandal.

He'd have to figure out the best way to get them to talk about her. As far as anyone knew, he did not even know she existed.

"Is everything all right, Andrew?"

He blinked, startled by Billie's query. She'd placed her hand on his arm and was watching him with an expression of curiosity. Or maybe concern.

"Of course," he said. "Why?"

"I don't know. You just seem different, that's all."

"Thinner," he confirmed.

She did not look convinced, but she did not press him further. "Well," she said briskly, "your mother is at the vicarage. She was up in London for a few days, but she returned yesterday."

"Is Nicholas home?" Andrew asked. It had been far too long since he'd seen his younger brother.

"Not at this precise moment, no. He and George went off for a ride with your father. But they should all be back soon. Dinner is at seven, so they won't be much longer."

Speaking of which . . .

"I should clean up before dinner," Andrew said.

"Go on up to your room," Billie said. "I'll see about having a bath drawn."

"I am not certain I can adequately express how heavenly that sounds."

"Go," Billie said with a smile. "I will see you at dinner."

A good meal, a good sleep, Andrew thought as he headed upstairs. It was exactly what he needed before heading out in the morning for a good woman.

His good woman.

His Poppy.

"DARLING, ARE YOU sure you're feeling well enough for dinner?"

Poppy turned to Lady Bridgerton, grateful that the dim lighting in the carriage prevented the older woman from seeing just how wan her smile was. "I'm well, Aunt," she said. "Just tired."

"I cannot imagine why. We have done nothing requiring any great exertions recently, have we?"

"Poppy took a walk today," Georgie said. "A really, really long one."

Poppy looked at her cousin with surprise. Georgie knew quite well that Poppy had not taken a long walk that day. She'd barely made it to the far end of the garden.

"I did not realize that," Lady Bridgerton said. "I do hope you were not caught out in the rain."

"No, I was most fortunate," Poppy said. It had begun to rain about an hour after she and Georgie returned to Aubrey Hall. Just a sprinkle at first, but it had been growing in intensity ever since. The smack of the drops against the carriage was almost too loud for conversation.

"Helen will have footmen waiting with umbrellas," Lady Bridgerton assured her. "We will not get very wet going from carriage to house."

"Will Edmund and Violet be there?" Georgie asked.

"I'm not sure," her mother replied. "Violet is getting very near to the end of her confinement. I imagine it depends on how she feels."

"I'm sure she's fine," Georgie said. "She loves being pregnant."

"Have they thought of a name?" Poppy asked. Her cousin Edmund had married quite young—he was barely nineteen at his wedding. But he and his bride were wildly happy by all accounts and currently expecting their second child. They lived close to Aubrey Hall, in a charming manor house given to them as a wedding gift from Edmund's parents.

"Benedict if it's a boy," Lady Bridgerton said. "Beatrice for a girl."

"How very Shakespearean," Poppy murmured. Benedick and Beatrice were the lovers from *Much Ado About Nothing*. She'd quoted Balthasar's song from that very play when she and Andrew had had their battle of the Shakespearean quotes.

It was ridiculous how much fun that had been.

"Bene*dict*," Georgie said. "Not Benedick."

"Sigh no more," Poppy murmured. "Sigh no more."

Georgie gave her a sideways glance. "Men were deceivers ever?"

"Not all men," came a grumble from the opposite corner.

Poppy jerked with surprise. She'd quite forgotten Lord Bridgerton was there.

"I thought you were sleeping," Lady Bridgerton said, patting her husband on the knee.

"I was," he said with a *hmmph*. "I'd like to be still."

"Were we so very loud, Uncle?" Poppy inquired. "I'm sorry that we woke you."

"It's just the rain," he said, waving away her apology. "Makes my joints ache. Was that Shakespeare you were reciting?"

"From *Much Ado About Nothing*," Poppy said.

"Well . . ." He rolled his hand in the air, urging her on. "Have at it."

"You want me to recite it?"

He looked at Georgie. "Do you know it?"

"Not in its entirety," she admitted.

"Then yes," he said, turning back to Poppy. "I want you to recite it."

"Very well." She swallowed, trying to melt the lump that had started to form in her throat.

"*Sigh no more, ladies, sigh no more, Men were deceivers ever; One foot in sea—*" Her voice caught. Choked.

What had happened to him? Would she ever know?

"Poppy?" Her aunt leaned forward, concerned.

Poppy stared into space.

"*Poppy?*"

She lurched back to attention. "Sorry. I was just, er . . . remembering something." She cleared her throat. "*One foot in sea, and one on shore, To one thing constant never.*"

"Men are flighty creatures," Lady Bridgerton said.

"Not all men," her husband said.

"Darling, *no*," she said. "Just no."

"*Then sigh not so, but let them go*," Poppy continued, barely hearing the conversation around her. "*And be you blithe and bonny, Converting all your sounds of woe . . .*"

Would Shakespeare always make her think of Andrew? Would *everything* make her think of him?

"*Into Hey nonny, nonny*," Georgie finished for her. She gave Poppy a queer look before turning to her father. "I knew that part."

He yawned and closed his eyes.

"He always falls asleep in carriages," Georgie said.

"It's a skill," Lord Bridgerton said.

"Well, it's a skill that shall have no reward this evening," Lady Bridgerton said. "We've arrived."

Lord Bridgerton sighed audibly, and the rest of them gathered their gloves and bags and whatnot, preparing to alight.

As Lady Bridgerton had predicted, they were led inside under the cover of umbrellas, but the wind had picked up, and they all got a bit wet on the way in.

"Thank you, Wheelock," Lady Bridgerton said to the butler as he took her cloak. "It is so very dreary tonight."

"Indeed, my lady." He handed the cloak to a footman and moved to help Georgie and Poppy. "We shall dry these as best we can during dinner."

"Is the family in the drawing room?"

"They are, my lady."

"Wonderful. No need to take us in. I know the way."

Poppy shrugged her arms from her cloak and followed her aunt and uncle to the drawing room.

"Have you ever been here before?" Georgie asked.

"I don't think so. I haven't really spent that much time in Kent." It was true. Poppy saw her cousins in London far more than she did in the country.

"You will adore Lady Manston," Georgie assured her. "She is like a second mother to me. To all of us. Dining here is always informal. It's just like family."

"*Informal* is a relative term," Poppy murmured. Back on the *Infinity* she hadn't worn shoes for a week. Tonight she had dressed just as grandly as she would for any meal out in society. The pink dress she'd borrowed from Georgie was a hair too short, but it wasn't very noticeable. And the color seemed to suit her.

She was trying to get on with her life. She really was.

The hard part was that there was nothing she could do. She did not know where Andrew was from, who his family was. It certainly did not help that the surname he used was James—surely one of the most common in all of England.

How many common surnames were also common Christian names? James, Thomas, Adam, Charles . . . They all seemed to be male names. Even Andrew could be a surname. Hadn't she met someone before with that name? In London, perhaps . . .

"Poppy!"

She looked up. How was she in the drawing room already? Her cousin Billie was regarding her with amusement.

"Sorry," Poppy mumbled. "Just woolgathering."

"I dare not ask what you were thinking about. It is always the strangest thing." But Billie said this with the greatest affection. She took Poppy's hands and leaned in for a double-cheeked kiss. "I'm so glad you're here. You'll get to meet George's brother."

"Yes," Poppy murmured. She hoped they weren't trying to match her with Nicholas. She was sure he was perfectly amiable, but the last thing she wanted right now was a flirtation. And wasn't he quite young? Just a year older than she was.

"He's not down yet," Billie said. "He was quite travel-worn when he arrived."

From London? How difficult was it to travel from London?

"Let me get you a glass of sherry. I'm sure you need it. The weather is frightful. You'd hardly know it's summer."

Poppy accepted the glass and took a sip, wondering who the young gentleman across the room was if not Nicholas. He looked the correct age, and he and Georgiana were laughing like old friends.

But Billie had said he had not come down yet.

Odd. Poppy gave a mental shrug. She wasn't curious enough to ask, so she took a few steps farther into the room, smiling politely as she watched Lady Manston enter the drawing room through a doorway in the far wall.

"Alexandra!" Lady Manston called out, hurrying

over to embrace Lady Bridgerton. "You will never guess who arrived this afternoon."

Georgie appeared at her side and tugged her sleeve. "Come over and meet Nicholas."

Nicholas? Poppy frowned. Then who—

"Andrew!" Lady Bridgerton cried.

Andrew. Poppy looked away from the gathering, horrified by the moisture pooling in her eyes. Another common name, just like James. Why couldn't the bloody man have been named Marmaduke? Or Nimrod?

Enough. She had to get through the evening. With renewed determination she turned back to the room, her eyes finding her aunt, who was now across the room, embracing someone.

Someone with brown hair, sun-streaked with gold.

Pulled back in a tidy queue.

Dear God, he looked just like—

Andrew.

She didn't feel her glass of sherry slip through her fingers, didn't even know she'd dropped it until Billie, standing next to her, cried out, "Oh!" and caught it, splashing them both from face to hem.

But before she could say anything, even *think* anything other than his name, Billie deftly spun her around and started moving them both toward another door Poppy hadn't realized was literally right behind them.

"We'll get you cleaned up," Billie was saying. "Oh my goodness, it's in your eyelashes!"

"Billie!" someone called from across the room. "What are you—"

Billie swiped her sleeve across her face and poked her head back out into the drawing room. "Please do go in to dinner, we will follow presently. No no, I insist."

And then she turned back to survey Poppy briefly before summoning a maid for some water and a rag. "We'll get this righted in just a moment and everything will be back as it was."

Back as it was.

Poppy almost started to laugh.

Chapter 23

Five minutes later, Andrew was seated in his usual spot at the table in his family's formal dining room. He wasn't sure he had ever been quite so happy to be home . . . *or* so eager to leave.

It had been glorious to wash in an actual full-sized bathtub, and he was very much looking forward to a proper meal, but his head—and his heart—were already one foot on the road toward Poppy.

"George!" his mother exclaimed. "We are waiting for your wife. She said she would be here presently."

Andrew looked across the table with a bit of a smirk. His older brother had a half-eaten dinner roll in his hand.

"You're as hungry as I am," George said to him. "You just haven't the guts to go ahead with it."

"And defy *her*?" Andrew returned, with a tip of his head toward their mother. "Never."

"It's why he's my favorite," Lady Manston said to the table at large. "For this evening, at least."

"Feel free to demote me tomorrow," Andrew said cheerfully. He was quite sure she would, once she realized he'd left home again, but there was no need to inform her of his plans just yet.

George took a sip of his wine. "Billie could be three minutes or thirty. She told us not to wait."

Lady Manston did not look convinced, but any further objection was cut off at the pass by Lord Manston, who picked up *his* roll and said, "I'm starving. I say we eat. Billie will understand."

And thus the soup was served.

Oyster bisque. Andrew's favorite. He barely resisted the urge to pick up the bowl and slurp the whole thing down.

"This is delicious," Lady Bridgerton said to Lady Manston. "Is it a new recipe?"

"I don't think so. It might have a touch more salt, but other than that . . ."

Andrew paid no attention as he savored each spoonful. After the last drop, he actually closed his eyes in appreciation and sighed.

"Sorry to be delayed," he heard Billie call out. "I'm so glad you did not wait."

Andrew heard all of the chairs move as the gentlemen stood. He opened his eyes, glancing down to catch his napkin as he too rose to his feet. A lady had entered the room, after all.

And then time seemed to slow. Billie swished into the room, saying something over her shoulder to another woman, who was looking down, fiddling with something on her dress.

And yet as she moved, as the light hit her hair . . .

As she *breathed* . . .

He knew.

It was Poppy.

It made no sense, but then—of course it made sense. These were her cousins. And if Poppy had also been put on a boat to Kent instead of Dorset . . .

But it made no difference why . . . She was *here*.

He had half a mind to leap over the table just to get to her faster.

But she had not seen him yet.

Or he didn't think she had. She seemed to be examining a floral arrangement in the far corner of the room.

She certainly wasn't looking anywhere near the table.

Even as she walked *to* the table, she wasn't looking anywhere near it.

She knew he was there.

Andrew was suddenly filled with crashing, warring emotions—relief, elation, and that gravest fear of all men: female fury.

He stared at her like a starving man, a huge, stupid smile battling the requisite bland countenance required by manners.

He had a feeling the huge, stupid smile was winning.

But she wasn't going to be able to avoid him all night. There were only two empty seats at the table: one to his left, and one directly across. And he was fairly certain Billie planned to take the one across.

"Poppy and I decided the sherry was so tasty we ought to incorporate it into our wardrobe." She swept her hand across her mid-section as if to say, *Just like so.*

"Will I be forgiven if I do not follow suit?" Georgiana teased, and everyone laughed at that.

Except Poppy, who was staring ferociously at a spot on the wall behind Billie.

And Andrew, who could not stop staring at Poppy.

And Nicholas, who Andrew suddenly realized was also watching Poppy with rather a lot of interest.

That was going to have to be nipped in the bud. It would not do for his brother to be ogling his wife.

Because, *oh yes*, he was going to marry this woman. This amazing, brave, clever, and beautiful woman was going to be his wife.

Though first she'd need to look at him.

Actually, first she'd need to be formally introduced to him.

"Poppy," Billie said, stopping by Nicholas's chair, "may I present George's youngest brother, Mr. Nicholas Rokesby? He is recently graduated from Cambridge. Nicholas, this is Miss Poppy Bridgerton of Somerset. My cousin."

Nicholas took Poppy's hand and brushed his lips across the back.

Andrew gritted his teeth. *Turn to me, damn it. To me.*

"And this," Billie said, "is yet another of George's brothers, Captain Andrew Rokesby. He returned only just today from a voyage at sea. To . . ." Billie's brow furrowed. "Spain?"

"Portugal," Andrew said, never taking his eyes from Poppy's face.

"Portugal. Yes, of course. It must be lovely there this time of year."

"It is," Andrew said.

Finally, Poppy looked up.

"Miss Bridgerton," he murmured. He pressed his lips to the back of her hand and held it longer than propriety allowed.

Her breathing was shallow; he could see it. But he could not tell what was in her eyes.

Anger?

Yearning?

Both?

"Captain," she said quietly.

"Andrew," he insisted as he released her hand.

"Andrew," she said, unable to rip her gaze from his.

"Andrew!" his mother exclaimed.

Because it was far too soon for him to ask a lady to use his given name. They all knew that.

"Do allow Miss Bridgerton to take her seat," his mother added. Her tone was studiously mild, signaling clearly that she had *many* questions.

He didn't care. Poppy had just sat down right next to him. The world had become a very bright place indeed.

"You almost missed the soup, Miss Bridgerton," Nicholas said.

"I—" Her voice cracked. She was clearly flustered. Andrew lost the battle to suppress his grin. But then he looked up and saw Lady Bridgerton looking very intently at Poppy, and his mother looking even more intently at him.

Oh yes, there would be questions.

"It's very good," Nicholas said, sending an awkward glance around the table. He clearly did not know what to make of the strange atmosphere. "Oyster bisque."

A bowl was set down before Poppy. She stared at it as if looking away might cause her ruin.

"I love the soup," Andrew said to her.

He saw her swallow. Still, she stared down at her bowl.

He fixed his gaze on her face, willing her to look up as he said, "I really, *truly* love it."

"Andrew," admonished Billie, sitting across from him, "she hasn't even had the chance to try it."

Poppy didn't move. He could see the tension in her shoulders. Everyone was watching her by now, and he knew he shouldn't have put her at the center of attention, but he did not know what else to do.

Slowly, she picked up her spoon and dipped it into the oyster bisque.

"Do you like it?" Nicholas asked, once she'd taken a very small sip.

She nodded, a tiny, jerky motion. "It's very good. Thank you."

Andrew could no longer restrain himself. Under the table he reached out and took her hand.

She did not pull away.

Softly, he asked, "Do you think you might want more?"

Her neck seemed to go rigid, as if it was taking every ounce of her will just to hold herself steady.

And then she seemed to snap. Her chair lurched backward as she ripped her hand from his.

"I really really love the soup," she cried out. "But I also hate it *so much*."

And she ran from the room.

POPPY HAD NO idea where she was going. She'd never been to Crake House, but weren't all these grand homes *somewhat* the same? There would be a long row of public rooms and if she just kept running through them she'd end up . . .

Somewhere.

She didn't even know *why* she was running. She only knew that she couldn't remain in that dining room for one second longer, with everyone looking at her, and Andrew saying how much he loved the soup, and they both knew he wasn't talking about soup, and it was all just too much.

He was alive.

He was alive and—*goddamn it*—he was a Rokesby. How could he have kept that from her?

And now—and now—

Had she just told him that she loved him?

Had she just said it in front of his family and hers?

Either that, or the entire county of Kent would soon think she'd gone stark, raving mad.

Which was also possible.

To wit: she was running blindly through the home of the Earl of Manston, she could not see a thing for the tears streaming down her face, and she had just wailed something about soup.

She was never eating soup again. Never.

She skidded around a corner into what looked like a smaller drawing room and paused briefly to catch her breath. The rain was still coming down, hard now, and it beat against the window in a furious tattoo.

It beat against the whole house. Zeus or Thor or whatever god was in charge this miserable day *hated* her.

"Poppy!"

She jumped. It was Andrew.

"Poppy!" he bellowed.

She looked frantically around the room. She wasn't ready to see him.

"Poppy!"

He was getting closer. She heard a stumble, then a crash, followed by "Bloody hell."

She almost laughed. She might have smiled a little.

She was still crying, though.

"Pop—"

Lightning streaked through the sky, and for a split second the entire room was illuminated. *There* was the door!

Poppy ran toward it, flinching when thunder cracked the night open. Good heavens, that was loud.

"There you are," Andrew growled from the opposite doorway. "Jesus Christ, Poppy, would you hold still?"

She paused with her hand at the door. "Are you limping?"

"I think I broke my mother's favorite vase."

She swallowed. "So it's not from . . . Portugal?"

"No, it's from chasing you through the bloody dark. What the hell were you thinking?"

"I thought you were dead!" she cried.

He looked at her. "I'm not."

"Well, I see that now."

They stood there for several moments, watching each other from across the room. Not warily, just . . . with care.

"How did you get free?" she asked. She had so many questions, but this seemed the most important.

"Mr. Walpole arranged it. It took almost a fortnight, though. And then I needed several days in Lisbon to settle my affairs."

"Senhor Farias?"

"He is well. His daughter had the baby. A boy."

"Oh, that's lovely. He must be so pleased."

Andrew nodded, but his eyes stayed on hers in a way that reminded her that they had other things to discuss.

"What did everybody say?" she asked. "In the dining room."

"Well, I think they've figured out that we know each other."

A horrified laugh welled up in her throat. She looked over at the door—the one both she and Andrew had entered through. "Are they coming after us?"

"Not yet," he said. "George has it minded."

"George?"

Andrew shrugged. "He nodded when I looked at

him and said his name as I left the room. I think he knew what I meant."

"Brothers," she said with a nod.

Another bolt of lightning shot through the air, and Poppy braced herself for the thunder. "My aunt is going to kill me," she said.

"No." Andrew waited through the boom. "But she's going to have questions."

"Questions." Another hysterical bubble of laughter jumped within her. "Oh dear God."

"Poppy."

What was she going to say to her family? What was he going to say to his?

"*Poppy.*"

She looked at him.

"I'm going to start walking toward you," he said.

Her lips parted. She wasn't sure why he was saying this so explicitly. Or why it made her so nervous.

"Because," he said, once he'd halved the distance between them, "if I don't kiss you right now, I think . . . I might . . ."

"Die?" she whispered.

He nodded solemnly, and then he took her face in his hands, and he kissed her. He kissed her so long and so thoroughly she forgot everything, even the thunder and the lightning, which flashed and crashed around them. He kissed her until they were both breathless—literally—and they pulled apart, gasping as if they didn't know which they needed more—air or each other.

"I love you, you stupid man," she mumbled, swiping her arm across her face to mop up the tears and the sweat and God knew what else.

He stared at her, dumbfounded. "What did you say?"

"I said I love you, you stupid man, but I'm just so . . . bloody . . . *angry* right now."

"With me?"

"With everyone."

"But mostly with me?"

"With—" *What?* Her mouth fell open. "Do you *want* it to be mostly with you?"

"I'm just trying to figure out what I'm up against."

She eyed him suspiciously. "What do you mean?"

He reached out and took her hand, twining their fingers one by one. "You did say that you love me."

"Against my better judgment, I assure you." But when she looked down at their hands, she realized she didn't want him to let go. *She* didn't want to let go.

And sure enough, his fingers seemed to tighten around hers. "*Saying* it was against your better judgment? Or actually falling in love?"

"Both. I don't know. I don't know anything anymore. It's just— I thought you were dead."

"I know," he said solemnly. "I'm sorry."

"You don't know what that feels like."

"I do," he said. "A little. I did not know if you'd reached Mr. Walpole safely until I was rescued nearly two weeks later."

Poppy went still. It had never occurred to her that he might have gone through the same anguish that she had. "I'm sorry," she whispered. "Oh my God, I'm sorry. I'm so selfish."

"No," he said, and his voice shook just a little as he brought her hand to his mouth for a kiss. "No. You're not. I've known you were safe since I spoke with Walpole. I was on my way to find you. I was going to leave in the morning. I thought you were in Dorset. Or maybe Somerset."

"No, I was here," she said, even though it was obvious.

He nodded, and his eyes glistened as he said, "I love you, Poppy."

She wiped her nose inelegantly with the back of her hand. "I know."

A surprised smile touched his face. "You do?"

"You'd have to, wouldn't you? To have run after me? To argue with me like this?"

"I had no trouble arguing with you before I fell in love."

"Well, that's just you," she muttered. "You're very argumentative."

He leaned his forehead on hers. "Poppy Louise Bridgerton, will you marry me?"

She tried to speak. She tried to nod, but she didn't quite seem to have control over herself, and anyway, right at that moment they heard the sound of people coming their way.

Lots of people.

"Wait," Andrew said. "Don't answer yet. Come with me."

Anywhere, she thought as he took her hand. Anywhere.

THEY DID NOT get far. Even Andrew had to admit that there could be no debauchery with his mother, his father, two of his brothers, two of her cousins, and her aunt and uncle all bearing down on them.

As Andrew had predicted, there were questions. The interrogation had taken over two hours, and by the end of it, he and Poppy had told their families everything.

Almost everything.

In the initial commotion, though, Andrew had managed to pull Lord Bridgerton aside to assure him that he fully intended to marry Poppy.

But he did not want his proposal to take place in a crowded drawing room. Or worse, immediately following an angry demand from her relatives.

They agreed that Andrew would call upon her the following morning, but as it turned out, the Bridgertons couldn't leave that night. The thunderstorm took a violent turn, and it was not deemed safe for them to make even the short journey home.

Which was how Andrew came to be standing outside the door to Poppy's bedroom a few hours past midnight.

He couldn't sleep. And neither, he suspected, could she.

The door opened before he could knock.

"I heard you outside," she whispered.

"Impossible." He had been moving with great stealth, well aware that hers was not the only bedroom on this hall.

"I might have been listening for you," she admitted.

He grinned as he stepped inside. "You're very resourceful."

She was wearing a white nightgown—whose, he did not know—and her hair had been twisted into a sleeping plait.

He reached out for the end.

"Are you going to pull my hair?" she murmured.

"Maybe." He gave it a tiny tug, just enough to urge her forward by half a step. "Or," he said, his voice growing low and husky with need, "I might finally indulge myself."

She looked at the tip of her braid, and then up at him, her eyes bright with amusement.

He started to unwind the three sections, slowly, savoring the silky strands that played across his fingers until the whole length of it spilled across her shoulders.

She was so beautiful. The entire time he was back in Lisbon, in that godforsaken room waiting for rescue, he'd thought of her. He'd closed his eyes and pictured her face—her impish smile, the way her eyes seemed extra green just before the sun went down.

But his imagination was nothing next to the real thing.

"I love you," he said. "I love you so much."

"I love you too," she whispered, and it sang through his heart.

They kissed, and they laughed, and the rain beat steadily against the window. It seemed fitting somehow, but not because it was stormy.

It was because here, inside this room, they were warm and safe.

And together.

"I have a question," he said, after they'd tumbled onto her bed.

"Oh?"

"Can we agree that I've thoroughly ruined you?"

"I don't know if I'd call it ruined," she said with faux thoughtfulness. "That would seem to imply I'm upset about the outcome."

He rolled his hand in the air, palm down to palm up. "Nevertheless . . ."

"And not to put too fine a point on it, but the only people who have any idea that something untoward occurred are your family and mine. Surely they would not breathe a word of hurtful gossip."

"True, but we mustn't forget Mr. Walpole."

"Hmmm. He's a problem."

"A huge problem."

"But then again," she said, clearly enjoying the conversation, "he's quite bullish on national security. I don't think he would ever acknowledge having met me."

"So you don't want to invite him to the wedding."

"The wedding?" She gave him a sly glance. "I don't recall accepting a proposal."

He leaned in. Wolfishly. "I did ruin you."

"I believe we were still debating that."

"It's settled fact," he said firmly. "More to the point, we need to decide what to do about *now*."

"Now?"

He nipped at her bottom lip. "I very much wish to make love to you."

"You do?" Her voice came out a bit like a squeak. He thought it delightful.

"I do," he confirmed. "And while I do understand that it is not quite de rigueur to anticipate our vows in such a thorough manner—"

"A *thorough* manner?" she repeated. But she was smiling. She was definitely smiling.

"When I make love to you," he said, "I hope to do it very thoroughly."

She caught her lip between her teeth. It made him want to bite her.

Good Lord, she was practically turning him feral. He crawled over her, grinning as she giggled.

"Quiet," he whispered. "Your reputation . . ."

"Oh, I think that ship has sailed."

"Bad pun, Miss Bridgerton. Very bad pun."

"Time and tide wait for no man."

He drew back an inch. "I'm not sure how that's relevant."

"It was all I could think of," she admitted. "And you know, you never let me answer your question."

"I didn't?"

She shook her head.

"And which question is that?"

"You'll have to ask it again, Captain."

"Very well. Will—"

He kissed her nose.

"You."

Her left cheek.

"Marry."

Her right cheek.

"Me?"

Her mouth. Her beautiful, perfect mouth.

But just a light kiss. Swift. She still needed to answer.

She smiled, and it was glorious. "Yes," she said. "Yes, I'll marry you."

He wasn't sure there were words for such a moment, even among two so glib as they. So he kissed her instead. He kissed her mouth, worshipping her in all the ways he'd dreamed of these last few weeks. He kissed her cheek, her neck, the perfect hollow above her collarbone.

"I love you, Poppy Bridgerton," he murmured. "More than I could ever imagine. More than I can even conceive."

But not, he thought, more than he could show her. He slid her nightgown from her body, and his own dressing robe somehow melted away. For the first time, they were skin to skin.

"So beautiful," he whispered, gazing at her as they kneeled in front of each other. He wanted to kiss her everywhere, to taste the salt of her skin, the creamy essence between her thighs. He wanted to swirl his tongue around the tight pink buds of her breasts. She'd liked that, he remembered, but what if he nibbled? What if he tugged?

"Lie down," he ordered.

She gave him an amused, questioning look.

His lips found her ear in a hungry growl. "I have plans for you."

He felt her pulse leap, and she started to lower herself down. When her bottom touched the bedsheets, he scooted her legs out from under her, leaving her breathlessly on her back.

"You were too slow," he said with a wolfish smile. She didn't say anything, just watched him with a glazed passion, her breasts rising and falling with each breath.

"I hardly know where to start," he murmured.

She licked her lips.

"But I think . . ." He trailed his finger down her body, from her shoulder to her hip. "I'll start . . ." He moved inward, then lower. "Here."

Both of his hands moved to her hips, his thumbs pressing against the soft skin of her inner thighs. He slid her open, and then he lowered his head for the most intimate of kisses.

"Andrew!" she gasped.

He smiled as he licked. He loved making her gasp.

She tasted like heaven, like sweet wine and tangy nectar, and he could not resist sliding a finger inside her, glorying in the way she instinctively tightened around him.

She was close. He could take her over the edge with one single graze of his teeth, but he was selfish, and when she came, he wanted to be inside her.

She moaned with frustration when he drew back, but he quickly replaced his mouth with his cock. He nudged at her opening, his body shuddering with desire as her legs wrapped around his. "Do you want me to stop?" he whispered.

Their eyes met.

"Never," she said.

And so he pushed forward, finding a home in her warmth, wondering how he had lived twenty-nine years on this earth without making love to this woman. He slipped into a rhythm, each stroke bringing him closer to the edge, but he held back, straining against his own release until she found hers.

"Andrew," she gasped, arching beneath him.

He leaned down, rolled his tongue across her breast.

She whimpered. She moaned.

He turned his attention to the other one, this time giving it a little suck.

She let out a keening cry, high-pitched but quiet, and her body tightened beneath him.

Around him.

It was his undoing. He pumped forward once, then again. And then he exploded within her, losing himself in her scent, her essence.

In *her*. He lost himself in *her*, but somehow, in that moment, he found his home.

Several minutes later, when he'd finally caught his breath and was lying on his back beside her, he reached down between their bodies to hold her hand.

"I saw stars," he said, still amazed.

He *heard* her smile. "On the insides of your eyelids?"

"I think I saw them on the insides of yours."

She laughed, and the bed shook.

And then, far sooner than he would have anticipated, they shook the bed again.

Epilogue

Nine months later

Andrew had thought that he wanted a girl, but as he held his newborn son in his arms, he could only think that this amazing miraculous creature was perfect in every way.

There would be plenty of time to make more babies.

"Ten fingers," he told Poppy, who was resting with her eyes closed in their bed. "Ten toes."

"You counted?" she murmured.

"You didn't?"

She opened one eye. "I was busy."

He chuckled as he touched his son's tiny little nose. "Your mother is very tired."

"I think he looks like you," Poppy said.

"Well, he's certainly handsome."

She rolled her eyes. Even with her eyes closed he could see that she rolled them.

Andrew turned his attention back to the baby. "He's very clever."

"Of course he is."

He looked over at her. "Open your eyes, Pops."

She did, with a look of surprise at the nickname. He'd never used it. Not once.

"I think we should name him Roger," he said.

Poppy's eyes grew round and wet, and her lips trembled before she spoke. "I think that's an excellent idea."

"Roger William," Andrew decided.

"William?"

"Billy would like that, don't you think?"

Poppy smiled widely. Billy had come to live at Crake several months earlier. They'd found him a position in the stables, although it was understood that he was to be given time off every day to attend school. He was doing very well, although the stable-master had complained about the number of cats now taking up residence.

Andrew and Poppy were also living at Crake, although not for much longer. The house that Andrew had been building in his mind for so many years was almost a reality. Another month, maybe two, and they would be able to move in. There was a large, sunny nursery, a library just waiting to be filled with books, and even a small greenhouse, where Andrew planned to cultivate some of the seeds he'd collected on his many travels.

"I will have to take you outside when it's warmer," Andrew said to Roger as he walked him around the room. "I shall show you the stars."

"They won't look the same as they do from the *Infinity*," Poppy said softly.

"I know. We will make do." He glanced at her over his shoulder. "I will tell him how the ancient gods built a ship so tall and so strong that the mast split the sky and all the stars fell out like diamonds."

This earned him a smile. "Oh, you'll tell him that, will you?"

"It's the best explanation I've ever heard." He walked over to the bed, settling Roger in his mother's arms before stretching out next to both of them. "Certainly the most romantic."

Poppy smiled, and he smiled, and even though he had been told by *many* women that newborns did not smile, he liked to think that Roger did, too.

"Do you think we'll ever see the *Infinity* again?" Poppy asked.

"Probably not. But maybe a different ship."

She turned to look at him. "Are you feeling restless?"

"No." He didn't even have to think about it. "Everything I need is right here."

Her elbow jabbed gently into his side. "That's far too pat an answer, and you know it."

"I take back everything I've ever said about you being romantic," he said. "Even that bit about the stars."

She gave him a look as if to say, *I'm waiting*.

"I have found," he said thoughtfully, "that I rather like building things."

"Our new home?"

He looked down at Roger. "And our family."

Poppy smiled, and she and the baby drifted off to sleep. Andrew sat next to them for a long while, marveling at his good fortune. Everything he needed really *was* right here.

"It wasn't too pat an answer," he murmured. Then he waited; he wouldn't put it past his wife to say, even in her sleep, "Yes, it was."

But she didn't, and he eased himself off the bed and walked over to the French doors that led out to a small Juliet balcony. It was close to midnight and perhaps a little too cold to be going out in stocking feet, but Andrew felt a strange pull toward the inky night.

It was overcast, though, and not a single star twinkled above. Until . . .

He squinted up at the sky. There was a patch that was much darker than the rest. The wind must have cleared a small hole in the clouds.

"*En garde*," he murmured, and with his imaginary épée, he jousted with the heavens. He laughed as he lunged forward, aiming straight for that one spot. And then . . .

He went still. Was that a star?

It twinkled merrily, and as Andrew stared up in wonder, it was joined by another, and then another. Three stars in all, but the first, he decided, was his favorite. It was a fighter.

He didn't really *need* a lucky star.

But maybe . . .

He glanced back through the window, where Poppy and Roger dozed peacefully in the bed.

Maybe he'd had one all along.

Do you love historical fiction?

Want the chance to hear news about your favourite authors (and the chance to win free books)?

Mary Balogh
Lenora Bell
Charlotte Betts
Jessica Blair
Frances Brody
Grace Burrowes
Gaelen Foley
Pamela Hart
Elizabeth Hoyt
Eloisa James
Lisa Kleypas
Stephanie Laurens
Sarah MacLean
Amanda Quick
Julia Quinn

Then visit the Piatkus website
www.piatkusentice.co.uk

And follow us on Facebook and Twitter
www.facebook.com/piatkusfiction | @piatkusentice

piatkus

BETTWS

Julia Quinn started writing her first book one month after finishing college and has been tapping away at her keyboard ever since. She is the author of award-winning historical romance novels, including the *New York Times* bestselling Bridgerton series. She is a graduate of Harvard and Radcliffe colleges and lives with her family in Colorado.

Please visit Julia Quinn online:

www.juliaquinn.com
www.facebook.com/AuthorJuliaQuinn
@JQAuthor